P9-DGR-492

FROM THE Library of

Margaret McKiernan

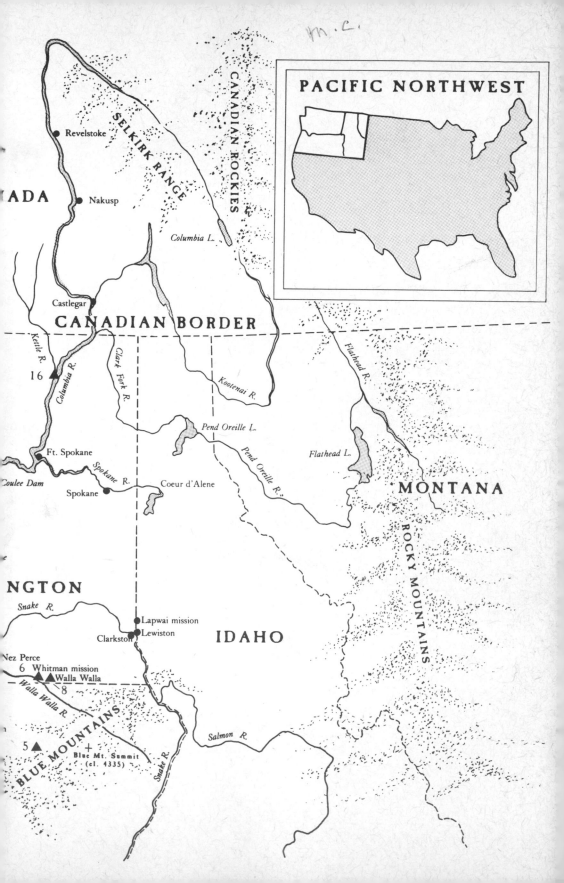

PAMELA JEKEL

ST. MARTIN'S PRESS • NEW YORK

"The Day the Earth Spat Warthogs," by Tom Robbins. Published by *Esquire* magazine, 1985. Used by permission of author.

"The Frozen Logger," words and music by James Stevens. TRO © Copyright 1951 and renewed 1979 Folkways Music Publishers, Inc., New York, N.Y. Used by Permission.

"Roll On, Columbia," words by Woody Guthrie. Music based on "Goodnight, Irene" by Huddie Ledbetter and John Lomax. TRO © Copyright 1936 (renewed 1964), 1957 (renewed 1985), and 1963 Ludlow Music, Inc., New York, N.Y. Used by Permission.

Children of the Raven, by H. R. Hays. © Copyright 1975 Hoffman Reynolds Hays. Published by McGraw-Hill Book Company, New York, N.Y. Used by Permission.

Indian Legends of the Pacific Northwest, by Ella E. Clark. Published by University of California Press, Berkeley, California, 1953. Used by Permission.

"the song of the trappers," in *John McLoughlin: Father of Oregon,* by Robert C. Johnson. Published by Binford & Mort, Publishers, Portland, Oregon, 1958. Used by Permission

The Empire Builders, by R. O. Case. Published by Binford & Mort, Publishers, Portland, Oregon, 1949. Used by Permission.

COLUMBIA. Copyright © 1986 by Pamela Jekel. All rights reserved. Printed in the United States of America. No part of this book may be used or reproduced in any manner whatsoever without written permission except in the case of brief quotations embodied in critical articles or reviews. For information, address St. Martin's Press, 175 Fifth Avenue, New York, N.Y. 10010.

Design by Paolo Pepe

Library of Congress Cataloging in Publication Data

Jekel, Dr.
Columbia.

I. Title.
PS3560.E46C6   1986   813'.54   86-3656
ISBN 0-312-15096-2

First Edition
10 9 8 7 6 5 4 3 2 1

For my grandmother,
Leona Laudert Roth,
who has lived most of her life on the River,
providing a place to hunt blackberries
every summer of my childhood.
She made a religion of resilience,
and faced each of life's treacheries
with a healthy curse and a smile.
She gave each of us,
her daughter and her granddaughters,
a piece of her marrow
and still, still,
stands straight as any cedar.
This is not her life, but it is her song.

Contents

Preface

The Columbia River is the absolute monarch of the Pacific Northwest, the last wilderness in continental America. In this land of boisterously lethal volcanoes, dense misty forests of primeval fern, and the prehistoric Sasquatch, who still, according to local tribal lore, roams the virgin mountains, the Columbia circles the Northwest, acting as both conduit and wall for her people, through twelve hundred miles of moving water.

A young river, the Columbia is the fourth largest in all of North America, ten times the size of the Colorado, and at its birth, its waters gouged canyons a thousand feet deep, spewing cataracts to rival Niagara at over four miles wide. The river's discovery by a Yankee captain gave America her first and most important foothold on the Pacific and, ultimately, right of domain to the entire continent. And because it supplies more hydroelectricity than any river on earth, indeed energy that made the aluminum for seventy percent of American planes and half of her atomic power, the Columbia can even be credited with helping to win World War II.

From its fountainhead in a still, cold lake deep in the heart of Canada to its mouth, twisting in deep green violence as it foams into the Pacific, this wilderness highway claims waters from British Columbia, Utah, Wyoming, Nevada, Montana, Idaho, Washington, and Oregon, draining more than a quarter of a million square miles. The story of the people who struggled for control of the Columbia and its power is the story of America's last continental frontier, an epic struggle in keeping with this river of dark forests that presides over our nation's farthest corner.

Time, like an ever-rolling stream,

Bears all its sons away. . . .

PART ONE

Nine Thousand
Years Before Present

For a million years, the warm primeval sea stretched inland to the Blue Mountains. The earth shrugged its shoulders balefully, and the Cascades pushed from the depths, thundering mud and boiling rock into the sea, throwing up storm clouds of exploding steam. In another million years, the sea withdrew, and soon the swampy land was covered with giant ferns and ginkgoes. Lumbering great lizards and flying reptiles ruled the jungle.

The earth twisted restlessly once more, and a three-hundred-mile ring of volcanoes erupted along the Cascades, gushing out rivers of molten lava and heaping up sheer cones of stone. As the fires burned down, the snow began to fall, whitening the new peaks and the tender new growth. It snowed for centuries without pause, and huge ice fields began to fill the valleys. Solid white walls of rumbling death gouged the earth, sweeping the jungles and the reigning lizards into oblivion. Finally, the snow stopped, and spring came again to the land.

The glaciers began to soften, then to melt, and vast lakes formed, blocked by still stubborn remnants of ice. To the east of the mountains, in a valley archaeologists would one day call the Okanogan, glaciers plugged the infant flow of water, forcing the rising river to find its way across the lava plateau. Impatient to reach the sea, the green waters cut through the earth, ploughing a canyon eight hundred feet deep, five miles across, and fifty miles long, and the roar of its cataracts could be heard across one hundred miles. Soon, man would come over the top of the world, following the animals, to the banks of the great river.

FIRST BOY HUNKERED DOWN IN THE GRAY VOLCANIC ASH THAT BLANKETED the cliff, clutching his spear to his side. Soon, the sun would be high overhead, and the great maned mastodon would move to the deeper shade and the narrow walls of the Canyon. Then he would make his kill.

He stared, never moving, as the hairy beast slowly waved its lethal tusks from side to side, wrenching leaves from one bush, then another, oblivious to the stalking hunter. Bend your head, breathed the boy, willing the old tusker to move. He saw that its legs were stiff, and its shaggy hump was silvered. No matter. It was an enviable kill, one in which even a seasoned hunter might take pride. The Old Ones told of ample herds of the great Walkers, many seasons past, when their tusks dug furrows through the cattails, and their moon-feet left deep pocks in the mud flats. But now, their tracks were gone. He wondered how far this mastodon had roamed, searching for others of his kind. Old or not, this Walker would get him his name.

First Boy thought of his father, Hyak Chak Chak, named for the swiftest eagle in the Canyon. It was hard to follow such a man in the eyes of the People. What words would brand *him,* all his life, letting him shrug off his child name, First Boy, like the skin of the lizard? He knew that like the beast before him, his name must be large in the mouth and full of power.

As he watched, the mastodon browsed closer to the canyon rock, down a trickling stream where the reeds grew thick in mud, and the sheer walls leaned closer. Ten feet at the shoulder, with six-foot tusks, the beast was almost twice as tall as the boy, shielded by a shaggy mane so thick that not even the sharpest obsidian flint traded from the tribes to the east could pierce its hide. And First Boy had but a basalt spear, ample for small game and the red fish but too weak for the neck of such a monster. Yet kill he must, or go back to the tribe forever a youth, the target of all men's—and his father's—contempt.

The mastodon shuffled further down the Canyon, wuffling from side to side, drawn deeper into the narrow gorge by the soft cattails with their succulent stems. First Boy eased away from the edge of the cliff, keeping his eyes averted from his prey lest his excitement shine forth and startle the beast.

Time passed, and the sun climbed higher over the Canyon of the River. In the distance, far away, the mastodon could smell the great waters and the ice fields, could hear the faint roar of the cataracts. It browsed slowly, reaching always with its sensitive trunk-fingers for tempting leaves, gradually rounding a curve in the narrow canyon. Ahead, a large clump of shrubs clustered together, set back from the stream bed. The beast tossed its tusks from side to side but sensed no danger. Ambling forward, the mastodon shouldered the bushes aside to stretch its trunk toward the thick, damp foliage.

First Boy was waiting, crouched in a stifling pit, silent as the rocks themselves, gazing up through the woven mats covered with brush. For what seemed a season he had squatted, smeared with mud to mask his scent, scarcely breathing, stalking the Walker in his mind though he moved not a muscle. He willed the brute forward just as it was now, its neck stretched, its trunk grasping delicately at the piled shrubs, its soft underbelly swaying just over his hidden head. As its rank odor filled the pit, First Boy thrust upwards though the mats with all his strength, screaming a call to whatever spirits watched him now, twisting and jabbing his spear deep into the monster's bowels.

The mastodon matched his shriek with an astonished trumpet of pain and savage outrage, half-rearing on its massive legs, flashing its tusks at the air, at the unseen foe, the well-known scent of man.

First Boy scrambled out of the pit, twisted his body away from the beast, and thrust again and again between the angry tusks, the rearing legs, just as one mighty foot crashed through the mats and the covering of the brush into the pit. Half in, half out of the hole now, the mastodon whirled white sword tusks on the boy, bellowing its defiance. First Boy stumbled, fell forward, and clutched at the Walker's hide. He jumped back as though burned, made one last dodge to the beast's flanks and shoved his spear with all his might, both fists clenched at its shaft, deep into the tusker's ribs. There was a hollow snap, a crack that echoed up the walls, a single red glare from two pain-glazed eyes under a matted mane, and the mastodon sank with a burbling grunt to its knees. As First Boy stood panting, less than a spear length from this demon of his dreams, the huge animal moaned. Its trunk snaked feebly out toward the boy, back to the spear shaft protruding from its ribs; then it fell heavily to its side.

First Boy sank to his knees, following the red glaring eyes to the ground. He swayed back and forth, holding his sides, breathing heavily. He had made the kill, he had made the kill, his mind pulsed exultantly. Alone, he had faced the tusker of death and toppled those tree-trunk legs to the mud. I have fulfilled my quest, he thought.

For ten days, he had hunted the draws alone, searching for his spirit guide. For these days, he had little but dried berries and cold water to sustain him, a cedar cinch at his waist so he would not weaken from the pain of hunger. For ten days, he had dreamed in the shade of the Canyon, rarely sleeping, only making careful rock piles and playing the stick game with the spirits, waiting for his own private vision, his personal power to come to him. Now he stared, mesmerized, as the dark blood pumped slowly down the maned side of the monster. Never before had he been so close to such a large death.

A movement drew his eye. The sun seemed to tilt, and from out of the canyon wall into a patch of yellow heat, a large rattlesnake silently slid, its black tongue thrusting into the air.

First Boy held his breath, and a spell of exhaustion and shock hit him, causing him to roll on his heels. The snake seemed to look directly into his eyes as it came endlessly closer, black opaque eyes that bored into him, unblinking. The ringed body slid effortlessly, circling tightly in the sand, until it had gathered into a massive basket of coils. Nothing moved but its forked tongue, which quested in and out silently.

First Boy held himself still with an effort. He felt no fear, only a singing exhilaration that made him tremble. Here, then, was his spirit vision. He, First Boy, would be First Boy no more. Now he would take the name of Sin tehla, Snake with Teeth. And the message of his vision was clear. His spear would be always sharp, true, and deadly like that of his spirit guide, the Rattletail, who had witnessed and now guarded his kill.

Deliberately, the boy held out his hands to the snake, palms up, to show that he understood the message of his vision. He eased his knife from the leather thong at his waist and walked carefully, reverently, his bare feet and legs within inches of the flickering tongue of the reptile, to the head of the dead behemoth. With all his strength, he pried the mastodon's jaws open and hacked off a piece of its tongue. Returning to within a foot of the snake, he carefully placed the bloody meat before its flat, spear-shaped head.

"Always," he whispered solemnly, as sibilant as the snake's rustling scales, "always, I will save the best, the tongue, for you, my helper. I will carry you forever with me until my death. I, Sin tehla, speak."

Motionless, the snake seemed to listen, its head hovering just above its last heavy coil.

Someone else had anxiously watched the afternoon shadows move over the canyon walls. On the ledge of the tribal cave, Wacawin, Flower Woman, sat grinding wapato roots, keeping one eye on the riverbed below and one on the toddler, Second Boy, at her knee. Her firstborn had been gone for ten days now, gone to find his spirit partner alone. For ten days, her hands had moved to their tasks, had gathered seeds from the meadows, had dug the onion bulbs, and had caulked the mats against the coming winter cold. But always, her mind's eye returned to two brown legs hunting—where? To two black eyes seeing—what dangers? She said nothing of course, even to her man, Hyak Chak Chak, for to name her fear for First Boy would be unseemly.

She absently swung her hair back over her bare shoulders and held her second son's grasping hands away from her breasts as his mouth sought her nipple. He tugged playfully, causing her to wince. He was not really hungry for her milk, only for her gaze. She set him on his sturdy legs again and murmured a reprimand, softly lest his father hear.

Her man sat silently, drilling a small hole into an owl's claw. It was the season of falling fruit, and soon the red fish would surge up the river in packs so dense that a child could walk their backs. The tribe must be ready. The men made the spears, sharpened the cutters, and netted together the great weirs with which to harvest the fish. And one man, he with eyes keen as the hawk whose name he carried—her man—made the ritual gifts for the fish spirits that would appease them and ensure their return.

Few men could make the great trip to the ice fields in the north, to capture the frozen blue rock to lay at the head of the river and feed the water's power. Few men knew how to mix bone marrow and earth to paint the magic signs on the river rocks to direct the fish into the weirs. Of all the tribe, only her man could turn an owl's claw into a spirit amulet, a powerful thing of bone and rock that would call the red fish to his spear.

She ducked her head lest someone see the pride wet her eyes. Truly, the People were blessed to share such power. And she was blessed above most. Wife to such a man. Mother to two sons. When she left her father's crowded pithouse on the lake of the Sun People, the Spukane, she had not envisioned such a destiny. Indeed, her bride-price had been small, her father grateful to lose the third of five daughters. After her village of a hundred or more, she was at first wary of the wandering tribe with which her man made his home. Like the dogs they kept for the hunt, this tribe moved as often as the seasons.

In early spring, the women covered miles of prairie, digging camas, bitterroot, biscuit root, and hemp, stuffing the harvest into willowbark bags, and rendering all that forage into ground cakes dried in the sun. After the roots came the berries—the currants, the chokecherries, the huckleberries—all to be gathered and dried, mixed with meat, or pounded into slabs for travel. The game was best in the summer, of course, before the rutting, and then the pithouses were filled with hides to be cleaned, meat to be jerked, horns, hooves, and bones to be split and stored. And now, the season of the red fish.

Life was good, thanks to the bounty of the river and the earth. The tribe ended each year in the winter cave for the dark nights and days, when the old stories circled round the walls like smoke. The unseen spirits protected the People from empty bellies and enemy arrows, for each man here had eaten a vision and found a partner. A spirit partner such as First Boy sought now. Once more, her eyes followed the winding trail from the Canyon up the steep cliff. Still no sign of his return.

The sun dropped, and the people gathered within the lip of the cave, the smoke curling overhead to smudge a spot on the basalt ceiling that had been blackened through the millenniums. Wacawin fed elk meat into the boiling water, water she kept rolling by adding heated rocks carefully, one by one. One of the Old Ones, mother to a man called Eyanpaha, Camp Crier, squatted close to the flames and extended her bony hands out for warmth.

"Uhunh," she moaned, rocking on her heels. "First Boy's quest takes him far. What will you give me if I tell you his fate?" The ancient mother peered through the smoke at Wacawin, watching with wary eyes for Hyak Chak Chak, who worked now over a stone bowl. She kept her voice low.

Wacawin tried to ignore the woman, but respect and curiosity made her speak. "Do you see him in the smoke, Old One?"

"Waugh!" The Elder spat in the flames, her eyes darting. "I need no fire to show me his feet. I see his tracks in my head."

Wacawin crouched low over the old woman. Ostensibly rearranging the cooling stones, she cautiously passed a delicate bone needle to the wizened palm, a small treasure, but all she could spare. "Tell me, then. I listen."

The old woman wheezed and rocked on her haunches, staring into the flames. "He partners with death, your firstborn."

Wacawin stiffened, instantly sorry she had asked. Around her, the People ate and smoked and talked. None saw her face tighten with pain. The old woman grinned suddenly, gripping her knees with relish. "He brings death now in his two hands. And more power than he can hold."

Alive, then. First Boy lives, Wacawin thought. She moved away, keeping her eyes down and her tongue stilled. She did not want to know more, did not want to kill whatever power lay in the mystery of her son's future.

The old woman's voice rose louder, however, and some stopped to listen. "Never since the Old Ones came across the seabridge have we had such a one as he. Since the time of the floods, the People have known no power as his!"

Wacawin sank to her knees and averted her eyes, keeping her hands busy with the cooking. She had heard the talks each winter since she was a child. All members of the tribe knew how the Elders had come across the great land to the north, following the game, that they had settled near the river only to be swept away by the great flood, and how those few who ran to high ground became the People today. She had heard it so often, she no longer listened. And as she looked about the cave, she saw with some relief that few others listened either. Except her man. He appraised the old woman with curious eyes, his hands paused in their work. His eyes narrowed as he gazed back into the night.

He misses nothing, his wife thought as she glanced sideways at his turned head. Especially when it is of First Boy. First Boy, who reminds him always that his own eyes see now from aged canyons, his own hands not quite so strong. She stood slowly, easing her stiffened knees, and looked out into the night. A warm wind came up from the river, the fingers of the sun still on its edges, but she felt its cold underbelly. Winter would be on them soon, and it would be time for heavy robes against the winds. She wondered if she would have two men to clothe or only one. Then she thrust her fear from her and turned back to the fire.

The next morning as light seeped over the Canyon, the Night Watcher called to the waking People, "E-eeh-hah! He comes!" Hyak Chak Chak was at the ledge, peering down into the valley floor before the Watcher ceased his warning.

Down the stone cliff, down the sliding gravel paths, down the yellow rock to the riverbed, his eyes followed the shadows until he saw the moving brown spot that was his son, First Boy. He thought, "So he comes. And judging by the speed of his step, he brings with him a spirit power." He turned to the tribe and shouted, "Hear me, my People! A man comes!"

As First Boy trudged up the last few steps of path, he held his arms high over his head, beating together two gourds filled with pebbles. He sang his spirit song loudly up the Canyon.

> "I, son of Swiftest Eagle, I, son of the People
> I go out and speak with Spirits of the Earth,
> Spirits of Mountains, of Rivers, of Creatures,
> And I, son of all the Spirits,
> Bring back the voice of One! E-eeh-hah! E-eeh-hah!
> I speak with the power of the Rattletail.
> I, Sin tehla, Snake with Teeth,
> My spear shall be sharp and true and deadly,
> My song is one of warning and power!
> I, Sin tehla, Snake with Teeth, E-eeh-hah!"

The three Elders gathered slowly at the mouth of the cave. They had heard many youths come home in such a fever, yet few proved worthy of their own boasts. One wizened old man frowned toward Hyak Chak Chak. "He sings loud for fifteen summers."

The father lowered his eyes and squatted in the sight of the People, waiting. His role was finished now. Though he would share whatever pride or shame was coming, he could say no more.

Suddenly the boy was there, framed by light in the mouth of the cave. The People faced him silently in a half-moon circle, the three Elders in the middle, judging, listening. He took a deep breath and shouted, "It is I, Sin tehla. Hear my voice, O Grandfathers! See my dance, my People!" The boy laid his gifts on the ground. A brief gasp of wonder rippled round the circle like a breeze through the rushes. In the dust lay two huge rattlesnake fangs and the crusted end of a mastodon tongue.

There was silence. In the smoky depths of the cave, the boy sought out his mother's eyes, but the shadows were dark after the sun of the canyon, and he could not find her face.

Slowly now with a sinuous grace, he began his spirit dance, the personal dance he would carry with him all his life. He lifted his eyes to the walls of the cave and sang his spirit song, a song which would call his spirit partner, the Rattletail, to his aid whenever he needed its power. Moving faster, he writhed and twisted, and his rattle mesmerized in the stillness. Weaving at the waist, the boy made circles in the dust, seeming to grow larger and yet more slender before the watchers, chanting a sibilant, lyrical song which also made circles over their heads in the gloom. As he danced, he plucked two huge rattles from out of his cedar waist cinch, and these he put in his mouth so that as he sang, they buzzed sharply. Finally, his voice died away, and his feet were still.

One Elder spoke with tight dignity. "A Walker and a Rattletail. Powerful spirits for one unripe."

The boy felt his magic sitting on his shoulder, and it gave him courage to speak. "These are a shaman's spirits. I, Sin tehla, shall be shaman to the People."

Again, a gasp, one more audible, even outraged, circled the cave. Slowly, another Elder spoke. "Your father is a caller of fish, his father before him a caller of elk. No one before you has had the magic."

From the shadows came another voice, quavering but clear, his mother. Behind the many heads, he still could not see her, but he heard her voice as a thirsty man hears falling water. "Some have," she said. "His People to the north had the seeds of such within them. My mother called the Rattletail her brother. Of all the Sun People, she alone owned such magic."

Such an interruption of the Elders was a rare thing, but they were patient men. After a pause, one Elder spoke again. "And your mother was shaman to the Spukane?"

Even in the darkness, the boy could sense his mother's bowed head. "No, for she was a woman. But she knew the secret ways of the Rattletail, and she used the powers he holds in his teeth!"

Several of the women shifted position slightly, their knees making a rubbing sound in the dirt, their only comment. They had heard of the practices of some tribes who knew how to grind the Rattletail into dust and give the powder to women who wanted their bellies emptied of fertile seed. But they knew, too, that some had died by such means.

The boy spoke up, "I, Sin tehla, will learn these things, my People. My spirit power will teach me. He has already given me one gift." He knelt beside the mother of Camp Crier. "Does your mouth still hurt you, Old One?"

The elder nodded, her black eyes watching him carefully.

"Show me where," he whispered.

She opened her mouth and pointed back to a straggled row of blackened teeth. He peered inside her mouth and saw a hole in one large molar, ground down nearly to the gum. From his waist, he took another rattlesnake fang and gently poked it into the rusty cavity. He sensed all eyes on his back.

Another voice called out from the circle. Black Elk, a brooding man, spoke harshly. "I will have no blunt-horned calf for my shaman!"

Against all custom, his father's voice interrupted the speaker. "Every shaman was once such."

Suddenly, an old voice stopped the rising murmur around the circle. "Augh! I speak!" The old woman rose unsteadily to her feet, glaring at the People. She pointed to her jaw. "Already, he sees with his mother's mother's eyes. My tooth no longer pains me." She spat in the dust, glancing with bright eyes at the boy. "Let him tell the story. We heard his song and saw his dance, and my jaw aches no more. Let him tell the story!"

The Elders glanced at each other somberly. Rarely did any tell the stories save the Old Ones. Never a boy of fifteen summers. Finally, an old man lifted a gaunt hand as if in benediction. "Tell the story, then. And if the spirit of Sin tehla sits on your shoulders, we will hear him."

The boy stepped to the middle of the circle, his eyes gleaming bright with controlled excitement. He took rapid deep breaths as if he had a race to run. He felt his whole body fill with a lightening, a quickened rhythm down to his fingers, a tautness in his flesh. He began his dance, slowly rising to his toes so that he swayed, a dandelion on its stalk in an unseen wind. His feet made rustling sounds in the sand like the scales of the Rattletail; he began to writhe and twist, coiling his arms around his head, drawing the listeners' eyes to the movements he made in the dust. He felt the power sit on his shoulder, felt Sin tehla in his soul, and he began.

"Long, long ago," he sang, "when the sun was young and no bigger than a star, there was an island far off in the middle of the great water to the west. It was called Samah-tunie-whoo-lah. And on it lived a race of giants, white giants with hair as black as night." He drew his hands up over his head, bending and pulling at the air to show their height. All eyes followed him. "Their chief was a tall white woman called Scomalt."

A rustle went through the People, but the boy raised his voice and drew each ear back to him. "And she was great and strong and she had Sin tehla's powers of life and death and more! She could make whatever she wanted in the world."

And now he began to move jerkily about the circle, thrusting, feinting, and dodging, emulating battle. "For many years, the giants lived in peace, but at last they quarreled. And then they warred! The noise of battle was heard over the land!"—and here, the boy picked up his rattle gourds and crashed them together suddenly. "Scomalt was very angry!"

He crouched down quickly and whispered, a sound more riveting than a shout, "And so she said, 'I shall drive the wicked ones of these people far from me. Never no more shall my heart be made sick by them.'"

Now the boy changed his dance again, his song became one of lyric beauty, a haunting quest dance that made the listeners feel as they did on their first spring journey to the south each year. "And so she drove the wicked giants to one end of the island. And when they were gathered together in one place, she snapped off that piece of land"—and here, the boy broke a stick in half, the sound ringing sharply through the cave—"and she pushed it into the sea. For many days, the floating island drifted on the waves and winds. All the people on it died except one man," and he whirled in the dust suddenly, crouching on his knees, "and one woman."

He heard the old woman moan softly in cadence with his song, but he dared not heed her. He saw that all eyes were on him, as birds watch a snake coil. He made his gestures larger still, his body held all the winds and waters of the world, and he seemed to mold them in the air with his hands.

"And s-s-so . . ." he hissed softly, "they floated and drifted for many more days. The sun beat down upon them, and ocean storms swept them until they came to some islands across the sea. They steered their way through them and at last reached the land. On one side was the sea, on the other side was ice. They walked between the water and the great ice prairies toward the rising of the sun. On and on they walked until the man and the woman came to the great river, *our* river, and there, they stopped."

Several of the women began to add their voices to the Old One's, chanting and swaying in time to the boy's music, for they all knew what was coming next. But suddenly, the boy broke the expected rhythms and stood straight and tall, his arms stretched up to the roof of the cave. Slowly, he opened his arms as if to embrace all the people at once.

"Hear me, my People. It is I, Sin tehla, who speaks. And I tell you what is to come. In times to be, far past the death of our children's children, the ice will come again and the river will be tamed like a dog. Then the land will float, and the red fish will come no more. It will be the end of the world and the end of the People."

There was an abrupt silence in the cave as the boy stopped his song, ended his dance, and kneeled before the circle, his head bowed. This was an unfamiliar end to the story, one which no listener knew how to interpret or judge. The boy did not look up, though he sensed his mother's gaze on him, though he felt his father's stare.

Finally, one quavering voice took up the last few notes of his song. It was the most withered Elder of the tribe. The Old One got slowly to his feet, leaning on his two comrades with palsied hands. The silence in the cave seemed to press into the back of the boy's neck, bowing him still further.

"We will go, then, and see this kill," the Elder said.

The boy's heart surged forward violently in his chest, but he kept his face impassive.

As he led the band down the Canyon, along the river, and toward the spot where the mastodon had fallen, he breathed a silent prayer to Sin tehla that all would be well. He had covered the bloody carcass with shrubs and had carefully urinated at its four corners, leaving his mark to drive away any scavenging beasts.

Still, there was always a chance that his spirit power would leave him, even briefly, and if he were forsaken by Sin tehla now, he was lost. He glanced behind him to the clan, which followed in single file on the full day's journey it would take to reach the narrow canyon of the kill. He dared not meet his father's eyes for fear someone would notice his glance and be reminded of his youth. With this act, he would either make himself a place of power in the tribe, or he would mark himself forever a useless youth, invisible and nearly dead to all eyes. He forged ahead, mindful of the Old Ones and the children behind him, counting off the distance in his mind.

And when the tribe was finally gathered around the mastodon, he showed the Elders the sacred hole of the Rattletail in the canyon wall where Sin tehla had led him. Alone, he crawled past the boulders, among the snakes, whispering to them gently, soothing their flickering tongues, and the People's eyes grew large, their mouths silent with wonder. A few ventured to the edge of the sacred hole, and they saw the hundreds of Crawling People, some dead, some alive but sleeping in the cold darkness. The boy walked among the snakes that guarded his kill, driving them back, and then the People saw the power of his spear, still embedded deeply in the great Walker's ribs. At this, the Old Ones lifted their ancient voices in praise as they walked arm in arm to the river. Over the water, over the sound of the distant rapids and up the Canyon, they sent their chorus, as the people sang behind them.

> Henceforth this man shall be called
> Sin tehla, the Rattletail,
> Favored of all the Crawling People, Snake with Teeth!
> Henceforth, this man shall be boy no more but Shaman
> To the People until his power wanes, e-eeh-hah!
> O River, tell the Winds and the Sun,
> This man is Sin tehla, Snake with Teeth, eeehhah!

PART TWO

The River People,
1792–1825

For mankind is ever the same and nothing is lost out of
nature, though everything is altered.
—John Dryden,
"On the Characters in The Canterbury Tales,*"*
Preface, Fables, Ancient and Modern

*T*he great river begins high in the icy blue fields of the Canadian north, twisting and shoving its way through glacial canyons and raw granite, carrying its memories of a cold woods-lake birth, running green with rock salts and youthful power. It surges past the Selkirks and the Valhalla Mountains, out of what men will call British Columbia in its honor, south to the new land of America. The river itself is new now, younger than the rocks, younger than the sea to which it flees, but older than the packs of Chinook salmon that leap Kettle Falls and Grand Rapids, older than the deep woods, and far, far older than the men who follow its waters of promise.

Past the Canadian border, the river turns west and swallows up the Spokane, carves the Grand Coulee Canyon, and thunders over falls four-hundred feet high. It rolls over the desert lands, smooth and cool as a mother's palm, feeding Wenatchee with her apple orchards and Richland with her wheat.

Now, the river meets the Snake, turns west again, feels the tug of the sea, and thunders through deep woods and high mountains, past The Dalles, Mount Hood, Vancouver, Portland, Longview, through locks and under mighty ships, and stretches out wide arms and powerful fingers of currents, eating away the edges of Astoria and Ilwaco, racing into the ocean's embrace . . . names of places which man will build, names of mountains which man will climb, but none were named when the river and this story began, and only its voice split the silence of the wilderness. Look on your map for the river, follow it with your finger or your feet, but know that its waters carved the land before maps were drawn or eyes opened to see.

A THOUSAND YEARS PASSED, AND THE PEOPLE MOVED SLOWLY DOWN THE river, down the canyons, following the game. Long after Sin tehla was dust, long after the ice fields melted, the People reached a bend of the river where it turned to run to the sea, and they called it the "place of the snake," after their greatest shaman.

Three thousand years more, and the nomad tribe moved further west, meeting with and melting into the Okanogans, the San Poil, the Yakimas, the Klickitats, and the Wenatchi bands. Along the trail, the People forgot some customs and adopted new ways, but always, the river provided their rhythms and ordered their lives.

By the time Christ was born, Sin tehla's band called themselves the Chinooks, and they were the lords of the great river, which they named Wauna, the Source. Where Wauna met the sea in a five-mile mouth of twisting currents and treacherous sandbars, the Chinooks controlled the north shore of the mighty water and therefore all commerce up its twelve hundred miles.

Because of the river's resources, the People became the richest tribe in North America, masters of an intricate and far-flung system of trade that filled their cedar longhouses to overflowing with incredible bounty—a bounty which would finally, in this year of 1792, draw the attention of George Washington's newborn nation, across the span of the continent.

It was a dark winter night on the river. The Chinook village was silent, shrouded by heavy fog and the whispering fringed arms of the cedar trees. Outside the main lodge, the wind howled, its mouth full of snow. Ice frosted the canoes lined on the shore; the river rapped on their crusted sides. The salmon-drying racks were empty now and snow-dusted.

This was Qwatsamuts, the village of the People. It sprawled on a wide plain by the river, a village of twenty-two lodges and over three hundred Chinooks. Each lodge housed several families and their slaves, clans knit together by intricate and rigid marriage and birth ties. The tyee's lodge was the largest and most crowded with kin, for as chief of the Chinooks, Comcomly must care for all those who had nowhere else to go.

Inside the tyee's lodge, an acrid haze from the fires hung at the smoke hole, and the odors of damp blankets, dried salmon, dogs, and children made the air dense. Caches were full, and the little olachen, the herring so fat with oil that they burned like torches, were strung along the ridgepoles.

It was the month when every animal in its mother's womb starts to have hair, the season when men stay in the lodges, and the stories floated from fire to fire like embers on the smoke. This was the time when Talapas, the Coyote-Trickster, Yehlh, the Creator, and the Raven all made tamanawas, spirit power. Ilchee, Moon-girl, sat and listened to the tales. Wrapped in furs, she huddled on a pallet above the dogs and the fleas, dreaming idly as she watched the men smoke and the slaves care for the children. Comcomly, her father and tyee of the Chinooks, was laughing softly with Wallulah, her mother. She smiled to herself with pride.

Her mother was Comcomly's youngest wife, and even the Old Ones cackling at the fires had to admit she was also the most comely. A tyee's daughter in her own Scappoose tribe, Wallulah had come to Comcomly with a bride-price larger than any could remember. And after thirteen years on his pallet, having borne him only Ilchee, a girl-child, she was still the tyee's favorite. Would that *I* grow to such a place, Ilchee wished silently.

An old grandmother coughed and moved closer to the fire, interrupting Ilchee's thoughts. She tapped her pipe importantly, spilling the kinnikinnick ashes into the flames. She asked loudly, "If I tell the stories, what will you give me, neh?"

One voice quickly offered, "Dried salmon."

"No," she spat.

Another voice called, "Dried salal berries and whale oil."

She rocked on her heels, pondering this barter. Finally, "No," she grunted, shaking her gray braids.

Then Comcomly stood up, brushing aside his wife's legs. He was less than forty winters, yet already his stocky frame leaned slightly, as if he sought to peer deeper into whatever met his gaze . . . a gaze of only one eye, for the other had been lost long ago to the sickness-that-makes-holes-in-face. His knees and ankles were thick from years of squatting in the long canoes, his arms heavy as a sockeye. "Old One," he said, "tell us the stories, and I will give you the penis of an elk to put in your waist bag and warm you at night." He grinned broadly when the lodge laughed as one man.

"Hee-hee!" the Old One cackled, tossing her head like a young girl before a warrior. Her eyes fixed on the fire then, and her voice rose above the winds in the firs.

"Raven was going there, and when he got to the river where the Clatsops live, he saw a man dragging a cedar from the woods."

"Ah-ah-ah. . . ." A sigh of delight rippled through the lodge, followed by a few stifled snickers, for they knew this story well. Last cold season, it was the Klickitats so named.

"Raven was curious, and when he asked the man what he was doing, the Clatsop man said, 'My wife is having a baby, and she told me to bring wood for the fire.' "

At this, the People began to rock back and forth as though they felt a single, silent beat. Ilchee began the low humming song, and the rest of the young women took up the chant.

The Old One shuffled around the fire, flapping imaginary wings. "Well, and Raven flew down next to the Clatsop man and said, 'You are a fool to do battle with such a giant,' and he cut the wood up properly and piled it on his wings." She bent over as if she had a huge bundle on her back. "And so Raven carried home the Clatsop man's wood for him."

Several children hopped up and pretended to be old men carrying wood, in palsied, humpbacked staggers.

"Now . . ." the old woman went on, "Raven looked around some and peered into the lodge and said, 'Where is this woman who is having a child?' " Here and there, percussions of laughter punctuated her story.

"And the Clatsop man showed Raven his wife, stretched naked out on the furs and moaning, with a doeskin wrapped around her thigh. Raven looked and saw a sliver of cedar in her swollen skin, so he drew close to her and pecked and poked with his lo-n-g, brown beak—until he got it out." Here, the old woman rolled her eyes and rubbed her belly salaciously so none would miss the point of the story. As she chanted, many of the women joined in, for they knew the words well.

"And now Raven said, 'I will show you how to make a child,' and he hopped right on that Clatsop woman and enjoyed her while her husband stood by, grinning."

At this, the lodge rocked with laughter, and even small children, not quite knowing why, glanced at their elders and giggled with excited delight.

"And then?" prodded the Old One.

Now the whole lodge answered as one, "And when the child was born, Raven said to the Clatsop man, 'Here is your child. I give him to you. But he shall be called *Chinook!* ' "

Ilchee laughed aloud with the rest of the lodge and glanced toward her cousin, Soleme, Little Cranberry. She was pregnant with her first child, and she held her bulging belly as she giggled, her hand over her mouth. For an instant, the fires dimmed, Ilchee's eyes glazed, and she could see her cousin in a different season, her hands clutching her belly in birth. Soleme panted like a dog in the summer heat as the midwife drew a squalling, black-haired boy from her body. The child was bloodied from his battle for life, slippery and squirming, and then her mind's eye closed, and Ilchee saw no more.

"Well, and Raven will bring you a son next, my cousin," Ilchee called to Soleme, "and he *also* shall be called Chinook!"

Wallulah turned quickly and stared at her daughter, wondering how she knew such a thing, but the moment was lost in the noise of the lodge as the Old Ones began to speak of the news from northern tribes. There had been tales recently that strangers had come to the village of the Nootkas.

"They say that these sea-men arrived on the backs of huge black birds with white wings!" a woman whispered in awe.

"Ah-na, ah-na," chorused her sisters, making the sound of amazement and covering their mouths.

An Elder spoke up gravely, "The Old Ones of the Choppunish say that these white strangers are coming in great numbers, across the mountains. They have seen them in dreams."

"And what do they want with us, neh?" asked an old woman, leaning forward into the firelight.

Comcomly spoke out. "They want to trade, of course. Why else would they come this great distance?"

The people nodded as though with one head, and grunts of agreement circled the fires. The Elders began to speak of other things, and Ilchee settled back on the pallet to string more ta-cope shells for the spring barters.

The season of the cold moons was her favorite, the time of tsit-sika, winter magic, when everything was not real. Then, the shaman visited each lodge, telling his dreams of the future in exchange for oil, game, and spears. And only then were the story-songs told from mouth to mouth, while the earth slept and the People rested for the seasons ahead.

The People needed the winter magic but they feared it as well. The shaman was welcome only during the cold moon months, and many women shivered with relief when he had finished his prophesies and gone on to the next lodge. Never had there been a woman shaman in the tribe, in any tribe so far as Ilchee knew, and so the power of visions belonged only to men, who could not always be trusted to use them wisely . . . or gently.

Ilchee knew that most tribes on the river punished those who practiced magic without the approval of the Elders. The Clatsop forced witches into the forest to die. The Klickitats burned off their hair, and the Kwakiutl, the most barbarous of all, exacted the worst punishment. Ilchee shuddered as she recalled the whispered horrors which she had heard. A suspected Kwakiutl witch was bound and blindfolded, and a sharp green stick, heated in ceremonial fire, was rammed up her rectum with such power as to force the evil out her throat or mouth. Thus, the witch was made to walk about the village, stick in place, until she died.

Ilchee felt a sudden draft shiver up her spine. The life of a shaman was one of power, she thought—but also one of peril, as were all lives somehow separated from the rest of the tribe.

Ilchee became a woman after ten winters. Her first blood started as she strained to shove her little canoe up the beach after a day of hunting ducks in a quiet cove. She was not alarmed, of course, for she knew that her time was approaching, and she had been carefully prepared by her mother.

"Why does a boy become a man little by little," she had asked Wallulah, "and a girl turns to a woman overnight?"

"Perhaps it takes them longer," her mother had laughed softly. "And you will see in time."

To Ilchee's irritation, there were countless tests her brothers had endured to earn the solemn approval of the village, yet none she might share. She watched as Comcomly pounded wooden pegs into the sand, close to the fire, as was the custom. Cassakas, her half-brother, crouched close and tugged at them, ignoring his scorched face and singed hair. Then her father placed a hot coal on his son's forearm and keep it there until it hissed, while the boy suppressed his cries. It was said that Cassakas was brave, for his arm was scarred up and down.

But when Ilchee thrust out her own arm for the coal, her father gently pushed her back. "A woman has her own tests. Do not seek those of a man."

She had scowled fiercely at him. "I am as brave as my brother! Test me, my father. I will not shame you!"

But he had only laughed softly. "Well, and does the sapling argue with the wind? Run and tell your mother that the bowls are empty."

"I paddle my own canoe, and I shall—"

"Aye," her father said testily. "And that alone is a thing to be wondered at and told from fire to fire, that Comcomly feeds a little fool in his lodge. No other girl has her own canoe."

"Those who talk the loudest are the same mouths which my canoe passed in last season's races." She smiled quietly.

Comcomly rolled his one eye to the skies, as if only the gods could explain such a daughter. "You are like your mother. Arguing with her is like cutting water with a knife. When I shout at her, I wake to find her in the women's lodge, where she does not come out for seven days. Either my words start her flow, or she has a spirit willing to start it for her. Soon enough, you will make your own visit there, my daughter."

And now, her time had come. She almost relished it, so eager was she to prove herself. She hurried to the lodge to tell her mother. She was surprised to see Wallulah's dark eyes fill with water when she heard the news.

"So. My daughter is a woman at last. And soon she will leave her old mother and go to another's lodge to be wife."

Ilchee grimaced and burrowed deeper into Wallulah's arms. "Such a time is still fifty seasons off, Mother. Who would have this skinny child in his pallet, neh?"

But her mother only smiled.

While the Drummer called the news, Ilchee walked to the women's place, carefully, with dignity, as though she carried a cup of water between her knees. This women's place, the refuge for a hundred generations of females, was a small hut outside the village, away from the berry bushes and facing the woods.

The Old Ones came soon, those women well versed in the ways of making-a-woman time. They brought with them the special skirt Ilchee must wear, a soft cedar apron with detachable panels and a doeskin waist cinch. They bathed her repeatedly in warm water, chanting the woman songs to her, teaching her the taboos.

She must sit quietly on a special woman's mat, secluded for thirty suns. She would see only her mother and the Old Ones during that long time, and she must stay inside. She could have no fire lest the evil spirits be drawn to her; she could eat no fresh meat or salmon, lest the game be offended and leave the village forever. She could have only four sips of water each day, or her belly would grow stout. She was not to speak at all without reason, and she was to think of nothing save her duties as a woman and a wife.

Ilchee listened to her instructors patiently, hiding her resentment behind a bland face, her head low. But when the Old Ones left, she turned to her mother in anger. "This is not a trial! Not a real test of courage. This is a prison!"

"It is indeed a trial, my daughter. Women and men must have different forms of courage."

"I would rather endure the hot coals or eat of the grizzly's heart as my brothers do! They are told, 'you must,' while I am only told, 'you must not.' Of what use am I to the village locked up here? It takes no courage. Anyone can do this."

"A man could not," her mother said quietly and left her to her own thoughts.

The women's hut was dark and cold at nights, with no fire. Ilchee could hear the faint sounds of the village behind her, and she felt deeply alone. Once, she was so lost in reverie that she was startled by a raven cawing as he flew out to sea one morning. The day seemed to float by, and she heard him again as he flew home to the woods to roost.

She sang spirit songs to herself, chanted the old stories, and floated outside her body to visit her sisters, her mother, her kinsmen. At times, the loneliness seemed a black hole that swallowed her slowly, from the edges inward, but she pushed it away and sang her songs even louder.

One night, as she dozed in her hut, she heard voices close behind her. She was instantly awake, tensed in the darkness. These were not the voices of the People, but of another tribe—the warring Quinaults up the coast. She could understand part of the words, but most were lost in the guttural, unfamiliar accent. Her heart was thudding in her chest, and she froze as a twig snapped under a foot. She reached cautiously for her knife and crouched in the farthest corner of the hut.

Suddenly, the mat covering was wrenched aside, and Ilchee saw two dark hulks against the night sky. One gruff voice whispered something—she could understand only the words "tyee" and "woman"—but Ilchee did not wait for the unintelligible hiss to cease. She leaped upward from the shadows, scratching and clawing at the intruders, thrusting wildly with her knife. Hands gripped her shoulders, bending her back, and she smelled a rank rutting odor close to her face. She twisted violently, reached up and hit at whatever held her. She felt a slick braid slip through her fingers and she pulled with all her strength, kicking upward to an unseen groin, stabbing in all directions. A man grunted and let out a few startled coughs. She heard one stark yelp as her knife slid into a leg—and they were gone, crashing through the brush, as suddenly as they'd come.

She lay down panting, chanting a warrior's song between her gasps. "The weapon flew into my hands, wah! And I cut them and drove them away. I drove off their madness, hai! Now hear my warrior's song, Raven, hear my woman's song!"

I did not cry out, she whispered furiously. I battled alone. And now, I will not go screaming into the village, crying out in fear. But when my trial is over, all will know the shame of the Quinaults. She smiled in the darkness, her heart quiet now. Men must have the whole village witness their acts of courage. My mother is right, she thought. A woman's courage is private; her victories are secrets to carry in silence.

When one full moon had passed, Ilchee's trial was finished. Now, she was ready for the cleansing ceremony which would protect her in life and ensure that she marry into a family with high prestige. The Old Ones bathed her, brushed her gently with cedar boughs, oiled her limbs and her hair, and painted her with red ochre, marking her with the signs of the moon, her own suin, her magic. They laid her on a pallet and dotted her body with tattoos, ashes rubbed into cuts made with beaver teeth. She never winced. They pulled out the stray hairs on her forehead and cut her nails and plucked her brows. Finally, she was ready.

At daybreak, Ilchee was awakened by a light tapping on her head. Her mother stood before her, knocking her gently with a cedar branch. "This will give you protection against browbeating, my daughter," Wallulah smiled. "Now, come. The dancers are waiting."

Ilchee was dressed carefully in her finest cedar robes and walked through the village, curtained by four blankets that the Old Ones held about her. They entered the lodge, and many voices rose in song on all sides. The fires burned high, and in the light, Ilchee could see Comcomly arrayed in his ceremonial brimmed hat, carrying his personal totem stick. Soleme smiled from the edge of the fire, her new son on her back, and Wallulah stood waiting proudly.

To one side of the fire, four masked young men stood in a row. Each was painted with red figures as she was; each held a pair of tongs. Ilchee thought she knew two of them, but in the darkness, she could not be sure.

The drummers began, and the stick-beaters kept time. The women sang the being-born song and shook their rattles. The lodge throbbed with music and rhythm, and behind the blankets, the Old Ones readied four baskets full of water and winter ferns.

The young men began to dance before the blankets that sheltered Ilchee, moving up toward her in a line, and then away. As they came forward a fourth time, they each plucked a hot rock from the fire and dropped it into a basket which the Old Ones had placed outside the circle of blankets.

As the water heated, the voices rose louder, and the drums beat faster. The Old Ones removed Ilchee's robes and began to bathe her, chanting her spirit song, letting the warm, scented water roll down her limbs, brushing her gently with the wet fern leaves. Ilchee began to tremble, and it was as though the drums were within her. She felt a heat begin in her legs, move to her belly, and she began to sway with the voices, humming inside.

The Old Ones stripped away her blankets and she stood, naked and wet before the clan. A buzzing filled her heart, and she drew her head high, looking past the dancers, past the fire, past even her mother into some distant light place which she could see in her mind. For the first time in her life, she felt beautiful, powerful, and her eyes watered with the fierce pride of it.

The drums beat faster still, and she felt her legs respond to the beat. She danced alone before the People, her black hair swinging about her breasts, her oiled legs catching the fire, a whirl of wet skin and red paint twisting in a blur of color. Faster and faster she moved, lifting her legs higher, feeling the glory of her body. She danced before the young men, never looking at them, seeing only the vision of herself as woman.

One warrior sprang forward, dancing close to her in the firelight. He circled her, drawing nearer and then moving away, his body never quite touching hers. Then another warrior danced close, closer still, brushing against her. For an instant, she almost cried out at the throbbing she felt in her belly, the rush of moisture, the trembling of her loins. She could feel the heat of his flesh, could almost taste the sweat on his skin, and when he finally grasped her hips, bent her back, and penetrated her with a thrust of pain and pleasure, she wailed as she had heard a hundred women wail before her. The drums thundered, and the women's voices rose high, keening, and full of triumph. Ilchee wrenched herself free, whirling between the dancing men, the woman's blood on her thighs. Her eyes closed in ecstasy, and she danced alone, as the warriors melted back into the crowd.

Finally, the drums slowed, finished, and Ilchee stood silent, trembling. The Old Ones gave a signal, and the women scrambled to tear her blankets, for a piece of such magic brought great luck.

Comcomly stepped forward and took Ilchee by the hand, leading her to the center of the lodge, before all eyes. "My daughter, Ilchee, is now no longer a girl but a woman. From this time on, she shall be known by the name Ilchee, Moon-woman, and is favored in my heart. Let all who see and all who hear know this to be true. I say so."

In the following moon, Comcomly gave a potlatch, a gifting ceremony to honor Ilchee's coming of age. He had counted his blankets, furs, canoes, and slaves, keeping a record of all he owned by tying knots in a cord, one knot for each guest he planned to gift, for the potlatch was as much investment as ceremony. Those gifted in this season would return the favor in kind—but each would try to best the other—and in this way, trade became as urgent as life, and wealth could only increase.

Ilchee sat at the center fire, flanked by her mother and sisters, watching as the guests arrived. There were the Modoc, smeared with their red clay from the lands to the south; the Kwakiutl, who wore shells jutting from their lower lips; and the Chopunnish with their pierced noses. Only the river people, she noticed with pride, could boast the flattened head of the aristocrat. All the other tribes had rounded heads like slaves.

Comcomly strode the center of the lodge, welcoming kinsmen from both sides of the river, bowing and striking his chest with his totem stick to show his unworthiness for their attention. Ilchee was whispering with her sisters, judging each new arrival, when suddenly she saw outside the lodge a cluster of men tying their canoes in the shallows. As though the walls melted away, she heard their voices calling one to the other, shouting orders to their slaves, the same guttural rhythms she remembered from over a moon before. The Quinault party was here, and with them, the two men who had tried to shame her that night.

She stiffened as the Quinaults entered the lodge. They bowed to Comcomly and took their places by the fire. One of the Quinault warriors, a man with long black hair and a hooked nose, limped slightly from a wound hidden by his robes. Now, Comcomly was passing around the inner circle of most honored guests, those seated closest to the fire, as he dispersed notched sticks, markers for furs, baskets, canoes, and slaves, which those so chosen could claim at the end of the ceremony.

The Quinault warriors sat at the outer edges of the circle, their tyee in their midst. Just before the Quinault tyee could take a

marker from Comcomly's hand, Ilchee walked to the center of the
lodge and held up her arms before the fire. All eyes turned to her,
for never before had a woman, even a favored daughter, interrupted
the potlatch.

"Hear me, my People!" Ilchee's words rang round the lodge, but
she kept her eyes on her father. His jaw was open in amazement,
his face rigid with disapproval. Before he could speak, she whirled
on the Quinault party, pointing a shaking finger at two of their
warriors. "There sit two who would have shamed Comcomly's
lodge! Two who came in the night to the women's place, bearing
their private parts like weapons before them!"

A shocked mutter rumbled round the lodge as all eyes turned
from the Quinault party to Comcomly, whose face grew dark with
anger. "What is this?" her father asked, his voice low, ominous.

The Quinault tyee stood and faced the crowd, deliberately turning his back to Ilchee. "What is what, the whimpers of a child? Do
the People listen to a frightened doe who cries at footsteps in the
dark and brings her dreams to a council of men?"

Now, Ilchee knew that these were her attackers, indeed. And
more ominous, their tyee knew as well.

Comcomly pointed to the two warriors on the fringe of the Quinaults. "Is there truth to this shame?"

The Quinault tyee pulled himself to his full height, wrapping his
cedar robes about him. "We have not come to be accused, and we
will not stay to be judged." He turned to go, and the Quinault party
rose to their feet as one man.

Ilchee spoke again, her voice a quiet command in the silence. For
the moment, she was not a girl, but a warrior. "There is one carrion
crow here who limps. Ask him with the long beak to tell how he
came by the wound on his left leg, just below the knee . . . a wound
which the healing herbs still have not closed. A wound which
matches this!" and she yanked her knife from beneath her feasting
robes and held it high before the flames.

A gasp came from behind her, her mother's cry of outrage and
painful knowledge, but Ilchee ignored it. She started toward the
glowering Quinault, her knife before her, but a hand reached out
and grasped her arm.

The Clatsop tyee, a friend to her father, pushed her gently aside
and said, "Perhaps Comcomly's daughter wounded a Sasquatch in
the night. If the warrior's leg is unscarred . . ."

But the Quinault tyee spat with contempt. "Have all on this river gone mad? To insult the feasting with the croaks of a girl-frog? She has shamed herself, her father, and her people with her dreams. She sees ghosts where none exist."

The Quinaults pushed quickly toward the door of the lodge, but Comcomly caught the hook-nosed warrior by the arm, whirled him around, and whipped aside his cedar robe. A reddened wound sliced across the man's calf, an ugly scar, as yet unhealed from Ilchee's knife. Comcomly stared at the exposed leg, as the mutters round the lodge rose to an angry rumble.

"First, like wolves, you come in the night to steal my daughter's honor. Now, you come to steal my wealth as well." He turned to the guests, his arms outstretched over them as though in benediction. "Hear me, my People. These cowards are unwelcome on the river. We will buy none of their goods, neither will their refuse be bartered in our lodges. I say so." Majestically, Comcomly turned his back to the Quinaults, but they were already gone.

As though a chill wind had just blown through the lodge and then out again, the incident was quickly forgotten. The guests settled down to the business of feasting, but to Ilchee's surprise, few spoke to her. She felt eyes slide over her and then swiftly away. She felt a sharp stab of loneliness, and she wondered if she should have kept silent, after all.

Wallulah finished her duties to the guests, moving gracefully among the slaves, directing the feasting, and then she sat down next to her daughter.

"They do not look at me, Mother," Ilchee said softly.

But Wallulah's voice seemed almost gay. "No, they will not. They wonder what else you see, besides unhealed wounds under cedar robes."

"Perhaps I should have kept silent. You told me that a woman's bravery must be private."

"It is hard for them to hear a woman accuse a warrior, even of another tribe. They look away because they are confused. And perhaps afraid of what they do not understand. But I am proud, my daughter." She took a mouthful of salmon and gazed out over the crowd, her face bland. "Did you see his wound in your heart? A vision, perhaps?"

Ilchee scowled. "No. I felt my knife cut him that night in the dark and I remembered and that is all."

Wallulah patted her knee gently, rising to serve the herring eggs. "Well, and that is enough, my Moon-girl. They will forget before the pipes are passed. You must do the same."

The smoke rose higher and thicker in the lodge, and finally, the feasting was over. The men took out their pipes, long-stemmed bowls of stone and horn filled with kinnikinnick, the herb that settled all good food. Taking great draughts of smoke in their mouths, they relieved their bellies and punctuated the air with enthusiastic belches.

As Ilchee crept out the door, seeking a quiet spot to think over this night's happenings, she heard an old man murmur, "Aiya, the potlatch was good. A shaming of enemies and a filling of bellies. This lodge is now poorer but filled with honor."

She smiled to herself ruefully. So long as the guests got their share of blankets and gifts, so long as the feasting was ample, then all else was simply sport, amusement they would trade up and down the river like so many ta-cope, to be passed from mouth to mouth, each time growing larger with the telling.

She sat on a log up the beach, her feet dangling in the shallows. I faced my attackers, she thought, and I shamed them before the People, my knife in my hand. Then why, she wondered, do I feel empty of pride? If I were a young warrior, the People would be feasting my courage. But because I am a woman, their eyes pluck at me and then move away.

She hear her mother's voice in her ear once more: "A vision, perhaps?" Suddenly she gasped. She had seen Soleme crouching over the birth place, and now, she carried a son on her back. A son she saw in her cousin's belly before he ever took a breath. She had seen the Quinaults before they entered the lodge, seen them tying their boats, heard their voices over the tumult of the arriving guests, seen them, seen them, as though her eyes had floated outside her body, alive with their own vision. She had known which leg carried her knife's brand before they had even entered.

A flood of awe and panic rolled through her, and Ilchee bowed her head in lonely anguish. What is coming to me? she wondered. Will these visions make me mad? Will I be the object of murmuring tongues all my days? Will I always feel outside myself, separate and apart from my people?

She clenched her jaw, fighting down the ache in her throat. I will not open my mind to these voices, she vowed. Yes, she had seen things which no one else had seen. But no one need know. And never would she speak of it again.

Four moons later on a foggy night at high tide, twenty canoes silently paddled into the small bay north of the Chinook village. Fifty Quinault warriors tied their craft in the shallows and crept along the shore. They were almost upon the Chinook camp when the Drummer sighted them.

Ilchee woke with a start and cried, "The enemy!" before she heard the alarm cry, and when the Drummer called "Waloo! Waloo! To the woods!" she was running from the lodge with the rest of the clan before she was even fully alert. The young and the Old Ones rushed to the shelter of the trees, while Comcomly called the warriors to the beach.

Somehow in the confusion, Ilchee was separated from her mother, and she crouched, shivering in the mist, behind a cluster of huckleberry bushes. The forest itself seemed hushed. No bird called, the fog grew thicker, and she heard only the steady drip from the cedar trees. Suddenly, her neck hairs bristled up like a rising tide, and she was instantly, completely, afraid. She sensed a step behind her, and she whirled to see several hulking shadows creeping through the trees. The Quinaults had cut through the woods behind the warriors to capture the women and children. Ilchee shouted, a child screamed, and abruptly, the trees were alive with bodies. The women struggled, but several wives heavy with child were help-lessly bent over, shielding their bellies. Wallulah was among them, fighting savagely, while a Quinault warrior hauled her roughly to the canoes. Without thought, Ilchee jumped on his back and plunged her knife into the man's neck, growling in rage and terror. He writhed under her, she felt the knife scrape bone and rode him to the ground, where he twitched convulsively at her feet. She grabbed for Wallulah's hand, and instantly, she was in the middle of battle as Chinook warriors cut down the enemy in the thicket all around her. She crouched down, pulled her mother to her knees, and twisted under the brush for protection.

The Quinaults, still holding six captives, beat their way to their canoes, trying to hold the Chinooks at bay. When they got to the river, they found that the tide was out. They tried desperately to dislodge their heavy war canoes from the mud flats, shouting threats over their shoulders at the oncoming Chinooks.

Ilchee reached the beach and saw the women huddled by the side of a canoe, herded together by two Quinaults. "Run!" she shouted, picking up a rock and hurling it at the guards, racing directly toward them. The women heard her shout, saw the band running to their rescue, and turned on their captors, ripping and tearing at their faces.

The Chinooks surged down the beach, trapping the Quinaults between the mud flats and the woods. With swords, sticks, and poison arrows, they destroyed the enemy in moments. Dead bodies littered the mud, and the Old Ones and children crept in to kick at the muddied corpses. The band camped there at the mouth of the bay, waiting for the tide to return. The dogfish came, attracted by the scent of death. Comcomly retrieved one partially eaten head of a Quinault warrior to send back to the tribe as a warning.

The lodges that night rang with story-songs to Comcomly, to the warriors, and to Ilchee, who had climbed the enemy's back. Once again, she felt eyes slide over her and then away, as she sat beside her father. Few women had been honored in this way, she knew. She knew, also, that some wondered just what sort of daughter Comcomly had birthed with his Scappoose wife. But this night, she did not care, and she straightened her shoulders as the warriors did, holding her head high. And when it came time for her to sing her song of victory, she sang a special spirit song to the dogfish who had helped vanquish the enemy. But she kept her voice soft and low, as befitted a woman.

The shores of the river, silent in winter, now pulsed with the spring excitement. Ilchee stood at the door of the lodge, watching as the slaves carried baskets of dried clams from the canoes. The harvest at Willapa Bay had been good this year. She smiled to herself. Trade would be rich.

"Place those on the drying racks," she directed a slave, and then she looked up to see a huge canoe crossing the mouth of the river, its sails flapping like the mythical white wings of the Thunderbird, its back crowded with men.

Aboard the two-hundred-ton, two-decker ship *Columbia Rediviva*, Captain Robert Gray peered warily at the shifting currents and sandbars on both sides of his vessel. "Damn it to hell, Boit! Watch for that shoal to port!"

John Boit, fifth mate, pulled his eyes away from the lush panorama of river and woodland before him and helped wrestle the ship to quieter waters. He was still in awe of the formidable tides of this river. Even nine miles from its green maw, they had let down a bucket and brought up fresh water.

A sailor shouted, "Savages, Captain!" and all eyes turned fearfully toward shore.

The People shouted alarm warnings as women and children raced for the safety of the forest. Ilchee crouched in the door of the lodge and then crept closer, kneeling behind a canoe. The warriors circled around Comcomly at the river's edge, watching the ship nervously and avoiding the fear in each other's eyes.

"Hiyaa!" shouted Comcomly anxiously. "Hold your arms up and spread out! We must look like many!"

Now, Ilchee knew what the Nootka Elders had felt when they saw such a monster in their waters. Aiya, and their story-talk was true! She remembered, with a great cold silence in her breast, the tales of these big canoes with their barking guns that bit, sometimes to the death.

"It is the white castaways," Comcomly said calmly, regaining his composure. "We have heard of such, neh? Let us greet them like warriors, not women."

Ilchee shrank back in the lodge. Well, and she would wait and see, she thought. That night, the village gathered in the longhouse to debate the wisdom of commerce with the strangers.

"Are we so much stronger than our brothers to the north? That we should barter with these whites and win, when others have lost, neh?" one old man called anxiously.

"Our People have always bested our brothers in trade. It follows that we shall best these white castaways as well," answered a warrior impatiently.

"Ay-y-y!" shouted an old woman. "But it is said they bring the shaking sickness and the sickness-that-makes-holes-in-face! The Shoshoni say they make it and slip it in with their trade goods, so as to weaken the People."

"For what purpose?" shouted Comcomly. "Why should these white strangers seek to harm us?"

"To take our land," a young wife spoke up, and the women sitting near her nodded in agreement.

Comcomly grinned. "To take land? You speak as though the land can be stolen like canoes or bartered like blankets. The land is here, like the river and the wind. Does anyone take these?" He smiled sideways at the warriors about him. "Unless the whites can move mountains and put them on the backs of their canoes, the land will stay." The warriors laughed loudly and appreciatively. "And we will stay as well."

Ilchee said nothing, but she felt a familiar prickle at the back of her neck when the men laughed together. She glanced at her mother, but Wallulah only shrugged. The warriors were proud of their reputation as the fiercest traders on the river. If the whites had goods to barter, no tyee could keep the People away, and new wealth would fill every lodge. But a small patch of cold fear spread in her belly, despite the fire's warmth.

The next morning, twenty canoes filled with eager Chinooks and their trade goods headed for the great ship. Captain Gray watched from the deck as they approached. "Dirty and naked like every godforsaken savage on this coast," he muttered to Boit.

"Aye, sir. But some o' their women are handsome," Boit observed as he watched the canoes maneuver next to the ship.

"You been out of Boston too long, Boit, if you think bandy legs and dragging tits are handsome!" Gray guffawed.

Ilchee rode in the back of her father's canoe, and she saw the white men peering over the side. She covered her mouth in astonishment. These white strangers were so tall, a full head over her father! Their faces were not white like the gull, but pink, the color of clams rotting in the sun. Small mouths—Raven must have wanted them thin. No tattoos, no shells on their ears or noses, a stink like wet dogs, wild hair all over their faces, and the round heads of slaves. And if they wore so many clothes in this, the hottest season, what must they do in the winter moons, neh? No wonder they traded for all the Nootka furs, she thought. They even try to grow their own on their faces! All in all, they were a grotesque people, and she wondered that they could manage such a ship, so ungainly did they seem.

Her father led the trading party on board, and Ilchee eased around the edge of the men, trying to watch the sailors and keep out of sight. She looked about for the other women but they stayed at the rail, ready to fly over the edge of the ship in a moment.

Captain Gray was uneasy with so many savages onboard, and he kept his men back, edging toward Comcomly as he might a colorful snake of an unfamiliar species. Suddenly, he spied Ilchee, naked to the waist, with her cedar skirt about her loins, peering around the men, a bundle on her back. Surely, they could not be hostile, he thought, if they let a young woman with her child up close.

Grinning broadly to Comcomly, he bowed, then carefully, slowly, offered his two open palms to Ilchee, watching always for signs of danger from the natives. His men tensed behind him. Ilchee shrank back against the railing, glancing to her father and at the women huddled like frightened quail. To her surprise, Comcomly gently shoved her forward.

"The strangers find my daughter beautiful!" he shouted in Chinook. "Trade will be good this day!"

Ilchee shyly stepped to the center of the men. She unrolled her blanket on the deck, revealing not a baby but the trade goods she had made with her own hands—woven baskets, hides, and shell necklaces. She held out her palms in the gesture of trade.

Bartering was brisk then, and when Ilchee lowered herself down to the canoe once more, she carried six roots of the magic rock—nails, the men called them—and ten gold buttons wrapped in the folds of her blanket. The white tyee is ugly, she shuddered, but openhanded in trade. Especially to women.

The white ships came more frequently to the river in the following seasons, but the rhythms of the People were unchanged. When the leaves began to fall, Ilchee prepared to go on a spirit quest. She told her mother and received only a bowed head in reply. Her father, however, squinted his one eye in anger.

"Already, the young men look sideways at you," he said. "Already, they talk of you in the lodges. 'She *sees* things,' they say, and they do not come offering me a bride-price for you. A woman has no need of dreams!"

But to Ilchee's surprise, her mother stood against her father and refused to dissuade her from the dream walk. When two more ships dropped anchor in the river, Comcomly was soon too distracted to fight both women.

Ilchee prepared for her journey with days of fasting and frequent cold baths to fortify herself. She tied a wide cinch about her waist to stave off hunger, shouldered her bow, and slipped away from the village. She struck out across the well-worn paths, up the mountain where the woods were deep.

As she walked, Soleme's words came to her. "You must not make the Searching," her cousin had begged. "Do you think Raven will come to you? Or Talapas, or Thunderbird? Not a single woman in the village has received such a vision. You play a child's game. And what if Tatoosh makes the mountain smoke and rumble while you are at his feet?"

"I have been to the women's place," Ilchee had explained patiently. "I have worked over netting and rush baskets until my fingers are sore. I have held my sisters' children and quieted their cries on my breast. None of this fills my heart. The mountains, where the gods walk, is where I must go. And if Tatoosh rumbles, well, and I will listen to his words."

Now as she reached the timberline and turned to look back at the river, she was content with her decision. I am looking into the faces of the oldest gods, she thought, and their power is hovering over me. How many have seen them before me? What other searching souls are with me now, besides those of the gods?

Far in the distance, she could see the river-with-one-edge, what the whites called the ocean. The sky above it was oily and dark, and she tasted rain in the wind. She kept walking upward. By nightfall, she felt the irritation rise in her, and she remembered her brother's warning of olo latate, the hungry-head.

Cassakas had made the dream walk the year before and had reluctantly counseled her, even as she swore him to secrecy. "This you must control," he had said. "The hungry-head will lie to you and give you blind advice. Do not heed it."

She lay down and dozed fitfully. When the rain splattered on her, she pulled her blanket close and slept again, a sleep full of flitting dreams and the consciousness of cold and wet. She awoke at daybreak with the sharp grinding of hunger in her belly. Pulling her cinch tighter, she stood and walked again, towards the jagged peaks. It was time to find her spirit place.

She came to a clearing, ringed by ferns. Feeling more at peace than she had for two days, she sat down, drawing her knees up to her chin. She felt her body sinking into the earth as if into a mother's lap. This, then, is my place of Searching, she thought, and she waited.

Another day and night passed, and Ilchee prayed and whispered chants of steadfastness to the gods, asking them to support her in her Searching. On the night of the fourth day, she felt a lightness well up from her body, a tingling that began in her fingers and her toes and crept up her limbs until she felt a warm core at her heart and little else. She sensed that her soul was being purified, strengthened for a great vision. And then she fell asleep.

In her dream, she saw two great darknesses like separate clouds moving up the river. Both shadows settled over the People's lodges, and as from a great distance, she could hear the death wails of the village. She shivered violently in her sleep with despair. But way off in the sea, she saw a light hovering over a faraway island. She drew nearer and flew over the island like a gull, dipping closer to investigate.

In the middle of the island was a clearing. A white man stood alone, and on his arm he held a huge eagle. She knew instinctively that this was the man she had come to find. Suddenly, it was as if *she* were the eagle, bound and tied. She could feel the ropes on her talons, could hear the panicked blood beat in her feathered breast as she flapped her wings. Now, she was above the man, watching him calmly. The eagle grew larger and darker until it became a giant raven, and it turned and plucked out the eye of the white man, swallowing it like a berry, leaving him blind and gasping. The raven flapped its black wings and left the man's arm, coming right toward her in the sky.

Ilchee felt a gust of fear, for she knew she was too weak to fight. Abruptly, she realized her spirit partner was upon her, and the shock of her vision awakened her.

She looked about and could see nothing in the dusk. She heard a rustling in the spruce. High on a limb directly above her, a large raven sat, cocking its black eye at her calmly.

So. Raven sits above me, calling out to me even in my dreams. Raven is my spirit partner. He has shown me a great evil which will come from the white man and descend upon my People. And shown me somehow—how, I am not sure—that I must warn them. Raven, the god with the strongest magic of all the creatures, he of cunning and wisdom, has come to *me*. She was flushed with pride and a fierce sense of duty.

She stood slowly, holding her hands up to the large bird. "Thank you, O Raven, for my vision. For bringing me to this place of Searching to meet my spirit power. I see and I understand."

Ilchee began her spirit dance, moving her arms as the raven did, cocking her head as she sang. Her faintness was gone from her now, and she felt only a great joy which forced water from the corners of her eyes. As she danced, the raven spread his wings wide and opened his bill as though to speak. There was no question in his eyes, no fear, no startled movement, only a welcoming warmth as he seemed to listen to her song. Her heart rose to meet him, and she felt a singing hum through her soul.

My Searching is successful, she thought. I will bring a mighty spirit partner back to the village and tell of my vision. *I* have had a vision that can now bring pride to my father's fire. And Raven will show my People how to fight the black clouds of death, the evil of the whites which will come from the river and the sea to cover the lodges. Raven will tell me, and I will tell the People.

But when Ilchee returned from her Searching, she found the People deaf to her vision. She told of Raven's warning, and mouths muttered quietly before she had even finished.

"It was only an empty belly talking," an old man sneered. "Perhaps an empty head, as well."

Ilchee glanced at her mother in astonishment and saw Wallulah's eyes flood with pain. Her father watched her carefully, his eyes narrowed with—what? she wondered. Suspicion? Doubt? Finally, he rose to his feet and motioned for silence.

"Moon-woman has seen a dream. Perhaps it was Raven speaking to her, perhaps only the shadows of the mountain. But in this lodge, all may tell their dreams and be heard. Whether the People will believe, well, and that is for each to say alone."

A woman spoke from the back of the fire. "The trade has been good. The big ships bring great wealth, and the lodges are filled with busy hands this season. Should we drive off the whites on the word of one who cannot see her *own* path clearly? One who flits blindly, like the bat, after unseen phantoms?"

Ilchee gasped in outrage. The bat was neither bird nor beast but a poor creature caught between two worlds, belonging nowhere. Before she could speak, her father motioned her still.

"Let us wait and see. No dream, however muddied, can hurt us, neh? The gods do not speak to women, well, and we all know this. But it is also true that even the seasons change. I will hear no more talk of dreams and visions this night. Elowah!" he called to her sister. "This oil has grown cold with talking." And he sat down to eat, averting his head from his women.

In the next moons, strangers came more often to the river. A Spanish ship anchored off the bay for days, and the People paddled to and fro with goods to trade, bartering hundreds of otter skins, elk hides, beaver, and salmon for swords, nails, and copper tea kettles, which they hung from their lodges as ornaments.

Increasingly, the women of the village took control of the ship trade, for naked, they were more welcome onboard than their men, who could not be persuaded to barter without their weapons about them. When Captain James Baker from Boston anchored the *Jenny* in the Columbia's shallows, one older woman paddled a canoe full of young girls, both slave and free, alongside his ship.

"You buy ripe girls, neh?" she shouted, gesturing to their naked flanks. "Bring you pleasure and warm your old bones!" she cackled in Chinook.

This was the first time the Boston captain had seen such a display in these waters, and he asked his Nootka interpreter why it was allowed.

The man shrugged laconically. "Chinook woman want canoe. Chinook man get fishhooks."

"You mean they're married? And their husbands take their—they *pander* for them?"

"Chinook woman get five fishhooks. She give fishhooks to husband. Husband count up fishhooks and get her canoe when he has plenty. Good for everybody, neh?"

The following season, a young slave girl gave birth to a son. The child was the result of shipboard sport with Mister Williams, first officer of the *Jenny*, for which the girl received eight fishhooks, a bonus of three. Because the child was white, with light hair and eyes, he was fed to the river.

Other women, fearing that their husbands might reject such babies and them as well, took herbal tonics to rid their bellies of the white seeds or pressed themselves violently over sticks or fallen logs to expel the unwanted life. The Elders muttered against such evil, but the women still went to the ships, and their men still collected the fishhooks.

Because of her vision, Ilchee never again set foot onboard a white ship, but the other women in the village eagerly discovered what was most wanted and provided it. Those women with slaves were able to gain still more wealth by bartering them to the sailors. If they had no slaves, they offered themselves or their daughters. No lodge could afford to ignore the white trade; to do so would mean relative poverty in less than a season.

It came to be that the women learned more of the Boston-men's speech and made better trade than their men ever had. The white man was strangely vulnerable to the wiles of females, Comcomly told the council. He wondered aloud if the Boston-men had any women of their own, so lustful did they seem.

"Perhaps the white women have hair between their legs as the white man does on his face," laughed an old man. "Perhaps the white man cannot even find her womanhole for all that hair."

Ilchee listened, and her heart was torn. Her mind told her that the growing power of the women in the band was a good thing. Even her youngest sisters no longer bowed their heads and turned their eyes away when a man came to the lodge. And knowledge of the white strangers must be good, as well—but at what cost?

Since her Searching, she had no more dreams. Indeed, she sometimes wondered if Raven remembered her at all. A small, throbbing voice of doubt plagued her. Had she only wished so hard that she made it so? Was she, as some said, chasing only phantoms of her mind? She waited and watched, wondering what else the People were trading from the whites.

Kathla, the third daughter of the canoemaker, was stricken with a new sickness. She had many running sores on her legs and lips, and she winced and cried out when she had to walk or lift her arms. The shaman was called, but he could do nothing to ease her pain or to stop the swelling under her limbs. Finally, fearing a brother of the sickness-that-makes-holes-in-face, the People cast her out. She was banished to a hut far outside the village, to an isolated point deep in the woods. Her old grandmother, whose life was of little value to anyone, went with the stricken one to care for her.

Each morning, the canoemaker went to the rocks near their hut and placed food and herbal remedies there, shouting out his instructions and concern for Kathla, who answered from the woods.

One day, he returned grim-faced, his arms full of the food he had not left. When Ilchee met him on the path, she asked about Kathla and the old woman, but the canoemaker only set his jaw. "The wolves took them," he said and walked down the beach alone.

When the season of the cold moon came again, the People heard the news that the white man was coming—and this time by land, not by water. In November 1805, the Lewis and Clark party reached the Chinook village. Wallulah, as Comcomly's favored wife, led the women's trading party out to greet the strangers and returned with tales of a Shoshoni woman, called Sacajawea, Bird-woman, who had led RedBeard and his men through the mountains.

Ilchee refused to greet the strangers, but she accepted a blue-beaded sash that her mother had traded from the Shoshoni. Ilchee stood and silently fingered this thing of rare beauty, trying to imagine all the wonders it had seen, coming over the mountains. It was as though she could almost see the lands herself, as her fingers counted the beads.

But the whites slept among the People in their lodges, and this was a new thing which troubled Ilchee. She went to her mother and asked, "Do you see the whites with your heart or are you blinded by their gifts? You go to them with open palms and take their trade, you bring them slaves for their pallets, you feast them at our fires—what of my vision? Raven told me—"

"That was *your* vision, my Moon-girl. Your father has had no such dream."

"He dreams only of wealth, neh? Of captains' hats and sailors' coats. How many canoes can his slaves paddle? Can he not see the danger?"

"Well, and it is not for the daughter to criticize her father's will," Wallulah said with some heat. "Especially not when his skins have bought her a blue-beaded sash that she wears even as she speaks ill of his wisdom. Especially not when her own dreams have kept the young warriors from her door."

Ilchee flushed and turned away, fingering the sash reluctantly.

Wallulah said softly, "He sees danger enough, my daughter. He sees the danger of turning away the strangers, when many other lodges are open to them, and welcome. There are many warriors who would like to carry the tyee's totem stick, neh?"

"So you will stay silent? You will help him bring the strangers into our waters? By our fires?"

Wallulah straightened proudly. "I am tlesast, favored wife of Comcomly, Chinook tyee. You are his favored daughter. We will speak no more of it."

RedBeard, the white leader called Clark, stayed with his band at the Chinook lodges one moon, and then crossed the river to live in the Clatsop village for the rest of the winter. In truth, the People were not sorry to see them go. These white men were poor traders, complaining frequently that they could not meet the prices of the great ships. And RedBeard blamed the women loudly for the sore-sickness that visited his men.

Wallulah said, "I told this RedBeard that the sickness was one of his own people, and surely his women must have told him how to cure it." She turned away. "But he ordered me out like a slave. Wah! These whites are quarrelsome as the bear in rut! At *me,* he shouted, with his finger wagging and his face red!"

Ilchee heard her mother's mutterings and pulled her cedar robes about her like a shroud, her eyes far away.

And so, the great white ships came and went on the river. Ilchee listened to the news ebb and flow around her, waiting always for Raven to whisper in her ear, but her dreams were silent, and she was left alone to wonder if her spirit partner had forsaken her.

Many women were also alone, for they had been turned out of the lodges for the sore-sickness, the disease that pained their parts and turned a man's water to fire. The Old Ones could find no cure; no herbs nor salves from the spruce gum would stop the sickness. Now, only slaves were bartered to the whites, and women began to keep their daughters away from the ships. Some did not tell their husbands when they grew sore, hoping it would go away. And sometimes it did. Other times, it left them and went to their husbands instead. This made the men look sideways at their women, and there was less laughter in the pallets at night.

Meanwhile, the Old Ones bickered among themselves, and none could see what was coming. Boston-men and King-George-men built their own lodges near the ocean now, and the Clatsops showed new arrogance since the white men had wintered with them, even daring to threaten Comcomly's power.

Finally, Comcomly stood before the council to quiet the mutterings. He pointed to the huge boulder that lay atop the mountain behind the village and shouted, "So long as that rock remains in place, so shall no one question the power of my People!"

Trade patterns were shifting once more. Only last moon-of-the-falling-fruit, a young male slave brought ten blankets. This season, one King-George-man refused to accept a slave in trade at all, while another Boston-man would give only five blankets. Yet the plateau people, who were having to go farther and farther afield to capture slaves, had warned that soon the price for a good slave might be as high as fifteen blankets, if they could find any healthy slaves at all.

Ilchee thought of these things as she stood and gazed across the river at the smoke from the white man's fires. His lodges had grown huge, twice as tall as those of her people and ringed all round with high walls. Her recent dreams were troubled paths of dark shadows and fearsome enemies, but as always, Raven was silent. She dreamed of walking meadow paths where she heard dry rustles, as unseen creatures slithered into the brush just ahead of her feet. In her dreams, the warning rustles did not make her turn back, but neither could she take her eye from the path and enjoy the sight of the mountains, lest she tread on death.

One night, the Chief Factor of the white village across the river came to be feasted. He was called Duncan McDougall, a tall man with a full, red beard and burly brows. Her mother said he was something called a Scot, and Ilchee sensed that he was special in some ways which she could not see. Certainly, he came with enough warriors to impress any tyee, she thought. But he seemed angry often, and his teeth shone through his red beard like clam shells in the dark sand.

Ilchee could not escape her duties as a grown daughter this night. With her mother and her sisters, she served the men quietly, carefully holding her head down and her eyes away from the sight of their fiercely hairy faces.

As she passed close to the Chief Factor, however, she felt his eyes on her. The back hairs on her neck lifted as though she had stepped in cold water. As if her eyes were on a string, they moved to his, and she was struck by the questions in his eyes, eyes the color of sea ice. Her nipples hardened, and she trembled slightly, yet she felt a warmth flush her face.

Quickly, she moved behind her mother, busying her hands with serving bowls and wondering at her confusion. She could not recall a man's eyes staring at her so frankly, with such questions in them. She vowed to go no more by this white man, lest he steal her suin, her spirit power, with his piercing eyes.

A wind came up that night, and Comcomly urged his guests to stay in his lodge, warning them that the river was too dangerous to cross. But the Chief Factor insisted that they could not stay, and his men loaded their canoes and pushed out into the currents. Comcomly and his warriors stood on the shore watching as, suddenly, a gust of wind and water upset both canoes, tossing the white men into the water. The men wore heavy furs, and they could barely fight the currents. McDougall floundered violently, struggling to keep his head above the roiling river.

"He tries to fight the river!" Comcomly said anxiously, peering through the rain. "How can these warriors be so clever in their ships and so stupid in the water?"

Swiftly, he ordered several warriors into their canoes, and finally, all but two of the white men were dragged to shore. The Chief Factor was taken back to Comcomly's lodge, dripping and semiconscious. Wallulah and Ilchee cared for him, covering him with dry furs, warming stones for his pallet, and when Ilchee put a herbal tonic to his lips, he opened his eyes. Hers was the first face he saw.

In two moons, her father came to her. The white tyee, McDougall, wanted her as wife.

She shrank against her mother, her eyes huge in her face. "My vision warned me to stay away from all things of the white man! You know what Raven has shown me!" she cried.

"I know you had a dream," Comcomly said, "and you think Raven sits on your shoulder. But I also know that the whites have been friends. Such an alliance between our lodge and theirs can only bring power to our village. And even if the whites become an enemy . . ." He held up his hand to silence her protest. "Even then, we would be wise to have ears in an enemy camp."

"But the sore-sickness! I will be unclean!"

"I have it from the Clatsops that his man's parts are free from it. Two of their women say so. It is an honor, daughter. He has chosen few to share his pallet. He chooses only one for wife." He crossed his arms adamantly. "And he is the only one who has chosen you at all. Even when you walk the bride-path, you will be far older than all the rest of your sisters, neh?"

She bowed her head. No daughter could refuse such an offer when brought from her father. Not when no other warrior had asked for her hand in all her winters. Not when her father was tyee, and all eyes watched the drift of the smoke from his lodge.

She glanced at her mother for support. A trembling smile played over Wallulah's lips, a smile Ilchee could not read. She said nothing, but her eyes shone with quick tears.

"He has sent two white warriors to bid a handsome bride-price for you," her father went on. "If you find you cannot live in his lodge, I have his promise that the bride-price is yours to keep." Still, her mother said nothing.

Ilchee thought swiftly of those cold blue eyes that followed her
about the lodge, that mouth that rarely smiled, those huge shoulders
which did not slump under the heaviest furs. "Well, and I will think
on this," she said, her voice low. "I will ask Raven." And she turned
and walked to the river before her father could speak again.

She went to the women's place to bathe, moving along the bank
until she was hidden in the birches. Once she was sheltered from
all village eyes, she gave herself up to quiet sobs. She had never felt
so small, so helpless, so lost.

Finally, her tears stopped, and the hitches in her breast calmed to
regular breaths. She turned sideways and tried to peer at her profile
in the water. Her nose was scarcely large enough for piercing, and
she could only wear one hiqua shell, while SongBird could wear
three. The eye of the moon, my mother has called me, for my light
skin. But I am not beautiful—not like others in the village who have
plump legs, brown round arms, and large ears, which even a child
knows are the mark of passion.

She sighed and walked through the waist-deep water, trailing her
hands behind her. Always, she thought, I have pressed myself to
serve the People. And now . . . is this the new path I must choose?
She firmed her jaw and hit at the current, striding deeper into the
pull and tug of the river. No warrior comes to the door of a girl who
has dreams, she grimaced. One who talks of them before her father's fire, who sees Raven on her shoulder, when most warriors
must be content with lesser spirit partners. Only a white man would
take such a bride, she frowned. Only one who could not see beyond
her father's totem stick.

Raven, she whispered, come to me now. She knelt swiftly in the
cold river, letting the water cover her belly, her breasts, then her
head, holding her breath. I will not breathe, she thought fiercely, not
until I hear Raven calling me, leading me to life. She held her breath
until her chest ached, until the weight of the water on her felt like
a cold death, until her eyes swam and her limbs tingled, and finally
let it out in a whoosh, staggering to her feet and grasping.

Raven did not perch in the birch tree, watching her. Raven did
not call out his raucous cry as he flew to the sea. Raven did not come
to her at all. She knew, then, what she must do. With no fresh sign
to tell her otherwise, she had no choice.

Ilchee left the river and stood on the shore, gazing across at the
fort which jutted out and faced the sea. When I cross the river, I will

join a different world, she thought. Not a different world such as my mother joined when she left the Scappoose tribe for the Chinooks, but a wholly strange world of alien men with ugly faces. And he who goes with wolves, the Old Ones say, learns to howl. Once I cross the river, I will leave the People as irrevocably as if I had crossed the mountains, no matter what this McDougall vows.

Her mother would send slaves with her, of course, but where would she go when she had her woman's time? How would she feast her husband's guests in such a lodge? Who would spear the first salmon, and what shaman would assure that the fish was properly appeased to ensure a good harvest? There were too many questions she could not see. "Oh Raven," she breathed silently, "keep me strong for this new trial. Let me not shame my People."

She walked into her father's lodge and stood before him. He was sitting at the fire, as though he knew her answer before she spoke.

"I—I will be . . . wife to this white tyee, father. If there is to be evil, I shall know it sooner."

Her father stood and took her braids in his hands, gently piling them on her head as she would wear them when wed. He grinned down at her. "You will bring honor to my lodge, little Raven. And beauty to the lodge of the white man."

And so, it was time for Ilchee to be wife. She was taken from her father's lodge, supported on each side by her mother and her sisters, her head bowed as was seemly lest she seem too eager. She wore the wedding robes of fur and many loops of hiqua at her breasts, blue beads of royalty in her ears and her nose, and new-wife tattoos down her arms. As though in a dream, she moved woodenly through her duties, never feeling more distant from herself, wondering vaguely if all brides felt so detached.

The People lined the river as she came, and many canoes laden with foods and gifts gathered in the shallows. Her sisters paddled her across in her bridal canoe, while her father and mother rode ahead in his larger one.

When she stepped on the opposite shore, she saw a long path of otter skins that her father's slaves had laid down on the sand. Barefoot, she walked on them; flushed and pleased at this show of honor, she kept her head low. As she came to where her father and her husband stood, she glanced sideways at her sister, SongBird, and read in her face that this man had kept his promise.

Two days before the wedding, the white tyee had sent a message by his clerks that he would make a husband's request. When it was told round the lodge, the women rounded their mouths in astonishment.

He wanted Ilchee well-bathed before he took her to wife, he said, her breasts covered with robes though it was the hot months, and her skin and hair free of all oil and paint. The Elders argued against such carelessness, for any number of evil spirits could enter a woman so unprotected.

Ilchee had gasped indignantly at the news that she should be made wife in such a slavelike fashion, without the proper adornments of her class and status. "I will not do this! Not if I remain unmarried all my days!"

But Wallulah silenced her with a low word of caution. "Do as he bids, my daughter. Now is when you may bid one another and see all things done as you ask. Only after must you obey him and ask no favor in return."

The thought of asking a favor for herself had not entered Ilchee's mind, but once her mother's words pricked her, she knew what she would barter for her oil and paint.

Now, Ilchee raised her eyes to look at her man for the first time since she crossed the river, and her smile rose unbidden to her mouth despite her efforts to be solemn. His red beard was gone.

His face was not completely naked, to be sure. A small, red brush still bristled between his nose and his mouth, but that wide wrap of hair at his cheeks and chin had disappeared.

Without that brush, she smiled quietly to herself, he was almost pleasant to look on. And she did not begrudge him a minor alteration of her favor. She herself wore two small patches of red paint on her cheeks—under her skirt where none could see.

Comcomly gestured for the drummers to begin, and the women raised their voices in the wedding chant.

"Now comes my daughter, Ilchee, Moon-woman, of my favored wife, Wallulah of the Scappoose," he said in Chinook. "She shall be wed to this man, the white Chief Factor, and her soul shall be in his hands for all time." He added in English, "Princess Raven, my daughter made wife. McDougall, my son."

Ilchee glanced at him quickly when she heard the strange words "Princess Raven," a white meaning, for the People had no such titles. Her father grinned at her, and then she understood. He was giving her one last gift, one which the whites could best appreciate —the gift of royalty.

He took Ilchee's hand and placed it in McDougall's. Ilchee, her head still bowed, noticed that her own skin was no darker than her husband's. "It is a good sign," she breathed. "So long as Raven sits on my shoulder, I will see the white man's evil before it comes for my People. Perhaps our tribes can be kinsmen, after all." She turned her face up to McDougall and smiled, and in the radiance of her smile, his own face creased, and he squeezed her hand gently.

That night, as she lay on her husband's pallet, she let her thoughts roam as she waited for the throbbing in her lower parts to cease.

It happened quickly, she thought, my wiving. He had scarcely taught her his name, "Mac-doog-al," when he led her to his lodge. There, he had removed her cedar robes, her fur mantle, and her hiqua shells, carefully, as though he feared she might start like a doe. She watched his blue eyes to see if they would change color in the shadows, but they stayed clear as they roamed over her body.

She waited to see what he would want her to do—and then, slowly, he pulled her down, gripping her shoulders. She turned her face to him and gently licked his lips, the sign that a woman makes to a man that she is ready. "Mac-doog-al, husband," she whispered, wondering at the heat that began in her belly.

He put his mouth on hers and pressed his lips into her teeth. She felt his hair bristle against her mouth, but she tried to give herself to this new sensation. He slid his tongue inside her mouth; she sucked it gently, and he began to moan deep in his chest. She knew then that she pleased him, and she pressed her body against his, her arms went round his neck, and she flicked her tongue hotly at his lips. He took his hands from her shoulders and moved them down to her flat belly, stroking her ribs, gripping her waist with his huge hands. His hands moved up, then, cupping her breasts, and she breathed a quick prayer that he might find her beautiful. When he bent his head and tongued her nipples, she wondered at this strange man who would do as a babe did. He seemed to draw her inside up to his mouth.

Swiftly, he moved over her, and she drew him inside her with her fingers, opening her most private places, pulling him past the shock of invasion, deeper into her body, moving under him like a canoe over rapids. She was silent throughout, listening to his moans of pleasure, until she could no longer hear anything but her own blood pulsing through her loins.

And now Ilchee lay in the darkness quietly, for she was too shy to go outside her man's lodge while the wiving must still show in her eyes. She had seen men and women coupling, for the lodges were full and the nights long. She had also spoken with a young cousin, a girl who had gone to the traders' ships.

"Do the white men rut in strange ways?" Ilchee asked.

"No," the girl had giggled. "They all search for the Small Death and the Great Birth as our men. Their male roots are large and red when angry, and they have hair there as on their cheeks."

At that, Ilchee had grimaced. "No wonder their women let them leave for so many moons. Is there no place they are without this hair?"

"None that I could find," the girl laughed lustily. "But it does not get in their way!"

Indeed, it had not.

McDougall lay quietly next to this Indian princess and listened to her heartbeat. He was still amazed that she was his wife. At first, he had been disgusted with her, as he was by most of these savages. Her ankles were thick from squatting in a canoe, her body was short and covered with black tattoos—and her head! Squashed to a slant like the peak of Hood's mountain. But, he thought, it was clear that her intellect had been in no way impaired. It was obvious in her eyes, those bright black beads that followed him each time he came to her lodge, that she was a smart one. She wasn't young, but at least her skin was lighter than most. That's what had made him notice her at first, he grinned to himself . . . that and her arse.

He groaned loudly, throwing one leg across her hip. She would be a good addition to the barracks. God knows, they needed a woman about. McDougall glanced at her sideways. Despite her squashed head and her bandy legs, she pleasured him in bed. And the winter was coming on.

Ilchee was soon used to her husband's ways and quickly became part of the white man's fort. She learned English: first the husband-wife words of the bed, then the words of anger, and finally those of trade. The following moon, she stood on the shore of the river watching as her sister, SongBird, was paddled across. Once more, Comcomly gave a daughter as wife to a white man. Archibald MacDonald, company clerk, took SongBird's hand and led her to his lodge. Ilchee's heart was full at the thought that her sister would be close to her again.

The fort on the tip of land which the whites called Astoria was quickly becoming the focus of river people from both shores. At first, the Chinooks and the Clatsops watched the high walls rise with pleasure, for they felt sure they would be asked to camp inside as a gesture of hospitality, a gesture they had extended to the white strangers many times over. But once the walls were high and strong, McDougall ordered all the People outside the fort at dusk. Except for those few wives taken by the officers, no natives were allowed. And though they protested, the Clatsops assuring him that they were "no Chinooks, no Chinooks!"—certain that the tribe across the river had somehow offended him—and the Chinooks calling just as loudly, "No Clatsops, no Clatsops!" still, McDougall closed the great doors on their backs each nightfall.

Ilchee stood and watched from the sentry post as the two tribes camped outside in resignation. The smoke from their fires mingled in the black sky with the smoke of the whites that drifted outside the walls. Just as a tongue turns always to an aching tooth, her mind turned to her own emptiness. She walked restlessly past the walls, stopping to peer out when she could.

I am alone here, she thought, and separate from my People. She remembered the potlatches her father gave each season, where peoples from all the tribes were welcome to feast at his fires, to sleep on his furs, to fish his river and hunt his game. For the People, hospitality and trade go hand in hand, she thought. But for the whites, once trade begins, friendship becomes suspect. Will I ever feel at home, anywhere? But such thoughts made her weary and heavy, so she turned away and went back to her husband's lodge, where he waited for the plates to be filled.

Even though the natives were kept outside the fort at dusk, the new crews arriving from the east were uneasy. They shuddered as they saw legions of savages camped about them, moving to and fro within their barracks by day and surrounding them by night.

"It's particular bad during the cold months," an officer complained to McDougall. "Hell, those robes could hide any number of weapons, sir, and we won't stand a chance if they decide to use 'em."

Finally, McDougall summoned Comcomly to him. Reluctantly, he explained that from now on, only the tyees could trade for the tribes. "You must keep your people outside the fort," he said, folding his arms across his chest.

"But that is not our way," Comcomly protested. "Each trades for himself. I cannot tell them—"

"Either that, or *nobody* comes in," McDougall interrupted.

Comcomly was aghast. To threaten the trade in such a willful way was worse than wrong; it was akin to madness. He began to explain, to persuade, to attempt to wheedle his son-in-law, but McDougall held up his hands and turned away. "I won't be accused of favors," he vowed, "just on account of my bed being warmed every night." Finally, in frustration, he pulled a black horse-liniment bottle from his pocket. He held it before the tyee's face and glared at him fiercely.

"You see this vial, Chief?"

Comcomly squinted his one eye and nodded.

"This holds the smallpox sickness. You kwass? The death bottle. It is mine." He thumped his great chest.

Comcomly's mouth flew open in astonishment, but then he coughed politely, not wanting to shame his son-in-law with his disbelief. He whispered, "Sickness-that-makes-holes-in-face?"

McDougall nodded solemnly. "So you see, you must tell them to stay away."

Comcomly left instantly, and before nightfall, all the Clatsops knew that Chief Factor McDougall had a suin, a magic bottle that held the sickness, that he was angry with the Clatsops, and that if he grew more angry, he would release the magic and kill them all. From then on, McDougall was referred to privately, in the safety of the lodges, as the memaloose chief, the white who held death-in-a-bottle.

After two years, McDougall finally paid his bride-price in full, by dint of hard work and tight trading. Ilchee had watched him daily as he labored unceasingly at the post, and though she was proud of his wealth, she could not understand what pulled him back to the trade counter day after day. Often, she had tugged at him, coaxing him back into the pallet in the morning, sitting on his great belly and twisting his chest hairs until he rolled over her, rigid with desire. But always, eventually, he would leave her and go to work. Finally, she confronted him.

"You are great chief," she said, drawing him away from the trade counter, nodding to the clerks who stood by, sly-eyed.

"Aye," he grimaced. "Great tyee, that's me."

She nodded solemnly. "Yet you work so hard you cannot rest after you eat. You cannot pass a day in your lodge with your wife." She tugged him to the door and pointed to a pig which rolled outside the barracks in the mud.

"See there," she chided softly. "That is the true chief. He does no work like a slave. When hungry, he eats. When tired, he lies in the sun."

"Woman," McDougall snapped, loud enough for all to hear, "I have more to do than wallow in the mud and lie in the sun. That's for pigs and dogs and . . . Clatsops."

She flashed him an angry look and whirled from the store. He had not had to say the word; she could read it in his heart. He almost said "Chinooks."

In the moon when bears begin to get fat, Ilchee knew she was with child. She had been sleeping restlessly, wakened by dark dreams with flapping shadows. She knew Raven was speaking to her, but she could not make out his words. Often, now, she dreamed in English as well as Chinook, and she wondered if her own thoughts were driving away her spirit partner before she could hear him. But when she had missed her woman's time twice, she no longer wondered. Perhaps I simply cannot hear Raven so well with the child's ear next to my heart, she thought. She hurried to Song-Bird's lodge, grateful for once that all husbands were at the trading store.

"The child will have skin like a gull!" SongBird giggled, her brown breasts jiggling. "Between you and your white tyee!"

"He will be a shaman," Ilchee said.

"And how do you know such a thing, neh?"

"Raven tells me."

Her sister frowned. "Well, and we have need of such a one. The Old Ones say the snows will be three squaws deep this winter. The shaking sickness is in the village again, and three mothers are singing the death song already."

"More and more whites come each moon," Ilchee nodded.

SongBird shrugged. "The Boston-men are few, and the People are as many as summer stars. Let them come."

But Ilchee felt the black feathers of Raven whispering in her ear, louder than she had for many seasons, and in her mind's eye, she saw the dark clouds coming up from the sea and coiling over the river . . . and she shivered, holding her belly.

As she bathed herself that night in the river, still scorning the iron tub of the barracks, she thought of the latest argument she had had with her husband. In an effort to draw closer to him, she had decided to tell him of her vision, the Searching, and her spirit partner. But to her horror, he had only laughed, pulling her into his lap.

"The white man does not need such a power," he smiled.

She had opened her mouth in astonishment that he would tempt the gods in such a way. Not need a spirit partner? Not need the partner who would give him direction in life, who would show him how his strength works? Not need the god-on-the-shoulder who would be the companion and core of his being for all his life?

Patiently, she explained. She told him of the discipline that the young boys must endure. "They are like the bows and arrows of the People," she said. "Their backs must be strong and their aim true. They learn and fast and bathe and bend their wills to the wills of the gods, and when they are ready, they go to seek their spirit partner, clean and alone." She added, with quiet pride, "Some women do so as well."

"Damn few, I hear," he snorted.

"That is so. But it is hard to hear the words of the gods in the crowded lodges with the smell of cooking and the cry of babies."

"Well, our God likes the people to be all together. That way, he only has to say things once." McDougall grinned.

Her eyes widened at his laughter. She closed her eyes in frustration. How could any white man understand? She had seen long ago that he saw only the ripples on the river, knew only the surface of the world. To him, to all white men perhaps, a tree was only for building or burning. The creatures, only for eating or harnessing. These men did not know that some things must be believed to be seen. They thought that they were not part of the earth and the earth was not part of them. It was as though they spoke a different language with words that could never make sense, no matter how many papers they signed and gave one another.

But she accepted that for him, it was true. It is not my place to teach my husband such things, she vowed. She shuddered at his vision of a cold and lonely world, a world of waiting death and unmet desires and searching with no end. What must it be like, she wondered, never touching the earth, never knowing what healing powers waited, untapped, in his own belly? To live blind and help-less always as a strapped infant on its board? She knew that she would never understand.

Though the whites did not believe in the messages from the gods, Ilchee could see that the gods had their will with them, nevertheless. Once, McDougall called the fort together and opened up the walls to the bands outside. He stood on a wooden box and spread his arms, speaking loudly to all who listened.

A white man, Pelton, had been killed when he went trapping on Tillamook lands. McDougall called for the capture and punishment of the murderers. Comcomly listened quietly to all his son-in-law had to say and then waited to find him alone.

"These were evil men of the north, they who do this bad thing," Comcomly said. "Let us pay the blood-price for your Pelton and end it. If my people go tracking for the evil men, there will be war between the bands. Many more will die."

"If you do not bring me the murderers, many will suffer for the evil of a few," McDougall argued. "They will say I covered up for you because of your daughter. The Boston-men will punish your people over and over for this murder."

"Even though it was not Chinooks who do this?"

"Aye, even so."

"Even if those who do this thing pay a blood-price?"

"The Boston-men don't want your money, Chief, they want an eye for an eye. And if you don't help them get it, they'll fill your land like fleas and hunt your people down with guns, make no mistake. And they won't stop to ask who did what."

Comcomly curled his lip in disgust. "Well, and they are mad dogs, then, to seek blood for blood and make a war for one man. Who makes their laws for them, neh?"

McDougall shrugged. "That's the way we do it, old man. And if you won't help me, the Clatsop tyee will."

And so, the tracking began. Three Tillamooks were taken by a party of six white men and ten Chinooks. The guilty were dragged back to the fort before a jury of whites and Indians and then sen-tenced to hang. After the executions, McDougall gathered the na-tives together in the great hall of the fort and gave gifts and smokes for their services. Mourning relatives, both those of the executed Tillamooks and those of the four Chinooks killed in the capture attempt, silently carried away their dead.

For two generations after, the word "pelton" in the Chinook tongue meant one who made foolish waste. And the gods were angry, Ilchee knew. She told her dreams over the fires outside the fort, finding new courage with each word she spoke. The Old Ones covered their heads at her visions, but the young warriors began to listen.

When she left the fires, one warrior muttered, "She has the ear of Raven, that one."

An old woman answered, her head still hidden in her blanket, "Perhaps she has the ear of the white god as well. Perhaps the two gods war in her heart."

One morning, as Ilchee walked through the meadow picking horsetail and thimbleberry, the first greens of the season, her water broke and she felt her pains begin. She kept picking to the length of the meadow where SongBird knelt, digging wild onions.

"My son is coming," Ilchee said, holding her hands over her taut belly.

Her sister looked up quickly. "You have seen him, neh?"

"In dreams. And he comes now."

SongBird stood and felt Ilchee's stomach, knelt and put her ear to her skin. "You are right. He comes quickly."

The women walked slowly to the beach, out to the wet sand where Ilchee could feel the rhythms of the green water. There, SongBird dug a pit for her and helped her to kneel over it.

Ilchee was beginning to pant with the labor now, and between breaths, she chanted the tamanawas words commanding the child to come forth. SongBird tied a cedar bark cinch above her sister's abdomen to encourage the child to move. Then, she tied another bark strap to a piece of driftwood, pounded it deep in the sand, and put the other end in Ilchee's hands.

Ilchee squatted over the pit, her face creased with strain, her thighs trembling with exertion. She pulled at the cord each time the pains came and repeated the birthing chants, coaxing her son between spasms. SongBird rubbed dogfish oil on her birthhole, down her legs, and over her belly, smoothing the skin in rhythmic strokes, crooning to the unborn child.

Ilchee felt Raven all about her, flapping his great wings, hissing in her ear, and she pulled at her knees, straining to send her infant forth. She began to groan, her voice low and harsh; there was a long time when she felt the head lodge between her hips, and she cried

out once, twice, her hand fluttering down between her legs, as if to
pull the life from her, and then up again for help, and finally,
twisting convulsively, she felt the babe slip free.

As from a high, lonely ridge, she heard SongBird call, "You saw
him clearly! A son with a head like the moon!"

Her last words snapped Ilchee back into the present, and she
focused on the child. His hair was light brown and hung in damp
curls about his face. But his eyes, when they fluttered open, were
a dark brown. In a whirl of savage feeling, she bent over the child's
face, and her tears fell hot on his head.

His skin and hair are as light as his father's, she thought, and his
head, oh his head, is as large and round as any slave's! My child—
bone of my bone, blood of my blood, a piece of the earth and the
sky—looks to be little of my own. Only his eyes look like mine.
McDougall's seed has conquered, and my son is not much of the
People.

"Well, and he is a handsome child," SongBird said softly.

Ilchee pulled herself together and picked up the child, holding
him to her breast. "He is white," she said. "O'-na shall be his first
name. Little Clam. For he rests in the space between two peoples,
as the clam between the water and the land."

She held her infant son and rocked slowly, facing the river, feeling her body move to the rhythms of the breeze in the firs, the
ripples in the water, the beat of the earth itself. She felt, for an
instant, as if she sat in the palm of life's hand, felt the pulse of all
things living and dead and and reborn run through her veins. Something new rides the winds, she thought, something fleet and white
with a dark underbelly of the void.

The child moved in her arms, stirring to life. Ilchee took its right
hand gently, so it would always pull things to it properly, and held
her son up to the sky. He was a red and bloodied man-child, victori-
ous in his first test of courage. As she gazed into his unblinking eyes,
it did not matter that his hair and skin were light, only that he lived.
She crooned to him, calling his name immediately, for she knew that
the babe could understand unexpressed thoughts and might die if
not welcomed to the world at once.

She carried her son to the river, cleaned the blood from the creases
of his legs with soft seaweed, and while SongBird cut the cord, sang
his first spirit song, telling O'-na of his courage. Finally, Ilchee
walked back to the fort, holding her son before her for his people

to see. When she reached the lodge, she placed the tiny, white-skinned infant in his father's arms. McDougall touched the silky brown hair and laughed aloud. He stroked his beard thoughtfully, appraising the boy.

"His name is Caleb," he said finally. "It means faithful, like a dog. And it comes from the Bible, I think."

Ilchee's breath went out in a shocked hiss. "You will name your son for a dog? For that which is unclean?"

He motioned her away impatiently. "Unclean? It was my father's name, woman." He picked up the child and held him high in the air. "My father's name and his father's middle name before him. Caleb Douglas McDougall."

The next morning, Ilchee strapped Caleb to his cradle board, padded the slanting cedar slab that would hold and mold his head, and braided the harness with which she would carry him about. She mashed crabs and rubbed them over his little limbs to make them strong, and then she bound him onto the board, pressing his arms and legs in place so they would grow straight. She laced a cedar root over his forehead to flatten it into the high slope which was the sign of rank among the People.

As she was pulling the cording tight over her son's brow, McDougall entered the lodge. He shouted, "What in God's name do you think you're doing there, woman!"

Ilchee started at the anger in his voice and gestured in confusion to the child. "I fix his head. He is a highborn child. Son of tyee and princess. Grandson of Comcomly."

McDougall strode to where she knelt and snatched the cradle board from her hands. The infant winced, blinked, and began to whimper.

"No son of mine is going to have his head squashed like a damned bug." He pointed to the baby, his eyes narrowed. "Look again. His hair is like mine and his skin is lighter than yours. He can pass for white, and he's mine!"

Caleb started and began to cry. Ilchee gazed at her man in amazement. Once more, she felt Raven hunched in her ear, and she almost closed her eyes, so dizzy did she feel. Like a croaking bird, the words mine, mine, mine echoed in her head. Without thinking, she reached and blindly closed the baby's mouth, stifling his cry. Highborn children do not screech like the crane, one part of her mind whispered. But the rest of her tightened as if for battle.

She stood slowly, her mouth hardening. "Would you have him be a slave, then? Would you have him be called roundhead by every lowborn clam-eater on the river? Would you have him be an outcast in the villages, a shame to his people?"

"His people? *I* am his people! I'll have him be called Caleb, and I'll have no head squashing, that's for damned sure!" He ripped the child from the cradle, laid him on the bed, and threw the board to the ground, glowering at Ilchee. "Or I'll not have him at all." He stalked out the door.

Ilchee knelt then and took the baby in her arms, rocking and crooning him to silence. "My little O'-na," she murmured. "Ah-na, ah-na, ten-as, my son. No kwass, do not fear. Raven will sit on your shoulder as he does mine. We will find the way. You will not be a slave."

She held the child and thought of all the slaves she had owned herself. Captives of war, most of them. Thin and frightened and less than human. Or orphans. Children whose parents had died or who had lost status and could no longer keep them were often sold into slavery rather than be left to starve. Squayyetz, slaves, were lower even than taltsaus, the poor. Though they were never whipped, they could not marry save to other slaves, and then only with permission. It was the slaves who cleaned the fish, buried the entrails, swept the refuse from the lodges, and dug the pits where the People emptied their bowels. When a master died, a slave was often tied to a burial canoe to starve, lest the rich man have no one to serve him in the land of the spirits. Slaves could not gamble, for they owned no property. They had no spirit power, knew no magic, and did not dance. Indeed, she grimaced, they were less alive than even the whites.

She shuddered and clutched the child closer to her breast. She would drown him now, right now in the cold shallows, before he reached his soul birth in one moon, rather than let him live his life in such shame. Then she looked down at the child. He had the hair of his father, it was true, and the skin as well. But his eyes—the holes to his soul—were those of the People, wide and brown.

"You will not be a roundhead, my son," she whispered. "I, your mother, say this."

She quickly strapped the infant into the tum chasas, the cradle board, and firmly pulled the cedar cinch tight across the tiny forehead. The child twisted and whimpered, but Ilchee closed her ears to his protests. She gave him a wad of duck fat to suck, looped the board on her back, covered it with a blanket, and left her husband's quarters.

For the next months, she spent long hours out at the river, in the meadow, and in the woods, gathering roots and digging camas. Only when she returned to the fort did she remove the cedar cinch. When she did, she covered the baby's head with a hat or a blanket.

In her heart, she heard voices whispering to her—in her memory, she heard the Old Ones say, "A woman must never let her husband get accustomed to her absence." But then her son would mew, and she walked still farther away, out of sight from the high walls of the fort. Soon, Caleb's small head began to slant slightly from the brow up to the crown, and McDougall, increasingly absorbed with the troubles at the fort, had not noticed.

More and more traders, both English and American, came to the mouth of the Columbia. As war between England and America grew imminent, McDougall saw that he could not hold all the northwest with only one fort and a small knot of soldiers. Sometimes he shouted with frustration, "I should just give the whole damn thing back to the Clatsops, let *them* meet John Bull's ships! Fur takes are short, we're running low on *everything,* and the godrotting rain never stops!"

The Clatsops and the Chinooks were restless and discontent with the quality and quantity of trade goods offered, for they had bartered much—many of them, their daughters—to remain middlemen on the river. Now, they saw less trade and more whites, and anger grew in the lodges.

After too many seasons of hardship and tension, the British sloop of war *Racoon* sailed up the river to take the fort, girded for a long siege. McDougall reasoned that there was little left to take and that there would be less if they had to withstand the sloop's twenty-six guns, so he announced to the British that he would sell the fort for a fair price.

When news of the sale reached Comcomly, he dressed in his finest war robes and captain's hat and indignantly demanded to see his son-in-law. "See those few King-George-men?" he asked, pointing to the ship anchored several hundred yards offshore. "They are poor, they have no rank, yet you fear them! You give your lodge and all your goods to them, and now King-George-men come to carry you off as slaves. Well, and *we* are not afraid of King-George-men. My warriors will not let them take you."

With that, Comcomly took his men and they prepared to conceal themselves in the nearby woods, determined to fight to the death. But McDougall only thanked him for his loyalty and gave him a new set of clothes as a gift. Comcomly went back to his lodge bewildered, shaking his head over this new sea change.

When Captain Black of the *Raccoon* ordered the Union Jack run up over the fort, he looked about and muttered to his lieutenant, "Is *this* the fort that was supposed to be so mighty? Christ, I could knock it over with a four-pounder in two hours."

Three guns were fired as a tribute to the *Raccoon,* three cheers given, and an eleven-gun salute answered from the fort's cannons in a toast to His Majesty's health. Comcomly refused to attend the ceremony but sent his son, Cassakas, to represent him. When the tyee did finally come to the fort, the Nor'westers, the Boston-men, and the tribes were sampling a new water brought from the King-George ship.

Comcomly found Cassakas slumped against the barracks wall, vomiting and moaning. Assuming that his son had been poisoned, he searched out McDougall to arrange for his revenge. But when he found the Chief Factor, he was amazed to see him just as befouled. In fact, as he looked about the fort, it seemed most were shouting mindless songs, or asleep in the shadows.

He found Ilchee in her quarters, nursing the babe. "They call it dam-fine-lum, father," she replied to his questions. "It is fools' water, and it makes men mad."

"We must keep it from the People," Comcomly said firmly. "If the Boston-men choose to let their enemies weaken them, that is for them, but the People will not follow their madness."

Comcomly went to McDougall the next day and asked that no more fools' water be traded to his people. Ilchee listened while her father tried to explain why this must be so, but the new clerk for the Nor'westers only smirked and spoke out of his mouth sideways to her husband. "I can't keep 'em out. Tell the old chief to order them not to buy."

Comcomly saw the men smile, thought that all was agreed, and left the trading post content. But Ilchee knew that no solution had been reached. Later, she pulled McDougall aside. "You do not understand, I think. My father is tyee, aye, and that is true. But he cannot tell the People what to do or how to live. He cannot make laws to keep the People away from what harms them. We have no kings like the whites. But you must not sell the fools' water to those who will be poisoned by it."

McDougall shrugged. "If you know how to live, then you don't need us to keep the whiskey locked up. If your father can't keep them from it, what kind of chief is he?"

"He is not chief, that is a white word. He is tyee. He leads the People only so long as they wish it. When they will no longer follow, another will lead in his place."

"Look, you said if they want to, they'll drink it. Well, it looks to me like they want it, all right. And if they want to buy it, we've got to sell it to them."

"Why? When they wanted guns, you would not sell. Cannot the fools' water be as that?"

He glared at her, now impatient himself. "Listen, I'm not chief here now. Go and talk to them that is, if you're so damned concerned about it."

She turned away, her head down. She knew that if her own husband would not speak for her, none would listen. No one from the King-George ship knew that she was Princess Raven. The whites had forgotten that her father once spoke for more warriors than ten ships could carry.

In the days that followed, Ilchee passed word among the People that Raven was very angry when they drank fools' water and shamed themselves before the gods and their enemies. She told of her vision that Raven would make all their male roots deaden and rot if they drank the white man's dam-fine water. Some warriors scoffed, but others quietly clutched their private parts and remembered that, indeed, they had been unable to pleasure their wives when full of that strange liquid.

McDougall shouted with laughter when he heard the rumors. After all, it was no longer his profit to worry about. "Did you really tell them you'd make their parts all turn soft and fall off?" he asked her, grinning.

"Not I," she said solemnly. "Raven said. I only said his words."

McDougall snorted. "I'd like to see him try."

She smiled softly. "Would you? Well, and *they* would not."

A new breed of man came with the ships that season. Five settlers came to Comcomly's lodge and smoked and feasted with him, but they did not seek trade—they wanted land. Comcomly heard their offer of great wealth for plots to dig, and he sent them away that he might discuss this new request with the People.

That night, he whispered to Wallulah on his pallet. "Our young men do not agree as they did in the old days. Some would keep the white man on the other side of the river. Others would welcome him here with his guns and his iron pots and his cloth."

Wallulah said, "They are like the young fish in the water. They jump at whatever is thrown."

"Ahhya," muttered her husband. "And this bait I cannot see clearly."

But when he asked the council, most of the warriors approved the plan to give land to the whites. Only the Old Ones raised their voices in anger. One Elder pounded his stick and shouted, "We must stop our ears! This land holds our fathers' bones. We must never give it up!"

But the warriors did not want to hear the old winds, and Comcomly saw that they gazed at one another and then into the fire with feverish eyes, eyes bright and glazed with visions of wealth.

Yet who, truly, could sell the land? he wondered. Not even he, tyee of all the river people. "We will not sell the land," Comcomly finally decided, holding up his hands for silence, "but only take payment for its use. As we do the clam beds when we let the Willapas dig and the berry bushes when we let the Clatsops pick. But the land will be ours for always."

When the whites returned, they traded the People fifty blankets and twenty guns for some flat bottom land down by the river. Later, Comcomly smiled in the darkness of the lodge. "Well, and it is a good bargain for the People," he whispered to Wallulah. "We received many things and loaned only poor land in return. No berries grow there. No game trails cross that useless meadow. The People will not miss such land. And when the cold moons come, the Old Ones will be grateful for the blankets, and the young men will be happy with the guns, and all will call me a great tyee. Ahh-ya, it was a good trade!"

Ilchee was sitting in her husband's lodge mashing camas into paste when he came in smiling. She looked up and her heart warmed, for he did not smile often these days. He pulled her to her feet. "The *Pedlar* sails tomorrow for Boston."

She said nothing. His smile slid from his mouth, but she could still see it in his eyes. "I'll be on her," he added.

She almost sagged in his arms but caught herself and then stood stiffly, willing herself to remain calm. She bent silently and picked up her son, covering his head as she always did. "We will be ready," she whispered.

But he turned away abruptly, his face twisted. "I'll not be taking you or the bairn. I go alone."

She caught her breath. "When will you return?"

"Soon. Next season," he said. But he answered too quickly.

The child began to whimper, for Ilchee was unconsciously squeezing him. "When will you return, neh?" she repeated more firmly.

Angrily, he whirled on her and yanked off his son's head covering. "To what? To a godrotting hovel with a bandy-legged squaw and a pointy-head brat? You made my child a fucking savage!" He shrugged contemptuously. "You're not a fit wife for an officer."

Her eyes flared in anger, but she swallowed her sharp retort. "You will not return then," she said stolidly.

"No, by God," he snarled. "Let the thieving King George fops deal with your father. I'm done with it." He jammed his hat on his head and strode from the room.

Ilchee slumped on the pallet, laying the child gently at her side. I will not weep, she thought dully. She thought swiftly of Tet-sui, wife of a petty officer, who had a child on her back when her husband sent her packing to her People. She had gathered up her belongings, lingering over her small bundles as long as she could. Tet-sui did not cry out, nor did she plead. But for days after, she left little gifts of berries and game on his doorstep. When he went out for duties, she was standing quietly in the shadows holding her son, not daring to ask to be taken back, only hoping that his mood might change and he would welcome her again. Finally, she crept back to the village in shame. The People shunned her lodge, and with no hunter to provide for them, her old father soon took milk from Tet-sui's breasts, half-kneeling, leaning on her, sharing with her son. Later, when the infant died, it was said that Raven punished her for her unworthy ways. Perhaps she ended her son's life herself, Ilchee thought. For a white man's son with a round head is less than a dog in the village.

She listened now for McDougall's returning footsteps. She waited through the night, but the silence in the lodge was complete. So then, she thought the next morning, he will leave me. But I will not be as Tet-sui. I am Ilchee, Princess Raven. I will not wait in the shadows for him to take us back.

"Your people are not my people," she whispered. "And day and night cannot dwell together." Her eyes were so dry that they burned. It was as though the last five years had been a dream, and her heart had dried from the outside in like a rain puddle in the sun.

She quickly packed her bundles. I will not even wait for his farewell, she swore. Let him look for me in my father's lodge. And she breathed a grateful prayer to Raven for giving her the courage to prepare her son properly for her people.

The whites are poison, she grimaced, Raven warned me, and he was right. They have lost their souls; their hearts are hard and shriveled as last season's berries. She looked down at her young son sleeping in the corner. He is white, she thought, but perhaps his soul can be salvaged. When McDougall returned to pack, Ilchee and the child were gone.

And so, Ilchee returned to her father's lodge. Her mother embraced her silently and then turned to her grandson, uncovering his limbs and examining him carefully as he kicked and crowed. "He is a strong man-child for barely two winters," Wallulah said.

Ilchee sighed hugely. "He looks like his father."

"That is so. But he has your eyes. Perhaps he will have your vision, as well."

"Well, and I will pray to Raven that he does not. What does my father say of my return?"

Wallulah turned away slightly, her head bowed but her voice calm. "He will accept it in time. It is a great shame, but then you have always held a large piece of his heart. Let him hear the child cry and hold him. He will be reconciled soon enough."

"And the rest of the People?"

Wallulah shrugged. "They will say what they will say."

The village had changed much in her absence, and Ilchee scarcely recognized the nearby fields where the white huts crowded together like toadstools. She heard white words in every mouth, saw their trade goods in each lodge, and smelled their fires just over the rise to the meadow. She began to sit apart and walk alone.

She never saw SongBird now, though she knew she had a son. It was as though her sister had been swallowed by a great beast, and the fort walls were its belly.

Trade was dwindling, and more whites traveled a hundred miles to the upriver bands to find new and cheaper goods to barter. There were no more inamucks, sea otters, to hunt. In other seasons, she could remember hearing their klack-klack-klack drifting right into the lodge, as they floated on their backs in the kelp, holding clams on their chests, beating them with rocks. But now, they were gone. And the waterfowl which once kept the People awake with the noise of their comings and goings and jostlings for mates were also fewer on the river.

But most ominous of all, the People themselves had altered. Round the fires at night, they spoke not of story-songs or children or hunts or the Old Ones but of trade—and of other bands who were stealing the whites away.

"They paddle upriver to see Kesano!" Comcomly complained bitterly. "What does the tyee of the Willamette dogs offer that I cannot? I—*I* have given them three daughters! Yet, Kesano wears a King-George medal about his neck and a King-George flag flies on his lodge. Ai! The wealth he must have hoarded in his rafters!"

He gestured brusquely for Ilchee to bring him more oil. Since her return, he rarely spoke to her directly, showing his disapproval in his silence.

"Next season's potlatch will be costly," an Old One muttered. "An alliance between tribes would be good. Perhaps a daughter from Comcomly's lodge to Kesano's, neh?"

Ilchee kept silent, casting her eyes down. Her father had no more daughters to offer. Chowla still lived with a trader in the lower meadow. Kau-at-loh had been paddled across the river only last season, as bride to Louis Rondeau, trapper. The other women in the lodge were either too young, too old, or unworthy for an important alliance. And Kesano would never consider herself as bride. An abandoned wife, a white man's woman who had borne a white man's child, she could hardly be wife to any man at her age, least of all a tyee.

"What I need is more sons," Comcomly snorted. "Daughters, wah! One might as well raise gulls."

The seasons flowed by, and Ilchee became more invisible outside her father's lodge. Girls were made brides, boys grew to manhood, but because she had no lodge of her own, no man, and only a child who was as invisible as herself, Ilchee was separate from the rhythms of her People. She retreated into her dreams, and Raven came to her more frequently now. She fingered her blue-beaded sash, and her visions rolled through her mind like water over stones, carrying memories and bits of the future.

Her days were spent watching O'-na, Little Clam, who was growing to be a sturdy boy with bright eyes and a ready laugh. When he was outside the lodge, he played quietly alone. But once away from the eyes of the village, he climbed easily into Comcomly's lap, crowing triumphantly as he scaled the bony knees to perch himself where he might take a chewed morsel from the old man's lips and have it for himself. He clung to Wallulah, holding to her bowed legs and laughing up into her face, and through him, Comcomly eventually was reconciled to his daughter's presence.

Never did Ilchee allow the boy to be called by his white name, however. Even when whites came to the lodge to be feasted and spoke to him, reaching out to touch his light brown curls, he answered them only in Chinook, saying, "Call me O'-na."

Comcomly's lodge still hosted many white traders, and Ilchee found that she could not avoid them so easily. Because she spoke the white tongue, her father pressed her to sit next to him as trade began. And when the whites discovered that she had been wife to McDougall and had borne him a son, they leaned closer to her, assuming that she must admire all their kind. They gripped her hand and pumped it up and down in a great display of friendship. She suffered their coarseness and their touches for her father's sake, but she hurried to the river as soon as they left, to wash herself and clear her mind of anger.

One day, two white men in long robes came to the village and asked to speak. Comcomly welcomed them politely as white etaminuas, priests, and invited the People to his lodge to listen while Ilchee interpreted.

They talked far into the night, telling of the white god and his son who died for all men. They called their god Saghalie Tyee, Highest Chief, and spoke of sin and hell and heaven. At first, the People listened eagerly, for it was winter and the story-talk time. But soon, their attention waned as the black-robes went on and on.

Finally, one priest pointed at those nodding by the fire and shouted, "It is *those* evil, lazy ones who will be plagued by eternal sickness! The Saghalie Tyee will strike down those who still make room in their hearts for false gods!"

Ilchee stopped translating and fell silent, staring into the fire. When the priests prodded her to continue, she snapped at them, her face flushed with quiet anger. "You listen now while I speak. We do not come onto your ships or into your lodges and tell you that you must sing and dance for Yehlh or Raven or Talapas. Yet you come into our village and tell us that our gods are dead, that if we do not worship your Saghalie Tyee and your Jesus, we will not go to the land of the spirits. You tell us it is wrong to flatten our babies' heads, but we do not tell you it is wrong to squeeze your women's bellies with whale bone. Our babies are not your concern; neither are our gods. If you kill the gods, the People will perish."

"But you have been married to a white man," said the priest, "you have a white child. You know the truth of what we say!"

She shook her head sadly. "Well, and I know of your gods, but I know nothing of their truth. Your gods are only words."

"Don't you want your people to have the blessings of God, my daughter?" asked one old priest gently. "Do you want them to live and die in sin?"

She shrugged impatiently. "What is sin? You cannot tell us. You whites, you break your own laws, and you make war on all that stands in your way. You come to a tree and you cut it down, never offering thanks or the gift of a salmon head at its roots that it may live again. Yet the tree wishes you no harm. You could go around it in peace."

She sighed and pulled her robes closer about her. "We cannot keep you away. You will come, more and more, for that is your way, to go everywhere. But we do not have to make room for your gods as well."

She stood abruptly and went for the door, brushing off their pleas and protests like jumping dogs about her feet. Some of the People followed her with their eyes, and she saw flickers of admiration there. But many others turned to the black-robes with smiles and gestures of appeasement, hoping that new trade goods would emerge from their packs, now that the talk of gods was ended.

White forts were springing up along the river like mushrooms in the rain. As the otters moved out, the settlers moved in. Those who came needed land for farming, and the land near Fort George was marshy and unfit to plough. They clamored for trade nearer their cabins, and in 1824, George Simpson, governor of the Hudson's Bay Company, spied a piece of land on the green river that seemed to him a fitting site for a new fort. It had well-wooded hills, natural meadows, fertile soil covered with rich grass, and a carpet of blue lupin. He sent his subordinate, Chief Factor Dr. John McLoughlin, to investigate the possibility of moving Fort George to this new site up the river.

McLoughlin arrived on the Columbia in O'-na's ninth spring. The new Chief Factor was forty years old, with eighteen years of experience in the fur trade under his belt. He stood six feet tall, carried most of his weight in his shoulders and chest, and his prematurely white hair wreathed his face like wood smoke. When Comcomly first saw McLoughlin at Fort George, he named him the White-Headed Eagle, and the People up and down the river called him this for twenty years.

The Chinooks were gathering camas in the upriver meadows when the new Chief Factor arrived. Twelve canoes filled with officers, soldiers, workers, carpenters, buglers, and pipers landed on the bank, making more noise than a thousand geese. The bagpipes squealed as the men drove the mighty cedar posts in the ground. The People drew closer to watch. O'-na winced and covered his ears.

Ilchee said, "Do not let them see you afraid, my son. They scare away the spirits with this noise, and then they will build. First, they will build the walls, neh?"

As they watched, the Union Jack unfurled over the site, followed by the flag of the Hudson's Bay Company, a flag blue as the sea with a beaver on it. The whites called their new fort Vancouver.

Comcomly hurried to present himself to the Chief Factor and came back grinning. "Trade will be even better than before! He has promised this. We will have all from the river's mouth to this place, and Kesano will eat his totem stick when he hears!"

Before the river crested with the spring runs, the whites built an impressive village. The walls were twenty feet high, enclosing more than forty buildings: offices, barracks, storehouses, a bakery, a chemist's shop, two trade stores, one for the natives and one for the whites, and workshops for carpenters, smiths, coopers, tinners, and wheelwrights. Every new moon, great ships anchored at Fort Vancouver's docks, bringing settlers from all the way around the Horn.

The best camas plots were lost, but the People spoke only of the new trade.

Ilchee tried to ignore the talk of the new fort, but one rumor intrigued her. It was said that this White-Headed Eagle had a wife of the People. She had brown skin, it was talked in the lodges, and she was of some faraway tribe. When the whites gathered for feasting in the great hall, she ate alone in her man's lodge, as was fitting.

The women of the village placed bets as to who would be the first to see her and tell the others of her dress, her appearance, her manners. The men, however, bet to see who would be invited to feast first with the Chief Factor—Comcomly or Kesano.

Because there were so many new ships on the river, the white captains set markers in the water to show bars and currents, even all the way to the sea. "I would see these water totem sticks," Comcomly said at the council fires. Soleme's son, now a grown warrior, paddled out to capture one of the water markers. He had scarcely reached the shore when he began to shiver, and he raced to his lodge, where his women covered him with blankets. They built a fire in the sweathouse and pushed him inside, but he trembled all the more.

The old shaman was called, and he stood staring down at the man with sadness. "It is the shaking sickness again," he said. "The white totem stick has poisoned him."

"Ai-i-i!" screamed Soleme, falling to her knees and clutching her son closely to her breast. "Then I will kill the evil thing!"

She picked up the marker and dragged it about the village, screaming aloud to the gods, beating the stick over rocks, through the river shallows, and cutting at it with her knife. Still, her son shook and moaned with the fever.

Finally, Soleme brought the cursed marker to Comcomly's fire. "Old man! Old man!" she cried. "Why did you let my son pluck death from the river!" Ilchee tried to calm her cousin, but Soleme only pulled away, glaring. "You!" she turned on Ilchee furiously. "You saw his birth! Why did you not see his death as well? What good are your dreams if they can't warn us of such evil! Aiya-a-a! Ask Raven, witch, how do I save my son?"

Ilchee's eyes burned with unshed tears. There was nothing she could say to comfort Soleme. She tried to hold her, whispering words of hope, but Soleme wrenched out of her arms and pushed her away. She hurried back to her lodge to find her son dead of the shaking sickness.

And as if the gods intended further punishment, the captain of the ship flew into a rage when he learned that his water marker had been moved. He hung an evil sail in a tree near the village and warned that any man who touched either his sail or his marker would perish slowly in painful agony. No one went near the white captain's totems, but their caution did not save the village.

Within two moons, as one wet blanket dampens a dry one, the shaking sickness struck again, spreading from lodge to lodge. The People doused themselves with herbal tonics and sat in sweathouses until they had used up all dry timber within a mile of the village, and still, many were plagued with violent chills, drenching sweats, and skin that felt like hot rocks in the sun. As the deaths began, every lodge was a place of sorrow; each man cut his hair to the shoulders, for all had lost a kinsman. Every woman wailed in grief, and even the dogs were ominously silent. Two hundred death canoes lined the river, their noses pointed to the setting sun, towards the memaloose illahee, the place of the spirits.

The young and the old succumbed first, and Ilchee watched O'-na carefully, keeping him far away from the sick ones, holding him next to her at night, feeling his small limbs often for fever. She clutched him frequently, sniffing at his neck like an animal mother until he squirmed away from her impatiently and would not sleep under her blanket.

But one morning, as she went to his pallet, O'-na opened his eyes and stared at her mournfully. There were smudged dark rings under his eyes, and his hair was plastered to his head with sweat. "Why is it so hot?" he asked, his voice petulant and weary.

Ilchee's heart froze, and her hand unconsciously went to her throat. She pulled him from under the furs, his body strangely wooden in her arms. Quite suddenly he began to cry, and Ilchee remembered exactly how he had looked as a baby, his mouth drawing together in a bow, the tears running down his cheeks.

She held him tightly, half-carrying him to her pallet. She brought him a cup of water, watching as he drank it down greedily. His eyes darted towards the shadows of the lodge as though he saw spirits hovering near him. She gathered him into her arms and crooned the songs which once had soothed him to sleep.

In a haze of long hours, the shaman danced and rubbed her son with oils and herbs; Comcomly carried him to the sweathouse and back again, weaker and more vague. O'-na did not speak, and his lips were swollen with the fires that burned inside him.

Late in the night, he began to cough between shivers, great gasping whoops, animal choking sounds that caused panic to leap into her throat in a rush of sour bile. Ilchee grabbed him and slapped his back, startled at the frailness of his body. His life is growing lighter, she thought frantically. It is no longer strong in his bones but ready to soar away, at the breath of the slightest wind. She rocked him, calling his name over and over.

Little Clam, I named him, she thought, because he is between two worlds. And I thought he could live in either. But in truth, he belongs no place, just as I belong no place. She wept softly, stroking his hot forehead. And yet if he lives, it will be because of his white blood, that very essence which sets him apart. His white blood is his strongest ally against the white sickness. "Oh Raven," she cried, her voice hoarse, "save my son, and I will follow your visions wherever they lead. I will shout my dreams to the rafters, even if the People drive me out like a mad dog!"

When the morning came, O'-na opened his eyes and asked for water. His cough was quieter; his skin was cool. Ilchee fed him a bowl of broth, made him comfortable, and then walked to the river, her head reeling with exhausted relief. Mourners were wailing outside the lodges, and she realized dimly that she had been tending her son for four days—and more death canoes lined the shore. My son has fought with death and nearly been eaten by it, she thought. While he lived, many more have died.

A woman passed her, wailing a mourning song, following a line of kinsmen who carried a small cedar box. "Where has my daughter gone?" she sang wearily. "Come, all you people from strange lands, hear my death song. Oh, she had plump arms and dark eyes and she laughed when her brothers pulled her braids. She is gone. My daughter! My heart!"

The woman walked to the beach where the mourners were placing the death box in a canoe. Her husband prepared to tie a young slave girl to the coffin, to accompany his daughter in death. The wailing mother grabbed his arm. "There has been enough death," she said. "Let her care for the living."

The husband wrenched his arm away in anger, but then his wife added, "My daughter has clever hands. Surely she can braid her own hair, even in the dark lands."

The husband hesitated, scowling, then slowly untied the slave. It was unheard of that a daughter of a prosperous lodge should be sent into death with no handmaiden. But a mother's voice must be heeded. Ilchee bowed her head at the woman's courage.

That night, Ilchee tried to sleep, but her eyes opened, straying to O'-na's pallet where he rested. Each cough jerked her out of dreams; each restless turn in the furs made her lift up and gaze at him in darkness. She had asked for his life, it had been given back to her, and now Raven hissed and whispered in her ear, reminding her of her promise. Finally, she touched her son one last time and crept out into the darkness toward the river.

She sat on a stone in the shallows, vaguely aware of the night sounds, seeing only old memories in her mind: the tug of his lips at her breast, the way he used to smile when she tickled his cheek with her braid, his joyous kicking chortle when she freed him from his cradle board, the last time he came running with a shell in his hand, eager to show his treasure and then hide it away from his cousins. Almost, she thought, it is as though he had actually died, so clearly do I feel a loss. Something has been taken from me, and I can never again feel he is wholly mine or completely safe.

A cold tranquillity settled over her, and she wondered in some distant part of her mind if she would ever feel whole again. There is nothing more for me, she thought, but my promise. A woman has never been shaman, neh? Well, and one will be shaman now. A woman does not dream? Well, and this one will shout her dreams until the woods ring. And then a blackness welled up, perhaps from the river, perhaps from her heart, and her eyes swam, her chest heaved with pounding blood. Raven's voice came clearly, and she heard the flapping of his wings.

Once more, she was standing on the top of a ridge, looking down at the village below. Just as she had stood a lifetime ago on her Searching, she watched as the dark clouds rolled toward the lodges, faster this time, blacker and with deadly searching fingers. A hundred voices buzzed in her ears: her mother's, those of many grandmothers, spirits of shamans long dust, and one, a young man's voice, who sang his spirit song and danced in spirals through her mind, chanting in a language she could not comprehend, shaking a rattlesnake's tail, warning her of something coming, some dread evil destruction of even the river itself; his voice grew louder, more harsh, became a croaking raven in the sky.

Once more, she saw a light hovering over the sea, leading her to an island. A white man stood alone on the island, and on his arm, he held a huge eagle. The great bird was bound and tied to his wrist, struggling, gasping, shrieking for its freedom, and Ilchee felt the cords as though they wrapped her own flesh, panted as though her own screams rent the silence. And then she was watching again, and the eagle swelled to become a giant raven, black and powerful with rage. Raven twisted and turned and plucked out the eye of the white man, holding the eye aloft like a berry, just as he had done in her first vision, and she clearly saw, for the first time, the berry he held in his bill—the eye! The eye of the white man from her vision! Raven opened his bill, and the eye fell down into the river, rolling over and over toward the sea—whose eye? What did it mean?

Ilchee recoiled in horror, snapping herself back to awareness. The vision slowly receded, the death wails whipped through her ears like a departing wind, and she bowed her head, weeping helplessly. Perhaps it is too late for my son, she sobbed, too late for me as well. We will, neither of us, ever be part of the tribe's heart. But it is not too late for the People.

She wiped her face, hurried back to the lodge, and peered inside. O'-na slept, his arm thrown over his eyes as though to ward off things he would not see. Wallulah sat silently, stirring the fire. It suddenly seemed to her that always her mother had known when it was better to have both eyes open, had known when her daughter might need her.

"Raven has come to me, my mother," Ilchee said quietly, mindful of the kinsmen sleeping around her.

Wallulah nodded, as though she had expected such news. Ilchee felt another sharp anguish. When had her mother's eyes become so sunken, her hair so wispy and frail? When had her fingers grown so twisted and small?

She went on, "It was the same vision of my Searching, only stronger this time. We must take the People and leave the river, leave it to the whites and go into the mountains. This is the only way we can escape the pestilence they bring and survive. Raven has said so."

Wallulah dropped her head and her lips moved silently, as though arguing with some unseen enemy. Finally she gazed up at Ilchee, her head cocked like an old crow. "And you will lead them?" Her voice

was so weary, so slow. "You will lead the old ones? The babies on
their boards? The warriors with their rafters full of the white man's
wealth?"

"I will lead them away from the death canoes. Those who can still
stand. Those who will follow. You and my father and I. *We* will lead
them. Just as soon as O'-na can walk."

"Your father will never leave the river. The White-Headed Eagle,
McLoughlin, has offered him the job of a river pilot. He will help
the great ships find their pallets more safely. And he will once again
fill his rafters with the wealth of a tyee."

As though he'd been listening, her father reared up on one elbow,
his harsh whisper slicing through the silence. "What new madness
is this, neh? Come to bed, wife."

Ilchee glared at him, her eyes flashing with rare impatience. "This
is *not* madness, my father." She grasped her mother's arm. "Don't
rush to him like a slave. Raven has warned me—"

"Raven again!" Comcomly interrupted her. "Always he comes
when you call him. I wish he would teach you how to be a proper
wife and daughter instead of packing your head full of wild dreams.
A man deserves some peace in his gray years!"

"There will be no peace until we leave this place," Ilchee said
angrily. "Until we have gone where the whites will not follow! Are
you blind as well as stubborn?"

"They will follow everywhere," Wallulah said softly. "That
much even *I* can see."

But Ilchee did not answer. She picked up her robe and strode out
of the lodge, up the path toward the women's place. He is old, she
muttered to herself, old and blinded by greed and habit. But surely
there are others who will listen, who will follow a vision, even if
it comes from the mouth of a woman.

When the Drummer called the People to bathe the next morning,
Ilchee waited on the shore, her arms raised to capture their attention. "Hear me, my People!" she called. "Raven has come to me once
more!"

"Always something with that one," an old man sneered. "She
gets a bellyful of bad salmon, and she has a dream. Her son gets the
shaking sickness, and she has a vision." Someone laughed, and a
few made as though to push past, but she stopped them.

"Are you so safe, then, that you will not listen? So sure, as you fill the death canoes with your kinsmen, that there is no other way? Will there even be any Chinooks left to carry you to your own canoe, when your time comes? Hear me, my People!"

One mother choked back a sob. Her husband, with newly shorn hair, said quietly, "Tell us quickly and leave us to our sorrow."

All eyes turned to Ilchee. "You all know where the sickness begins," she said. "The whites live in your meadows, their goods fill your lodges—and their pestilence kills your children."

"Some children live, neh?" a warrior called angrily. "Some who have *white* blood in their hearts!"

"It is true, my son lives," Ilchee answered him calmly. "I have promised Raven my life in exchange for his. And now, I stand before you, with Raven's words. I have had a dream, an old dream, of a shaman who saw this truth long ago. Soon, the river will be tamed like a dog, and the land will float, and the red fish will come no more. It will be the end of the People. We must go to the mountain where the gods walk. I will take all who wish to escape this evil, and we will go where no pestilence can find us. Come with me and live!"

An old man muttered querulously, "Live on what? Roots and rocks? One winter will kill more than ten seasons of sickness."

Ilchee turned from the old man and opened her arms to the crowd. "We will follow the creatures. They were wise enough to leave the river long ago. We will take what we need, and we will live in peace."

"For how long?" shouted a voice, and Ilchee looked up to see Comcomly hobbling toward the crowd. "For how long before the whites find you once more, neh? My daughter speaks well for a woman, but her heart flies higher than her feet can follow. Well, and if the whites bring the sickness, they also bring the cure. Better she should go to them, with Raven's tongue in her mouth, and get the medicine from them that will heal our People!"

The crowd turned from Ilchee and faced Comcomly as though one breathing creature. "Aiya!" a man shouted. "The medicine! We need the magic medicine!"

"The whites listen to women! Who better than she who was wedded to one of their own?" Comcomly added.

Several heads turned back to Ilchee; a few women gazed at her with compassion, even pity. One old wife touched her arm gently. "I remember when your name was sung round the fires. A warrior-

girl, they said. It is not easy, neh? Even for one who killed a Quinault before she knew thirteen winters."

"Will you go for us?" a young wife whispered. "Will you ask the
whites, in the name of your son? And your husband?"

Ilchee sighed heavily and closed her eyes. No one will come with
me, she thought dully. Not until they have no other choice.

Comcomly called to her, "So, my daughter! What does Raven say
now!"

I must break with him, she thought, even as I break with the past,
all tradition, all—all safety.

Her eyes filled with hot tears, but she lifted her chin and spoke
firmly. "Raven has spoken. *I* say, I will go and do this thing. And
when it is done . . ." She faltered, turned away, her voice low.
"When it is done, well, and we shall see."

Ilchee walked up to the front of the fort with O'-na at her side.
The walls stretched across the meadow, almost blocking out the
sun. A few of the Willamette tribe huddled nearby; some lay on the
ground. Ilchee directed her son to sit where he might watch and
listen, and then she approached the guard at the gate.

"I would see Chief Factor McLoughlin," she said in her most
careful English.

"On what business?" the guard asked. "You the princess that
used to be wife to McDougall, right? I saw you before. If you come
for more medicine, we give out the last to these boys, here."

"My People have had no medicine," she said quietly. "Tell the
Chief Factor I come for my father, Comcomly. And for my son."

The guard eyed O'-na narrowly and then shrugged. "I'll tell him,
but I can't say for sure he'll come. You wait here, eh?"

Ilchee leaned against the fort walls wearily, but when she saw
that the Willamette warriors were watching, she straightened and
stood stiffly, holding her robes tightly against her breast. After a
long while, she caught a glimpse of white hair and tall shoulders
coming through the gate. The guards parted for him, and Chief
Factor McLoughlin was before her. "You are the one they call Princess Raven?" he asked. "Comcomly's daughter?"

She paused, unsure for an instant. "And wife of McDougall. I
come for medicine."

McLoughlin peered at her kindly. "We have very little left, I'm
afraid. We've given all we can spare right now to the other tribes.
If you had come sooner—"

"Our children are dying," she said, her voice low and harsh.

He sighed mightily and looked away for a moment. "You kill yourself with ignorance, my child. Your people get the ague and then drag themselves into sweathouses and throw themselves into the river. Naturally, they're dead by morning, and without even a thy will be done on their lips. We, too, have the sickness inside, but we do what the doctors tell us, and we survive."

"And you have the medicine."

McLoughlin shrugged. "Yes, we have that, for what it's worth. I can manage to spare you some, but not enough for the whole tribe."

The guard stepped forward. "Shall I run 'er off, sir?"

McLoughlin said dryly, "No need, Sergeant, though I surely do appreciate your concern. Tell the doctor to make up a small packet of quinine and bring it out to—Missus McDougall." As the man walked away, McLoughlin asked, "And your father is well?"

Ilchee nodded.

"He sees a great deal with that one eye of his, doesn't he?" McLoughlin chuckled. "And this is your son?" He glanced towards O'-na, who dropped his head shyly. "Handsome lad."

"He still has some of the sickness."

"So do most of my men, princess." He nodded quickly. "This is the devil's own land, and no doubt about it. Between the rain and the mildew, the croup, the festerations, and the putrid fevers, it's a wonder any of us make it at all. Tell your father I look forward to the spring runs. Word in from the traps is that the plews are prime this season. Ah, here's the sergeant with your quinine—" and he was gone.

Ilchee walked over to O'-na and looked down at him. He was still watching the gate where McLoughlin had disappeared, his eyes wide with wonder. She took his hand and led him back down to the river.

As Ilchee pulled her canoe up the beach, she sensed an unfamiliar silence from her father's lodge. No slaves rushed to take her packs; no dogs raced to bark their raucous welcome. When she went inside, the pallets were crowded with kinsmen, yet no one called a greeting. In the center of the lodge, Wallulah lay on a bed of furs. Ilchee drew near, and her mother opened her eyes, wide and ghastly in the shadows.

"I told them you would come," she whispered, her voice like the scratching of birch branches.

"Aiya, my mother, what is this?" Ilchee cried.

Comcomly spoke from a corner. "She was taken two days after you left."

Ilchee rummaged in her pack feverishly. "I have the white medicine, my mother, and you will soon be well." She handed the quinine to a slave who quickly dissolved it in warm water. Ilchee cradled her mother's head in her lap and began to spoon the liquid between Wallulah's lips. Her eyes are so red and her skin so hot! Ilchee thought frantically, but she kept her voice steady. "It is bitter, neh?" she said softly. "Like the acorn in the spring. But it will make you strong again."

Wallulah took two mouthfuls of the medicine obediently, but then she began to gasp and cough, her chest heaving spasmodically. She feebly twisted her head away and struggled to speak.

"The rock is gone," she whispered hoarsely.

Bewildered, Ilchee looked up at her father.

"The Chinook rock has been stolen," Comcomly scowled. "The damned Clatsop thieves have taken it and rolled it to the river. But we will have it back before another moon has passed. And they will pay for their insults!" The boulder that had always stood for the power of the Chinooks was no more.

"Well, and do not worry yourself," Ilchee said, stroking her mother's brow. "It will be back in place by the time you are well enough to see it."

"You must take them," Wallulah said, her voice weaker now. "Away from death."

Ilchee bent low to hear her. "But they will not follow," she whispered, her back to the listening ears. "They call me the 'white wife' behind my back. They say my son has a white heart. And besides, they will not heed the words of a woman."

"You are not the first to have dreams. My mother before you spoke with Raven."

Ilchee's eyes grew wide. "You never told me."

"You are only the first to speak your dreams before all fires," her mother went on swiftly, as though she gathered strength with every word. "You bring the medicine. And you bring the dreams." She coughed violently. "Take those who are not blinded and go." She struggled to continue, her face contorted.

Ilchee shushed her with low words of comfort and began to spoon the medicine into her mouth once more. But her hands shook so badly that some of the liquid spilled down her mother's neck. Ilchee reached for a fur to wipe the spill and turned back to see her mother smile softly at her, a shimmering tremble of love and gratitude. Her eyes closed, and the breath of life hissed from her lungs into the larger silence.

Ilchee walked ahead of the line of mourners, her mind blank with pain. Comcomly stood on the beach, wailing over the river's roar, singing the death chant for his wife who lay in the canoe. Memory flooded over Ilchee and for an instant she staggered, dizzy with the sight and the shock of death. She took the blue-beaded sash from her waist and laid it gently on her mother's breast, and the mourners began the farewell songs.

She told me to go, Ilchee remembered, told me to take them and run from death. What did she see for me? For my son? And what of my father? Now, Comcomly wept unashamedly, staggering blindly, leaning on a slave. Blindly.

Sudden, certain knowledge slashed through her, and she gasped aloud. Her *father* was the man in her vision, her father was the true white man, despite his color, the figure who stood alone on the island beckoning to her. Her father's was the arm that had tethered her, like an eagle, bound and tied with ropes on her talons, until she was saved by Raven, who plucked out his eye like a berry. Her father—loving and brave, jealous and willful, greedy and blind—Comcomly. However innocent was his blindness, however well meant his ambition, he had brought certain destruction to the People by whoring for the whites.

I have been fearing an enemy who would come from outside, she thought, when all along the real danger came from within, from our own tyee who could not see past what he could hold in his hands.

The mourners picked up the canoe and carried Wallulah to the river. Her canoe dipped and bobbed gently in the eddied current, circling round jagged rocks as though it had its destination clearly in mind, its nose pointing downstream. Gradually, the stronger currents caught it, and Wallulah sailed out of view. The last thing Ilchee saw was a bright flash of sun, a blue-edged spear of light from the beaded sash draped on her mother's breast.

Soleme embraced her, leading her slowly back to the lodge. Comcomly and the mourners followed. Ilchee was dimly aware that at this time she should offer her father some comfort, but she could scarcely look at him, much less take his arm.

"Perhaps this is not the time to speak," Soleme said, her voice low and hesitant. "But your mother would not mind. There are those who are ready to listen, I think."

Ilchee looked up, bewildered. "What?"

"They will follow you. Away from the whites and this death. Into the mountains." She grasped Ilchee by the arms and said, "You could be shaman now. They will listen to your dreams."

Ilchee stammered in confusion. "How many?"

"Enough, I think, to survive. I would go—and Sarca, the Drummer. And Whatsma, the hunter. And Keego and Timit and their women."

Ilchee thought for a moment. "All those who have lost children to the sickness."

"And others. More will follow once we begin."

Ilchee touched Soleme's cheek lightly. Do *I* look so old? she wondered vaguely. Are *my* eyes so worn and ancient? She thanked her cousin and went inside the lodge to find O'-na.

He was huddled in the corner of the lodge, playing quietly with his grandfather's totem stick. Ilchee knelt beside him and took it from his hands.

"Is grandmother riding the river?" he asked softly.

She nodded. "But you are alive, my son. Do you know why? Because I made Raven a promise. And now, it is time I redeemed that promise. Soon, I will take the People, those who will follow, away from the river and the death canoes into the mountains where the gods walk. Because it is my duty. Do you understand what a duty is?"

The boy nodded warily. "To do for those who have done for us. I will hunt game for your fires in the mountains, my mother."

She smiled sadly. "There are others who can do this. But there is one thing that only you can do for me—survive. And there is only one place where you can do this, your duty."

O'-na's eyes widened. "I will not go to the whites," he whispered. "You cannot make me!"

She gripped his arms and pulled him close. "Listen to me, listen! There is no other way. The shaking sickness still rides your back, and even if it did not, I cannot take you where even the strongest among us may die, empty and frozen. I have promised Raven *my* life, but not yours as well!"

He struggled to free himself, wrenching away from her in fury. "I will kill them as they sleep! I will run away!"

"It will not be forever. Once the sickness has passed, I will come back for you—"

He doubled his fists and began to beat on her chest, his head butting against her, his voice breaking in wretched despair. "Grandfather was right! You are *not* a fit woman, *not* a fit *mother!* What of your duty to me? To me! Always, you see only Raven!"

Ilchee stiffened herself against his blows, and tears rolled down her cheeks. She did not try to shield herself, and when he saw that she offered no defense, he twisted away, his face hidden in his hands. For a long moment, they sat, and the only sound was the rhythmic hitching of his sobs. She placed Comcomly's totem stick on his knees.

"It is not for a son to judge the vision of his mother." She thought for a moment and added, almost to herself, "No, nor a daughter that of a father. Keep this by you, so that you will know who you are."

He picked up the totem stick and hurled it angrily across the lodge. She gasped as it clattered down behind the pallets. "You are more blind than grandfather," he said. With dignity, he rose to his feet and walked out the door.

Fort Vancouver looked even larger to Ilchee the third time she stood before it. She pulled her robes tightly over her head and tied O'-na's rush hat low over his brow. "Do not speak," she whispered. "Not until I say so." She took his hand.

She sighed with relief that the guard was one she did not know. "Your business?" he asked, glancing at her with bored eyes.

She patted her pack and shook her head as though she could not speak English. He waved her inside. "Trading post is that corner barracks," he said, pointing, and she shuffled past him, pushing O'-na before her.

The small barracks that served as the trading post for the compound was crowded with customers, both white and brown. Ilchee edged up to one side, keeping O'-na beside her. She scanned the people carefully. This is the time, she thought quickly. I remember that this was when the white women came to barter for trade goods. Always the same time each day—and she stepped back into the shadows as several officers' wives came up to the counter.

Among the women, one stood out as starkly as a crow among a flock of gulls. She was dressed in white women's garments, her waist cinched in tightly, her hair piled on top of her head. But her eyes were dark and her skin was the color of warm beach sand.

Ilchee knew instinctively that she was looking at the wife of the White-Headed Eagle. She moved closer and asked softly, "You are wife of Chief Factor McLoughlin?"

The woman turned in surprise at Ilchee's careful English. "Yes?" she said. "Who are you?"

Ilchee pulled her robes from her head. "I am Princess Raven, favorite daughter of Comcomly, tyee of the Chinooks." She reached down and nudged O'-na closer. "This is the son of Chief Factor McDougall. I bring him to his father's world."

Several women clustered closer, and Ilchee spoke more rapidly, her hands tightening on O'-na's shoulders. "He is sound and brave, and has his father's hands. He is ten years and can work at any task."

One of the women leaned nearer and asked, "But surely you don't mean to leave him here? All alone?"

"He is not alone. He will be with his people. And I will come back for him when the sickness is past."

McLoughlin's wife asked gently, "And his kinsmen?"

"They are dead. Those who are left are leaving the river and fleeing to the mountains. He cannot go along."

"Well, he certainly can't stay here," one of the women said quickly. "They'll never allow it."

There was a long breathless moment. McLoughlin's wife peered at O'-na with kind eyes. Then she turned to a woman who had been watching silently. "Have you room in your cabin, Missus Demers? Just until we can decide what to do with the boy?"

Ilchee looked up and caught a flare of pain on the woman's face, hovering about her courteous smile. She had brown hair, shelf-like breasts, and large, pensive eyes. This one has lost a son, she thought quickly. On an instinct, she swiftly pulled O'-na's robes down from his face and chest and lifted his hat.

"Why, he's white!" one of the women said in a shocked whisper. "And they've bound his head!"

"It's not as bad as some I've seen," Mrs. Demers said and bent down to gaze in O'-na's face. "What are you called, lad?"

There was a long moment of silence. Ilchee held her breath. Finally, in perfect English, her son said, "Caleb McDougall."

"Do you want to stay here?" Mrs. Demers asked.

Another pause. You know what you must say, Ilchee thought frantically, we have talked it through so many times, you have wept, you have raged, but there is no other way. I must take them to the mountains, where half of them may die in the winter snows. Here, you will be safe; here, you will have a chance at a better life. Please, my son, remember that I will come back for you, remember that I love you, remember your duty.

O'-na did not look at Ilchee. He said solemnly, "I will stay."

Mrs. Demers smiled thoughtfully, one hand on his shoulder. "He looks like a good boy. I guess we can find a bed for him. Until you come back."

When Ilchee rounded the bend of the river and first caught a glimpse of the village, she was startled to see the People massed on the shore. They raised their arms in greeting, and she heard several shout, "Ilchee! Ilchee! She has returned!"

O Raven, she breathed, they are waiting for me. She scanned the beach: nearly forty people—there were Soleme and Sarca and Whatsma and Keego—more than half of all those still alive in the lodges thronged the shore, waving to her. There was a time long ago, she remembered suddenly, when all I wished was to be like my mother, the favorite wife of a powerful tyee. And now, they wait for me. As she drew nearer, she heard Soleme cry, "Ilchee is shaman! A woman-warrior for our shaman!"

It was for this, she thought swiftly, for this that my nights were haunted with dreams, my days rent with visions, for this that I have been kept apart from my People, for this, the hardest of all your commands, O Raven, that my son sleeps in a white man's bed tonight, and my own father scorns me. I am not alone, others have walked this path, but my words, *mine* shall lead them now. She was almost dizzy with the fierce pride and the pain, the hot flood of love for them all, the sense of completeness she felt for the first time in her life. She stepped from the canoe and the crowd fell silent.

She braced her shoulders and lifted her voice above the roar of the river. "Hear me, my People!" she cried. "We will go to the place where the gods walk and death cannot follow!"

The warriors began the chants, pounding their totem sticks on the ground in unison, and the women's voices raised the song over the trees, up toward the mountains in triumph.

"Raven has spoken and he will be with us!" Ilchee shouted. "I say so!"

*   *   *

But death did follow them up the mountain, hidden in the guise of whirling winds and snow, in the face of high, jagged peaks, and in the cramping numbness of hunger. Ilchee led those who would leave the river, thirty-eight in all, some of them old before they began, all of them older by the time they reached the plateau where she finally stopped the relentless climb and said, "Here, my people, here where Raven first spoke to me, is where we shall make our refuge."

Whatsma, the hunter, called out wearily, "I have seen no deer sign since the sun moved to the sea. We are too high for even the whistling marmot to follow. What are we to eat in such a place? No salmon, no camas . . ."

"Raven will show us," Ilchee said calmly.

"Will Raven also shelter us with his wings?" Timit's woman grumbled. "Even trees do not grow so high, neh?"

"And neither does the white man's sickness," Ilchee said.

Soleme stepped forward behind her and added, "Look, there are trees enough, though they do not grow so tall for the wind—Sarca, you and the others gather branches for the women; Keego, you and Whatsma dig the pits for the fires"—and in that way, the camp at the top of the mountain began.

Shaman she might be, but never would they accept a woman for their tyee, even these who had found the courage to break with all tradition, most of the community, and much of the past. Whatsma, the hunter, as the strongest man among them, quickly assumed a position of leadership, for many remembered that his lodge had been the richest in trade goods. Ilchee was content with their decision, for it was still her voice which led them, her dreams they followed, no matter whose fire was the largest.

In the first moon on the mountain, the band buried three of their fellow pilgrims: an old mother whose legs would no longer carry her, a young woman who had fallen from a precipice while gathering huckleberries, and a child, too weak from his battle with the white man's sickness to survive. As Ilchee sang the death songs over their bodies, she breathed a grateful prayer to Raven that he had given her the strength to leave O'-na behind.

But having buried one child, she could no longer rest until she saw her own once more. Alone, Ilchee made the lonely pilgrimage down the mountain, walking much slower this time for her legs were no longer young, stopping often to sit beneath a tree and listen to Raven flap and whisper in her ear—for he was always with her now—until she came at last to the edge of the vast meadow and could smell the fires of Vancouver, could see the glint of the river shining beyond the fort and the many cabins clustered around its high walls.

She sat in the bracken at the edge of a field of cut wheat, her blanket pulled up round her head, and crooned an old cradle board song to herself. He would come this way, she knew, for she had seen him so many times in dreams, and as the sun moved overhead slowly, she remembered his birth time, the way he sneezed when she turned his face to the sun, the way he laughed when she blew on his neck and growled like a dog.

He came, finally, in a pack of other boys, with his arms full of skins. As she watched, he threw down his burden, wiped his brow with a red kerchief, and said something to a comrade beside him. Her heart turned over. Like the others, he bent and picked up a skin, shook it out, and spread it, hide down, in the stubble to dry. So tall, in only a few moons, so *white*, with a hat over his light brown curls, a white man's shirt on his back, and trousers on his long legs! And yet, she would have known him anywhere, in a herd of a hundred white boys, as her own.

From out of one of the cabins, a woman came and stood, her hand shading her eyes, looking across to the wheat field. Her voice rose above the hum and buzz of the insects, the heat, but Ilchee could not hear her. O'-na turned leisurely from his work and waved, then back again to the skins, and Ilchee realized with a shock that the woman had called the words "Caleb! Oh, Caleb!"—such a foreign sound, she had not even understood it, but her son responded as easily as though he had taken in the name with his mother's milk.

The boys were finished now, and they scattered to the small cabins, O'-na running away with the rest, a whoop of laughter carrying back to her hiding place on the breeze. She closed her eyes, a wave of dizziness washed her, and she realized she had been clenching her hands together tightly. For an instant, she hated that white woman with all her soul, and her voice, the way she had called to O'-na as though she had a right to him, like nettles, poison barbs, fishhooks, clawed at Ilchee's mind with a terrible malignance. But over her hatred, she heard Raven's whispers, reminding her, pulling her back in time to a vision of her father's face, contorted in grief, her mother's voice, "You must take them away, you must save them!" to the horrifying heat of death that had come from her son's skin in the sickness, and she sank back, exhausted. Ilchee lay in the bracken, inviting her dreams, wishing for darkness, silence, a small truce of the gods between living and dying, and she put out of her mind her memories, willing herself to remember only his laugh, the last sound she had heard as he left her again.

When she had rested, she took the trail up the mountain once more. One day, he would forgive her this lie, she knew, the lie that he had to stay behind to avoid the sickness. It was part of the truth, of course, but not all. How could she explain, make him believe, that Raven's prophecy of the river and the fate of the People was coming as surely as next season's snows, that *he* was a part of that prophecy, as she was herself, whether he believed or not, and that his destiny lay in the white world? He will learn new dreams, she vowed, but I will never let him forget the old ones, and he will carry my voice within him until he dies, aye, and even beyond.

When she reached the plateau at last, Soleme and her man waited by the fire with warm meat and blankets. "There is news," Soleme called out gleefully, as soon as Ilchee had received the greetings of the band and settled herself wearily. "Sarca's woman is with child!"

From a corner of the makeshift shelter, Sarca proudly drew the shy woman forth, and the moment she looked into her eyes, Ilchee saw the birth in her mind, as she had a lifetime ago when Soleme had expected her firstborn, she saw a red, squalling infant taken from this woman, washed into life not with water from the river but with spring water from the highest mountains.

"It is very good," Ilchee said, her voice thick with tears and laughter which she could not separate, "a new beginning, neh?" An old memory of an ancient tale prodded her. She added, "And when the child is born, he shall be called *Chinook!*"

PART THREE

The River Settlers, 1845–1850

A frontier is never a place; it is a time and a way of life.

Frontiers pass, but they endure in their people.

—Hal Borlund,

High, Wide and Lonesome

*A*nd so the river flowed on, in a ten-mile mouth of green deep power, bordered on the north by Washington, on the south by Oregon . . . two states still to be born, but already created by the river itself.

Wandering men told of this mighty "River of the West," and tales of its teeming life and emerald promise spread seductive fingers back east, farther even than the Columbia's own watershed. Men like David Douglas, distinguished botanist, John Scouler, surgeon-naturalist, Benjamin Bonneville, Jedediah Smith, the Sublette brothers, and Jim Bridger all carried visions of the river: of its lush rain forests of giant cedars, ferns, and waterfalls, of its schools of red salmon and its wooded banks where game thrived and berries grew so fast and thick that travel was possible only by cutting a swath or floating the waters.

This last, the wandering men warned, was no easy task, for the Columbia held a deep churning violence and power beyond anything they had seen on the Clearwater, the Snake, or the Mississippi. But the risk was worth it, they vowed, for the valleys that gripped this mighty river were large pockets of paradise. By 1840, tales of the new Eden rushed back to the east coast like the Columbia's own tidal current. Men who could find no toeholds in the crowded Tidewater or the patchwork farms of the Ohio valleys began to turn their eyes to the west.

West . . . where the land was fair, the earth was fat and fed by sweet waters, and hope, like the blessed breezes, blew warm from every quarter. West . . . where a goodly part of the nation seemed to be moving in a hurry. A man could get left behind, if he dawdled.

THE WAGON TRAIN HAD MADE NEAR TWENTY MILES, AND SUZANNA WIPED the dust from her lips, squinting far ahead to the lead driver. The sun was like iron in a brass sky, and after five hours of leading the cow column, last in line behind twenty schooners, she ached to lay down the reins.

Her father trotted up on Big Ben, yanked down a faded bandanna covering all but his eyes, and hollered, "Anytime now, Suz!" over the whine of the wind.

"Ain't I ready, too!" she shouted back, shielding her mouth against the dust with her bonnet brim.

He grinned at her and galloped off, his lanky shoulders hunched. That grin'll cost him a gritty bite next time he chomps down, she thought wryly. But it's good to see it all the same, wrinkling his dear ol' face like a hound's. God knows, the two of us have blessed little to grin at these days.

Her mind wandered again—anything to pull her from the heat and the dust and the endless prairie. Nothing else to do but recollect and look, she thought. And fret, maybe, if a body took any pleasure from it. She pulled Buck and Bright, the two lead oxen, to a straighter line and let her thoughts wheel away like buzzards in the sky, this time to a familiar chant from childhood. Suzanna Blue . . . where are you? She was fifteen, and it'd been years since she'd heard her mother sing it. And two months since she'd had a mother to sing anything to her at all.

She squinted and let an image of her mother's face come up, shimmering through the heat, as she'd seen her last spring at St. Joe. She was in fine fettle then, and spry-looking as most any woman on the whole train, with her high pink cheeks and her yellow hair. That was the last time she looked like the mother Suzanna wanted to remember.

"The Lord giveth and the Lord taketh away," the preacher had said, and it gave no comfort then and less now. A damned dried-up ol' Bible-banger, her pa called him. Suzanna shifted her weight on the buckboard, tugged the reins tighter, and tried to yank her mind as well from the scene she inevitably returned to—her mother's face as she had seen her last. She grimaced. Both of them deserved something better than that final memory of twisted agony and desperate, mewling, feverish clawing at life. Suzanna had hollered at the midwife to do something, anything, her mother screaming like a mad woman, the harsh copper stench of blood in the air, the guttering candle casting weird shadows on the canvas. To die trying to pull that bleeding bit of flesh from her body, not even a real baby yet, crying for it to live even as she was dying—Suzanna reached up quickly to wipe the ache from her eyes. It was too dry to cry. And too late besides. I will never marry, she vowed again fervently. Lately, the familiar words, like a catechism, brought some comfort just in the saying of them. If that's what sharing a pillow gets you, I'll sleep alone. Besides, she smiled ruefully, I'm all Pa's got.

It was the summer of '45, and Isaac Blue and his daughter, Suzanna, were two months out on the Platte, two years behind the "Great Emigration," which saw over a thousand wagons trundling west. Already, it seemed the wilderness was getting winnowed away.

Isaac had been at the store the day Win Jessup read the paper for the week. The Missouri *Republican* was the favorite around those parts, and a goodly crowd gathered to hear old Win drawl out the news and to watch him polish his spectacles.

"Why, they say here that goin' west's no more'n a pleasure excursion," Win intoned solemnly. "Yessir, right here, says so. Can make it in forty-four days, an' scarcely raise a blister. Just like goin' from St. Lou to Philadelphia was no more'n thirty-five years ago. Can you figure that?"

Isaac slipped away from the back of the crowd with a fever in his blood. The prospect of living out his life on the small plot wedged between relations had often filled him with a cold, numbing dread. Now, he put on his best black waistcoat and rode into St. Louis with his jaw well set. When he returned, he announced to his pregnant wife and his daughter, Suzanna, that he had found a buyer for their land.

"Eliza, I weren't cut out to make a farmer. I ain't got the back for it," he confessed. "If a man wants his dreams to come true, he best wake up. I'm a good hand with the stock, an' I hear tell they need such a man out west. Plenty of horses an' cattle to tend. An' not many who can tend 'em like me."

That was a long speech for Isaac Blue, accustomed as he was to having his wife and his daughter take up most of the talking space. But he said his piece, and he waited.

Suzanna watched her mother, rocking by the fire. She'd learned that the answer to their future often lay in the lines of her mother's mouth. When the calf was weaned, when egg money was to go for a new span of fence, when it was time to switch from corn to wheat, her mother mostly signaled these and other decisions in neat furrows that carved from her nose to her thin lips, and now, those lips tightened and deepened in silence.

But to Suzanna's surprise, her mother didn't rear. Instead, a strange, half-exultant, half-astonished laughter bubbled out of her, and for an instant, the girl she'd been a lifetime ago sat there in the old rocker, her eyes gleaming. "My God an' little fishes . . . Oregon! 'Tis just a blank spot on the map. A dark corner full of woods an' wild rivers an' thunderin' mountains. Why not just say the moon, an' have done with it?"

Isaac forgot his daughter was watching, and he grinned, grabbed Elizabeth round the waist, and pulled her to him. "If I did, pretty woman, would you tag along?"

Elizabeth was even shorter than Isaac, both of them slender as fenceposts from pounding anything extra they had into their plot of Missouri flatland. But she was strong, too, and she pulled away and glanced at Suzanna quickly. In that look, Suzanna saw Elizabeth measure her daughter's chances and throw up her hands: fifteen, pert enough but hardly gets a second look in town, no bachelors buzzing round yet so no harm done and might be a blessing besides, to take her where the men are many and it don't take beauty and fifty acres to catch one.

Elizabeth smoothed her skirts and her back hair, her old self again. "Well, of course you silly fool, an' I expect you'll drag me there soon enough. But we'll talk on it later."

But Suzanna laughed aloud once she was alone in her bed. They were going to Oregon. She knew it even then.

May was when the grass was up, and October was when the mountains filled with snow, and anybody going west knew their travel had to be fenced by those two months. Though that's about all Isaac and his family knew of the journey, they left the farm to strangers, pocketed their banknotes, and made it as far as Fort Kearny by early June. There, they stopped to bury Elizabeth Blue and her scarce-born infant in the army cemetery up the hill. She only got as far as the first five hundred miles.

Suzanna and her father stood at the grave together, each lost in a private bewilderment. The shadows slowly lengthened, and Suzanna sat down on one of the rocks they'd piled to keep the wolves from disturbing the two bodies. Two doesn't hardly describe them, she thought dully, since one was just small enough to be cradled against her mother's breast through eternity.

"We just as well go on, Suz," her father muttered from the back of his throat. "There's nothin' for us back in Mis'oura now."

She silently slipped her hand in his and listened for the wind to come up, a wind which had sat down on its haunches and whined and howled at her each night since they'd begun.

"You still got me, Pa," she said quietly. "We still got each other. An' I won't ever leave you."

"Don't say such a thing," he said harshly. "It ain't right for mortal human bein's to make promises like that to each other. Promises they cain't never keep."

Somewhere, a coyote howled dismally, and the stars became more visible on the tail end of the dying sun. The moon rose, bigger and brighter than any moon she'd ever seen in Missouri. Isaac slumped down next to her with a weary sigh and slipped his arm around her shoulders, cradling her head, and they listened to each other's heartbeat for comfort.

The next morning, they started out again, trailing in line, part of Captain Jackson's column crossing the prairie. Suzanna looked back at the fort over her shoulder until it was lost in the dust, trying to fix her mother's resting place in her mind.

After three months of rocking travel, they passed Fort Laramie, Independence Rock, Devil's Gate, and Bridger's station. By late August, Suzanna could understand why one old-timer at Kearny had called it "the pee-poorest country this side of hell."

In two days, they looked to reach Fort Hall on the Snake. But for right now, she thought, I'd settle for just getting down off this dusty, hard-as-nails, slab-sided wagon and standing on my own two legs. If they don't give way beneath me.

Suzanna pulled the team tighter behind the back tongue of the Carter schooner and wondered for the tenth time just why they were going, except her father said there was more to life than stay in one place, root, hog, and die. Finally, she heard the "haul up!" call, and Isaac appeared through the dust to lead the team into the circle for the night. Lordylord, she winced, as she rubbed her back gingerly, stretching her long legs out before her. Another mile, and I'd 'a been three inches shorter.

She jumped down and ran around back to open up the grub box that was nailed to the tail of the wagon. There was a rust-spotted bit of mirror under its lid, and it never failed to catch her eye. Nobody could say you're a beauty, Miss Blue, she frowned to herself. Hair pale and thin and tucked up under a raggedy old bonnet, nose no more than an afterthought, and a chin that led the way. Only her blue eyes kept her gazing, for they were cool pools of light and shadow on an everyday sort of face. She grinned pertly, but she didn't like what that did to her chin, so she slammed back the lid and got to work.

The coffee pot was the first thing out, and she rummaged round the dutch oven and the camp kettle to get it. She climbed up the wagon rail to the water bucket to fill her pail.

Lord, what a land, she thought. You got to climb to fetch water and dig to get wood. She checked the butter bucket—the bouncing and rolling of the wagon had churned it nicely. As she started supper, she heard the sound of a woman crying, a familiar refrain at one time or another up and down the line.

She stuck her head around the wagon and spied Philura Carter sitting on a pile of trunks. Too often on the trail, something was needed at the bottom of the packed goods, which meant that a woman had to drag it all out, barrel by barrel, trunks and baskets and baggage, for whatever it was she'd tucked where she'd thought she'd never look at it 'til Oregon. Then, she had to repack the whole mess from Dan to Beersheba and tight as a tick besides, lest she wanted to lose it with the first good jolt of the wheels.

Philura sniffled quietly as Suzanna approached. Her eyes were red with dust and vexation. "I was jest sittin' here thinkin' how there's nowhere soft to sit after ten hours on the hind end of a wagon," she said with a wail, "an' how easeful my pa's ol' hogs were to sit astride when I'd a mind!"

Suzanna smiled gently and climbed up on a trunk next to her. Philura was a new bride, and John Carter was doing his level best to make the trail an easy one. He did most of the driving, took some pranking for it, too, from the other married men, while Philura sat inside, out of the wind and the dust.

"You got your coffee started yet?" Suzanna asked briskly. "You an' Mister Carter are more'n welcome to share a bite of supper with Pa an' me." She looked away to give the woman a chance to collect herself.

Philura was only three years older, and already her stomach bulged slightly under her skirts with the evidence of her new bride status. She shrugged, tossing her head as though she just recalled her matron state. "Thanks, but I reckon I can handle it," she said.

Proud as any man, Suzanna thought. She'll make it fine. She gave the girl a quick pat and hurried back to her own fire. As she fried the sidemeat, she thought of Missus Ketcham, traveling with her husband and her two sons from Iowa. They'd joined up at Kearny, and Rebecca Ketcham hadn't quit muling all the way up the Platte. She hollered and she wailed and she fussed, saying that the trip would be the death of them all and why by the Sweet Mary and Joseph she'd ever left Iowa, she'd never know.

Finally, when they got to Laramie, she simply sat down in the road like a flaxed-out cow and refused to budge. Her husband pleaded and argued for most of three hours, but she never took her eyes off the fort, and she never made a move for the wagon.

Captain said to go on, let her set. Mister Ketcham packed up the two boys and drove off. Along about sunset, his wife borrowed a horse and met up with the train down the trail. Meanwhile, the poor man had sent back his oldest son to fetch her. When he saw Missus Ketcham astride a horse in the middle of the road, he asked, "Did you see the boy, Rebecca?"

"Aye, Mister Ketcham," she said calmly. "And I blew his brains out with a pistol rather than let you drag him to hell."

Well, of course, not a soul believed her, but that poor man had to go fetch the boy, and as he rode off down the trail, he looked back to see black clouds of smoke billowing from his wagon. She'd set fire to the whole thing, lock, stock, and barrel. He came running back, doused the fire, and gave her a good flogging with his oxen whip. Women sometimes went a mite crack-brained on the trail, Isaac said.

"An' what'd you do if I was to throw such a fit?" Suzanna had asked her father.

"Well," he drawled, "on general principles, I'm opposed to female floggin'. But damned if I can judge the man sorely who leastwhys carries his whip handy. It's like startin' a balky horse, I guess. You show him your crop an' fill his mouth with gravel, an' it gives him somethin' else to think about."

She grinned as she recalled his words. "Pa, supper's on!" she called, and whistled tunelessly under her breath. He came round the wagon, carrying his whip in his hand. She started and laughed aloud, almost dropping the fry pan.

"What's so blamed funny 'bout a frazzled whip, I'd like to know?" he asked, his forehead wrinkled in bewilderment.

But she could only shake her head in speechless merriment as she served up his hoecakes.

The long miles of the prairie spread ahead of her like a vast sea. At night, she could hear the chorus of coyotes, as though they laughed at folks who tried to cross this blister of a land. It don't do nothing by halves, she thought. Either there was no game for miles, or the herds of buffalo were so thick that you couldn't see the ground beneath their hooves. Either the wind about blew your tongue back in your mouth, or there wasn't a breath of air, stifling as the inside of a corn crib in August.

And always, the wolves. They traveled in packs behind the game, their yellow eyes watching for a stray calf or a crippled bull too old to keep up. She'd seen them snarl and scrap over a cow mired in a sinkhole, taking great bites from her haunches even as she struggled to pull free with what was left of her legs. And all the while, the buzzards wheeled overhead like they had all the time in the world. I never thought to see such things, but now I have, I'm not sorry, she thought. A land of hard beauty, Pa called it. Cow skulls laying about, picked bare as the back of your hand, and rattlesnakes coiled up, waiting for a careless foot, and the sun and the wind and the endless horizon. The weight of the space all around her sometimes seemed so hot and heavy that it smothered her and left her gasping. Yet her eyes watered with pride as she watched their lonely wagon train wend its way across the flatlands, saw the people stubbornly bend and then melt into it, all the while making it their own by their presence. The yondering restlessness they felt made no sense, but in her heart, she understood.

When the wagons circled for the night, she liked to sit and listen to the men and women talk over their dreams and hopes for new lives. It seemed she could feel their futures coming up, shimmering all around them like the firelight.

Some dreamed of land, some of riches, others of—salvation. There were a powerful lot of preachers on the train, and hardly a one had a good word to say about the other. Their wives scrapped over everything from children to pot space at the fires, and their menfolk argued over who would save the heathen. When they weren't splitting up Paradise between them, they told some fearsome tales.

"I heard some of the white men've even taken—squaws as wives," one of the Methodist mothers whispered, glancing at the wagons to be sure no children spied. "Livin' in sin, they say!"

"No decent white man would do such a thing," the Baptist preacher said quickly. "Open cohabitation with savages! Women who are probably diseased and *certainly* unclean. I, for one, could never countenance it." He warmed to his subject. "Might could be I'd have to write a letter to the proper authorities about such wrong-thinkin'."

"Letters won't keep them apart," a priest said mildly. "The thing to do is marry the couples immediately so that they can redeem themselves in the eyes of God."

The concept shocked the circle of believers to silence. Not even a sputter erupted from the Baptist preacher, but he went white and clutched at his Bible with one hand, his wife with the other. Abruptly, they rose and retired to their wagon.

In the silence, the priest added, "Why, Doctor McLoughlin, himself, has an Indian wife. Four children by her, at last count."

The Methodist minister recovered and said quietly, "Which is why we're making this trip. I think it's clear enough that papist policies aren't savin' souls. The wilderness needs us, sure. The day of salvation for the unwashed is at hand."

Isaac got up abruptly and passed Suzanna on the way to the wagon. "High-minded blowflies," he muttered, and she followed him, threading her way through the sleeping train until they climbed into the high, white canvas which was home.

When they reached the Sweetwater River valley, they could see a dark line of wagons straggling ahead of them, trailing clouds of dust. Captain rode ahead to ask if they wanted company, and by nightfall, both trains had circled into a community of travelers. Captain John Sutter led them, a troop of six schooners dwarfed by the huge herds of cattle they shepherded.

Suzanna sat at the edge of the campfire, patching her father's cotton shirts. It had been a hard ride that day, and her eyes smarted from the dust and the smoke. But Sutter's tales of grizzly fights and Indian wars kept her wide awake, even though her body ached with weariness.

"Don't you fear the savages, man?" John Carter asked. "I wager a herd this size'd draw every one for miles."

"I don't fear nothin' that walks on two legs," Sutter grinned. "Or four, neither. But I do keep a keen watch out. I promised the Methodists I'd bring 'em a herd, an' I aim to keep that promise. Time we Yanks stopped bein' beholden to ol' HBC."

"HBC?" Carter frowned, bewildered.

"Ol' 'Here Before Christ', boy! Hudson Bay Company!"

Carter blushed and was quiet.

"But are there markets for that much stock?" a farmer called from the edge of the fire.

"Damn an' hellation, man, there's no bother 'bout markets out there. Stiff markets, too. Why, you can get fifty cents for corn an' a dollar for wheat, an' pert' near name your own price for good beef."

"Who pays that kind of cash money?" another wife asked, her eyes wide with wonder.

Sutter laughed slyly. "Hudson Bay Company, o' course. They's the only ones who can. An' then, they turn around an' sell it to you newcomers for a purty profit. Sooner or later, you got to pay it."

Silence greeted this announcement. Sutter lit his pipe and leaned back, the smoke curling over his head. " 'Course, if you bring in your own beef, you can ship it down to the ports, like Saint Francisco, and sell it to the English yourself. They'd never even know where it come from. An' you'd get better prices an' better stock an' not be beholden for nothin'." Sutter looked around the ring of listeners intently, leaning forward into the firelight. "An' when the time comes for war, you be rich an' ready, owin' nothin' to nobody."

"You think war's coming?" Brother Wilson asked quickly.

"Talk's of it, aye, up both ends of the trail, an' this chile believes it, too. Can't get a bellyful of English an' Yanks on the same land an' expect nothin' less. Got to come. An' when it does, every man best be able to butter his own biscuit."

The idea caught fire. Suzanna could see it circle the camp in the eyes of the men, drawing down the mouths of the women, and she held her breath. War wasn't something they counted on, she thought swiftly. Lots of talk of fifty-four forty or fight, I recall, but nobody's figured to join some wilderness army.

"Tell us about the meeting at Champoeg," a man asked. 'I hear tell they got together a petition."

"Sure did," Sutter drawled. "Got a little meetin' goin' in the Willamette Valley, all hot an' rarin' to go, an' voted in a Yankee government for all lands south of the river. Got 'em a judge, a sheriff, an' a damned treasurer. An' a captain of the troops, though they ain't got no troops to command, last I heard. Sent a paper to Congress an' said they was the new territory."

"Damned Bay boys can't keep it all to themselves forever," another man said. " 'Bout time they moved out anyways. Polk'll pass that new treaty, if he hasn't already. Take it first and then argue the fact later, I say."

Suzanna watched the men closely. We're coming, she thought. Sure as spring rain, and back of us will come still more. When she thought of it, she felt restless, eager to be going again, somewhere, anywhere. We will cross the mountains, grind through the dust, ford the rivers, bringing the future in our hands. She felt a tingling in her flesh and could see that others felt it, too. I wish Ma was here, she thought for the hundredth time. Nearly halfway. Lord give me strength.

Paradise, the people called it, always looking toward the west, following the sun every day until their eyes ached with watching. But paradise doesn't look much like I figured it to, Suzanna thought often. And doesn't act like it, neither. Like the Israelites, we're just following our Moses across the desert. Only our Moses isn't a man, it's a dream. And as for plagues, we're about even with the Hebrews on that score, too.

One day, as they stopped for water, a dark cloud moved over the horizon and came toward them, like a black tide in the sky.

"Locusts!" Captain hollered, and he hurried everybody into the shelter of the wagons.

"Whyn't we run?" Suzanna asked her father as she tied the side flaps down securely.

"Oxen'd be blind—'sides, we'd never outrun 'em!" her father shouted hastily, throwing the grub box in the wagon.

Then, with a loudly growing hum, the insects were all around them. They plopped against the wagon like hail and covered the ground so thick that there was no place to set a boot without smashing their bodies. The sky was black with them, and the sun was blotted out. Horses screamed and pitched and bucked, but their hobbles held them fast. The lumbering cattle and oxen stood by helplessly while the locusts crawled all over them, into their eyes, ears, and nostrils.

Suzanna tried to watch outside from a tiny rent in the canvas, but all of a sudden, the bugs were inside as well, hundreds of crawling bodies wriggling over boxes and bedding and arms and legs. She heard children screaming in the other wagons, and she gasped as the vermin writhed through her hair and down her neck. Her father cursed and tied his trouser legs frantically, beating at his thighs where the bugs scurried up his ankles.

One team broke and tried to run, dragging a wagon behind, but the bodies of the insects were so thick that they only squashed, and the wheels slid as though they were on marsh mud. The horses squealed and crashed heavily into one another, trying to escape the roar and the maddening insects.

After long moments, the noise began to slack off. Gradually, there were fewer and fewer locusts, and the buzzing of their wings droned away. Suzanna stuck her head out of the wagon and saw a huge black shadow moving westward in the sky.

Philura Carter jumped out of her wagon, her face pale as the canvas. She'd been wearing a canary yellow skirt with green stripes, fixed for Sunday meeting. The hoppers had eaten every stitch of green from her waist to her feet. Her skirts hung at her knees in tatters, and her underlinen fluttered in the breeze. Suzanna ran to check Buck and Bright and saw that every piece of harness and reins had been chewed through, particularly where the leather was damp with sweat from animals or man.

"They like the salt, I reckon," her father muttered, and he cursed again when he saw the repairs to be made.

There was not a single blade of grass as far as she could see. The willows down by the creek were stripped of their leaves as though it was the coldest winter. The creek water was so thick and clogged with bodies that it was unfit to drink, and an unholy hush lay over the land.

"Hell an' Maria!" her father shouted suddenly, as though the silence gave him the willies. "I be damned if I can see the use such critters have on God's green earth!"

There was nothing for it but to drive on.

There was so much to see on the trail that sometimes Suzanna forgot to be weary. She liked to go out and look at the buffalo herds, much as she used to hitch up to see the peddlers' fair back home. The great shaggy beasts wallowed in the mounds made by the ground dogs, kicking their spindly legs in the air and puffing and groaning. The bulls snorted and roared at each other, butting and shoving the cows from one end of the plains to the other, the calves scampering along, wide-eyed and plaintive.

And then there were the Indians. They hadn't seen many on the trail, but they watched for them constantly. Sometimes, hunting parties crossed the horizon, the dust signaling their presence, and the savages came into camp on their horses, their squaws trailing behind them. Captain said when they had their women, there was nothing to fear, but each man held his rifle ready, even so.

The Indians Suzanna saw were mostly scraggly sorts, short and squatty with louse-ridden hair in lanky braids. They wore only pieces of hide at their loins, and their women were covered with shapeless leather aprons. Dogs followed them everywhere, noisome and pesty as starlings. The preacher said they were accurst of God for they didn't toil; neither did they spin. Suzanna noticed they didn't smell much like the lilies of the field either. She recalled the talk of whites marrying squaws, and she gaped at them, trying to picture it. I believe I'd rather marry a coyote, she thought staunchly. If I married at all.

Once, they were camped on the banks of the Sweetwater so the women could do the wash. A pack of Indians watched them idly from the trees. Mrs. Riley's two-year-old, Berta, wandered up to a squaw, and when the squaw beckoned to her, she lifted up her arms to be held. The squaw carried Berta to her mother and gestured with signs, asking Mrs. Riley how much she would take for her daughter.

"The child's not for sale," Mrs. Riley said, glancing nervously around for the men.

The squaw offered to trade her own child for Berta, pushing a young boy forward.

"No, not for trade neither," Mrs. Riley said firmly, picking up her daughter and hurrying away.

But the squaw stood still, watching, and Suzanna kept her eyes on her all the while she washed. Finally, when Mrs. Riley turned her back for an instant, the squaw swooped in, grabbed Berta, and ran for the timber. Suzanna hollered for the men and chased her, catching her just as she reached her pony. She grabbed the horse's halter, jumping back from the kicking feet of the furious woman. The men were on them in a moment, and though the squaw fought and shouted, they pulled Berta from her arms.

Berta began to cry as Suzanna led her back to her mother's embrace. "Pony!" she shrieked, pointing over her shoulder.

"That pony'd take you places you'd rather not be goin', little one," Suzanna said. "An' next time, you might think to holler *afore* you get rescued!"

Fort Hall was filled with wild and hairy French-Canadian trappers when the travelers pulled in, so the women kept close to the wagons. Suzanna was disappointed at the fort's smallness after Laramie, and on top of that, the Bannock village was empty.

"They're up at the falls for the salmon run," Captain said, and she wondered when she would get to taste this red fish that she had heard so much about. The salmon, folks said, fought their way up the rivers to breed and die. Did dying often follow breeding, she wondered vaguely, or did it just seem so?

Her father prowled the settlement and then came back puffing and blowing like a hobbled steer. "They expect a man to pay three dollars for heatin' an' refittin' a blamed wheel rim! Hell, that's a four-bit job back home. An' a dollar a pound for beans!"

"Well, 'less you're fixin' to make it to Oregon on hoecakes an' coffee, 'pears like we got to meet that price, Pa."

"Damn me! I told the man he ought to wear a mask an' carry a gun, an' I ain't goin' back to him now. You go, Suz. An' don't worry me with what it costs, just buy the blamed stuff."

So Suzanna smoothed her back hair and strode to the trading post. She stepped inside and surveyed the rough planked shelves. Sniffing hungrily, she relished the rich smells of coffee, spices, tobacco, powder, and smoked game. To smell such all the day would be like eating white bread every meal, she thought to herself.

Really, we don't need much, she shrugged, wrenching away with difficulty from the urge to buy an armful of everything. Now that Mother is gone, the larder is my say-so. If Pa wants to go all the way to China, I mean for him to have the grub to do it on. Game was still good . . . perhaps she could get by with meal, beans, and coffee.

She finished her trading quickly, refusing to wince at the prices. Moving outside the store, she edged round a pig and a dog quarreling over a scrap of something, and past the tavern where the trappers were having a drinking and swearing contest, judging by the ruckus. Outside the gates, she came to a clear, sparkling creek which wandered across the meadow. The Portneuf, they called it, and now in September it was low and noisy like creeks back home. Some of the boys were fishing; she could hear their shouts of victory as they jerked flopping trout from the water. The younger children were wading, tossing rocks, and running as though they'd never get enough of the air and the open space. She sat down on the creek bank, just off from a ridge-runner. She glanced over at him, smiled briefly, and then looked away.

Mountain men they were called out here, she knew, but back in Missouri, they were just ridge-runners, and no-count to boot. Mostly cold-eyed rascals who wouldn't do an honest day's work and beat their women. Pa said that ridge-runners liked their game high-flavored, their whisky raw, and their women salty. But this one looked different. He was husky, tall, and wind-chapped, and his face creased in comfortable lines like a favorite boot.

Suddenly, there was a commotion upcreek, and one of the men —Riley it was, she could him plainly now—came galloping toward them shouting, "Shoot her, shoot her!" His horse was pounding up the bank, and right behind, swiping at his flanks, was a huge she-bear, roaring mad.

"Sweet Jesus," the mountain man cursed softly and yanked his musket from the shade of a willow. "Must'a come on her cubs a-fishin'." He put the gun to his shoulder, winked one eye, and slowly—while Suzanna held her breath and made to run if he missed—squeezed off a single shot.

Riley's horse reared, and the grizzly screamed, a high-pitched whine of rage and pain, and stopped to bite frantically at her haunches, skidding along sideways, her long canines gleaming in a red mouth. With a great lumbering gait, she wheeled and bounded back down the bank, scattering onlookers on both sides.

The mountain man shouldered his musket and started after the bear.

"Where you goin'?" Suzanna called.

He turned and appraised her up and down casually. "Don't do to leave younguns to starve when ye put a bullet in their mammy. They's either hers," he grinned insolently, "or they's mine. Want to come along, sister?"

He wants me. The thought shot through her like cold water in a hot belly, and she quietly praised herself as she always did when she had a thought beyond her years.

She stuck out her chin and turned away. "No thank you, I'm sure, mister." She walked back up the bank and sensed his eyes follow her rump switching in her skirts. She felt a wild urge to pick up and run, but she fought it down and walked, her heart beating hard.

In two days, they left Fort Hall and the prairies, and they saw no more buffaloes, antelopes, or ground dogs. Suzanna was glad to leave the heat and the dust, but she missed the antelopes, those pert beasts with their quick turns and their high leaps and their twinkling white tails like flags. She even missed the buffaloes. I remember when I wrinkled my nose over the thought of boiling coffee over dried dung, she thought. But there's nothing like digging for roots and greenwood until your back is broken to make chips a mite easier to take. Now, she missed the prairies littered with easy fuel and the fragrant fires at night. Ma was right, she thought, pretty is as pretty does. And that goes for buffalo dung, as well.

After another week on the trail, the wagons began to rise steadily. The oxen always seemed to be pulling now, their flanks straining ahead of her. Early mornings and dusks had a bite to them, and the breeze was chill in the shadows. Summer skies with winter's eyes, Suzanna thought, and she hurried to finish the woolen shawl she was knitting.

High bare buttes rose before them, looming to the right and left like guards. They seemed to be close at hand when you looked at the tops of them, but when you looked again at the ground, they were still far away. The country rose higher and higher, and stands of pine, cool and green and dark, broke the edges of the hills. Off in the distance, Suzanna could see snow-topped peaks that seemed to go on forever into the sky.

Captain hurried them now, pushing for the passes before the heavy snows set in. Wolves came closer to the camp at night, and the men tied the horses within the circle of wagons rather than outside with the oxen. The dogs were forever growling deep in their throats and baying frantically at some unseen threat. Soon, even the oxen were moved in, and sleep was impossible as they lowed and stumbled about, bumping against the wagons in the dark.

They passed piles of cupboards and trunks, marked by lonesome signs, "Help yourself." Every mile or so, piles of boulders on an open stretch of ground marked the graves of those who had made it this far—but no farther.

Accidents seemed to happen more often now, and each mother warned her children to keep close to the wagons, moving or not. Most of the men were off hunting when John Weatherby fell under the team and broke his leg. Isaac was the only man close, so Missus Weatherby called him to help her boy, who was laid out on the ground, his leg twisted at a crazy angle.

Suzanna ran behind her father, carrying the medicine chest, wondering what in the world she would do if she had to cut something.

Isaac knelt and touched the boy's knee gently. He glanced up at Missus Weatherby. "I ain't no doctor, ma'm," he said, "but I reckon bones is bones. This one's broke."

John was sixteen and near a man, but he looked suddenly young and helpless on the ground with his face the color of early snow. Suzanna looked away, not wanting to shame him.

"Figure you can set it, Mister Blue?" John asked through clenched teeth.

Isaac said softly, "If you want me to. But it'll hurt like hell, sure enough, boy."

"Hurts like hell right now," he said, and Suzanna saw the sweat on his ashen skin.

"You want a snort of somethin' strong afore we start?"

John shook his head feebly, licking his lips. "Pa wouldn't like it. We's teetotalin' Methodists."

Isaac shrugged. "Well, that's fine, boy. You got grit in your mulligan. But I think I'll have my ownself a smart one afore I set to work."

Mrs. Weatherby snapped, "What do *you* need a drink for? You ain't the one with the broke leg!"

Suzanna impulsively reached out and patted her arm. She knew she was only speaking out of fear and anger, that her husband wasn't there when he was needed.

But her father just grinned. "I know, missus, but I'm just a calf-hearted sonofabitch." He grabbed the whiskey bottle, took a huge swig, and set to work.

Suzanna got in the habit of working her quilting nights before the lamp, piecing together the bits and bolts of color. She had started out with just a little swatch of calico, then she traded a bit there and a piece here, and of course, she had a length left over each time she mended a dress, and she took whatever happened to come and wove it all together. I guess this is what the preachers mean by predestination, she thought. She worked without a pattern, and her quilt became a live thing in her hands.

Isn't it odd, she thought, that you can give two women the same colors, even the same pieces, and one will turn out a Nine Patch and the other will put out a Wild Goose Chase, and there'll be two quilts made out of the same cloth and just as different as can be. Seems like that's the way it is with living, she mused, life brings in the pieces, but we can cut them out and put them together pretty much to suit ourselves.

She stood and draped the soft quilt over herself, watching as it curved to the wagon floor. Lately, she'd felt eyes on her back, flicking in her direction as she moved about, single eyes and even some of the married eyes, too. She wasn't pretty, she knew, but she was young and strong and her hair had lights in it before the fires at night. She turned and ran her hands down her hips slowly. Her breasts were full, even though her flanks were lean and long. My hands are big and so is my back, she thought, and maybe a man on the trail don't hanker to pretty so much as just healthy young flesh. The night they'd stayed over at Laramie and the dancing started, several held her elbows just a mite longer than they needed to and squeezed her waist firmly.

Her throat had been full of blood and her beating heart and the music, and in an instant, she saw how easy it would be to be wanton. And when a few of them whispered in her ear, "You're mighty purty tonight, Suzanna," and "My, can't she dance to beat all!" she had smiled and laughed but followed no one out into the darkness. Not for a few pretty words would she go following after her mother's mistakes. No man in her bed and no babe in her belly, she recited over and over to herself, until it became like a nun's rosary in her mind.

Finally, they reached the fearsome Blue Mountains, the last obstacle on the trail to the Columbia. The rocks loomed up dark and solid ahead, and now that they were this close, the prospect of failure, the very real possibility that they could die almost within sight of the river, was enough to make nightmares rumble through her mind. However, a refrain ran through the camp, "If the other trains could get through, we can," and no one spoke their worry out loud.

It started to snow two days into the mountains, and then the worst struggle began. They had to fashion ropes and pulleys and winches to haul the wagons up the canyons, and when they reached the plateau, they used the same ropes and winches and sheer muscle to hold back the wagons from running headlong over the oxen, plunging them all to the canyons below.

At the top of the passes, the snow was already deep, and the wind moaned desolately through the trees. The forest was so dense that little light filtered through the uppermost branches, nearly three hundred feet above their heads. Like a great, silent, frozen cathedral, Suzanna thought, and she shivered, part from cold, part from the bleakness of the deep woods.

They scrambled up the icy banks, leading the teams, stumbling from one foothold to another. Isaac's wagon was first in line, and Suzanna walked a little ahead, calling back to him warnings of boulders and windfalls. Captain had gone back down the line to help the stragglers.

Suddenly, she rounded a dense grove and saw an abandoned wagon, marooned beneath a great shoulder of rock that jutted out from the south wall. Two exhausted oxen had been turned loose, and they lay in the snow, lowing weakly. The faded canvas wagon top was mantled with snow. Icicles hung from the wagon spokes.

"My Lord," Suzanna whispered. "How long has it been sittin' here?" She called back to Isaac, who tied the team and stumbled through the snow to her shoulder.

"God ha' mercy," he said, and he ran toward the wagon. "Hallo-o-o!" he called. And then Suzanna saw a slight waft of smoke beating back from the wagon, nearly invisible in the wind.

Isaac saw the smoke, too. "Do Jesus, somebody's alive in there!" he hollered. "Hey, in there! Hallo-o-o!"

Suzanna heard a woman's voice from inside the wagon. "We're here! We're here! Thank God!"

They went to the wagon and looked inside. Suzanna saw a plain woman with blankets pulled about her, thin and pale, her young face lined with pain. She sat with seven children about her, some too weak from hunger to move.

"You got any extra victuals?" she asked softly.

Isaac pulled some jerked venison from his pocket and handed it to her. She passed it to the children, and they looked from Suzanna to Isaac with big, wondering eyes.

"Where's the rest of your train, ma'am?" Isaac asked. "And your man?"

"He went down the mountain three days past to get help. We got a broke axle an' can't budge. He left us plenty, but the wolves took it the first night—climb right up the tree an' yanked it down, where he'd stored it safe. So we been without, waitin' on him." She pushed back a grimy lock of hair from her eyes. "We got behind the rest, an' they couldn't wait. They feared the storms. You got room for us, you think?"

They helped the woman—Missus Elizabeth Smith was her name —lead her children to the Blue wagon. By now, the rest of the train waited in the trees, and Captain parceled out her family to the wagons. Missus Smith carried her youngest, a six-month baby. The oldest boy, no more than ten, Suzanna guessed, brought up the five younger children. Suzanna's eyes burned as she watched them, and she wiped away the water with the back of her hand.

Barefoot, the woman walked through the snow, leading her children, laughing weakly when she saw the waiting wagons. There are a thousand more like her behind us, Suzanna thought swiftly. And even the Blue Mountains can't keep them out.

They traveled for a week up and down the great canyons, and finally, they reached the peak, and they knew it was all downhill. The children were put off to lead the stock, and all who could push or shove or pull put their shoulders to the task.

Suzanna's father locked the wheels, tied a forty-foot fir behind as a drag, and zigzagged back and forth until he reached the bottom of the slope. Over and over, they cut new trees as brakes, moving slowly down the mountains. The branches dug like claws into the dark earth, Suzanna slid alongside the oxen's flanks to keep them steady, and finally, oh finally, the Columbia was in view.

She stood and gazed at its fast-flowing currents, awed by its silent power. Columbia . . . the river of the west, they called it, a name large, lovely, and full of promise in her mouth. Not like the old-man rivers back home, she thought, shaking her head. Everywhere, the surge of green water gave the feeling of strength, nowhere drifting in lazy circles in the sun, always rolling and churning in an excited pother, a silent struggle, intent on reaching the sea.

That night round the fires, important decisions had to be made. Which wagons would be going on downriver to the Willamette Valley, perhaps as far as the sea, and which would take a different fork and head for other destinations?

"I hear tell the river'll kill stock quicker than six Mis'oura winters," Brother Wilson said solemnly. "You got to cross it twice, an' through currents faster than what we seen so far."

"What other choices we got, Captain?" Isaac asked.

"Well, there's Fort Nez Perce right where the Snake comes in. Some folks call it Walla Walla. Anyhow, McKenzie built it, and it's sound. Between the river and a half-decent potato patch, a man can make out all right. And the Nez Perce are a peaceful sort, so far." Jackson kicked back and leaned against a saddle, stretching out long legs to the flames. "Then, there's Lapwai, the Spalding mission further up the Snake. They're doing right well with the Nez Perce, I hear. Lutherans, I think. Or maybe Congregationalists, hell, I don't know."

The Methodist minister spoke up. "That's where we'll be heading, leastways 'til we get the lay of things."

"And finally, you could go to Waiilatpu. I'd say that's about the closest from here. Probably the easiest route, too."

"What's goin' on there?" Isaac asked.

" 'Nother mission. And don't ask me what kind. The Whitmans run it. It's a damn sight bigger than Lapwai, but then they got to contend with the Cayuse, too, and that's an ornery bunch of siwash. But they got more land and more stock." Captain Jackson grinned. "And I hear tell that Narcissa Whitman's not too hard to look at, neither."

"We got to get across the river," a farmer called. "They say the Willamette's got the best land."

"That's so," Jackson said, "and I'll get you there. But for those who don't hanker to walk behind a plough, there's other spots that'll do 'em. And from here, you can make it by yourself. Just follow the river up 'til it hits the Snake, then you'll come to the fort. They can tell you how much further from there. You can be there in less than a week, I wager, if the snow holds."

The next morning, the Blue wagon and four other families turned north and made their way upriver.

"If he's got that much stock, he's got to need some hands," Isaac said. "An' if you can stand to work for Missus Whitman for a season or so, I can stand to work for the preacher-man himself."

"At this point, I don't care much, Pa," she said wearily. "I just want a hot bath, some clean clothes, and a bed that don't rock in the wind."

The Whitmans called their mission "Waiilatpu," the place of rye grass. Eden, more like, Suzanna thought, as she led the oxen behind the four other wagons who had decided to head north, rather than risk the Columbia crossing. At Fort Walla Walla, they'd heard that these Presbyterians were doing well among the heathens, but they were still surprised when they rounded the bend and saw several houses, sheds, warehouses, fenced pastures, and even mills for grain and lumber. All very substantial in the winter sun.

"God looks out for his own, don't he?" her pa said under his breath, as the oxen pulled the wagon into the deep ruts that said many others had been there before them.

The grass in the mission pastures even in the early winter was tall, dusky, and thick, so high that they could only see the backs of the horses and cattle. Chickens clucked and scratched in the dirt, and hogs wallowed in the mud by the creek. Suzanna felt a tightness in her throat, so much did it bring to mind Missouri. But she swallowed firmly and stepped down to meet the woman who came toward them, her arms outstretched.

She was tall and plump, this preacher's wife, with blue eyes and yellow braids piled on top of her head like a crown. "Welcome to Waiilatpu!" she called, and her smile was warm. But as she drew closer, Suzanna could see that her eyes searched the wagons intently as though she looked for trouble, and her back was stiff, unyielding as a rich widow's parlor chair.

"No sickness here, missus," Isaac spoke up quickly. "An' we all crossed with strength to spare."

Her eyes matched her smile then. "The Lord be praised," she said and walked them up to the white mission house.

Suzanna wondered how many wagons had whoaed up here to let off the weak and the sick to heal or die at her hands. I might just run off the next batch with a stick, she thought ruefully. But Mrs. Whitman hid whatever resentment she might have felt under a bland Christian smile, and in no time, she had herded them into the parlor to meet her husband, the Reverend Marcus Whitman.

Doctor Whitman was tall and older than his wife. His black hair was touched with gray, and he walked with stooped shoulders, like he thought too much, Suzanna noticed. But he seemed to take to her father and within the hour, Isaac Blue was the new stockman at Waiilatpu. Not much cash, her pa said later, but bed and victuals, leastways, and for now, that'd do.

They soon met more wayfarers who'd sought shelter at the mission: the seven orphaned Sager children and Helen Meek, daughter of Joe Meek, mountain man, and his Nez Perce wife; Mary Ann Bridger, child of another mountain man and a squaw, and at least a dozen other families who had made the Whitman station a refuge. Their first night at table, Suzanna quickly saw that it took a half-hour just to set the table. And any place that took two hours to wash up after was not going to be home for long. Not if they took her vote, anyways.

But what was intended to be only a temporary stop soon began to feel familiar, and Suzanna settled into life at the mission. Her father tended the stock, driving them out to pasture, milking the cows, poulticing their bug bites and cracked horns, and birthing their calves. His horse, Big Ben, hardly raised his head out of the long grass, as though he was determined to make up for the long months on the trail. Already, his ribs were fleshed out, and his straggly winter coat was glossy and sleek.

Suzanna found it easy to get along with most everybody; winter chores kept them all too busy to fret one another much. By spring, she felt she'd almost found a family. But John Sager, the oldest boy on the mission grounds, was one who vexed her. He watched her all the time and tried to put himself in her path. A tall, pale-faced lad who bit his nails down to the stubble, he was trying to grow a beard, but all he'd managed were a few scrawny tufts on his chin. When he sauntered up one day and asked, "Whyn't you an' me take a walk to the pasture?" Suzanna evenly replied, "I been to the pasture." She liked John well enough, but he made her uneasy. "Besides," she added, "I got chores to do."

"They can wait a mite, can't they?" He had an honest face, but his gaze didn't quite meet her eyes. She saw that he didn't really know her and couldn't see inside her at all.

"Now, that'd be a fine thing," she said lightly and turned to go.

"You're the fine thing," he blurted, and she flushed for him and for herself. She walked away, and he followed her, switching a rope against his thighs. She looked sideways at him under her lashes. Something in her wanted to prod him as a child pokes at a frog with a stick to see if she can make him jump.

"What you want to grow that beard for, John Sager?" she asked pertly. "Pa says I should never trust a man who wants to grow on his face what grows wild on his tail." And then she stopped, and a bright flush of confusion spread up her cheeks. Good Lord and little fishes, what a thing to say to a man! She picked up her skirts and ran for the barn.

Between the dishes, the mending, the sweeping, and the washday chores, Suzanna's favorite time quickly became Sunday, with its peace and quiet and unfettered freedom. The Indians started gathering right after breakfast, and soon the yard was full of them: tall and rangy, dark brooding Cayuse with black hair and patient eyes. They were wrapped in blankets in the winter and wore breeches in the summer, breeches they got from the Whitmans, mended by the mission girls. Their women wore long robes and kept their breasts covered, leastways when they were in plain sight of the mission houses.

The Indians seemed to like the singing best, and so the doctor sprinkled his sermons with plenty of pauses for music. But in between, he asked God to be merciful to poor sinners, to bless their harvests, and to protect them from the elements, the heathen, the wild beasts, the sicknesses, and the deadly accidents. After he'd finished his catalogue of disasters, each listener felt grateful just to be alive at all. He'd throw in a hymn, the restless in the crowd would calm a bit, and they'd listen once more.

Then he'd start up again with the glory of the Lord and the awfulness of wicked ways and the blessings of being a good Christian, and the shuffling would begin again so he'd break into song. And finally, he'd finish up with a rousing good bellow about the storms of winter and the shorn lamb and the abundance of the earth. Amen. Amen.

The words rolled out of his mouth like fruit, full and round and ripe, as if in offering to his own private altar. And what with one blessing and another, the doctor took long enough talking to God for Suzanna to watch an ant crawl from the toe of her boot, down near six strides of spring grass, not even counting the side trips up an occasional trouser leg or twig, and all the pauses in between to feel the air with its tiny feet.

Struck by a sudden truth, she thought, nobody can preach better than this ant, and he doesn't say a word.

But then, it was time for freedom, and her favorite way to spend it was to walk away from the mission and into the hills, following the creek toward the Walla Walla River. The air had a taste to it here, all high and sharp like spring clover and ice, and the bees droned over her head, up to their thighs in pollen.

She thought how the worlds of different people had different shapes. Somehow, inside herself, she carried all the space they'd traveled across. She thought back to the folks she'd known in Missouri—the girls she'd befriended, the families they'd met; they were far away and different now. Their lives were as changed from hers as her own was from the Indians. Yet each felt his life to be the best, the only one with any real meaning.

She marveled at how the savages would sit in rows on logs out in the yard, for all the world as if they sat in the finest church. They might sacrifice salmon to their own gods during the week, but on the Sabbath, the hallelujah shouts and the fervent hymns and the hollering got to even the most stubborn of them, Suzanna noticed, and they ran trembling to each other, tearfully begging forgiveness for their heathen ways.

Once or twice, she had to admit, she'd felt a strong desire to run up and down the rows, too, singing and shouting to the Lord. But the thought of her father's sideways grin acted like a cold slap of water, and she always settled back to watch.

If they just wouldn't holler out their sins so much! Suzanna grimaced. Sitting for hours, washing their hands and feet in the basins of water Mrs. Whitman set out for them, happy to splash the day away, singing and chanting. Sometimes, they got drunk on it, she thought, and then they sat for hours, rocking on the logs until dawn, shouting and praying for the Holy Spirit to carry them away.

Suzanna had watched while Doctor Whitman baptized a few of the most promising converts. Before all the congregation, two braves stood up and repeated after him, "From this moment on, I will be a white man." This was the Lord's work, everybody said, and it was good . . . even if no *other* work was getting done. However, Isaac grumbled that the stock couldn't eat hymns, and he hadn't met a cow yet who gave down milk to two praying hands.

She walked further and heard a bird sing, tremulously at first, and then it give full throat to a flame root of spring joy in its breast. Reverend and his wife are smart all right, she thought, full of book learning and gold words. But they still can't say why the birds sing like that. Or even why folks find it beautiful when they do.

That reminded her of the time she'd overheard the doctor and the Cayuse chief talking longside the creek. Doctor had said something about knowledge being power, but the heathen said, "No. That is not so." And he didn't say more. But when the doctor kept pestering him about preaching in the lodges, the chief finally stopped and gave him the strangest look, as though he'd just realized the man was deaf.

"We will not have your gods in our village," he said. "We will come and listen when it pleasures us, but we will not have your gods in our lodges. We are too full of gods."

"There's only one God—" Reverend began firmly.

But the chief cut him off. "Well, and that is not what the red robes say."

The Catholic priests had done their best to convert the Cayuse, sending up presents from Fort Walla Walla and generally pestering the heathens to death. "The red robes are wrong," Whitman repeated tirelessly. "They are men of good heart, but their gods are false."

The Cayuse chief shrugged hugely and turned away. "There is much we will learn from the whites. But we will not learn to fight over gods. We may quarrel with men over things on earth, but we never fight about the great spirit. We do not want to learn that." He added gently, "Perhaps the old ways are best. White medicine does not work for us. The black robes say one thing and the red robes say another, and the truth escapes while they hunt for it." He had walked away then without looking back.

Suzanna thought about what she'd heard long and hard. When she searched her heart, she knew that Mrs. Whitman would judge her as having gone to hell in a bushel basket. For I am proud and headstrong and thoughtless, she frowned. Full of go a piece, bide a spell, and hitch up and go again, as her pa would say. If she had a God at all, she guessed He was the One who made the sunshine and the lambs and the wildflowers and the singing birds. And she had the vague and pleasant notion that He made it all for her, that she might enjoy herself.

She would have liked to wander far, but she rarely strayed from the sight of the mission. The Cayuse had been fretful, Doctor said. They showed up for Sabbath sermon, regular as the seasons, but there was muttering in the lodges, and their children no longer baptized their corn-husk dolls in the mission creek.

And when Doctor Whitman called a council to teach the braves how to plant crops, they gathered, but not a one lifted a shovel. Patiently, he dug neat rows, showed them how to plant the seeds, how to hoe and weed and dirt, how to water—but the chief only stood silently, his face cold and closed.

Finally, an elder of the tribe said, "You tell us to plow the land. Shall we also take a knife and stab our mother in the chest? Dig under her skin for her bones? You say, plant the seed and cut the grain. Do we cut our own mother's hair?"

Doctor got angry then and allowed as how they wouldn't plant for themselves, but they sure had nothing against stealing the labors of others. The watermelons, for instance. The minute they got close to ripe, they disappeared from the fields, as did bushels of corn, beans, and apples.

But the watermelons were Mrs. Whitman's favorite. On a hot summer day, she kept two or three cooling in the creek, and said nothing eased her more when she was weary. When the savages kept stealing the fruit, she plugged a hole in the ends of the melons, filled them with emetic, and sealed them back up. Suzanna shook her head with a grimace when she pictured the scenes in those lodges. Terrible price to pay for a piece of melon.

And they were still mad over their dogs. Doctor said the wolves were bad last winter, so he put out some poisoned meat to kill the new pups, figuring that the bitches would haul it back to the dens and do them all in at once. Well, it worked fine, until some of the Cayuse dogs got hold of the meat and dragged back to the village to die.

The chief's son came to the house, red-faced and shouting that he'd kill a mission horse for every village dog that died. But the doctor calmed him down and he went away. Still, it don't hurt to go easy on the traipsing just now, Suzanna thought. Leastways, 'til they forget about it a mite. And she turned and walked back toward the mission house, her arms full of wildflowers.

In the fall when Suzanna was seventeen, a wagon train came trundling through, just before the first snows set in. They were on their way up to the Lapwai mission, but Isaac said, "They won't stick there a week before the Methodists kick 'em out. A rowdier bunch, I ain't seen since the Platte."

Six wagons, men mostly and a few grown sons, had come ahead of their womenfolk to settle land east of the Snake, free land, they hoped, since President Polk had signed the Oregon Treaty. They'd collected four trappers, two scouts, and a half-dozen catamount skins on their way, and they promptly invited the mission families to join them for a celebration dance.

Suzanna stayed up sewing by lamplight, piecing together some lace for the collar of her only best dress. Isaac sat down beside her, a raveled harness in his hands. He began to mend the leather, glancing at her under his brows. "You lookin' forward to this do-se-do?" he asked casually.

She looked up and grinned, and then bent again to her sewing.

"You're—uh—you're nigh a young woman now, eh?" He bent his head closer to his work. "Anything you need to ask me?"

She chuckled low in her throat. "Pa, I'm past a young woman.

Fact, I think I'm movin' up fast on spinster-lady. An' I don't guess I need to ask you about men, any." She looked up and smiled. "So you can wipe that worry off your face."

He paused. "Wouldn't want to see you get hurt."

"Well, we're both of a mind there, I guess." She slapped down her lace and suddenly laughed out loud. "Good Lord, Pa, it's just a dance! You're gettin' me so riled, I near stitched my thumb to my dress."

So the night came, the lanterns were strung in the barn, the tables crowded with pies and cakes and punch, and the families crowded in, hollering howdy like they hadn't just seen each other at breakfast. As if by instinct, the girls clustered in a covey by the lemonade barrel, and the children raced about shrieking and wrestling with the dogs.

One old trapper climbed on a haybale, put a fiddle to his chin, and began to saw. "Choose yore pardners!" he shouted, and the music crashed into life.

Suzanna was whirling in a crush of skirts and stomping feet, her hair flying out behind her, her mouth wide open in a laugh, before she even got her bearings.

> Git out o' the way, ol' Dan Tucker,
> Yore too late to git yore supper!

One partner after another grabbed her arms and swung her about, and she was bumping in a stepping-out getup of feet and rhythm, letting the fiddle carry her in and out of circles, through a blur of color and noise. She saw Isaac standing in a corner grinning, and then one of the widow-ladies hauled him out, and he sailed past, shouting something she could hardly hear.

Suddenly, a man stood before her, bowing deep, and she was in his arms, light and firm at once, and the music had the high beat of her heart in it, and her feet moved of themselves. The fiddle stopped and in the midst of the noise, her partner said, "You're Miss Blue, I reckon. I heard you was the prettiest gal on the place."

She flushed and groped for something clever to say, but could only manage, "Cain't imagine who'd tell you such a lie. But you got the name right, anyhow."

He was tall, dark, and scruffy-looking, but he had an easy confidence about him, a hardness from the trail and his years that made her feel flustered and tongue-tied. And when he took her elbow lightly and led her back to the dance, she felt a surge of heat run through her limbs.

"You come across with your pa?" he asked, his hand on her waist. Now, the blur of music and color had faded behind his head, his shoulders somewhere, and the touch of his hands on her back, her fingers, was more immediate than anything else.

"Sounds like you know all about me," she said, trying to be pert, but it came out sharper than she'd intended, so she smiled to take away the edge. He whirled her faster, and she had to go on her toes to keep up.

"I know you're not a preacher's daughter, an' I know you got the bluest eyes I seen this side of the Blue Mountains, an' I know"— he twirled her under his arm and out again—"that you dance like you got the fever. That so, Miss Blue?"—he bent her over slightly —"you got the fever in you?"

She couldn't answer for the tightness in her breast, and they danced harder, faster, and finally, the music fell away, and they stood panting in the corner. "The fiddler's quit sawin' for a spell," he said. He went to fetch a cup of cider, and she felt suddenly bereft. When he returned to her side, he said, "Let's go drink it outside," and she walked away with him, out into the night, her mind whirling.

It's so easy, she thought quickly. He spoke and there she was, natural as though she'd done this every night of her life. She felt powerful and wary all at once. They walked, and he didn't touch her, both of them cradling their cider cups as if they needed two hands. She talked swiftly, telling him of the trip across the mountains, the Cayuse, what crops had done well this year, and all the while, she watched him move, sensing the nearness of him.

He talked, his voice low and rumbling, his name was Jess, he said, and he came from Ohio, had some land back there, but it didn't amount to much, now he was looking to make his fortune out here, just passing through—and her mind stumbled to alertness.

Just passing through. She made her voice light as she could. "I heard you were goin' to Lapwai. Leavin' in a day or so?"

His eyes met hers and then skittered away, shadows from the moon carved on his face. "If you like, I can walk you back."

The sound of the fiddle came to her now, faint and squealing, and the lights from the barn looked impossibly distant. He reached out and pulled her to him, pressing his beard to her mouth, his lips to hers, and she felt his body lean and hard against her legs, the blood pounding in him like a galloped horse. A moment of wet heat, and she was conscious of his arms round her tightly, his tongue roaming her mouth, and in the silent roar of her heart, her mouth came alive and hungry. She cried out silently, her whole body reaching out, full into him. After one fierce moment, she pulled away, panting.

His eyes were dark and glowing, and she almost went back into his arms, but then she thought of her mother, and her mind reeled in horror. So this is how it happens, she thought swiftly, just this easy, just this fast. She stumbled back, catching up her skirts clumsily. He reached for her, but she twisted away and ran toward the lights, the music, the safety of the barn.

The next morning, the wagon train pulled out, and Suzanna stood under the trees, watching them go. Jess walked alongside the lead wagon, his rifle over his shoulder, a dog at his heels. In the daylight, he seemed more scraggly, more sun-cured, and she wondered what his lips would feel like now. There was bran smudged on the back of his trousers where a horse had nosed him. She stared at his shoulders, and he turned as though he felt her and smiled lightly. His eyes held her and took her measure without flinching. His jaw muscles were flat and hard.

Isaac came up behind her. "Wouldn't give much for the rest, but I purely hate to see that fiddle man go."

"Aye," she said softly. "He was a good one," and she walked away slowly, her hands trembling and hidden in her skirts.

The next year, another wagon train came through from the south. The wayfarers had no more than pulled down the road than the mission was struck by an epidemic of measles. "Trail fever," they called it, for it stuck on longer and harder than any measles they got back east of the Platte. It went through the children first, like locusts through wheat. Even after they were out of bed, most were weak and feeble. Suzanna caught only a small dose; likely she'd had the Missouri measles as a baby, and after that, she guessed the Oregon brand just couldn't stick too long on her.

But her father was struck hard. He came in five days after the wagons had passed, fretting that he felt growly and light-headed. The next morning, he wasn't to breakfast, and when she went out to his room in the barn, she found him hunched under a brace of blankets and shivering, even though it was fine outside.

"How you feelin', Pa?" she whispered.

He opened bloodshot eyes and gazed at her wearily. His voice seemed to come from deep inside his chest, but he smiled all the same. "Cold as the nose on a froze dog," he said slowly. And his teeth chattered as if to prove it.

She put her hand to his cheek and could not contain her quick gasp at the heat off his flesh. His smile slipped. "I'm stove up, eh?"

"Likely you just got the measles, Pa," she said softly. "But never you mind. It'll pass quick enough." She pulled up a chair close to his side. "Any spots?"

"Only afore my eyes." He thrust out an arm from beneath the covers, and she could see none on his skin. But she recalled how Katie Sager had the fever for five days before the rash came on.

She patted his hand briefly for comfort and went to get Mrs. Whitman. It was decided that her father should stay out in the barn, away from the rest of the house, for Doctor Whitman hadn't had the contagion yet, and there was no sense in passing it to those who'd escaped it so far.

Suzanna glowered at that. She wanted her father near her, but there was little she could do. Since she'd already had it once, she was put in charge of his care. For the first days, he slept all the time, rarely calling out for even a drink of water. Suzanna woke him often, put a cup to his lips, and he'd sip and then sleep some more. Once he smiled and said, "There's some good tunes on this ol' fiddle yet, Suz."

As she did her chores, she listened for his call and her eyes were turned often to the barn. One afternoon, she was laying down fall seed corn in furrowed rows, dropping it in one kernel at a time in the spaded earth. It was too cold to sprout, but the doctor wanted it under the earth just the same. When she looked behind her, old Jed, the rooster, was pecking up each kernel just as fast as she dropped it down.

"You no-count, plug-ugly bird!" she shouted, wincing as she realized the scolding she would probably get, seed being so dear. In a flash, she grabbed the rooster, hauled him squawking and flapping to the chopping block, wrung his neck, and cut open his craw. She carefully retrieved the kernels, replanted them, and then plucked the rooster for the supper pot. Somehow, she just couldn't brook any trespasses just now. Not after Jess. And Pa.

In a week, the measles jumped the creek and raced through the Cayuse village like a prairie fire. The death wails seemed to go on forever, as ever present as the wind. The doctor spent most of his time trying to help them, but he came home weary and dispirited from his failures.

"The fools will not listen!" she heard him holler one night after four children had died in the lodges. "They sit in those stinking sweathouses until their eyes pop, and they plunge themselves in that freezing river water. By God, I think if the snow was deep enough, they'd bury themselves up to the neck in it!"

He fussed until finally Suzanna heard Mrs. Whitman snap back at him. "Don't plague me with the Indians anymore, Marcus! I cannot bear it. I've got my hands full right here!"

Reverend Whitman had bellowed then, so all the house could hear, "Sometimes, Narcy, I wish to God that Adam had died with all his ribs in place!"

Suzanna was startled to hear them speak so sharply. There were sixty-five people in and about the mission now, some in houses of their own—families, workmen, and folks just dropping in for the winter. She felt a quick stab of guilt that she had helped so little since her father was sick. Their voices dropped, and she heard no more. She knew from months of watching that the doctor and his wife would never allow a quarrel to go aired in public.

"Remember," Mrs. Whitman always scolded them when the children cuffed each other, "the meek shall inherit the earth."

Her father got no better, and she soon forgot all her chores to sit by him and hold his hand. The doctor came as often as he could, but there was so much sickness in the lodges that he was usually called away until late at night.

Isaac lay covered so that nothing could be seen of him save his face, his eyes half-closed. Mrs. Whitman came and stood by her. "How is he?" she asked, her face calm.

Isaac stirred weakly and murmured something that Suzanna bent to hear. She took a towel from a little pile by her side and touched his forehead and mouth with it. "You want a drink, Pa?" she asked softly. She turned to Mrs. Whitman. "He's cold, he says. Always cold." She began to weep soundlessly. "Don't you know anything to do?"

Mrs. Whitman could barely look at her, sitting there silently, giving of her will and strength, trembling with despair. She did not look young now, and her face wore a mask of pain and patience that was not like youth at all. She stopped her weeping and gazed at her father's gaunt face fiercely, as though she could will him back to her.

"We've done all we know, child. The rest is in the Lord's hands." She wished Suzanna would break down and sob or scream and so ease herself, but she did not. Only quiet tears coursed down her cheeks.

The girl took her father's hand in both of hers. "Would whiskey help, you think?"

Mrs. Whitman shook her head. "You must wait. Ask for the Lord's help and wait."

Suddenly, Isaac stirred weakly, pulling his hand from Suzanna's. "Haw there, Bright," he said fretfully. "Get up there, Buck. Gee a mite."

Suzanna's eyes widened in wonder. He was back on the wagon. "Pa!" she shouted. "Pa, don't leave me!"

And in the next instant, he was gone. His chest sank, and the struggle eased from his face. She stared at him in terror, and then, gradually, a cold wave of calm settled over her.

I am alone now, completely, she thought. Now, no matter what she did or where she went, she had only herself to think of, to answer to, to lean on. She had no protection; neither did she have any reins. She recalled something her mother used to say—life is like licking honey from a thorn—and her mind was a quiet space of white wonder. The ache of her sorrow welled high in her, smothering her, closing her throat. After all, she thought, the saddest moment of my life can come only once. And she bent and kissed her father's lips softly, whispering goodbye in her heart.

Two days after her father was buried, while eleven people were still down with the measles, the Cayuse attacked. Mary Ann was working in the kitchen, and John was sitting on a stool winding twine. Suzanna was in the next room with Mrs. Whitman and several of the women, feeding the children. Dr. Whitman came in from the lodges and seated himself by the fire.

Suzanna heard Indian voices in the next room and recognized Telekaut, one of the chiefs, asking for more medicine. Suddenly, she heard a shriek, and Mary Ann stumbled into the room, her eyes wide and staring. "They're killin' us, they're killin' us!" she screamed. They ran into the kitchen and found Dr. Whitman lying in a dark pool, a gaping tomahawk wound in his scalp.

Narcissa Whitman screamed and fell to her knees in her husband's blood. Suzanna moaned and grasped at the door for support. John Sager was slumped on the floor, a knife jutting from his chest, his hand still groping for his gun. The kitchen door was open, and the sounds of rifle fire and galloping horses filled the awful silence.

They heard boots running to the door, and the children began to shriek in terror. Mr. Kimball burst into the room holding his ripped and bleeding arm. "The damned savages!" he cursed. "They've gone crazy!"

Mrs. Whitman keened loudly, and took the doctor's head in her lap. Suzanna knelt by John's head, trying to staunch the blood with her skirts, but she could scarcely sort out his features, they were so hacked. She felt numbed, shuddering with a mute horror, and somewhere, deep in her soul, she was appalled that she felt so little grief for him.

People rushed in, and there was no more time to cry or moan. Suzanna pulled herself away from John to help Mr. Kimball bind his wound. Mrs. Whitman was still calling piteously to the Doctor, but he never moved nor answered. More screams and shots came from outside, and Mary Ann went to the window, shouting, "They're killin' Mister Saunders!"

Mrs. Whitman went to the window to see, and a bullet shattered the glass, pierced her right shoulder, and dropped her to the ground. She moaned, "Lord God, save us," and was still. Now, the Indians began to batter at the door, yelping like wolves. Suzanna shouted for help, backing away from the door. She began to drag Mrs. Whitman upstairs, and others herded the children up, carrying those who were too sick to walk.

As she staggered up the stairs. Suzanna remembered an old broken gun barrel in the boys' room, and she ran to fetch it. She held it out to Mr. Rogers saying, "If we point it over the stairs at them, maybe they'll think we got a gun." He took it and steadied it on the stairwell. Suzanna managed to get Mrs. Whitman pushed into the bedroom upstairs in a corner. The children were still screaming in terror, and the shouts from downstairs grew louder, more frenzied.

As they crowded into the tiny bedroom, Mrs. Whitman awoke from her stupor and called to her husband, but he was past hearing. There was a burst of noise as the Indians broke the door downstairs and rushed in, whooping and overturning furniture.

A Cayuse brave, Tamsucky, called out, "Come down! No more kill!"

Mr. Rogers shouted back, "Come up alone!"

But Tamsucky saw the glint of the rifle barrel and would not come near the stairs. "We burn you out!" he shouted. "Send Whitman woman down! No kill!" The children began to scream and cry again, and Suzanna pulled Henrietta Sager to her lap, trying to soothe her.

Mrs. Whitman groaned, "We have no choice. If they set the place ablaze, we'll never get them all out alive. I will go down and you come after, children, if it's safe."

"You can't trust 'em!" Suzanna cried.

"I don't," Mrs. Whitman said calmly. "I trust in the Lord."

Mr. Rogers leaned back against the stairs, his face blanched and twisted with pain. "I'll go with you, then."

His wife began to sob quietly, but she said nothing.

Mrs. Whitman stood and leaned against Mr. Rogers. The two went out the door and started down the stairs. Suzanna could hear Mr. Rogers' voice calling down to Tamsucky, "We're coming! Hold your fire, for God's sake!" There was a volley of shots. Mrs. Whitman screamed once, twice, and Mrs. Rogers went for the door, but Suzanna grabbed her skirts and held her back.

They could hear Mrs. Whitman groaning. "You promised," she moaned once, clearly, and then she screamed in pain, "Oh, my dear God!" The Indians began to whoop and yell, the sounds of heavy steps clattering on the stairs. Suzanna jumped to the door and slammed it shut.

"Help me!" she called, and they pushed the bed in front of the door, Mrs. Rogers weeping loudly. "They've killed them!" she sobbed, "My husband is dead!"

Mrs. Rogers' son began to shriek, and she ran to him, clutching his head against her neck. Suzanna herded the children to the farthest corner. Mrs. Smith was silent and white, her mind seemingly snapped by the violence.

"We must wait and be still," Suzanna pleaded hoarsely. "Mary Ann, stop that cryin'! Make the babies hush. Maybe they'll go away now, an' leave us be!"

Mrs. Rogers clutched her boy and grew more frantic. "They'll kill us all!" she wailed, her eyes rolling back.

Suzanna reached out swiftly and slapped her cheek, one part of her mind recoiling even as she did so. "Not if you keep still! Hush, now, an' save your son!"

The whimpering began to cease, and the children clutched to each other for comfort. The enemy outside was suddenly less real than the blaze-eyed girl before them.

"We'll stand watch," Suzanna said quietly. "Miz' Rogers an' Miz' Smith—no, Mary Ann, you can take the second one, I guess. An' at least we'll know when they're comin'. In the meanwhile, you little ones close your eyes. Nobody's gonna sneak up on you without you knowin' it."

So through the night, they waited. Suzanna, Mary Ann, Mrs. Rogers, and Mrs. Smith—and twenty children huddled in the darkness.

Suzanna sat leaning against the wall, a child on each side of her, facing the door. Leastways, when they come, I want to see it, she thought. And I'll do my best to kill the bastard that touches me first. Three of the children were coughing in the corners, still sick with the measles. Mrs. Smith was lying in a corner, crumpled like dirty linen.

Oh Jesus, Suzanna moaned to herself, is this where it all comes to? All those miles, all those mountains, to die in a stifling room with a flock of crying babies and a mad woman? She bowed her head silently, and tears began to roll down her cheeks. She smudged them quickly with the heel of her hand. No time to cry, and no help for it if I do, she thought, gritting her teeth. They can only kill me once. And the hardest part will be the waiting. But since there was nothing else to do, she sat still and silent through the long night hours.

Dawn began to creep into the shadows of the room. Suzanna shifted carefully, trying to ease her legs without waking the two heads in her lap. One little girl began to sob quietly. "I got to have water," she said. "I'm so hot an' dry." Suzanna felt her brow and the fever there and said, "Just a little while longer." But soon, the rest of the sick ones were awake, pleading for water.

"I'm going down," Mrs. Rogers said. "My husband may still be alive." She shook herself clear of her son. "I'll bring back the bucket in the kitchen."

"Mama!" the boy shrieked once, and Suzanna grabbed her arm. "I'll go," she said. "I can move faster, an' you got to stay for him. If Mister Rogers is still alive, I can tend him."

Mrs. Rogers gripped Suzanna's arm, her face a confusion of pain and indecision. "I got nobody to leave behind," Suzanna added. And she pulled aside the bed that blocked the door.

She opened the door carefully, praying that no hinges would squeak. The stairs were empty, but the bottom planks were splashed with dark stains, blood that smeared the walls, the floor below. She crept down, one stair at a time, shifting her weight carefully to avoid the creaks. She put her hand out to steady herself, the other clutched her skirts so they would not rustle. She snatched her hand away when she saw her fingers had slid into a patch of sticky, dried blood on the banister; a handprint, small and red-edged, stained the wall.

She reached the bottom of the stairs and stopped. Her heart was thudding in her throat, roiling in her chest, and she would have liked to faint, she thought swiftly, to have someone else take care of her, of them upstairs, Pa, where are you?

There was no place else to go but forward, and so she went, creeping slowly from the stairs into the kitchen. She barely glanced into the sitting room, saw only that the desk was overturned, the chairs lay on their sides, the lamp smashed and the rugs askew, Mrs. Whitman would have a fit, her mind rattled, and then she pushed away the thought and the stark memory.

A dark streak of blood led through the kitchen doors, and she followed it, mesmerized by its thick edges, its obscene silent message, her hands trembling in her skirts. She peered around the doors.

Mrs. Whitman lay near the steps to the outside yard, her scalp half-ripped away, her blue eyes open and staring. Mr. Rogers lay where he'd dropped, half-in, half-out the door, his feet tangled like a drunken dancer's, face down in a puddle of dark blood. Dead. At least I don't have to see his eyes, she thought dazedly. Doctor Whitman curled in the corner, unmoved from where he'd fallen—was it only the day before? And John Sager sprawled where she'd left him.

She took a step toward the water bucket in the corner, pulling her eyes away from the blood crusted on Mrs. Whitman's blond hair, the flies droning around the open wounds. I'll never be able to drink a drop of water, she thought dully, not with this stench of death in my mouth, but as she clutched the bucket, her mouth went even drier. A step outside. She felt with her free hand in the knife drawer, facing the kitchen door. Slowly, the door creaked open, and Chief

Telekaut stood in the sunlight. She froze, and her hand arched up reflexively, the knife poised in the air. For a long instant, he stared at her, and his face swam before her eyes. She willed herself not to faint.

"The sick ones need water," she whispered finally, over the gravel in her throat.

"No more kill," he said quietly. Her knees gave way, and she eased to the ground, trembling.

The Indians quickly herded the rest of the women and the children together: the survivors from the mission house and the mill and the grounds, those who had been in the pasture or the barn or the chicken house. Of the seventy people at the mission, twenty-two were children, nineteen were men, and the rest, women. When the slaughter was over, most of the men were dead. Thirty-two women and children were bound together and marched to the Cayuse village, while the smoke and flames from the burning mission swirled behind them.

Suzanna walked with her head down and her shoulders stooped, but she knew in her heart that the attempt was futile. She was eighteen, and by that age, most Cayuse girls, indeed, most white women, were wives. If only Pa was here, she thought, but then, he would have been shot or tomahawked like the rest. At least, he does not have to witness my fear and the coming shame. She pulled herself into a secret place within her mind to hide from what she knew lay ahead.

They were herded into a large lodge in the village, and the old women and the little children were sent to another. The mothers cried and pleaded when they were pulled from their children, for many of the youngest were still feverish and weak. But the Cayuse seemed to have forgotten whatever English they knew, and they turned away. The lodge where Suzanna sat, huddled in the dim light, was stinking and foul with litter and mangy furs.

"At least, we don't have to share it with dogs," Mary Ann said, picking her way to a clear corner.

"Sweet Jesus, save us," one of the mothers sobbed. And others began to wail for their dead husbands and sons and brothers.

But Suzanna sat quietly, her eyes clenched shut. She had no one to mourn; though it had wrenched her to see John lying there all bloodied, and Mrs. Whitman, and the others, still she had no one to mourn save herself. I am alone, she chanted over and over, and have been since my father died. Even if he were alive, he could not help me now. What I must do is think. Think of survival and escape.

"I'll kill myself before I let a savage touch me!" cried a woman.

Yes, Suzanna said to herself. She had thought of that as well. But she knew she would never do it. Life was all there was, and she knew she would never willingly give it up. Certainly not for pride. I could throw a hissy, but it won't help. It didn't help when mother died, nor when Pa passed. The cadences of half-remembered sermons came to her. Those have I borne; this can I bear also.

A squaw came in carrying dried fish and water. She surveyed the room with visible contempt and threw the food to the floor. Helen groaned from the corner. "Water," she whispered, and Suzanna took her a share. The girl was shivering and half out of her head. "She needs a blanket," Suzanna said quietly.

"She's better off than the rest of us!" a woman cursed. "At least the damned heathens won't rape her!"

Now that the word had been said, silence settled over the lodge, and each woman grappled alone with her fear. For four days and nights they sat thus, listening for movement outside, peering through the cracks in the walls, and carefully dividing the food that was tossed to them twice a day. The corner where they made their toilet was soon reeking like the worst privy, and Suzanna began to wish that something, anything might happen, just to let them leave this prison.

Twice, she had tried to convince Mary Ann to escape, but she only shook her head stolidly and turned away. "There's no place to run," she said, "an' they'd hunt you down like a dog if you didn't freeze to death in the woods."

On the fifth night, Telekaut strode into the lodge. Elizabeth, who spoke more Cayuse than the rest, translated. "He says they won't kill us if we obey. We must sew for them an' do the work. He says, some'll be squaws an' some'll be slaves."

"What of the children!" a mother cried out.

Elizabeth waited for his reply, and when she answered, her face was twisted. "He says, there are no children. You must forget them."

"They've killed them!" another woman shrieked.

"No," Elizabeth said quickly. "They've sold them into the lodges. They're . . . Cayuse now."

There was a shocked hush, and some of the women began to sob. Telekaut shouted for silence. Elizabeth went on, "He says they'll be poisoned like our men poisoned his children if we don't obey. No more weepin', he says."

"We never poisoned his children!" Suzanna cried, angered now at their helplessness.

"Aye, he says three Indians went to Doctor for medicine. Two were sick an' one was pretendin'. The next day, all three died. He says Doctor had two medicines, one for the whites an' one for the Cayuse, an' the one for the Cayuse was poison. He says it has always been that way, an' other tribes downriver warned them that we keep death in magic bottles, an' let it out when we want to. Memaloose bottles. Death bottles. He says—well, anyway—" she faltered. "I can't get it all, but we're not the only ones to be punished, he says. Other tribes will make war on all whites in the territory."

"We should have let them *all* die when they took sick," a woman muttered, and then she looked up sharply to see if Telekaut had heard. His eyes narrowed, and he glared at her for a long moment. Finally, he turned and stalked out.

Within minutes, six braves came, and each went toward a woman, grabbed her, and dragged her out. Mrs. Kirby shrieked as she was pulled away, but the man slapped her viciously, and she fell silent.

A tall Cayuse with greased black hair and wide lips stepped before Suzanna and hauled her to her feet. He scrutinized her with cold eyes and then let out his breath in a long sigh as though he'd been bested in a barter. She was close enough to smell him and to count the pockmarks on his cheeks. She closed her eyes for an instant. When she opened them, she willed herself to smile tremulously. I am helpless, she thought quickly. And he can do as he pleases with me. She dropped her head as he led her out, and a wave of nausea and fear rolled through her belly. As she looked over her shoulder, she saw many more braves heading for the lodge.

She walked behind him in an early snow, trudging along, barely glancing at the Cayuse who clustered outside, staring at her. These are the same savages who sat on the mission logs rocking and praying, she thought dully. And now, they look at me as though they'd never seen me before. The man took her not to another lodge but to a tipi. A lesser brave with no other wife, she thought, he's no great shakes, so he has to take the plain one. She stepped inside the flap when he held it open and sat in the dark corner, waiting. He stirred the fire briefly, watching her out of the corners of his eyes.

She wished that she had learned more Cayuse and less Bible talk, but she tightened her lips determinedly. She knew that even if she could, she would not speak. The tipi was cold, and when she leaned against the stiff hide, a cold draught of air ran up her neck. She shivered, her eyes clenched shut. It can't be too bad, she reassured herself firmly, all wives do it. But inside, she felt numb as stone. He pointed to the fish in the corner. "Mamook piah muckamuck," he grunted.

Cook that fast, she thought. That much I know. She speared the fish over the flames, arranging them on the cooking stick. She tried not to meet his eyes while the food browned. But before the fish were finished, he grabbed her shoulders and pushed her back on the blanket. He shoved his knee between her legs and yanked her skirts up, fumbling at her linen. She lay still, willing him away with every muscle, her eyes shut tight. She felt a prodding, then a pain like a blade, and the ground was hard under her, and she could not flinch away and his breath was hot and foul on her face. He pressed into her and she had no space to breathe. He began to move inside her relentlessly, and she jerked with each thrust, twisting her head away, moaning as she felt him flood her insides with a stinging hot sap, hating him with all her soul.

Afterward, she wanted nothing but to cry, to be left alone and to sob while the night covered her. But she felt his hand on her, pulling her to sit up, and she opened her eyes. The fish were burnt. He gestured for her to get fresh ones and begin again. Trembling, she pulled down her skirts and went to work.

He took her back in the morning. The women came to the lodge, one by one, and no one asked and no one answered, and eyes shifted away. Helen had died in the night. Her body was cold and still. Mrs. Kirby began a prayer group in the corner, and for a while, Suzanna sat with them, her eyes closed and her mind searching for God. But she could not feel Him close to her, and soon, she withdrew and sat in her corner alone.

They came again the next night. The same brave stood before Suzanna and pulled her to her feet. She cooked one of the mission chickens, and he waited this time until the meal was cooked and eaten before he took her. She did not fight him but put all her mind to finding a safe place in her body where she could hide, could keep him away from some part of her. She shut her eyes and clenched her teeth. It was pointless to fight him, she sensed, and might even make him enjoy it more. He forced her, knees and elbows down on the furs. I will not resist, she winced, but I will not help him like it. She felt the hardness of him pierce her, flinched, and forced herself not to panic, to remain still, cold, apart. Once he was asleep, she crept quietly to the tipi flap and out into the night. She sat for an instant, confused, unsure which way to run. She knew the path back to the women's lodge, but which way was the mission?

Suddenly, he poked his head out the flap and said, "Chako!" Come. He was unworried at her absence, for he knew there was nowhere for her to go. She was furious with herself for not moving somewhere, anywhere, before he woke, but she dropped her head in what she hoped was the picture of obedience and crept back to the tipi. That night, he took her twice.

Peter Skene Ogden, chief officer of Fort Vancouver, assembled sixty men and paddled upriver to Fort Walla Walla. The Cayuse knew he was coming. Their powerful neighbors to the east, the Nez Perce, had sent Elders to tell the rebels that when the troops arrived, no other tribe would back them in their war.

"Only cowards take women and children to their lodges by force," one Elder glared at the Cayuse braves. "Children so green, the knife must be used. Waugh! We will not fight the Bostons so that you can keep your pallets full of white slaves."

"You did not see your mothers and your sisters fall to the red sickness!" shouted a man with his hair cut short in grief.

"Well, and neither did we follow the whites about like dogs, begging with both hands open! If you war, you war alone."

The Walla Wallas joined the Nez Perce, threatening to kill any Cayuse brave they could catch for ruining the trade season with war. But the captive women did not know this. In the lodges they waited, wondering if they would ever be white again.

When Ogden arrived at Fort Walla Walla and called a general meeting of all the upriver tribes, he stood with his back against the massive fort walls, sixty armed riflemen behind him.

Caleb McDougall stood in the ranks, holding a Bay Company musket on his arm. After ten years at the Methodist mission houses, and five more years working in Oregon City, he had signed up for militia duty at Fort Vancouver and was among the first to volunteer when word of the Whitman massacre rushed down the river. Old voices murmured in his mind: "His ma was a siwash, you know, some sort 'a shaman for the buggers downriver, I heard tell"; "His father was a Yank, at least, Duncan McDougall"; "Raised by the Bay boys, so I guess if it comes down to it, he'll take their side. Blood don't mean much, when it's such a mongrel mix as that"—voices he'd heard all his life, following him from the Demers shack, to the mission house, to Oregon City, and all points between. And now, he thought, I'm standing here under a HBC flag, ready to make war on my upriver cousins, to rescue some Yankee settlers. First, they'd come in a trickle, then in a tidal rush, and now that lands on both sides of the river were part of the Oregon Territory, he guessed he was an American, himself. If he was anything at all. It was all bewilderment and pain, the same inevitable pain he'd harbored forever, nothing to do about it then or now, so he pulled his mind to the job at hand, and gently fingered the gun stock.

A call went down the ranks, and all eyes focused on the woods beyond the fort. The snow was deep, the tree trunks dark and wet, and from the shadows, the Cayuse began to gather. Despite their frightening reputation, Caleb thought he had never seen so many raggedy members of humanity in his life. Over a hundred Indians slowly trooped in, clutching old blankets about their shoulders, shuffling sullenly through the snow. No women were present, and he wondered swiftly how many arrows, guns, and knives those raggedy blankets hid. It would be the final, highest irony if I were murdered by my people now, as I stand, he thought.

Ogden was subtle as a fist. Ignoring the young braves, he faced only the chiefs and the old men. The Honorable Bay Company was hyas solleks, he said, very angry. A Cayuse elder stood up and pointed at the braves clustered behind him. "It is the young men who seek this war, who buried their women and their mothers and sisters from the white man's sickness. It is the young men who take the whites to fill their empty lodges."

Ogden curled his lip in contempt and said quietly, "And it is a tribe of no-men who are ruled by such hasty heads. Do the Nez Perce let their young men run the tribe? Do the Walla Wallas? Do brave men take revenge on women and children?" He narrowed his eyes and spat on the ground.

Caleb shifted nervously behind him, watching the Indian eyes. Hooded, they were, under their blankets, like waiting snakes. He could feel their fear, their desperation, and he knew with a sudden swift insight that they were doomed to lose this and every conflict with so formidable an enemy.

In the tense silence, a Cayuse brave yelled out, "We will war!" He clenched his fists before him. "The whites must die! The moans of our dead still fill our lodges!"

"If you war," Ogden said matter-of-factly, "there will be no one left to hear the moans. The war will not end until every Cayuse brave is dead and his ears stopped with dirt." He paused, and his chin jutted out angrily. "And who will see to your women then, eh? Those who are left? Will your neighbors to the east and the south take them in? Or make them slaves as you have the whites?"

No one answered. Ogden turned to his men, gave a signal, and sixty rifles cracked smartly into place on sixty shoulders.

One chief spoke up quietly, "Well, and if we let you buy these slaves, will there be war?"

Ogden surveyed the whole lot of them with disdain. "I do not promise there will be no war. I cannot say. But the Bay Company will not war on those who return the prisoners. I have come to buy the women and children back. And that is all."

It was enough. The following morning, Caleb stood with the rest of the troops watching, as Cayuse braves carried off sixty-two blankets, a score of cotton shirts, handkerchiefs, twelve muskets, six hundred rounds of ammunition, and twelve flints as ransom. Then, they waited. It was snowing lightly, and he could scarcely see beyond the line of firs at the edge of the clearing.

"They're comin'!" shouted a sentry, and immediately, Caleb tightened into readiness. At the last moment, the Cayuse could slit the captives' throats before their eyes faster than they could stop them. They could take the ransom, save face, and force the whole territory into war.

There were over a hundred figures milling out there in the woods. Caleb could not tell which were Indians and which were whites, but he could see some women now, the Indians leading or pulling them, with the children trudging after through the snow. They stopped at the edge of the clearing, and an old man came forward, holding up his hands. Caleb heard the soldier next to him whisper, "I could pot that old bastard so easy from here."

Ogden stood before the troops, his weapon cocked and ready. Without seeming to move, he shifted imperceptibly so that his body was directly in front of the soldier's. He spoke quietly to the Elder, who then gestured to the Indians behind him. They faded off into the clearing as quietly as they had come.

For a brief instant, the blanket-clad figures stood packed together, silent as listening deer. Suddenly, one young woman broke and ran for the fort, and the others stumbled after, dragging clumsily through the snow, pulling the children, trailing their blankets behind them. Thirty or more, Caleb counted, some scarcely recognizable as white, raced past Ogden, shoved through the startled troops, and ran blindly, instinctively, into the fort.

What struck Caleb most forcefully when he thought of it later was that no one made a sound of welcome or relief. As though the captives feared their safety would be taken from them even as they grasped for it, they did not speak or wail or curse, but only fled headlong within the high walls.

Caleb had expected that it would take most of a week to get the women ready for their journey downriver. But after only one day of silence, while the wives of the fort tended them invisibly behind barracks walls, a few children ventured out to walk the grounds. Many of the girls were ill, the rumors reported, and some wished for death. Word trickled out from the army wives that four had died under Cayuse hands.

On the third day, as Caleb stood his watch at the tower, he saw a young woman leave the captives' quarters and walk slowly around the grounds. She was thin under her blanket, and her skirts trailed through the slush. Caleb could see a piece of blond hair, a swatch of pale face, and that was all. But there was something about the firmness of her gait and the set of her shoulders which drew his eye. Most all of the women walked arm in arm, as though they couldn't bear to let loose of a human being. But this girl walked alone. He watched her for most of an hour as she walked, never varying her direction, never looking from side to side. When he saw her two days later with the rest, he could pick her out just by the set of her head on her neck.

Caleb lay in the barracks at night, listening to the men talk about the women. "Jesus Christ," a bunkmate whispered, "a whole month in that godforsaken village. Bunch of damn heathens pawin' them day an' night. It's a wonder they didn't slit their own throats."

"I thank God none of 'em's mine," another man answered. "I'd be hard-pressed to take her back with that stink on her."

"An' some's bound to be birthin' half-breed bastards soon enough," a farmer muttered.

One man spoke up quietly in the dark. "An' I s'pose you'd kick-'em both out, eh, Johnson? Bag an' baggage." He was Joe Canfield, the rangy trapper, older than the rest of the men. Caleb had never heard him raise his voice. Indeed, he rarely spoke at all, not even when a loose paddle slipped from a soldier's hand coming upriver and splashed his pipe. He just clenched it and drew on as though it still glowed.

There was a long silence. "It'd be hard enough takin' some savage's leavings. Damned if I'd house his kid besides," the first man finally responded.

"What if she wouldn't give it up?" Canfield asked softly.

"A damned half-breed?" The man's voice rose to an ugly bawl. "Havin' him round all the time to remind me who had her?"

"Could be a reminder that she met a tough trail. An' that she got through it an' went on with some back to her."

There was another long silence. Finally, a third voice droned in. "A man can stand just so much, Canfield."

Three days later, the boats were loaded for downriver. The women and children stood on the shore, still silent. Most gazed at the water steadily as though they wore blinders, until they stepped quietly into the canoes. As they were pulling away, four Cayuse braves appeared on the bank and stood, watching them. Four of the women in the boats met their eyes.

A brave called out something in Cayuse, something Caleb didn't understand, but he heard the plea in his voice. One of the women flushed, went pale, and she raised one white hand as though in farewell. Another woman hissed a sharp, shocked command, and the white hand fluttered down to her lap.

The first day, few spoke. But as they went further downriver, some older women began to talk to each other, and finally, a few even asked questions of the men. The children spoke first, of course, and when no one silenced them, they grew more brave. Finally, the young girls raised their eyes and seemed to look about them all at once. The men had strict orders to make them comfortable and to leave off any painful subjects. For the married men, that was easy; most just didn't speak at all. But the bachelors in the troops soon found excuses to hover close to the girls, watching them carefully like spooked game.

Caleb picked her out at once, the girl who walked in circles round the grounds. When they made camp on the river, she didn't set back waiting to be fetched for, but got her own plate, filled it, and sat apart from the others. One of the women called her Suzanna.

The second day downriver, the women began to sing, faltering at first. They sang "Home Sweet Home," but when they got to the second verse and began, "O give me my lowly thatched cottage again," a few voices broke and began to weep loudly, wailing in chorus as though they'd all been released from the same tether. Caleb saw that some of the men wept as well, and his own throat ached with hurt. But Suzanna didn't cry. She drew herself away from the women and sat like a stone looking out over the river, her eyes blue gray and calm.

For an instant, Caleb wondered if she was feeble. Or maybe mindless with pain. But then she heaved a huge sigh and trailed her hand in the water. Her eyes swiveled to meet his. She gazed at him deeply, her mouth unflinching. He was startled by the directness of her stare and tried out a tremulous half-smile. She lifted her chin slightly, set her lips, and turned away.

That night, Caleb watched her again, but he couldn't go nearer. Somehow, the thought of the rage and pain that must lie behind those blue eyes pushed him off. When, finally, he got up the courage to go stand before her while she pushed food around her plate with her bread, he cleared his throat twice, but she did not look up. "Excuse me," he said softly. "Can I sit down?"

She said nothing.

"My name's Caleb Demers."

She didn't move along the log or shift her weight, but neither did she get up and walk off. Caleb sat gingerly by her side, easing his body down carefully so as not to jostle her. After a long moment, he said, "Your name's Suzanna?"

Her chin lifted then and she turned cool eyes on him at last. "Suzanna Blue, Mister Demers, an' I don't need your pity." Her voice was low and musical, but it jarred Caleb like a shout.

He blinked rapidly, confused. "I didn't think you did, ma'am, but I could use some company."

She shrugged and moved over slightly to give him more room. He watched her hands move deliberately from plate to mouth, short square fingers, no hesitation, no hurry. He wondered briefly what it would be like to feel those hands on him, and he shocked himself to silence. He finished his dinner, and he felt her eyes watch him warily as he walked away.

He half-expected her to pick a seat in another canoe the next morning, but no—there she was, climbing to the same spot. He pulled his hat lower on his brow so that he could watch her eyes move restlessly about the river edges.

That night, he came and stood by her again, saying not a word. When she didn't speak or move, he eased himself down at her side again, and they ate in silence. For three nights running, he sat close to her and could think of little to say. He began to dream of her at night, restless, haunting dreams that tossed him and teased him with the promise of something just out of his hands, just around the next curve of the river, unseen and uncomprehended. No one else spoke to her much, he noticed. The men spoke to Miss Bewley and Miss Smith and the others, but no one tried to take his place on Suzanna's log. He wondered if they saw something no-count about her that he couldn't see.

Finally, on the fourth day, he spoke to her again. "You have any kin downriver, Miss Suzanna?"

She started briefly, as though he had pulled her from a thousand miles away. "None," she said, shaking her head.

"Me neither. My folks moved to Canada a few years back. I went to the Willamette mission. Now, I work in Oregon City." He stretched out one leg cautiously and said, with just a touch of pride, "Worked on the Barlow Road some, too."

But she just stared blankly at him.

"The wagon trail over the mountains? Took us more than a year, but it's clear now. Wagons're crossing by the hundreds."

"Over the Blue mountains?" she said, and her eyes grew wistful. "Pa said they would someday."

Caleb looked at her quickly when she mentioned her father, but he said nothing. He felt as he had when he was twelve and tried to tame a doe who foraged near the fort. One sudden, ill-thought move, and she would melt back into the shadows.

But now that she had spoken, she seemed to breathe a little easier around him. And on the next morning, when she stepped into the canoe, he tried again with his smile. This time, a small shadowed creasing played about her mouth for an instant, and she ducked her head. When she raised it again, she looked right at him, smiled once briefly, and then turned away.

Caleb flushed, and his eyes almost watered with pleasure. It was worth waiting for, that smile. He couldn't keep his teeth covered as he rowed, his grin just lifted his lips right up, and he felt his soul must shine from his eyes.

Now he knew what he must do, he would win her. He would make her his wife. He felt he stood on a vast peak and looked at the world below. The way seemed open and easy and clear. She had no one, he had no one, they would cleave to one another. Biblical phrases from the mission house twisted through his head. He was vaguely aware that what he planned was supposed to be a solemn, reverential matter, but he could only grin with joy.

It took him all day to plan what he would say that evening, and he grew irritable with the slow crawling of the hours. He could never recall feeling so alive, as though all the river coursed through his veins. That night, he sat down by her and tried to sense her mood. She had been quiet all day, but that wasn't unusual. He smiled inside; after the mission ladies, it would be good to live with a woman who knew how to be still.

"Miss Blue," he began slowly, watching her all the while, "I've been thinking all day. You don't know a thing about me, but I'd be grateful if you'd listen to what I've got to say." He waited for an instant, half-expecting her to rise slowly and trail away. She sat straight and stiff as a cedar.

Encouraged, he rushed on. "I'm past thirty now and thinking it's time to fix myself properly. I've got a hundred dollars saved up, and my eye on a good piece of ground on the river." He saw that she began to chew her lower lip, so he talked faster. "I've been watching you, Miss Blue, and I think you're the best I've seen." He paused and took a deep breath. "I'm asking you to be my wife."

She sat stock still, her face straight ahead. Something told him to say no more. Then she laughed in a peculiar way, low in her throat, and she looked him full in the face, pity and contempt mixing in her features. "Mister Demers," she said slowly, "you're talkin' like a fool. I ask you to say no more about it."

She rose, but he caught hold of her arm and held her fast. He couldn't believe he had actually touched her, but now that he had, his pride rose in him, and he felt a slow anger start. "Hey, now."

She looked at his hand steadily, and he released her. "I'm sorry if I rushed you, but there's no call to rare up and call a man a fool. You're alone and I'm alone." He smiled tentatively. "I think we could make a go of it."

She whirled on him then, her eyes bright and hot in the pinched whiteness of her face. "A go of it? With a girl who just come from a Cayuse lodge? With the stink of the savage still on her?" She raised a trembling chin. "You're worse than a fool, Mister Demers. You're a coward."

That one reeled him back. "A coward?" he faltered.

"Aye, you ain't got the guts to find a proper woman. So you think to take a savage's scraps, figurin' on bein' above her all your life, gettin' a wife an' a slave all at once. Thinkin' she'd be so grateful to you, that it'd all be easy."

He felt the blood pump into his face. "I'm thinking no such thing. I'm thinking only that I've found a woman I could live with—and maybe love, if she'll let me—and I aim to find out if she'll have me. And that's all I'm thinking."

She closed her face to him. "I mean to have no one, Mister Demers." Her voice grew gravelly. "And I mean no one to have me."

She sat down slowly as though released from a long rope. Caleb stared at her, dumbstruck. As he watched, two abrupt drops of water leaped out of her eyes. "Oh, Lord," she said softly and rubbed the drops off with the heel of her hand. Then, as though it went against her whole soul, she began to cry. She didn't sob or wail, but the tears slid down her cheeks quietly and steadily as if she were alone with no one to see or hear her. He watched her for an instant, feeling numb and invisible, and then he walked away.

Suzanna felt rather than watched him go. Far away in the timber, a mourning dove was who-whoing alone, the saddest song in the world, she thought dully. A dirge for all the failed dreams, the disappointed hopes, for the innocent and the just plain stupid who have wandered out to this harsh place and been destroyed.

And now, this man comes to me, talking of marriage. As if I want to think of such a thing again, she winced to herself. As if I *ever* did. Once more, she remembered her mother, recalled bits and pieces of her manner, her gestures, the way the light hit her hair when it was loose in the mornings, the way she had of stretching her neck up as though to unhinge it from her shoulders when she was tired . . . the way her eyes had blazed when she fought for life.

Unbidden, however, other memories came as well. The way her

father had grasped her mother round the waist and danced her about the kitchen when she said she'd go to Oregon, the way she nestled her head in his neck as they walked along the fence, watching the stock at dusk.

She loved him, Suzanna thought. He loved her. And they would want that for me, I know. Pa had said, "A lot can happen 'tween here an' paradise," and he never spoke a truer word. Thank God, neither of them knew the half of it. An image of Jess floated suddenly up before her, leaving her startled and breathless . . . and even contemptuous of her heart, which began to beat as quickly as though she'd run a race. Caleb Demers doesn't make my heart race so, she noticed.

She had tried not to think about what had happened to her, to all of them. She made it into a story in her mind, a story that had happened to other women, people she didn't know, and told it to herself just to see how she took it. In her mind, the story didn't seem so bad. They were captured, they were—she winced—they were forced against their will. And they were rescued. It didn't happen *just* to me, she told herself, firming her jaw. Lots worse things happen, and people make out just fine. They go on, have happy lives, and tell their grandchildren all about it some day. It doesn't have to be such a tragedy.

But then, fingers of memory stretched into her heart, and she felt the weight on her belly, the rough hands ripping at her linen, the black emptiness, the ugliness, the hate—and she knew she would go mad if she sat and let it collect around her. She stood up and brushed off her skirts. Looking neither to the right nor to the left, she walked toward the river resolutely, leaving the campfires behind her.

Caleb's dreams that night were haunted by quite different images. After hours of restlessness, he finally rose and walked from the camp down to the river. He sat on a stone, watching the silver water slide endlessly to the sea.

He had known, of course, that most of the women, even some of the children, had been forced to the Cayuse lodges. Say it, he grimaced. To their beds. But somehow, it had never been real. Not until she said, "I mean no one to have me." The unspoken "ever again" lay in her mouth.

He tried to picture that sturdy, plain body crumpled in a heap of furs, naked, fighting off a huge-shouldered, greasy-headed . . . but he stopped and shook his head faintly, a sour taste of bile rising in his mouth. Now, I'm thinking like a white man, he scowled. Figuring that a Cayuse in her bed would be somehow different, somehow worse, than a trapper or a farmer or—even a missionary. The truth was, however, no picture was palatable at all.

As though in teasing torment, his mind pushed an alternate image at him: Suzanna naked on the same furs, lying back passively, even waiting, and maybe with that same shadowy smile he'd seen that morning in the canoe. The picture was so strong that he flinched.

Two women, I've had, he thought. One, that missionary's daughter when I was twenty, and Lucy Mack, the seamstress in Oregon City. Neither of them naked had made him feel what Suzanna had aroused in him, just sitting next to him on a log: the feeling of belonging, of a full sort of tenderness that made him want to reach out and take her hand and whisper secrets; the feeling that nothing else really mattered but being near her. A faint memory floated up of Wallulah, his grandmother, saying that when love is strong, two can make their bed on a knife blade; when weak, a pallet wide as the river is too narrow.

I know well enough what goes on between a man and a woman on pallets at night, he thought, on *any* pallet. He felt as betrayed as though she had belonged to him, yet he knew it made no sense. And then the darkest corner of his mind slid out his blackest pain for him to face. What if she carried a Cayuse half-breed in her belly, even now? A half-breed . . . like himself.

The words of the barracks jarred through him: half-breed bastard, always between them, always reminding him of what she was, whose she was before. That was the implicit fear all the women carried in their eyes, he knew. The one thing no one said as the days counted by. Some of them could be bred even now and don't know it, he thought. But they're waiting. Each one watching the other, wondering.

Far off upriver, he heard a long, quavering call, so faint that it almost blended with the night. The bay of a hunting wolf, the sound of the wilderness, shadowy and bleak. He felt suddenly drowned by loneliness, helpless before it all.

All my life, I've been confused about my proper place, where I belong, to which set of values, creeds, customs. My mother took her loneliness, and I guess it made her strong. But I have felt only bewildered and apart, he thought, and unsure in the world. It was a question he had somehow managed to refrain from asking himself until now: Is there a place for me, anywhere, in this land?

For a moment, the enormity of life and its twists and turns overwhelmed him. In a flash of instinct, he saw it. Though he had always done his best, had been what his foster father would call a good lad, it wouldn't come to him easily. He would have to settle for less than he wanted, and not just because he was half-Chinook, but because he was a man, and that was the way of life's treacheries.

Ah, Mother, he sighed. I have lived, waiting for you, building a life in the ruins of the village in my mind. I have had to live out of one life and into another—into many others—building upward as best I could, into the sun like a mushroom growing from the moldy decay of other lives. I thought I was the only one. But everyone is abandoned, everybody is building shelters in the midst of ruins, and I am losing myself. He put his face in his hands and mourned silently, for perfect things, broken.

The next morning, Suzanna took her customary place in the canoe as though nothing had happened. She looked so calm that he felt ashamed of his own discomfort. But she never glanced at him, not once. There were four more days to go before Fort Vancouver, they said, and Caleb half-wished them gone so he could be rid of her. As quickly as the wind turned round, though, he wished the days would halt, at least until he could clear his head.

That night, he stayed away from her and watched her covertly. She sat alone, as always, her plate on her knees. He could see nothing in the tilt of her head or the set of her shoulders that told her feelings. A cold woman, he thought. A pitiful waste.

The children were playing by the fire and fighting over a game of jackstraws in the corner of the camp. George Devine, ten, the oldest of the orphans, sauntered over to a group of little girls kneeling in the dirt over some prize or another, and suddenly, Caleb saw that he had a pistol in his hands. He rose and called sharply to George, wondering where the hell the kid snatched it and from whose tent, and instantly, there was a shot, a high shriek, and little Katie Sager stood screaming in a circle of frightened, silent children.

Suzanna reached her almost immediately, grabbed the pistol from the terrified boy, and pulled Katie to her breast. "Katie, you hurt?" she asked quickly.

The child hollered, "I'm shot!"

"Where're you shot?" Suzanna asked, calm now, gently feeling her all over.

The child put her hands to her cheeks, her eyes wide. "Through the head! He killed my ears!"

Suzanna laughed softly and pulled Katie to her, cuddling her as she kneeled in the dirt. She drew George to her with her free hand. "There, George, now you didn't mean it, I know. You won't play with guns no more, will you?"

"No'm," he said, his head down and his face flushed and wet with tears. She hugged them both, murmuring soft comforts, half-chuckling in her throat. Her eyes played across the camp to Caleb, who watched her, unable to turn away. In that moment, she seemed the most beautiful woman he had ever known.

Caleb found Joe Canfield by the edge of the river that night, rubbing down the canoes. The old trapper glanced up at him when he approached and then went back to his work. Couldn't ever sneak up on this one, Caleb thought, and he cleared his throat. "Think we'll make Vancouver in three days or so?"

"Should," the man said, moving his fist rhythmically over the cedar canoe, carefully cleaning its ribs of moss.

Caleb sat down gingerly on the bank, half-expecting the trapper to wave him away. When Joe said nothing more, he spoke up quietly. "You got a minute, Mister Canfield? I've been thinking on what you said back at the fort."

The old trapper looked up quizzically and then down again to his work. "I said a heap o' things."

"I've been thinking on what you said about how a woman might come through such a thing," Caleb rushed it out. He paused painfully. "I've been thinking of marrying."

Canfield looked up and a soft grin played at his mouth, but he said nothing.

"I've got no business bothering you with it, I guess," Caleb said. "A man wants to marry, he should just do it. But, I—well, sometimes, a man's got to . . ." he faltered and stopped.

"You think 'cause yer part siwash, it's different fer you?"

Caleb looked up, surprised.

Canfield shrugged. "That hat never leaves your head, boy. You shamed 'bout yer own blood?"

Caleb shook his head firmly. "No, but maybe *she* would be. I mean, considering."

"You mean, considerin' what they done to her? Ain't so hard to say it, man. They raped her. Happened before, an' 'twill happen again. But life goes on, will ye, nil ye."

Caleb pulled his hat down low, looking for the words. "Look, you seem to know a lot about such things. About women."

Canfield laughed, a short, friendly bark. "Ain't no fool knows 'em better or understands 'em less."

"Did you ever take a wife?"

The man scratched his head and stood looking out over the river, as though he surveyed the high lonely ridges of his life. "Aye . . . once," he said. He laughed again ruefully. "But this chile's like a damned tomcat who's sat hisself on a hot stove lid. He learned his lesson, see, an' he never sat on another hot lid again. Nor a cold one, neither."

"And you'd never take another?"

"Ain't sayin' that. Will say, you got to find out the answer fer yerself. If I was a mind to give out free advice—which I ain't—I might say that 'bout the worse thing I ever did was pull in my horse while he was a-leapin'. Ain't a man alive can make good headway in life doin' that regular."

Caleb thought another long moment. Finally he asked, low in his throat. "Suppose a man asked a woman. Asked her straight out. And she said she never would marry anybody 'cause she was so bad hurt and shamed."

Canfield said nothing.

"Suppose she said he was a fool for even thinking of it."

"Does this feller feel hisself a fool?"

Caleb jerked up his head and a tinge of anger edged his voice. "She said I was a coward." He kicked at the log beneath him. "Said I didn't have the guts to ask a proper woman."

" 'Pears to me, you did. 'Pears to me, she's the only one don't see it." Canfield laughed silently. "You been harkin' to too many other mouths, man. Ain't a one of us not strugglin' with some dream or 'nother, just to have it up an' die. But then 'long comes a new one shootin' up, green-growin' an' just as promisin'. Some men just lose their nerve, is all. Ugly men who take joy in croppin', no matter whose harvest. I hope to God I never get that hungry. You want her?"

Caleb answered quickly, firmly, "Aye. More than I ever wanted anything. But maybe she won't have me."

" 'Cause yer part siwash?"

"Don't even know if she knows it. Might be, she won't have anybody."

"Maybe not. Anyways, there's glory in the trailin' of her."

He looked up eagerly. "You think so?"

"Aye, I seen you sniffin' round her. She's a good one."

Caleb's voice wavered. "She sure keeps to herself, though."

Canfield shrugged, matter-of-fact. "I wouldn't have a dog who wagged his tail fer jes' anybody."

Caleb picked up a stick and made some aimless patterns in the coarse beach sand. "You know what they say, though," he muttered, his face turned. "She might have a baby."

"Then you got a headstart on most, man. Now, damn it, don't bother me no more." Canfield turned his back to him, crouching over the canoes. "I'm thinkin' maybe she's right. Maybe you *are* a fool or a coward to gnaw at such as that. Time you figgered who you are, an' live by it, 'pears to me. How many years you got on you, eh?"

Caleb shrugged. "Past thirty, best I can reckon."

" 'Bout time you acted like it. Hell, I had me a wife an' two younguns at yer age. Yer way behind."

He flushed. "You mean, start acting like a white man?"

"I mean, start actin' like a *man*. Stop whinin' 'bout what you want an' just go get it."

Caleb glared, stiffened—and then relaxed. He saw the grin on Joe's face, and he smiled slowly.

"You got yer answers, boy. Now leave this ol' man be."

Two days out from Vancouver, the boats stopped for the night at the only other white settlement on the north bank of the river. A small cluster of cabins sat back on the meadow called Washougal —"running waters" in Chinook—and the people came out eagerly to greet the travelers. News had swept downriver, and the women of the settlement were anxious to offer what comforts they could.

The sun was setting and the bats were stitching through the purple air when Caleb climbed a boulder to look at the river. It is a beautiful land, full of secret green majesty, and great dangers, he thought. And somehow, he couldn't place himself anyplace else.

Suzanna was walking toward the cabin when he found her later, deep in thought, her hand switching her skirts aimlessly through the light snow. The night was soft for winter, and she was so cushioned in her reverie that she scarcely heard him until he was at her side. She stopped and faced him quietly.

She thought that his face was pale in the night; a lock of dark hair fell boyishly over his brown eyes, out from under his hat. His mouth looked bruised, as though he held a hurt inside that pushed against his lips for release. She knew instinctively what he was about even before he spoke. And she felt a bubble of something rise through her, light but inevitable.

"Suzanna," he said quietly. "I've been looking for you."

"Aye, Mister Demers?"

"I gave a lot of thought to what you said, and it's just not true. I'm no fool, and I'm no coward. I've been trying to see myself without you, trying to place myself with another woman, in another place, doing something else, and I can't do it. I can't see it. I come right back to the truth every time I turn away. I want you for my wife, Suzanna."

She turned slightly as if to move off, and he grasped her gently by the elbow. She wrenched her arm away. "Don't touch me," she moaned, as if in pain.

He let her go. "I'd never force you, and I won't rush you. I just don't want you walking 'til I've said it all." He took both her hands gently, firmly, and pulled her to face him.

She looked up at him and felt a rush of warmth flood her, a wanting to brush that lock of hair back from his forehead.

"Could you ever learn to care for me, Suzanna?"

She closed her eyes and said through tight lips, "An' what of—"

"It doesn't matter," he said firmly. "Not a mite. You going to give up on your whole life, Suzanna? You want to cut off your leg 'cause your toe's stubbed?"

She stiffened. "I don't need you, Mister Demers. I don't need anybody. I can go it alone."

He smiled at her softly, a youthful confident grin. "You ever thought maybe I'm the one's who's doing the needing?" He took off his hat, and she gasped when she saw his head, slightly sloped from the old cradle board. "I'm half-Chinook," he said gently, "and all my life, I've been waiting for something good to happen to me. Somebody to come along and make me feel—like I belonged. When I first saw you, I knew you were the one. I know you been down a rough road or two, and I'm not promising that it'll always be easy from here on out. But I'm healthy." He chuckled softly. "I got a strong enough back to carry whatever loads you got. And I don't give up easy. You called me a coward, Suzanna. I'm wondering what it is *you're* so scared of, that you can't dig in and root longside of somebody who needs you. Afraid you might need somebody back?"

"I ain't afraid of anything, Mister Demers," she said quickly. "I seen your kind before. More than I care to."

"You haven't seen my kind before," he said gently. " 'Cause there's nobody like me on this river. Just like there's nobody like you. My mother was a Chinook. Not a Cayuse, not a Nez Perce, and not a Klickitat. My father was Chief Factor McDougall of Fort Astoria, before it went to the Bay boys. I was raised by whites, went to their schools, prayed their prayers and sang their hymns, and . . . joined their armies." He paused to let that sink in. "It's time for me to make a life of my own, past time, I guess. And I want you by my side while I do it."

She felt a cool breeze at her back and unconsciously, she swayed toward him slightly, her eyes focused on his face. All of a sudden, she felt so small, so insignificant, and the woods, the world, the man before her, seemed larger than she could control. "An' what if I'm —what if—"

"Then there'll be three to need instead of two, and it'll be just all the tighter bind." He pulled her slightly closer. "The land's big, Suzanna," he said, his voice husky. "It'll be needing plenty of babies. And each one'll have a different row to hoe. But each one you bear'll be ours, if you'll have me."

"Why do you want *me*?" she cried, her voice a hollow anguish.

He laughed, shaking his head. "First, you doubt I'm good enough for you, and now you doubt you're good enough for me? Time to stop doubting, Suzanna, and get on with it."

Her mind twisted away, running through the past frantically, and she saw her mother's wan face, her open red mouth shrieking, felt her father's arms, held his dying hands, cradled John Sager's bleeding head, and winced from rough hands on her buttocks, squeezing her, thrusting—then she stopped thinking, and pushed it all away. I'm stronger than that, she vowed.

Suddenly, it came into her mind the day she saw Rebecca Settle hauling on the reins of her runaway mule team, her black hair tumbling out of her bonnet and over her shoulders, her face set and white, while one small child clung with chattering teeth to the side of the rocking wagon and one baby brother bounced about on the floor in frozen terror. She finally got the team stopped, and the men clucked at her courage. But it took more than simple bravery to get back in that wagon, pick up the reins once more, and go on another thousand miles into the wilderness. It took spine. To keep going, no matter what.

As quietly as the first star coming out, she felt her heart ease, felt her mouth soften, as though it had its own mind. "Mister Demers," she said, "I don't believe I could ever marry. An' everything I ever knew says, if I did, 'twouldn't be to"—she couldn't bring herself to say words to hurt him—"to a man such as yourself. But we can be friends, I reckon. An'—" she faltered again. "An' I guess I can think on it."

His smile seemed to light up the woods, and she couldn't help but smile back, even though her heart felt queer and confused.

"Can I walk you back, then?" he asked quietly.

"Aye." She put her hand lightly on his arm.

They walked for a moment in silence, and the air was as cool and fresh as the other side of a pillow. He chuckled low in his throat. She looked questioningly at him.

"I was just thinking." he laughed. "Things'll probably come out all right for both of us. But Lord, it takes strong nerves sometimes just to watch!"

With a keen sense that she had absolutely nothing to laugh at, she felt a delicious, unreasoning bloom of joy bubble up in her mouth and she giggled as they walked through the darkness.

They arrived at the fort the next day, and the women and children were greeted by James Douglas, the new Chief Factor. They grew strangely quiet as they walked through the high walls, as though they were newly reminded of their recent torment.

Caleb felt a tug of loneliness when he stood inside his old home once more. The Demers had been gone now for nearly a decade, and there seemed little to remind him that they had ever sheltered him within these rough-hewn quarters. He was startled to see how small and constricted the grounds seemed, for at one time in his life they had encompassed his whole world.

The rescued women and children were parceled off to quarters to rest before they would be ferried to Portland. "There are many waiting to welcome you," Douglas said heartily to the group. "New families for the orphaned children and new lives for everyone.

Those who have hurt you and yours will be punished, but *you* have only to think about your futures."

There was a throttled sob from the back of the group, and the women closed in protectively about each other, keeping their faces averted from the officers who stood at attention nearby. Caleb caught Suzanna's eye, but she seemed distant, detached. She twisted her hands in her skirts, hiding them.

Later that day, he went to the women's quarters and asked her to walk with him down by the river. The snow was light, and the wind was calm, so they strolled away from the fort, following a path that cut through the meadow and the old camas fields.

"I never figured Vancouver to be so big," she said absently. "Had it so many stores an' cabins an' all when you were a lad?"

"Aye," he said, "guess it was the closest thing to a city on the whole river. We had scores of trappers and traders from Canada, merchants from Scotland, sailors from Liverpool, Kanakas from the Sandwich Islands—but not too many women." He grinned impishly. "I recall the chickens 'bout took over the dining halls every day, and we all took turns shooing them out. My main chore was beating and stacking furs. I thought I'd smell of beaver the rest of my days."

He was walking in front of her, clearing the snow out of the path and holding branches back. "My favorite times were when the couriers de bois arrived, I guess."

"The what?"

"Mountain men, you call them. Half-breeds, lots of them," he added, "just like me. French-Canadians, scouts, and trappers. They came in every spring, big brigades of them, just 'bout the time the ice started to break up, loaded down with pelts." He threw back his head and shouted, "Dans mon chemin, j'ai rencontre, deux cavaliers, très bien monte, l'un à cheval, l'autre à pied!"

She laughed in astonishment. "What in the world kind of tongue is that?"

"That's French. They sang that as they came up the river, bragging—they bragged 'bout everything from their pelts to their parts—and you could hear them coming a mile away. You know, I saw the Whitmans once."

"You did?"

"Aye, before they left for the mission. It was, oh, I guess, 'bout ten years back. They were the first white ladies to cross, they said, and they stopped in at the fort for supplies. That Missus Whitman was a fine lady. I remember, she sang 'Watchman, Tell Us of the Night.' Pretty yellow hair."

Suzanna began to shiver violently, and she pulled her shawl tighter about her shoulders. Caleb's face fell. "Jesus, I'm sorry. I didn't mean to—"

"It's all right. I just took a chill." She shook her head, her eyes closed briefly. "Just go on an' tell me somethin' else," she said quickly. "What's Portland like?"

He gazed at her a long moment, but she didn't lift her head. He said, "Big city. Growing fast. They used to call it Stump Town, because they had so many stumps left after they took down the trees. But, there's talk of making it the capital of the whole territory. Or Oregon City. That's up the Willamette, and I used to live there. But I guess I'll head for Portland, now. You know, we got a lot in common, you and I?"

She looked at him quizzically.

"Well, we both lived in the mission houses. The Demers, they're the ones who took me in and gave me a name, they sent me off with new breeches and a ten-dollar gold piece in my pocket for some Methodist learning. What I learnt pretty quick was that the preacher, Brother Lee, believed work in God's eyes was holy. I must 'a been about the holiest boy for miles."

Suzanna giggled helplessly. "I never prayed so hard for a miracle as I did every wash day!"

Caleb laughed and eased his arm around her shoulders, helping her past a thicket of blackberry brushed with snow. "Oh, they were good folks, I guess. I don't blame them. They're like everybody else, just trying to put the best face on broken dreams. Got all steamed up over God and gave up everything they had to come halfway round the world. And all their fine hopes didn't come to much, I reckon, after a few wet winters praying over a schoolhouse full of trappers' kids and half-breeds."

"Wish you wouldn't call yourself that."

"Doesn't hurt my feelings none. There's a passel of us in these parts, and nobody thinks much of it. Only newcomers, Yanks from Boston and such, feel called on to notice." He pushed his hat back slightly and brushed snow off his brow. "So we both got our fill of mission learning. And that's not all we got in common," he said softly. "We both got orphaned early on."

There was a moment of silence as they walked. "Why'd your mama leave you?" she finally asked.

"How'd you know she did?"

She shrugged gently. "I asked around. They say she was a princess."

"She was a shaman. That's even better. She took the people into the mountains to save them from the fever."

"Why didn't she take you, too?"

He paused, searching for the words. "I was young. And I'd just got over the sickness, and it would 'a been tougher in the mountains with winter coming on. And"—he faltered, remembering—"they said I had a white heart." He shrugged. "Half-white. And I guess they couldn't tolerate anything white just then. Not even the shaman's son. I tried to find her, walked up the mountain after her until it got so dark and cold I thought I'd die. And right then, I guess I wanted to. But the mountain's big, and her trail was hard to follow. Every time I came back to the fort, Missus Demers was waiting with hot biscuits and a warm bed and after awhile, I stopped running away. I never stopped waiting for her, though."

Her eyes widened. "So she never came back?"

"She may have," he said quickly, "but we moved upriver, and I went off to the mission school, and Mister Demers got moved up north to Fort Victoria. Then the Bay Company bought the village and put up a canning site and nobody was left. Anyway"—a taut smile—"I made out all right."

She thought for a moment. "But you've never tried to find her since?"

He turned away slightly, his head bent. "Not really. She said it wasn't for a son to judge his mother's vision. She saw visions, see, all the time. Raven, one of the old gods, spoke to her and she'd tell these visions to the people. But when it came time to choose, looked to me like she chose her dreams over me easy enough, just like she chose her dreams over my father."

"But," Suzanna asked, bewildered, "don't you wonder what happened to her? Where she is right now? After all, she's your ma . . ."

"All the time," he said softly. "Just like I wonder about a lot of things. But sooner or later, you put it aside and go on living, best you can."

"It's real hard to understand why a woman'd give up her child for visions and such," Suzanna said slowly, glancing up at him to see if the words wounded.

Caleb said nothing more, but his mouth was soft with memories. They walked along in silence. Suzanna remembered the words spun over the campfires that night on the trail. The preacher had said that no decent white men would take squaws for wives; diseased and unclean, he called them. Yet Caleb was the offspring of just such a union, and you couldn't ask for a more decent man, she thought. 'Course no one talked of it the other way around—a white woman wedded to a half-breed. She winced, the word itself was ugly. But when she glanced at him trudging next to her, the clean lines of his face, the set of his mouth, the heft of his shoulders, yes, even the slight slope of his head, she could find nothing ugly in such a countenance.

Something he was saying startled her out of her thoughts. "You know, Suzanna, once we get to Portland, things'll be different. They'll put you with some family or 'nother, and you'll be looking after somebody else's children, or cooking and cleaning in somebody else's place. You thought on it at all?"

Her voice was low and anguished. "I ain't hardly thought of anythin' else. But I got no choice, I got no place else to go—"

She saw something happen in his eyes, and he grabbed her hard and he was suddenly kissing her, not on the cheek or the brow, but hard and hungry on the mouth. It was a long, blind time before he let her pull away, and when she did, she stumbled slightly in the snow, falling against his chest.

"I'm sorry," he said. His hands were trembling, but his face was calm. "I'm not made of stone."

He took her arm and turned her back down the path. It was growing colder as the day waned, and ice had formed in their footsteps. Once, she slid on frozen earth, and she slipped her hand through his arm for support. She left it there, all the way back to the fort.

He lay in his bunk that night thinking, and finally rose to light a candle. The moment the light flooded the room, there was a low knock at the door. He opened it to find her standing in the passageway. "Suzanna!" he said, pulling her into the room and closing the door. "What—?"

But she put a finger to his lips and unwrapped her cloak. He watched her intently. It was the first intimate touch she had offered, and he was afraid to startle her into flight.

"You alone?" she asked, looking about the room cautiously.

"Aye," he smiled, "but I've no great desire to be. If I'd known you wanted company . . . "

She sighed, a deeply shuddering wind that moved through her chest and her shoulders and closed her eyes.

"What is it?" he whispered, suddenly afraid.

"I—I've come to you," she said softly, watching him all the while, pinning his eyes with her own.

He embraced her tentatively, and pressed a gentle kiss to her forehead. But the scent of her came to him strongly then, and the warmth of her flesh through the cloth, and he felt her muscles melt into his, and before he knew it, he was kissing her lips, softly at first, feeding on them gently, then hungrily, pulling her into his chest. She whimpered once, low in her throat, and her arms went about his neck. She returned his kisses, moving her mouth over his cheeks, his lips, and his neck.

He was shocked at the heat he felt from her, from himself, and in a confused swirl of power and awkwardness, he clutched her, murmuring heady words of love and desire. She drew him slowly to the pallet, and a small corner of his mind cried out in wonder and disbelief. But then, his body took over relentlessly, and his hands roamed over her hips, her waist, easing her from her clothes. He could not breathe, did not want to, and the candle made dancing gold shadows on her skin. Her hair tumbled about his hands, and her legs clung to his hips, and he was in her, moving, carried along soundlessly, exploding with the most painful joy he had ever known.

She clung to him after, her eyes clenched tight.

"Suzanna," he whispered, finally pulling back to look into her eyes. "I never would have—I didn't mean to—" He paused, searching frantically for some hint of her former smile.

But she only moved lower and cradled her head on his chest, willing him to silence. He held her, pulling the furs up about them gently, and waited.

Suzanna lay still, her eyes closed, feeling his breathing gentle. Now that she had done it, she ached inside with confusion and despair. She had rehearsed her actions in her mind over and over, but now they were together naked, and she felt a whirl of fear.

I've heard plenty 'bout the ways of men, she told herself. And though this one's better than some, he's still one of the breed. Led by their parts and ruled by their blood, Pa used to say. And only later, when they tire of it, do they look up and see they're hobbled to a woman they can't stomach. And so they punish her for their weakness the rest of her life. Well, now he's had me, she thought. And if he still wants me in the morning, maybe I'll be his. Maybe.

She felt the coarse underside of the furs against her skin, and remembered the quilt she'd worked so carefully on the trail. These are the pieces of my life, she thought. And it's up to me to put them together as I want them. Together, maybe we can make a pattern, him and me. This could be where it starts. Maybe the the truest wisdom is knowing what you have to accept, what your best choices are, and then learning to love them.

That had been the plan but somehow, now that it was started, she could not take comfort from it. She had expected to feel relief, like a chore done, but instead, she felt empty, alone, and unsure. It had been good when he held her. And she had forgotten herself in him, forgotten all but the wondrous touch of him, gentle and asking and giving and taking. But she was outside all rules now, she knew, everything that was right and decent. And if anything would make him despise her, make him remember her past, this night would do it. But she had to know.

Then he moved slightly, and in doing so, pulled the covering off her shoulder. Gently, he reached up and drew the fur up about her neck again, turning the edges close about her.

Without thinking, natural as breathing, while he thought she slept, he looked out for her. Maybe that's all there really is, she thought. Just making the way a little less difficult for each other as we go. And maybe it wasn't enough just to keep going. Maybe a body had to find the courage to forget and start over. There are no promises, she thought, that much I've learned. But that doesn't mean we can't take comfort from what's here, for now.

She felt rise up in her a love, an admiration for this man who held her so carefully. The constant hectoring of her mind seemed to cease for the moment, and she felt a peace that was finer than anything she had known in a long while, a resolution which closed the last place of her heart that had murmured so restlessly. She felt the tears seep through her lashes and wet his chest, and he pulled back with concern.

"What is it?" he asked softly.

She cleared her throat and smiled tentatively. "I've been thinkin' about what you asked me."

He rose up on one elbow and looked into her eyes intently. "I meant it, Suzanna. If you'll have me, I'll never leave you."

An echo of her father's words came to her quickly. "Don't say such a thing," she said firmly. "It isn't right to make promises like that. Promises you can't keep."

He chuckled softly. "There's lots of things I wasn't sure of in my life, and there'll be plenty more, I know. But there's one thing I can promise, and make it stick. I'll never leave you. I might get white and bent as an old birch, I might die first, you might wish to God I'd do it, but I'll never leave you. You'll never get rid of me, woman, so you might as well take me on."

In a bright flash of understanding, she saw that for the first time in a long while, here in his arms, she felt at home. She recalled the hazy words of the weddings she'd attended: in sickness and in health, for richer or for poorer, till death do us part. Her father had stood by her side in a wedding crowd and watched the bride and groom, their heads together in a radiant private joy. "It'll hold," he'd said gruffly, his highest praise. So will this, Pa, she thought, if I let it.

I said I'd never marry, never be a mother, never make my mother's mistakes, never *be* my mother, yet hers is the voice which sounds always in my ears. And what mistakes did she make? She fell in love, and the force of that one heart-step swept her along as surely as the river sweeps a fallen leaf to the sea. As she always did when she faced a dilemma, Suzanna turned it over in her mind, trying to see the darkest side, for she knew if she could stand the worse that might happen, she could make the choice. She thought of birthings and babies and standing in one place and hoeing and washing and two of them together, she and Caleb in the same bed, until the day she died. It was the most common of miracles. She saw that she was no longer just herself, but a thread in a tapestry, a piece in a larger quilt than even she had envisioned, a part of all the mothers and families who had gone before her and would come after her, from her, and the rhythm, the powerful rightness of it soothed her. She nestled closer to Caleb, her head in the sheltered crook of his shoulder.

"We need to find your ma," she said softly. At his look of surprise, she added, "A body can't get wed without family to witness, an' between us, she's all we got."

"After what you've been—? You'd go looking for a Chinook

shaman-woman to bless your vows? I don't even know if she's still alive, and even if I could *find* her, Lord, I—well—" and he sputtered to amazed silence.

"She's your mother, isn't she?" Suzanna asked calmly. "You should have done it long ago. No better time than a weddin' to mend old fences."

He stared at her wonderingly, at her steady gaze and her firm chin, and finally he drew her close. "We'll start out at first light."

Like so many things, that which seemed lost was only so until they looked, and then it was as though it had been there all along, Suzanna thought. Caleb found his mother in the first place he searched. In the old Clatsop village across the river, she lived in a rickety lodge surrounded by totem sticks, set back from the People's paths, apart and alone.

Suzanna stepped from the canoe and looked about the village sadly. There must have been a time, she thought, when more than dogs and gulls scrapped on this beach, a time when children ran laughing by the river's edge. But now, only one old woman looked up sullenly from her fire as they passed, and smoke drifted listlessly from the few lodges.

"You sure you want to come along?" Caleb asked. He pointed to the old lodge at the edge of the village. "They said she's there. But you could wait in the boat."

"I've come this far," Suzanna said lightly. She followed him up the beach, past the racks of drying salmon and the piles of empty clam shells, to the door of Ilchee's lodge.

Caleb coughed and scratched softly at the cedar door in the old way, bent his head, and then entered the dark shack. Suzanna took a deep breath and stepped within, waiting while her eyes adjusted to the shadows. In the middle of the lodge, a small fire burned. An old woman sat, scratching patterns in the sand with a painted stick. Suzanna stood quietly and watched while Caleb walked toward her.

The time fell away, and Caleb almost swayed with the shock of being once more in his mother's presence, before her fire. He squatted silently, his muscles assuming long-remembered postures with no protest. Without looking up, Ilchee said, "Well, and Raven said you would come, my O'na." She spoke in Chinook, and Caleb heard her as in a dream, the old rhythms rising and falling in his memory like falling water.

Old, old, she is so very old! his heart murmured, and he saw that her hand trembled as she drew the totem signs. "Did Raven tell you why I came, my mother?" he asked gently, in English.

"I did not need Raven to tell me you have found your woman," Ilchee answered him softly in the same tongue. "This, I can see." And she glanced up and smiled at Suzanna, who moved a little closer to the fire.

"You wish to take my son as husband?" Ilchee asked firmly, keeping her hands busy over the flames.

Suzanna glanced at Caleb and then said cautiously, "We're talking of it, aye."

"Who are your people?" Ilchee stared somewhere over Suzanna's head, as though she already knew the answer.

"I've got no living kin, but I come from Missouri, if that's what you mean." A moment of hesitation. "That's a state back east."

"She was took by the Cayuse," Caleb said gruffly. "I met her at Walla Walla."

Ilchee's eyes widened, and she motioned her son to silence. She turned to face Suzanna, searching her eyes for—what? Suzanna wondered. She stiffened and lifted her chin. "That's all over now. If you're looking for hate or vengeful feelings, ma'am, you'll find none here. What's past is past, and people got a lot more terrible things to bear than that." She took a deep breath and gave Ilchee a brilliant, fearless smile.

After a long moment, Ilchee returned her smile and nodded slowly. "Is your body as strong as your heart, then?"

Suzanna chuckled wryly, and in that instant, Ilchee recognized a sister-soul. "It hasn't failed me so far," Suzanna said softly. Ilchee put her head back and laughed, rocking and bobbing her head like a child while Caleb looked on, bewildered.

When Ilchee lifted her head, Caleb saw in the firelight that his mother was weeping; the tears made her withered cheeks glisten. He reached for her, and his voice cracked with pain. "Do you know how long I stood at the river and watched for your canoe!"

She put both her hands in his and laughed softly through her tears. "I came after three winters. The gods of the mountains would have sheltered the People if they had stayed, but they wanted to hear the river once more." She paused and listened, as if hearing the water's voice herself. Her voice dropped almost to a whisper. "The river will die, my son, and it will take the People with it." She chuckled wryly. "But who can leave it? Even *I* sit at its feet like an old frog, neh?"

"It is an ancient prophecy, my mother," Caleb said. "You have told it before."

"And others after me shall tell it again," she said. "Well, and so we returned. The dogs had the old village. Your grandfather's bones fed the cedars in the white way, and the guardman said Charles Demers took his wife and son upriver. He did not know where." She turned over one of his palms and looked closely at the lines there, as though searching for his life under her fingers. "The gods ate many on the mountain," she said, "those who were left needed Raven's words. I brought them here, to the Clatsops, that they might live or die together. And I asked Raven to bring you to my door when you were ready."

"When *I* was ready? You were the one sent me away, my mother, you and your prophecies."

"I did not send you away, my son, Raven did. You have never understood the difference."

"Neither did my father, I guess, or my grandfather either," he said bitterly, but she did not seem to hear him.

She looked up at the fire intently, "There was a time, long ago, when I feared the shamans myself. Many did, for they did not use their powers gently. But now I see that those with visions are only so strong as the People will allow them to be. And there are many ways the gods may choose to punish us who practice magic in the old ways."

He shook his head slowly. "Well, and I have come," he said in Chinook. In English, he added, "You might have hunted for me."

Suzanna said quietly, hesitantly, "Seems to me, what's past is past. You're here now, together, and that's what matters."

Caleb looked at Ilchee a long moment and then said firmly, "We want to be wed, mother. We want your blessing." He glanced again at Suzanna, saw her nod imperceptibly, and went on. "We want you to come and live with us. Or near us, anyways. So I can look after you."

Ilchee's eyes gleamed. "You have my blessing," she said in English, looking at Suzanna. "It is good. But I must stay with the People here, by the river. You do not need the old ways; they do. Raven will not speak in these old ears in the white man's places."

Suzanna spoke up quickly. "Caleb may not need you, but his

children will. As all children need their past, so they can see their future more clear. Please—" she added, "come with us . . . Princess Raven."

Ilchee laughed delightedly, a silvery youthful sound. "It is a long time since I heard such a name. You need not use it again, my daughter. My name is Ilchee, Moon-woman. And no, I will not come with you. Not now, while my people still need a shaman. Perhaps when another takes my place . . . but not yet. Besides," her mouth crinkled up in a grin, "you can bring my grandson to hear his old mother's words anytime, on any tide. Even now, he listens in your belly."

Suzanna gasped and flushed scarlet, glancing quickly at Caleb.

"Raven has told you this as well, my mother?" he asked.

"Make the wedding soon," Ilchee said calmly. "He waits to be born, a boy with his father's hair and his mother's eyes, blue and wide open, as is seemly. You may come for me at the marriage time; I shall come for him at the birthing time, and I will store up the old tales for the telling." She reached out and took her son's face in her hands. "I thought my heart had died when I left you, my O'na, but then I knew it had not, for it kept hurting for you, no matter which path I chose. You remember, I gave you my father's totem stick. Raven called you a shaman even at your birth. I, too, was afraid when I first knew I had visions. But you must not be afraid of them, my son. They are dreams of power."

Caleb smiled tautly. "And you remember, my mother, that I threw the totem stick across the fire. Raven does not know everything. I am not afraid; I simply do not see with your eyes anymore. You sent me to the whites. Now, their world is mine. You could make it yours as well."

She shook her head. "You were never far from my heart," Ilchee said softly, "in all these seasons, and you shall never be far from my eyes again. But we do not have to breathe each other's cooking fires, eh?"

She stood on the shore and waved them farewell, her long robes trailing behind her, her gray hair shining in the sun. When Caleb did not, could not, lift his arm to wave, Suzanna took his hand in hers and raised them both together, calling out a loud and cheerful goodbye over the rush of the water.

They were to travel that water many times, back and forth to Ilchee's lodge, as the land changed around them and the river drew more dreamers to its shores. Finally, they crossed the green Columbia for good and moved to Portland, where Caleb bought land for a cannery site.

Suzanna often thought of her father and smiled inside. "It's holding, Pa," she said silently to herself when she looked at her husband building their lives. Suzanna named her firstborn Isaac, after her father, and she imagined she could see a piece of him in the boy's ready laugh and quick hands. As she had promised, Ilchee crossed the river then to take him in her arms gently, solemnly, and hold him high in the air.

"He, too, has a head like the moon, like his father before him," she said. "You shall fill it full of new dreams, neh?"

Caleb put his arm around Ilchee's shoulders. "And you, with the old, my mother?"

Her eyes glimmered with some private promise. "Aye, perhaps. Raven has said that my seed shall lead the People. If it will not be you, then perhaps this round-headed gull, eh?" She took one of the infant's hands in hers. "There is building in these fingers, but a tearing down as well. I cannot see—" and she squinted as though to call up her vision more clearly.

Suzanna gently extricated the infant from his grandmother's arms. "Such talk, you two. This is one nation now, didn't the President just say so? Isaac'll have his own destiny, I reckon, just like every child born, and you can both tell him all the dreams you want, but let's not be putting his feet on any path afore he can even walk." She laughed lightly and patted Ilchee's arm, but there was a firmness to her chin that belied her smile.

Ilchee relinquished the child readily, but she gazed at a place just over his head, her eyes widening with secret wonder, an infinitesimal dimming of joy, and she said nothing more.

PART FOUR

The River
Sojourners,
1870–1880

History never repeats itself,

Man always does.

—Voltaire

*F*ar away from Ilchee's village, farther still from Caleb and Suzanna, the river's promise stretched tempting fingers, a wet prophecy of fertility and new lands. The river's voice, a green thunder of power, stretched even across the sea, and tales of its spring salmon, of its mossy banks, of its waiting fields and its ripe blackberries ran all the way to a land called the Middle Kingdom. There, the tales eddied and flowed upon the drought plains like spring rain, intoxicating and eternally new.

Tales of the river drank from the land and the people's hearts, even as the people drank up the power and promise of the tales. In the river's cascades, they imagined they could hear the songs of a million campfires, the beat of drums, the slap of paddles, the thud of hooves, the creak of wagon wheels, the sharp crack of muskets, the thunder of falling timber, the thwack of the pick and the shovel, and the rising voices, strange voices with new inflections, which spoke of unknown dreams.

And so they came, strangers before the river, and sojourners, as were all their fathers, and their days on the land were as shadows on its banks. They came with an enormous madness to eat the river and its roots, to devour its golden green secrets, to consume its incredible mirage of all their million shining hopes, but they were swallowed up instead, as all innocence was swallowed by the protean, phantasmal shape which was America becoming. With gemlike incandescence, they shone briefly and then were gone into the enormous darkness, but by their lights they helped define the birth, and still the river waited there, full and unending, patient and intractable, conveyor and confronter, to take what they brought and give back what they sought—and always it flowed by them, before them, to the sea.

NING HO, YOUNGEST DAUGHTER OF THE HOUSE OF NING, WAS TWO NIGHTS traveling from her village of Hsiao Chin to Guangzhou, and when her bearers came to a stop on a hill overlooking the harbor, she peered out of a small slit in the litter curtain and looked down, relieved to stop rocking at last.

Below the cliffs, she could see huge black ships at rest in the water, great wooden insects with their jointed-legged masts in the sky. Many sampans jostled about their flanks, like red ants scurrying around dead beetles. These, then, were the ships of the fan-qui, the foreign devils; she scowled, her moth-wing brows arching in disdain. With these ugly, awkward vessels, they had forced the Emperor to open the Middle Kingdom to their greedy barbarian

fists. By this year of the rat, in 1870, they had built great clumsy
houses in the port they renamed Canton, and the people told fearsome stories of their brutality. It was said they gave magic medicine
to the unwary to lure them aboard their ships and thence to the
country of the dog-headed race to be sold for their weight in silver.

Her litter reached the streets of Guangzhou, and she looked about
eagerly, amazed at the bustle and hurry. Hawkers jostled through
the throngs, shouting and thrusting their wares in the faces of those
who passed; fruit-sellers and pastrymen and spectacle-menders
fought for space on the crowded corners. Barbers shaved their customers out in the open air, scraping carefully around long, oiled
queues; fortune-tellers, herbalists, and money changers beckoned
from shadowed huts, and the sparks flew at a dozen blacksmiths'
and razor-grinders' benches.

Suddenly, she felt dizzy and wretchedly homesick for her father's
courtyard. She remembered her last night behind the walls, as she
sipped warm sweet wine and nibbled on delicate slices of ginger.
The moon rose through the branches of the mulberry trees while the
last cicadas whirred into silence. She wondered if she was ever again
to feel such peace in her new lord's house.

The litter moved swiftly through the crowds to a large moon gate
set back from the streets. The gate guard announced her arrival, and
she was quickly ushered within the high walls of the house of
Chang, one of the wealthiest in the district. Inside, a servant took
her to a private chamber where Ning Ho bathed and changed into
fresh robes. She scarcely had time to look about her, for the woman
prodded her constantly to hurry. The master was waiting impatiently.

Ning Ho wished fervently for nothing more than a cool bed and
an hour of solitude, but she bit back her short replies, knowing she
might have to depend on this servant in time. She remembered her
old amah saying, "Never spit in the well; you may have to drink
from it," and she quickened her preparations, carefully inspecting
her ivory face and her black eyes for any imperfections.

She was led to her master's chambers, a great room hung with
silken tapestries and lined with red-lacquered chairs. There, seated
on a high chair in the center of the floor, he waited. His brow was
deeply furrowed and his arms were crossed. His eyes restlessly
appraised her as she kowtowed before him, her head to the mat.

There was a long moment of painful silence, and Ning Ho became more anxious. She wanted to raise her head and gaze at him, but she didn't dare without leave. She was wearing her best red robes, and her hair was as glossy as a wet stone. Though she was unused to the powder and paint of a city woman, the servant had assured her that her efforts were not too clumsy. Surely, he was not displeased. . . .

But then he spoke, and his voice cracked, harsh and angry. Unbidden, Ning Ho jerked up her head in shock. By all the gods, this man is older than my own father! she gasped. Even with all his rich robes and oiled wigs, it was clear that the frame beneath the layers of wealth was an aged one, infirm and palsied, with skin as thin as carp scales. And worse, his dialect was scarcely intelligible, guttural and rough, not at all like the liquid tones of her village.

"I have been deceived!" he bellowed to his manservant. "That whore-dung of a matchmaker swore she was plump as a peach with the feet of a doe. Aiya, I shall slit her lying throat when I catch her! This one is all bones and *bullock-feet*. She shall never bear my sons!" He lurched from the room, kicking at her angrily as he passed.

Ning Ho sat frozen in an agony of humiliation. Never in her life had she been treated with such contempt. She pinched her thumb to keep from sobbing and waited, stolid-faced, to see who would come to take her away.

An hour passed. Her golden lilies ached with the pressure of kneeling. For the first time, she sorely regretted that the foot-binder had not made the dao-shang, the final cut, which would have made her tiny feet half their size. She wearily looked at them, curved and highly arched on the wooden shoes.

Her mother had said, "With the barbarians in our land, the old ways are changing. We shall do the binding, yes, but not the dao-shang. And that way, if she must move as quickly as the quail, she can." Ning Ho remembered her fond glance.

But Lao Tai-Tai, her father's mother, had sneered, "And what wealthy man will want such a horse-footed girl then, ma? The little fool is the only fruit of your loins who is imperfect, a female. Thank the gods, she is a beauty, but her beauty will count for nothing when the matchmakers ask, 'How small are her feet?' You will feed that pretty mouth to the end of your days!"

But her mother had insisted, and for once, her voice prevailed over that of Old Mother's. The foot-binder had come when she was seven, and her heels had been pressed downward, and salt-soaked

linen strips were wrapped tightly from her ankles to her toes, forcing them under so she walked on their tops. Some girls had their
arches cut so their feet would be no more than three inches in
length, but Ning Ho wore special wooden shoes, and though her
feet were almost twice as large, she still swayed on her crescent
moons with the gentle, mincing gate that men found so lovely. And
now, at fifteen, she found they scarcely hurt her at all when properly bandaged. She no longer had to sleep with her feet under her
mother as she had for two years, just to forget their agony; she no
longer had to crawl on her hands and knees just to keep from
sobbing. The healing herbs had done their job, and at least she could
walk without leaning on a servant's shoulder, something her mother
and her father's mother could not do. Last month, when she had
taken off the bindings to wash and oil them, one shriveled toe had
come away from her foot with the cloth. She had prayed to the
Goddess Kuang that she would lose more, and then no one would
ever know she had evaded the final cut. But Master Chang said she
had the feet of a bullock!

For another long hour, no servant called, no one came for her.
Three times she rose, determined to go to the only chamber she
knew in the great house and repack her trunk. But she dared not,
for fear he would beat her. A man who could kick could surely
thrash, and there would be no one who would stay his hand.

She was not to be wife, her father had said. "But you will be his
first concubine, much favored after his old wife, and your children
will be sons of the house of Chang. For this, you should burn seven
ris of incense to the gods so that you may have a male child and the
Celestial Hound of Heaven will not eat him up, so jealous will he
be of your good fortune."

And her mother had added, "Remember, my jewel. You are a
woman now, and as such should not expect happiness. Your satisfaction will come from serving others." So, her fate had been decided and now rested on the approval of her lord, at least until she
could attain the dignity and protection of being the mother of sons.
If she returned to her village, no man would believe she was still
virgin. No man would take her as wife.

She whined deep in her throat, a private sound like the helpless
keening of a trapped rabbit. All her life, she had depended on her
beauty and her charm to rescue her from trouble. If these weapons
are to no avail, she thought, I have nothing.

Just as she had resolved once more to go from her master's chamber and find her own way to a refuge, the servant entered. Now, there was no deference in her bow. Without speaking, she led Ning Ho to the waiting litter outside the moon gate. Within, the packed trunk was lashed and secure. The head bearer smiled insolently, as though he himself had bedded her and found her wanting. Instantly, Ning Ho's despair flamed into rage, and she had to grip her hands together to keep from slapping his grinning face.

She expected to see the litter turn down the same streets, back the way she had come, in the direction of the village. But instead, they went toward the waterfront. There, the litter stopped before a teahouse, and a man wearing the badge of the Co-Hong bowed her to a seat.

The Co-Hong were the wily government officers who dealt with the foreign devils, the only merchants the Emperor would trust to stand between the Dragon Throne and their grasping hairy hands. It was said that the Co-Hong controlled all goods moving in and out of the Middle Kingdom, even opium, which was forbidden. Under the supervision of the Hoppo, the Emperor's counselors, the Co-Hong ruled the ports and, ultimately, all ships that plied Chinese waters.

Ning Ho had never seen such a man, of course, but she had heard her brothers and her father talk of their power. Her stomach was roiling with fear, but she kept her eyes downcast and her mouth still. Perhaps this man knew her father and so was willing to help her. Inwardly, she was appalled to be on a public street and outside the protection of her curtained litter, with no veils to cover her face and no amah at her side. This, then was what came of praying to the Goddess Kuang. She vowed that she would shave her head and become a Buddhist nun before she would burn another ri of incense to such a faithless spirit.

The man called for tea and began to speak. "Before you refresh yourself, my child," he said quietly, "we must speak of your grave difficulties. The master of the house of Chang has found you . . . unsuitable . . . and has asked me to see to your care."

She dropped her eyes and turned her head away.

He smiled gently. "You must not feel shame, daughter of Ning. The old master's eyes are rheumy and calloused, and he has sent many away before you—though none so beautiful, to be sure."

Still, she kept silent. Her eyes strayed to the cup of tea next to her hand. She felt a sudden yearning to drink huge draughts of the hot liquid and then sleep, troubled only by the sounds of her father's courtyard just beyond her ears. But she listened carefully.

"Fortune has still smiled on you, even in your great trouble. The master has purchased your passage on the finest ship in port. You will go to Gum sam, the land of beautiful mountains. There, you will be welcomed as the honored wife of a wealthy lord, a scholar, Chun Ho, who went there five years ago and found gold on his lands." He chuckled amiably, "Chun Ho has but to bend over to harvest his riches. Your sons will grow to be mighty lords in the new land."

She raised her head slowly, shocked beyond all speech.

He rushed on, "You yourself have seen the men who come home from the land of the beautiful mountains. They tell of plucking gold off the streets; they come back with their pockets full. They are able to entertain their villages with great banquets and fireworks, and new temples are built to their glory. All honor these men."

She finally found her voice. "I shall go back to my village, then, and find such a man." She stiffened, and her black eyes flashed. "I am of the house of Ning, and what you suggest is impossible. If this Chun Ho would have a wife, tell him to come to my father's house and be welcome. But I will never go to the land of the fan-qui!"

She fumbled in her sleeve for her stiletto, the deadly safeguard all traveling women carried in their robes. "I shall slit my wrists before I hear another word of dishonor. I am not afraid to die."

But he stayed her hand gently. "Think a moment, my daughter. Your father cannot take you back."

Her mind recoiled. Not take her back? Aiya, he would do exactly that! Yes, there was dishonor, and yes, she knew that the stores were low and bellies were pinched, but her mother would never let her suffer such a fate. She shook her head vehemently, and picked up her cup. At least, she would refresh herself at this man's expense before she left him, gawking and open-mouthed at her courage. She said, "I will go home," and glared at him over the porcelain rim.

When she awoke, she was in a murky dampness. For an instant, she thought herself in her litter, but the rocking was more violent than she remembered. She sat up, her heart pounding in sudden icy terror, and the hair rose on the back of her neck. Then she realized she felt a draft on her head where she never had before. Trembling, she felt herself and found that her hair had been cut short like a laborer's, her neck shaved like a man's.

She looked about her in mute horror. It was dark, but dim light came from a hole above, and she could see shapes about her, leaning against the wooden planks. The floor she lay on was cold and dank as a root cellar. Suddenly, the heaves and pitches of the floor overwhelmed her, and she rolled to her side, retching miserably. After she had emptied her stomach, she began to sob weakly, and she sank down once more, her head throbbing.

When she awoke again, it was very black, and she sensed bodies close to her. There was a clanking in the distance as though a great blacksmith hammered at a forge underground. She opened her mouth to scream but then stifled herself in terror. Perhaps I am in the bowels of the spirit land, she thought, and if so, no one has properly lighted candles at my deathbed to guide me past the Yellow Springs. And now, the demons are hovering about me.

But then she heard a voice close to her ear—a cultured voice, speaking a scholarly dialect, though ill-pronounced. "Have no fear, my child. No one will harm you. The day will come soon."

Unable to see past her hand, Ning Ho crowded herself into the smallest ball she could manage, hoping to be overlooked by the demons. She slept, giving up a silent prayer that whatever kindly god had spoken would look after her through the night.

The next time she woke, light streamed through holes in the roof. Her head no longer thundered, but her mouth felt dry as millet chaff. A foreign devil sat beside her, reading from a small black book. No wonder her brother called them ghosts, she thought. This man's skin was white and his thin hair was pale as a six-month corpse. His black robes lapped over his lanky knees.

She eased up to a sitting position and leaned against the wooden wall. Most of the bodies that had crowded round her last night had disappeared. She supposed the demons must have eaten them. "Is there water?" she asked quietly, wondering who would answer.

"Ah, you've awakened, then," the fan-qui said.

Ning Ho was so astonished to hear the voice of her kindly god come out of a barbarian mouth that she could only gape in reply.

"I'll get you some water, my child," he said and crawled over to a bucket in the center of the room, filled a wooden cup, and brought it back to her. She drank it greedily. "Where are the demons?" she whispered. The room was no longer rocking so violently, but still she had to hold onto the walls to keep from lurching into the barbarian's shoulder.

"Demons? There are no demons here, my child," he sighed. "Only the sons of men. And that's evil enough, to be sure."

She did not understand all he said, but some words came through, and she began to feel more safe. "What is this place?" she asked, looking over her shoulder at a few men huddled in the corners. One watched her carefully.

"You're on the *Witchcraft,* bound for America. They brought you onboard drunk as a lord, and gave you over to that man, there." He pointed to the man who peered at them. The fan-qui lowered his voice. "You've nothing to fear from him, either, lass. He's a member of the Tong, and they'd probably torture him or worse if one of these lads lays a hand on you. He's here to see you safe to port."

She began to tremble, and she hugged herself hard to keep from falling, weeping, to the floor. "Why is my hair chopped like a slave? Where are my clothes?" She was dressed in a pair of coarse blue sahms, trousers, loose and baggy as the peasants wore. A shapeless blue jacket covered her slim body down to her knees. She wondered who had taken off her clothing, and she whitened.

He shrugged pityingly. "Who knows why they do what they do? I suppose they thought your own countrymen might molest you."

"Have I been dishonored?" she whispered.

He laughed shortly. "No more than the rest of us." He shook his head. "Nay, lass, you're safe, more or less. That Tong man will see to your maidenhead, if that's your worry. I wager someone's waiting to pay a pretty price for it in America."

His words shocked her into silence. She had been sold as a slave by the filthy Co-Hong. She leaned back, suddenly exhausted. Water slapped at the sides of the ship, smacking and sucking like a greedy child at the breast. Her trunk was gone, her jade necklaces, too. She was abandoned and alone, and if she lived, she would soon know dishonor and a life of drudging misery. The best I can hope for now is to be sold into a wealthy house, she thought dully, where I will care for the sons and daughters of other women, where the master's sons will take me and spread my legs whenever they wish, and my own sons will be sold as slaves. Or perhaps I will drown in a tai-fung, a Supreme Wind, or die from heartache, a slave in the land of the barbarians. I can be nothing else, as ugly as they've made me.

She stretched out her legs and peered down at her feet. They had removed her bandages and her carved wooden shoes. Now, her feet swam in clumsy peasant slippers. They ached as blood pumped into long-numbed nerves, and it seemed she could feel them getting flatter and bigger by the moment. Her mother's voice came back to her in a distant memory. She had asked plaintively, "Mother, why must my feet be bound so tightly? They hurt me so!" And her mother had replied, "Daughter, remember, only the most beautiful bird gets caged."

They had said she was beautiful. But now, that part of her life was over. Now, she must learn to think like a peasant and endure. She was once more overwhelmed by the boat's lurches and her despair, and she began to retch.

"Spew it up, lass," the barbarian said calmly. "If that pain goes down, it'll poison you sure."

In days, Ning Ho grew familiar with the rocking of the great ship, at least enough so that she no longer gagged up her food. The sailors seemed not to know she was a woman. They looked right through her as they did her countrymen. She had rigged up a small corner in the hold where she could perform her toilet in some privacy. A ragged bit of sail she had snatched from the cook served as a curtain; a rusty slop bucket was her bath. She no longer wept into the night silently. There was no one to hear her, and no one could help her if they heard.

She spent long tedious hours attempting to learn some of the fan-qui speech from the priest, for she knew instinctively that she must understand their strange hissing words if she was to survive in their land. Of course, she had heard of Mei-Kwok, the beautiful land, which was America. When she was a child, several men of the village had gone across the sea to find the gold that they swore lay in the streets like dung. They had never returned, but others did— and soon, even the meanest laborers heard the tales of Gum sam, the land of the golden mountains.

Some left their hoes and their fishing lines and went to the great ships, selling their water buffaloes for silver to pay for their passage. Families saved to send a favorite son, that he might make a fortune and uplift them all. When the droughts and the famines came in ever tighter circles, maps and pictures of the land of the golden mountains seemed to cover the villages like locusts. Even her own brother had brought a paper into the house, and read it aloud.

Americans are very rich people. They want the Chinaman to come and will make him welcome. There will be large houses, and food and clothing of the finest description. It is a nice country, without mandarins or soldiers. All alike; big man no larger than little man. There are a great many Chinamen there now, China God is there, and the agents of famous houses. Never fear, and you will be lucky.

But her father had shouted him to silence. "You will not go to this land of the barbarians! Not unless you leave a wife and a son behind. Else you will never return to bury these old bones, and I will curse you from the land of the spirits through all eternity!" And so, talk of Gum sam had ceased in the house of Ning, but Ning Ho recalled the stories, and now her mind curled away in awe.

One night, she listened as the men talked beyond her curtain. A low voice was speaking of his wife. "Aiya, the matchmaker cheated me!" he said. "It comes of having their feet free."

His comrade answered, "When we were boys, their feet were bound and they stayed at home properly." A bitter laugh. "Now, they run about like goats. Look at that one in the corner, who cannot wait to see the beautiful land and so cuts her hair like a shuey-kee."

The shuey-kee, the waterfowl, were the prostitutes who worked from the sampans, specializing in pleasing the barbarians. Ning Ho stiffened with white rage. So, they thought she had smuggled herself aboard this filthy floating hell! She whipped back her curtain, burst from her corner, and stood before the men, quaking with anger.

"Do you think *I* am here for my pleasure? A broken shoe to fit any man's foot? Some of you may be stupid enough to seek out such a fool's errand, but I—*I* was forced here against my will! My father is Ning, of the village Hsiao Chin, and I will not be insulted!"

With that, all the anger went out of her like a wind from sails, and she sullenly stomped back behind her curtain. She heard no more talk that night.

For two months, they were locked belowdecks as the *Witchcraft* ploughed the sea to Portland. Only the priest was allowed to walk in the fresh air, and she marveled that he would willingly come back down to the chu-tzekwan, the pigpens, as the men called the hold, just to speak of his gods.

He would sit for hours, holding his small black book, cajoling first one listener and then another to pray to his personal spirits. Ning Ho always listened carefully, for she wished to learn the speech and also the thoughts of such a man. Surely, there must be more like him in the land of golden mountains, she thought. They called him Shu-ho-ti, He-Who-Talks-Ceremony, for he was a peacemaker among them.

Once, Lo Tung accused his neighbor, Lin Ho, of stealing from his packet of ginger. Lo Tung prized his ginger, claiming that only tiny slivers added to the white barbarians' rice made it at all palatable.

"Your mother's filthy cunt!" he shouted at Lin Ho. "I curse your ancestors ten thousand times, you stinking dog vomit!"

But the peacemaker came between them, gentling Lo Tung's anger and saving Lin Ho's face. He wheedled them into silence with tales of the white demon, Jesus, and his mother, Mary.

The barbarians dropped buckets of rice and boiled fish to them, but Ning Ho grew increasingly weary of such fare. One man assured her that it was better now for the sojourners, as they called themselves, than it used to be. "The early golden mountain guests used to have to eat the same rotten food that the barbarians ate. Think of it—rancid pork and beef and hard biscuits. No fresh fish or vegetables. It's no wonder many arrived with their teeth loose as dice in a cup."

"Aiya!" the dentist laughed eagerly. "I will be a wealthy man in such a land. It's said that the barbarians don't know how to eat, even when they are in their own villages. So, of course, their teeth must be as rotten as their bellies!"

"Perhaps they have learned better ways by now," Ning Ho said. "Their rice is not well cooked, but at least the fish is firm."

The man snorted, "They have learned only that we will make trouble if they do not take care of us. Ten years ago, a white demon captain waited until his ship was out of sight of land and then told our countrymen that they must bathe and be shaved of their queues before they could step foot in the land of golden mountains."

Ning Ho gasped in outrage. To force a man to bathe against his will was to intrude into intimate areas of his life unthinkably. No man could stand such loss of face. And to cut off a man's queue was to doom him to wander forever, an outcast from the land of his ancestors. No Chinese could return to the Celestial Kingdom as woo-pien, tailless, for his queue was the sign of obedience to the Emperor.

"Did they cut their own throats in rebellion?" she asked.

"No, much better than that. They took over the ship, killed some of the white demons, and bound the captain with his own rope. They did not kill him, of course, but he lost so much face, he might as well have died."

Now, Ning Ho understood why they were kept in this dank hold for the duration of the journey. The white demons were afraid of many Chinese all together. It was something to think on.

The men passed the days in gossip, smoking and gambling at go and mah-jong to make the hours fly. Only one of their number had been to Gum sam and returned. He was a rich merchant from Guangzhou, and he had been to the port of kal-ee-for-nee-a, a land more beautiful, he said, than even the valleys of Guilin. Naturally, he was besieged by questions. "They will call you cool-lie," he would say, shaking his head in bemusement.

"Ku-li? Bitter strength? What sort of name is that for a man, ma?" Lin Ho questioned. He sat leaning against the ribs of the ship, scratching his feet in wonderment.

"Aiya, you know they cannot speak any language save their own. And they will change anything to suit them. Perhaps their ears are stopped with dung, who can say? But still"—the merchant grinned —"I am going back, because with what I earn in three years in the fan-qui land, I will be a rich man all the days of my life. My wife loves this old bone," and he patted his groin smugly, "but even she begs me to leave her and come back with my pockets full of the fan-qui gold."

The men laughed, for they knew well the ways of wives. Lo Tung shouted, "Aiya, and mine would have two servants to comb her hair rather than one, if she could!"

"She will have more than she can scold when you return," the sojourner said. "And your villages will honor your names forever. I go back willingly. There is enough wealth for all of us."

The men listened, bewitched with visions of distinguished ancestral halls, their wives decked in jade and silks, their pockets filled with tobacco and sweetmeats. Ning Ho looked about the hold. Many of them were indentured. They had offered themselves in a debt bondage to future employers in return for passage, making their marks, their thumbprints, on a long list which assured them of work. Some fortunate few had managed to scrape together their passage money, fifty dollars in silver, with the help of their clan or even their whole village, leaving behind a promise to share the wealth when they returned. None were drugged and smuggled aboard against their will to be slaves as she had been. She sighed deeply. The merchant said that there were few Chinese women in the land of golden mountains, and the white demonesses were so ugly that the sojourners would pay silver merely to look upon her face. She could hardly believe such tales to be truth, but she was past weeping, and she could only hope for the best.

Ah Goong, the fisherman, took off his jacket and bit the seams furiously to kill the lice and fleas. "Well, if we can survive the vermin and the poor rice and the stinking night buckets, we each deserve cash in our pockets," he said wearily. Not a man disagreed.

The *Witchcraft* finally reached the Bar and blew across in a rain squall, up the waters of the Columbia. The Chinese were allowed to come on deck for brief intervals to stretch and see the land. Ning Ho leaned on the rail and watched the shore move slowly past. The heavy dark trees and the tall mountains ringed with snow were so different from her village that her eyes watered and her throat ached. Never had she seen so much green. A man could feed many mouths with even a few li of this land, she thought. Even the water itself was green, from the glacial snows, the priest said, but Ning Ho felt it was because the water ate the land and so turned green from such fertile fodder.

Ning Ho was herded down the gangplank, the Tong man at her side. Her feet touched the hard, unmoving ground for the first time in many days, and she reeled unsteadily. A countryman, a labor agent, came forward, dressed in strange trousers and a jacket with some animal's fur about the collar. Quickly, he began to separate the Chinese into gangs of ten and twenty, rattling off commands in a dialect she could scarcely understand. When he came to her, he drew her aside, spoke to the Tong man briefly, and then bowed shortly to her. "You are the only woman?" he asked in a guttural speech.

She nodded, keeping her eyes downcast. To be so ugly in the hold of the ship was one thing indeed; to be gazed at in the open sunlight in this condition was dizzyingly shameful. He turned back to the men before him, directing them into one group or another. Each picked up his belongings and walked, single file, behind a wagon, into the city ahead. She climbed into the wagon and rode into

Portland, sitting between the Tong man and the labor agent, looking about her in wonder.

There were many tall buildings on both sides of the spacious street, square and many times higher than the highest walls round the richest houses in Guangzhou. The white demons walked about on wooden paths, so even the bottoms of their leather shoes would not touch the ground. Some of the houses were made of stone, like the Great Wall, and she rolled her eyes to think of how many slaves it had taken to build this city. The streets were wide and went in straight lines off into the distance as far as she could see. Evidently, the fan-qui were not scared of ghosts. In China, streets were always curved, for everyone knew that spirits could only travel in a straight line. Either their geomancers were stupid, or the white barbarians did not heed them.

The demonesses walked about unescorted by male guards or amahs, brazenly speaking to men on the street. She heard one of her comrades behind her laugh, "See those two boats going by!" She turned to see a demoness walking swiftly, showing her shoes. Indeed, it was true. Her feet were like sampans under her long, bell-like skirt!

Finally, their wagon turned down a small side street, and instantly, Ning Ho knew they were in a different city. The men who lounged about the little houses were Chinese, the Tang people; the shops were closer together; red strips of joss paper hung from many of the gates, dried ducks hung in the windows, and she caught the unmistakable odor of dau fu cooking close by. She felt her shoulders relax. It was true, then. There were Chinese here in Gum sam. At least, that promise had not been a lie. The wagon pulled up before a large building with letters in Chinese across the front. "Meeting Hall of the Middle Kingdom," they said, and two Tong men came down the steps to greet them.

"Welcome to the beautiful land, cousins!" one man cried out amiably. "We are here to help you arrange yourselves."

They quickly explained that they were representatives of the Six Companies, the Tongs or Benevolent Societies, which had been formed to help newcomers find their way into the fan-qui world. "If you need a place to sleep, we will give this to you," the Tong man continued. "If you need food or fuel or work, we give this as well. When you have earned your fortune, you will help others the same way." He nodded to his comrade. "Some of you will go to the Ning Yeung Company, some to the Hop Wo or the Sam Yup Companies, others to the Yeong Wo or the Kong Chow clans. We are the laws in our Tang village within the white city. If you die, we will ship your bones back to the lands of your ancestors. If you must borrow money or find a wife, we will help you."

The men began to splinter off into groups again, to follow the Tong men of their clan. The Tong man said nothing, but only clacked the reins against the horse's neck. The wagon drove on up the street and stopped at a small house wedged tightly between two tall buildings. On the front it said, "House of Joyous Relief" in bold red Chinese characters. The Tong man waited patiently while Ning Ho climbed down from the wagon, and then he bowed her solemnly inside.

"You are a lovely gem," Old Mother crooned to her, turning her around slowly. "You are not inclined to plumpness, a sign of fertility. That is good for business. You will make some rich gentleman whimper with delight, ma?" She laughed raucously. "But first, you must be worthy of the investments which have been made in your future."

"What must I do?" Ning Ho asked, keeping her chin firm.

"Why, you must please, of course, my daughter. And I will teach you how to do so, ah yes." She looked her over carefully. "It will be a quick three years, and perhaps some rich old gentlemen will buy your contract and build you a large house by the sea, ma?"

"I don't want a rich old gentleman," Ning Ho said, wrenching away her hands.

Old Mother's eyes narrowed. "Wei, the ass may bray a good deal before he shakes down the stars. What you want is of no interest to anyone, my daughter. Least of all, to the Ning Yeung Tong, ma? You will serve their needs for three years. If at that time some rich lord has bought your contract, you will be free to go with him. If not, you will, perhaps, be sent back to the empire. But until that time, you will serve your masters, and do so gladly. Unless you want to beg in the streets from the fan-qui instead."

Ning Ho slumped and turned her head away, her heart thudding with hatred.

"Now, sit beside me, my daughter, and hear what great joss you will have in the land of golden mountains. As a virgin, you will be sought by only the wealthiest men. We shall keep you intact for a while, for even untouched, you bring great value."

Ning Ho twisted away to evade her gleaming cat eyes.

"Aiya, you have spirit! That is good. It will raise a man's anticipation, and that is half his joy, ma? Many men believe that a virgin with spirit supplies vitality to their aged and withered roots. The old lords will pay much for dried dates soaked in your private places, believing them to be tonics. And then, of course, one lucky man will bid his wealth away to own those private places—two vultures with one arrow, ma? Perhaps too a young man with a wife will buy you as concubine, strictly for his own pleasure. But only if you heed my lessons well. No man pays for flesh alone, but for the illusion of beauty. We must give them what they wish."

For two days, Ning Ho was scrutinized by Old Mother, while servants dressed her hair, cleaned her teeth, and taught her to paint and powder her face. They prodded her to change her laugh to a high-pitched girlish noise, which they said drove men mad with desire. Her nails were buffed until they gleamed, her palms were perfumed, and every superfluous hair was plucked from her body.

She was finally dressed in fine silks and presented to Old Mother, who smacked her lips in glee. "You are more beautiful than I thought, my daughter! We will call you Tao Huo, Peach Blossom, a fitting name for one so rare in this barbarian wilderness."

Ning Ho winced. Peach Blossom—a flower accessible to any man, so unlike the lotus. Her father had named her Ho for that flower that floats above the mud, pristine and untouched by any hand.

"I think"—Old Mother narrowed her eyes—"aiya, I have decided! You shall be a pey par day, a sing-song girl. We can use your beauty as enticement, ma? The men will see you and lust for a woman, any woman, and we have plenty more to serve them. You will be trained in all the graces, and you will be given only to those who can afford to pay for the best. Do you agree?"

Ning Ho glared at her so fiercely that the rice powder on her smooth forehead sifted gently down on her silks. "I agree to nothing," she said coldly. "I shall escape or kill myself before I accept dishonor."

Old Mother cackled and clapped her hands. "Wei! You shall see your other choices, my daughter. And then you will beg me to make you such an offer once more."

Ning Ho was bundled roughly into shapeless clothing and taken to a large building in the center of Chinatown. Old Mother hustled her round back, through a side door, and into a dark corner behind a screen. An auction was underway, and Chinese men crowded into the hall, milling about the platform in the center of the room. On the platform stood fourteen women of different ages and descriptions. Most were young and slim; a few were stolid and heavy like peasants; one was old and fat. None were beautiful, but they all had been cleaned and groomed to show off their best features.

Some of the men in the crowd were wealthy gentlemen, dressed in heavy brocades with manservants at their side. Others were laborers, dressed in coarse cotton cloth with matted queues, pressing close to catch a glimpse of the women, smacking their lips at their beauty.

The Tong man running the auction tugged the first girl to the front of the platform. She was obviously frightened, and he had to pull her and curse loudly before she obeyed. As she stood before the men, he talked of her strength, her teeth, the length of her legs, turning her before the crowd. Suddenly, he reached to her neck and ripped the silk robe away from her body. She stood trembling and weeping, naked before the mass of gaping observers. The auctioneer turned her round again, forcing her to bend over, exposing her buttocks, letting her breasts dangle over the heads of those closest to the edge of the platform.

Meanwhile, the shouted bids from the crowd echoed round the room, until finally, an old gentleman reclining on a litter called out a high sum. From where she stood, Ning Ho could see his eyes glitter as the slave girl covered her face with her hands, weeping wretchedly, her breasts shaking with her sobs. The old man's servant went to the platform, threw a blanket about her shoulders, and led her away.

"She fetched a handsome price, ma?" Old Mother whispered. "And likely, he will never beat her. You know, that old fat sow at the end will not be so lucky. She will go to one of those alley-scum in the corner for less than a tael of gold."

Ning Ho looked where she pointed. A small gang of rough-looking wharf rats lounged against the back of the room, laughing coarsely at some private joke. She shuddered and turned away.

Old Mother took Ning Ho by the arm in a painful grip and led her outside and down a back alley. After several twists and turns, they stood before a long line of tiny cells, each with a wooden door.

Every door had a small window cut into it. Old Mother pushed Ning Ho up to the nearest door, and she stared in.

A girl sat on a wooden bunk at the back of the chamber. There was only enough room within for a washbowl, a wooden chair, and a narrow bed. She was pale under her gaudy paint and filthy robes, but she managed a tremulous smile in their direction. As Ning Ho stared, unable to wrench herself away, she heard voices from the adjoining windows pleading, cajoling, seducing, "I can please you better, beautiful sister. Please, come and knock on my door!"

Ning Ho put a hand to her mouth, stifled a low moan, and turned away wearily. "I have seen enough," she whispered.

"No, my daughter, there is one more place you must visit. I insist." Old Mother took her once more by the hand and dragged her to yet another dingy house, set back from the street.

"Where am I now?" Ning Ho groaned.

"This is the hospital where we take your sisters who have become too old, too sick, or too stubborn to pleasure their men any longer."

They entered, and Ning Ho stared into a dark, windowless cubicle. On the dirt floor lying on two old rice mats was a young girl no more than twenty. A small bowl of rice and a cup of water sat in the corner. By her side, a little metal oil lamp flickered. She lay with her eyes closed, her legs and arms curled up like an infant.

"Who cares for these unfortunates?" Ning Ho whispered.

Old Mother shook her head, bemused at her question. "No one, my Peach Blossom. They come here to die. If they have not accomplished this task by the time the oil lamp burns out, the doctors will do it for them."

Ning Ho began to gag wretchedly, and Old Mother led her away. That night, in a state of numbness, she signed a three-year contract, promising to be a sing-song girl for the Ning Yeung Tong and to deliver all her earnings to them in exchange for her room and food. She put her thumb into a smear of red ink and stamped it upon the paper. The red ink was for luck.

The first year was her hardest. After careful training, she could sing five or six lovely lilting Chinese ballads, do several simple, stylized dances, and play passably on the pipa. Then, Old Mother took her to a small neat house behind the alley of whores. Men came to her moon gate, eager to pay five dollars in gold just to sit and watch her dance, to hear her sing. Sometimes, they would simply wish to sit and listen to her speak. One miner told her he had come sixty miles downriver because he had not seen a Chinese woman in four years. Most of the men went directly from Ning Ho's house to the alley of whores close by. There, they paid one dollar to close their eyes, hold a woman, and pretend she was the beauty behind the gilded gate.

Occasionally, Old Mother would bring a wealthy lord to Ning Ho's private room, and she would do her best to gently pleasure him, for she knew he had paid one hundred dollars in gold for the privilege of sharing her bed for the night. She remembered distinctly her first man, an old merchant near the age of Master Chang, who had asked her if she was really a virgin or did she plan to trick him with goat's blood on the sheets? She covered her face and wept, and he believed her. Past the brief pain he inflicted and the relief she felt when he left, she remembered little else.

At the end of the second year, all the men ran together in her mind like the currents in the sea, and she could no longer recall what she had said to each in his turn, which needed wine, which preferred laughter, or only silence and gentle hands.

The time finally came when Ning Ho had only months to go on her contract. She knew several rich Tong men had asked to purchase her before her time was up, but none had been able to meet the price demanded. She was, she guessed, one of the most valuable commodities in Chinatown, perhaps in all of Portland. When she thought of such a thing, she almost smiled inside. But when she recalled all she'd had to do to earn such face, something inside her withered like a plucked flower laid on a hot rock.

Old Mother came to her and said that the Ning Yeung Tong had been offered one thousand dollars for her purchase, and she was to be married. "Aiya! He is so rich that he has fifty to work for him as fishermen. Even the fan-qui kowtow to him as he walks past. Your joss must be very good to catch the eyes of such a man, ma? And as wife, he wants you!" the old woman cackled.

Ning Ho held her breath in wonder when she heard the news. She was eighteen now, and had long ago given up any hope of being first wife to any man, much less such a one who was described.

"You obey him, or the bock tow doy, the hatchetmen, will come for you!" Old Mother warned.

Ning Ho knew she had no choice in the matter, even had she wanted to refuse the wedding. The Six Companies ran Chinatown and all within it, and the laws of the territory, it was said, stopped at Pine, the first street where the sojourners lived. "What clan is he?" she asked.

Old Mother set her thin lips firmly. "He is of the tangka," she said, "of Kwang Tung province."

Ning Ho gasped. "Of the boat-people? From a district known for its bandits? Why . . . they use eggs as money and never step foot on land. It is impossible! I am from the house of Ning, and never would my father allow—"

But Old Mother shouted her to silence. "Your father is the Ning Yeung Tong, you stupid sow, and the old ways mean nothing in the land of the barbarians!" She began to laugh coarsely. "His yang will be ample for your yin, I wager, and even if his male root is shriveled past all life, you will serve him eagerly." She went from the room, shaking her head at the young girl's foolishness.

Ning Ho had learned to act in the small things she could affect, while she pondered the large things she could not. And so, she concentrated on her good fortune to come. At least, there would be no mother-in-law to scold her. Two spoons in the same bowl could not help but knock together, but alone, she would be tai-tai, head mistress of his house at once without waiting for another to die. By the blessings of the gods, she might even bear him sons in time.

That night, she sat up late, watching the moths beat against the glass lantern, striving mightily to get to the flame, the source of the seductive light that lured them. She thought of all the men who had passed through her chambers; many she could barely recall. They had each wanted something from her, something she sensed quickly and then tried to give to them. Many wanted only to be admired; some wanted to be consoled. Most sought to take away some of her beauty and keep it for their own. She had often been asked for a keepsake, some small memento that they might cherish, which would warm them, when they were back in the mines or upriver, working on the railroads. When she could, she gave them something gladly, even if it was only a bit of linen she had worn next to her skin.

As she watched, one moth beat frenziedly against the glass, exhausting himself in determined circles, seeking some way to get closer to the light. On an impulse, she lifted the globe, let him fly into the flame, catch fire, and die. That night, she finally got to sleep by tallying in her mind all the old men in her village who had taken younger wives and had healthy sons within just a few years.

The fortune-teller had decreed that a certain day, ten days away, would be the most lucky time for her wedding, and so there was little time for the presentation of a hundred wedding cakes, fire-crackers, pigs' feet, geese, and other gifts, as would have arrived had they been in Guangzhou. But two days before the wedding, she received her wedding robes, delivered by her groom's manservant, and Old Mother and her slaves gathered about her in awe.

"He must be truly richer than the Emperor himself," sighed the old woman, "to spend silver on such robes in a barbarian land. I hope you will remember my many kindnesses, my daughter, when you are his tai-tai and eating white fowl every day."

Ning Ho fingered the rich red silks carefully, scarcely hearing her. In the back of her mind, she heard her mother's voice, and she longed to have her near. How she would have wept with joy to see her daughter so honored!

Back in the village, of course, her father would have nailed her into her coffin alive, shrieking for mercy, before he would have let her marry a tangka. But in this land, where so many barbarians were in positions of face and power, where everything seemed back-wards, a tangka could send red robes for the most beautiful sing-song girl in the city.

On the day of her wedding, she ate little, for she feared swallow-ing anything that might disturb the good omens. Her hair was oiled with jasmine, so slick that a fly's foot would slip on its surface. It was bound for the first time in the matron's knot, close to the back of her neck, and her face was covered by a heavy veil.

She was led from her chambers and seated in a high sedan chair in the front room of the house. Outside, she could hear the sound of fireworks and horns.

She was trembling, and she pressed her hands together to warm them. From a tiny slit in the side of the veil, she could see that the sedan was as richly decorated as her wedding robes. From behind her, she heard Old Mother and the servants begin the ritual wailing which was proper whenever a bride left her home, and she had to smother a startled laugh at their hypocrisy.

The wedding sedan moved slowly through the Chinese streets, preceded by a manservant carrying a large lighted lantern. Crowds of people gathered on the walkways, staring as the procession moved along. Ning Ho heard the admiring comments as she sat within the privacy of the red lacquered litter, and she smiled, carefully, so as not to disturb her face powder. Weddings in the land of the gold mountains were rare; formal weddings were unheard of, she knew.

When they reached the center of Chinatown, at Second and Alder, the horns screeched a signal, and the orchestra from the new theater poured out into the streets. She heard a flute, lyres, drums, and cymbals join the trumpets, and the gay noise was deafening. No evil spirits could possibly stand this din and will surely be chased away, she thought. How gracious it is of my groom to provide such face.

Her litter made its way out of familiar streets and down the back alleys of Portland. Now, instead of throngs of onlookers, they gathered little attention. Those few fan-qui who stopped to stare merely shook their heads in wonder, and a small pack of street children ran after her litter shouting,

> Chink, chink, Chinaman
> Sitting on a rail,
> 'Long came a white man
> And cut off his tail!

She could not understand their shouts and assumed that they hollered in excitement at the beauty and magnificence of the procession.

She peeked through a crack in the panels and watched the city rock by. It had grown quickly in the three years since she'd arrived. There were fewer horses in the streets now, and more of the metal carts she'd seen years ago—streetcars, the fan-qui called them. The white buildings were becoming grander and more crowded together, some reaching higher than the heavy black cords that crisscrossed the sky. The streets themselves were hard-packed with some substance that kept the dust from flying and the mud from miring, and as they passed the new railroad station, she stared at the great dragonlike engine which snorted and puffed, loading and unloading passengers.

There were more white women than ever on the streets, and though they still looked grotesque, she thought, they were no longer frightening. She knew that the fan-qui sometimes visited the

Tong brothels, for the girls whispered that the men were large, hairy, and intensely curious about how Celestial women were made. Some seemed disappointed, they giggled, and swore that there were no differences at all, as though tiny hands and feet, silken skin, and beautiful black hair and eyes were no differences worth counting. She shrugged. Fortunately, she had never had to serve such a man. Now, thanks to her excellent joss, she never would.

After several hours of travel, the litter stopped before a small wagon sitting by the docks. As she sat within, her litter was lifted and placed on the wagonbed. An unseen man clucked to the horses, and the wagon jerked into motion, bearing her up a dusty road. After what had seemed a season of journey, the wagon lurched to a stop.

Ning Ho sat silently within the litter, listening with every nerve, waiting for her groom's servants to help her balance her headdress as she stepped out. She expected, at any moment, to hear the voices of women, perhaps a friend or relation, calling, "Gung shi! Gung shi!"—the felicitous phrase that would welcome her to her groom's house and invite her to step down from the palanquin. She was astonished when a man's voice called, with some impatience, "Ning Ho, you are welcome in the house of Ah Fook. Come forth and pay proper respects to your husband."

She frowned. This voice sounded old and stern, and his immediate reference to paying respect did not please her, nor did the public shouting of her family name. But she adjusted her veil to cover her face completely and extended one slender white hand.

"We are not in the old country now," the voice said briskly, "and I cannot lead you about like a blind child. Put up your veil and step down please, and we will go inside."

She gasped audibly, for it was against all custom for a bride's face to be exposed to strangers or even to her own husband before they were properly bound. She hesitated for an instant, but he was moving away. I have no choice, she thought swiftly, and I cannot sit here for the rest of my days. She tossed back her veil gracefully and stepped from the litter, her head down, as was fitting.

The man took her hand wordlessly, and led her inside a cabin. It was a solid little house; one room in the front was for receiving guests, a side room held a table, chairs, and a stove, and the back room was for sleeping. Her groom led her immediately to the bed and stood beside her. She sensed when he was about to sit on its edge, and they both moved at the same time, each taking a place on the bridal bed. He tried to pin a portion of her skirt under him as he sat, but she moved too quickly and indeed, a fold of her robe lapped over his trousers. This was an omen, of course. If he had succeeded in sitting on her robes, it would have meant she was to be submissive to him all of her life. But her dress had lapped over him, which meant that she would preserve some independence in this union. She glanced sideways at him under her lashes. He was over twice her age, she guessed, but his face looked strong and alert. A tangka, she remembered, and she glanced at his hands. They were firm and well formed, but there were creases around his palms from handling fishing lines. And for all the wrinkles on his broad brow, there were no laugh lines around his mouth.

She sighed inwardly and straightened her spine. This one would need much tenderness to bring forth his soul. She knew that tenderness was the strongest weapon any woman could bear, and she vowed to bring at least that much into this man's heart. I shall do my best to please him, she thought, if he is kind to me. If he is not, I will—but she could think of no other action she might easily take.

Suddenly, he spoke. "I would see your crescent moons," he said, gesturing to her skirts. She was startled by his boldness, especially since he had never once been to the House of Joyous Relief as a guest. But she extended her feet slightly from beneath her robes, turning her face away, waiting for him to either accept or reject her at that moment. If he was not pleased with her, he could send her back to the Tong, claiming to have been swindled by feet that had not had the final cut.

He said nothing, but only nodded curtly, rising to bring two glasses of wine. She took a sip from one as he drank from the other. Then, they exchanged glasses, and each sipped from the same spot the other had touched. They stood and bowed deeply to each other, and they were married.

Ah Fook was the head boss of the Demers cannery, and fifty-three Chinese labored under his direction. He had come from Kwang Tung province ten years before with nets, his fishing gear, and a bedroll. He went to work as a butcher at the Demers cannery on the juncture of the Willamette and the Columbia rivers. He worked diligently for five years, a quiet methodical man, quick with his hands and sure with the Sheffield, a heavy knife curved at one end, capable of slicing through the thick backbone of a forty-pound Columbia River Chinook salmon like a paring knife through a ripe tomato.

The fish were caught in weirs by the whites, for no Chinaman was allowed to hook, net, or bait the salmon. They were boated to the cannery and piled by the thousands on the dock. The first worker cut off their heads; the next slashed open the bellies, throwing the entrails into the river and dropping the huge fish into the bleeding vat. Salmon bled like bulls, and most had to go through three vats, each filled with water, before their flesh was clean. The third Chinaman chopped the fish into tin-size chunks. A fourth dropped the chunks into brine; a fifth loaded the flesh into cans. Another Chinaman soldered the tops tightly, and finally, the cans were lowered, five hundred at a time, into boiling water to seal them firmly.

Ah Fook had worked at all levels of the cannery, moving up and down the line as the gang boss sent him, sliming the salmon, butchering them, filling the cans, sealing them, stacking the boxes, labeling them, and loading the wagons to be taken to the docks or to the railroad. After four years, the foreman named him China boss, leader of the whole crew. The only whites at the cannery were Caleb Demers, and he was rarely seen for he lived in Portland; his foreman and son, Isaac Demers; and the numbers man, who tallied up the books and gave out the silver at the end of the season.

As China boss, Ah Fook was entitled to temporary ownership of the small yellow wooden house at the back of the meadow, and so he was the only Chinaman to have a place to bring a wife. He had saved his wages for seven years to pay for a woman, for he knew that nothing else could bring him so much face or pleasure.

The rest of the crew lived in the China house, a bunkhouse boarded horizontally rather than vertically according to Chinese fashion, and lined with wooden pallets. Once, Demers had surprised the men by adding a mattress to every pallet. But the next morning, each mattress was stacked neatly outside in the dew, and the crew slept ever after on boards covered with their own blankets.

The China house had its own cook, of course, hired out of Portland for the six-month salmon season from the same Tong roster as the crew. He kept a hog pen on one side of the kitchen and a duck pen on the other, and the smell of duck fried in peanut oil was sometimes the only thing that would drive the odor of fish from a man's nostrils. Even across the meadow, the smell blew in with the wind off the river and stayed in the little house day and night. After a week or so, Ning Ho never noticed it, except on her husband's hands.

When her husband first saw her in her linen, in his bed, he fell on her and took her with a quick eager laugh. She did not mind, really, for she had expected little else. Even her wealthiest guests had often acted in such a manner, like peasants, too hurried to be polite. But when he tried to take her again in the night in the same manner, she slowed him with her hands, held him over her with her legs, teased him into gently exploring her body to give them both pleasure, and made him linger once inside her. After all, she told herself, he is old and cannot act the young rooster every night and live long. Soon, they were more accustomed to one another, and Ah Fook even smiled as he came in the door for his evening meal.

The great riches Old Mother had spoken of must be in the bucket that was hidden under the bed, Ning Ho thought, for her husband certainly did not mean to live like a wealthy lord. For the first time since she'd been on the *Witchcraft,* there were no maidservants to dress her hair and tend to her toilet. There was no cook to tempt her with sweetmeats when she awoke with wind in her bowels. If there was to be a meal on the table at night, there was no one but her to cook it, and aside from the hog pen out back and the carefully tended garden plot in the meadow, no food to cook it from. It was seven miles to Portland, and when Ning Ho suggested that perhaps the money should go to a Tong bank, Ah Fook only said curtly, "Money is like a man's wife. Strangers should not have their hands on it."

Ning Ho had known little training in her father's house, for until the last year as his daughter, there were many servants to do these things. But she learned quickly, and after several practice attempts and long whispered conversations with the cook at the crew house, conversations that she made him vow never to reveal lest her husband lose face, she was able to put simple meals on the table. Fortunately, Ah Fook did not expect her to be as adept in the kitchen as she was in his bed, so he was patient while she coaxed the rice to steam properly, fought with the layers of dust in the little cabin, and learned the difference between weeds and onion sprouts in the garden rows.

When she was finished with her work, she liked most to walk to the river, vast and shining in the sun. The path from the meadow to its banks took a wending way through a land which seemed to her to be inhabited by fairies and wood spirits. There were more colors of green than she knew names for, and the great trees and ferns made her feel small and ghostlike as she trod silently through their domain. Hundreds of feet above her head, the birds sang and nested in the sun, but below, where she walked, the air was damp and cool and shadowed. Newborn sprouts pushed their heads up overnight, crowding from the skeletons of moss-covered logs. The river was always cold, even on the warmest day, and in its mirrored jade surfaces, she could see the reflections of rows of aspen, the dark cedars behind them, and the tall mountains beyond them all. The roaring of the rapids was like the constant beating of a great heart.

In her mind's eye, under the surface of the river she could see the huge salmon moving in the depths, swirling through the riffles, jumping occasionally, a glint of sun on silver scales, a solitary splash, and by the time she turned her head, there was only a ripple. The salmon are such strong, godlike fish, she thought. The men called them bluebacks and "June hogs," the fat-bellied fish that threaded their way past the jaws of seals and sharks, through the islands, past the thundering currents and up the river. Moved by fierce and ancient rhythms, they fought to reach the sea and then to come back again, like the winds which moved up the river gorge in the storm season, buffeting themselves to death on the rocks.

In China, she thought, such a fish would be revered as sacred. Ah Fook had told her how the fish arrived upriver, bruised and scarred, how they went without food throughout their journey, and how, with the last ounce of her strength, the she-salmon hollowed out a nest in the stream gravel and hovered above it, enticing the male. Ning Ho could imagine the patient resignation of such a creature, waiting for her mate, waiting for that which would make her life have meaning. The male salmon swam tail to tail with her, Ah Fook said, and as she laid down her thousands of pink eggs, her yin, he released his yang, a stream of white milt. And six months later, her children start downriver, drawn to the sea, to live out their destinies.

Sometimes as she sat on the riverbank, she could see round the bend, Chin Gum, the sweeper, do his t'ai-chi movements, facing the great water. He would come while the others ate their noon meal, an old man, near seventy, with spectacles as thick as ale bottles. He stood on one leg like a gangly heron, his jaw fierce in concentration, forming intricate hand and foot patterns in the silence.

He never spoke, of course, for that would have been unseemly. None of the men ever addressed her directly, for she was wife to another man. If they had to refer to her in conversation, they might say, "Ask Ah Fook's wife if she would have the feet from this hog today," or "I see that Ah Fook's wife has made the melons bloom early this year." Indeed, no one spoke to her at all, save Ah Fook himself. And so, to watch the old sweeper and share the river with him, even though he never once looked in her direction, made her feel less lonely.

The crew worked from dawn to dusk with one hour off for their noon meal, six days a week, twelve to fourteen hours a day. When the fish were running fast, Ah'Fook had told her, the butchers could clean and cut twelve tons of fish a day, each man slicing a thirty-pound salmon in less than a minute. The season lasted from spring through the beginning of winter, and though each man was paid only at the end of his six-month contract, somehow each managed to scramble together enough silver to lay it down in the kite contests and mah-jong games that shattered the peace of the China house. Ah Fook rarely took part in these games, though he often sat in the open door of the cabin at dusk and listened to the laughter and jeers coming from across the meadow.

Gradually, Ning Ho began to feel at home in the yellow cabin at the edge of the meadow. To her surprise, the garden had become a true source of delight. At first, the hours spent with a cramped and numbed back over the close-set rows of turnips, kale, and onions were tedious beyond all endurance. She would stand and feel her muscles moan, wipe her sweat from her nose and forehead with the crook of her arm, and gaze over to the river, wishing for all the world to be a salmon or a waterfowl, anything rather than a be-grimed and laboring dirt-beetle. But then she had unbound her feet, ignoring the cramping pain that shot into long-unused muscles and tendons. Each day, she forced herself to work the soil barefoot or in loose slippers, feeling her feet broaden and become more strong. "I have been blessed once more," she told herself. "May the gods bring my mother joy for her far-seeing eyes."

She forced her feet into small slippers in the evening, that Ah Fook might not be disgusted by their new ungainliness. But secretly, she began to relish those moments when she felt the warm soil under her heels. She began to see the beauty of the earth, stretching away beneath her feet, as the last rays of the sun left the sky and the river mists moved up over the field. Long rows of cabbage, jade green and plump, yellow squash like slivers of sun, rhubarb and spinach, and green beans, dusty and firm to her fingers—and behind it all, the dark velvet woods threw cool shadows over the land.

At first, it had seemed she was a slave to these clamoring buds and shoots and roots, always calling to her, always needing water, weeding, tending, like a thousand infants squalling for their amahs. But now, she was aware of a feeling of kinship with this land, a shimmering bond of deep fulfillment, a vast tide of life. And to her satisfaction, she found that the rows and rows of growing things responded well to her hands. Even Ah Fook remarked that the yield had never been so plentiful nor so healthy.

Soon, there were more vegetables than the whole crew could consume, and Ning Ho began to think what to do with the bushels of cabbages, beans, and onions which would go to waste. She asked Ah Fook what he had done before with the surplus from the garden.

"There has never been so much," he said blankly. "I suppose you had better plough it under if the men cannot eat it."

She looked at him in dismay. To waste the food in such a way would be like spilling her own blood, she felt. As she looked out over the dew-washed plants, she could almost imagine the droplets as beads of her own sweat rather than water from the sky. "Can we not sell the vegetables and keep the money for ourselves?" she asked.

"Where would we take them, woman? It is too far to town, and I have no time to fool with turnips and beans. No, not even if the silver is to end in my own pockets."

"If I can find a way?"

He nodded absently. "Yes, yes. Do as you please with it."

After thinking about it for a day, she finally hung two baskets of fresh vegetables on her bien da, her pole, balanced it on her slim shoulders, and walked down the wagon path to the Demers house. Ah Fook had said that the Demers clan lived in a large two-story farmhouse, surrounded by porches and banks of roses. Ning Ho knew instinctively that this was not what Ah Fook had in mind when he gave her leave to dispose of her vegetables as she pleased. In fact, she knew that if the whites complained of her presence on their road, he would lose face and certainly shout at her. But she could not bear the thought of burying her harvest or leaving it to rot in the sun, and so she walked on, ignoring the throbbing in her feet, drawn by a strong desire to see those roses and the face of a white woman up close just once, even though it would most certainly be only a maidservant.

The sun was hot that day, and it was almost a mile between the cabin and the Demers house, with the cannery sitting between them. She found that her feet hurt but not unbearably, so long as she balanced her pole properly and moved with the small mincing steps that kept her hips swaying and her baskets bobbing. Finally, she reached the end of the wagon path, and the Demers house shone in the sun before her.

It was splendid, it seemed to her, jutting up from the dark woods with a sweeping view of the river beyond. As Ah Fook had said, the roses, all red and pink and white, clustered in heavy-headed and brilliant profusion against the sides of the porch. The scent of them hung in the heavy summer air and mingled with the heat and the dust. She stopped and put down her baskets for a moment, wiping her face and smoothing her hair. She was not at all afraid, and some part of her wondered at her curious willingness to approach the fan-qui, brazen as the village matchmaker. Surely, they cannot be insulted, she reassured herself. After all, I will not ask them for money. I make only a call of friendship. And if they find my vegetables pleasing, perhaps they may offer to buy another time.

She shouldered the baskets again, walked to the porch, and knocked softly on the screen door. But to her surprise, no maidservant answered her knock. Instead, Isaac Demers swung the door wide and grinned down at her. "Well!" he said cheerfully. "The China boss's wife!"

She was struck dumb, and what little voice she had left was railing at herself inside for being so stupid. This had happened to her before, she cursed, she had imagined something that had no basis in reality at all, had been swept along by her picture of how things would be, only to bump headlong into the way things really were. She felt a flush travel up her body to the roots of her hair, and her eyes watered with humiliation. She bowed her head in silence.

He bent and peered into her face, smiling quizzically. "Don't be afraid, mei-mei. I won't bite you."

Mei-mei, he called her! Little sister. Then she realized that he must have heard these words from the China crew at some time during his boyhood. She raised her head slowly, inwardly scolding herself for her cowardice. "Your pardon, boss," she said in halting English. "I bring gifts from China boss to house of Demers." She held out her baskets hesitantly, pulling aside the wet ferns which she had carefully wrapped about the vegetables to protect them from the sun. The plump tops of the radishes poked out, wet and ruddy.

To her amazement, he laughed again. "You walked all the way here just to bring us some radishes?"

Now, she cursed herself for being a fool as well as a coward. She turned to go, but he caught her arm.

"Wait, now. Didn't mean to hurt your feelings, Missus Fook. You just set here in the shade, and I'll be right back."

She sank down slowly to the porch, her eyes wide with wonder. How coarse these barbarians are, she marveled. Not only are they incapable of graciously accepting a gift, but they feel free to lay their hands on strangers as though they were lovers! She recalled how her guests had complained that the fan-qui were fond of shaking hands and clapping arms about a man's shoulders, laughing in his ear.

And yet, one had to admit that they were amiable enough. He had called her Fook, an inaccurate and even inexcusable breach—if he had to refer to her name at all, it should have been by her own family name, Ning, for no decent woman took her husband's family name unless she was an orphan or a concubine. But he seemed kindly, and surprisingly young, up close. She prayed quickly to Buddha that this man would not clap her about the shoulders, for she would surely flinch or screech with shock. And then she would have to throw herself in the river for shame.

Soon, he was back, slamming the screen door cheerfully, and sitting down beside her. He thrust a glass of cold lemon drink in her hand. He tapped his glass to hers lightly and drank, watching her over the edge. She drank slowly, luxuriating in the sweet-sour taste of the cool lemon sliding down her throat.

His eyes were blue and transparent as windows on the sky, and as he watched her, she became vaguely aware of the sheen of sweat on her nose, her black hair loosened about her neck, and the press of her trousers against her thighs. They sat for a long moment in silence. He said, "Say, it was good of you to come," and he glanced at her sideways. "But I'll bet this was your idea and not Ah Fook's, right?"

She smiled shyly and turned away.

"I get the picture," he grinned. "You made them grow, so you figure to take the profits from them as well. And that's fair enough, to my mind."

She frowned slightly. "A gift," she said firmly.

He stared at her a long moment. Finally, he chuckled and stood up. "Come with me for a minute. I want to show you something."

He led her back behind the house and there, stretched out for a hundred li in four directions, were a thousand rows of corn, peas, tomatoes, berries, and twenty other fruits and vegetables she could not even name. Ringing the vast fields were fifty fruit trees, heavily laden with apples and cherries and pears. "We appreciate the thought," he said softly, "But I'd hate to see you make another trip out here, carrying that pole the whole way for nothing."

Once again, she flushed hotly. She felt almost like spitting on her meager little baskets, so wretched did they seem next to this rich bounty spread out before her. Never before, even in the rich lands near the Pearl River, had she seen such fertility.

"We send crops in to the city twice a week," he said casually. "Over that wagon road you came up. Pa's been experimenting with different fruits out there, looking to find one that'd can good."

She watched him as he spoke, his hands gesturing over the land, his eyes moving from the edges of the fields to the trees beyond. He is a big man, she thought. The largest I have ever known. His arms and back are strong; his face is lined with laughter, even though he is young. His hair is brown like the earth, and it curls softly about his brows and just over his ears. He seemed like a strange earth god, ruler of the soil and the growing things.

"You are so tall," she murmured. "You must have been growing very long time, yes?" And not much older than myself, she thought.

He laughed. "Long enough to get the job done, I guess."

She was suddenly, intensely, aware of the fact that they stood together, alone in the field, with no one around. After today, she would have no face left before this man, she winced, but there was no sense in losing Ah Fook's as well. She bowed briefly and said, "I thank you for showing me your land." Then a thought struck her, and from somewhere, she plucked a last piece of bravado. "Please. You say you send twice a week?" She rushed on before she could lose her nerve. "If I carry here, you take mine to sell also?" When she saw his hesitation, she added quickly, "I give half my money to you?"

His eyes crinkled up at the corners. "You're a sharp gal, mei-mei. How old are you, anyway? Eighteen? Twenty? Couldn't be much more than that, I'd wager."

She didn't understand all he said, but she knew better than to speak again. She shifted her aching feet with impatience.

"Does ol' Ah Fook know he's got a Yankee trader on his hands?"

At the mention of his name, she panicked. "Please. My husband does not know I come. He would"—she hesitated, searching for the words—"he would fly with rage."

The man put back his head and laughed then, a loud joyous explosion of glee. It had been years since she had heard a man laugh so, and she giggled with delight, not quite sure why she did so.

"Sure, well, I can see that he would, at that. But there's no harm done, far's I know. You bring your stuff to me on Tuesdays and Fridays, and I'll see it goes." He chuckled. "No need to split your profits." He put out his hand and winked. "And no need to tell Ah Fook, either. You've got yourself a deal."

She grinned hugely, remembering to put her hand over her mouth. Men hated the sight of a woman's open red mouth, Old Mother had said, and she did not want to offend him. But he took her hand away gently.

"Don't do that," he said softly. "You've got a beautiful smile."

She was no longer startled by his audaciousness; indeed, she would have expected almost anything at that moment. She turned and scanned the land, counting up the different crops in her mind. She would grow the vegetables that this Demers man did not, she decided, and she would push the edges of her little field farther into the woods, now that she was assured nothing would be wasted. I have a secret with a white barbarian, she thought in amazement. Soon, of course, I will tell Ah Fook, but only when I can go to him with silver in my hands.

Isaac Demers watched her walk away, her hips swaying slightly, her black hair bobbing. Somehow, for the first time, he saw his own fields with a new eye. He recalled how her face had glowed as she looked over his rows of vegetables and fruit trees, as though she worshiped at a private altar.

He turned to survey the land. She was right, he told himself, nodding his head unconsciously. You couldn't ask for more. He knew she wouldn't understand if he'd called it God's country, like his mother did. But he'd seen the same sentiment in her eyes, just the same. And damn if it didn't make him feel good just to be next to such a plucky little thing, to catch just a whiff of the wonder she felt.

Ning Ho walked back down the road in a daze of happiness, recalling each nuance of the conversation, wishing she had said this or that. But inside, she was very proud, even smug, that she had found the courage to make such a bargain happen. This, she reasoned, was how great houses were founded. By a small step into new ways, with courage and a good deal of luck. This was how dynasties began. Well, she certainly had the luck, she knew, and she was discovering the courage. Now, if she could only bring forth a son upon which to build this great future, her joy would be complete.

Ning Ho had thought she would be with child before this. She was careful to encourage Ah Fook's ardor at auspicious times and had hung red papers which read "Healthy Sons, Ripe Grain, and Fat Fowl" over their bed. The red fortunes came from one of Chinatown's most respected astrologers . . . but still, no seed lodged in her belly. In her own village, there would have been a midwife to help with charms and spells, but here in this barbarian land, the closest woman was an old Indian priestess who lived in a shack by the river.

Ning Ho had seen her many times, gathering driftwood along the bank. She was more bent and wizened than even Old Mother, shuffling along with a blanket about her shoulders, usually accompanied by a slave. When Ning Ho questioned Ah Fook, he said only, "She is a healer for the savages, and the motherless fools come from many lis around to listen to her talk nonsense in eight directions."

"Does she speak only to the barbarian gods?"

Ah Fook moved his tongue around a large piece of pork and said, "How should I know? Old Master Demers goes to her cabin sometimes, probably to tell her to clean up the piles of stinking fishheads on the beach, but no one else goes near."

"Then she must speak the fan-qui tongue."

"Aiya, I have a curious monkey at my table, ma? I don't know, and it is of no concern of ours. Is there no more dau fu, then, wife?" And she dared not ask him more.

Several days passed, and Ning Ho kept one eye bent toward the river while she worked her vegetable rows. When she once again saw the old siwash walking along the water, she dropped her hoe, hid her face under her broad straw hat, and ventured nearer. She followed the woman at some distance until she disappeared into a shabby cabin, marked only by a well-worn path. Ning Ho took a deep breath and scratched softly at her cedar door.

The door opened, and a withered, shrunken crone beckoned her inside. Her long wispy hair was white and thin, but her black eyes darted over Ning Ho with the eager curiosity of a child, and her wrinkled face was open. "Well, and who is there?" she asked calmly in a small voice, no trace of a quiver.

"A stranger, Old Mother," Ning Ho said nervously in faltering English. "Wife of Ah Fook, China boss."

"There are no strangers to this door," the siwash said gently. "You are welcome here."

Ning Ho looked into her dark, restless eyes and felt a surge of hope. This one has seen the river flow for more years than I have been alive, she thought. She stepped inside and stared at the priestess, sensing an immediate kinship. Though her head was misshapen and her skin was brown, her eyes were slanted over wide cheekbones much like Ning Ho's own, as though, long ago, they had lived in the same village or had been of neighboring clans.

Ning Ho pushed the thought of Ah Fook's scowl from her mind and said quickly, before she could lose her courage, "I have come, Madame Priestess, for ginseng to put fire in my man's stalk, for I am an empty vessel without seed."

The old woman looked her over carefully. "Well, and you are a Celestial, neh? But do not call me 'madam,' little sister. My people do not use such white words. The name my mother gave me is all I need. Ilchee, Moon-woman, you may call me. I am a Kellalle woman, a shaman, but I cannot bring a babe to your belly." She gestured to her pallet, a dark slab of cedar in a shadowed corner. "Sit here, child."

Ning Ho sat and looked about quietly. The cabin was damp and ancient. Cedar boxes of herbs and bone talismans hung from the walls. The old woman sat beside her, painfully arranging her bent and crooked limbs on the dirt floor. "Why do you come to Ilchee and not to your own kind? My people tell me that the sojourners have strong medicines of their own."

"My people are far away, and if my man knew I asked for such a thing . . ." Ning Ho said, her voice falling away, "it would be a great shame. Will your gods help a stranger?"

Ilchee shrugged. "They are not *my* gods, sojourner, but the land's.

You are here, and so perhaps they will listen." She bade Ning Ho lie on the floor, and from a box over her head, she took herbs and sand, making an outline around her body. She chanted strange guttural songs over her, rubbing and pulling at her limbs, patting her abdomen with gentle, searching fingers.

"Aii, Raven, come to my eyes, speak to my heart," Ning Ho heard her sing, but then she could not understand the rest of the old woman's chantings, and she relaxed under her hands, feeling a warmth begin in her loins and move into her belly.

It has been so long, so long, Ning Ho smiled to herself, since I have felt hands with such comfort, and her mind whirled away to a season long ago when she sat on her mother's lap and felt the sandlewood comb move smoothly through her long, black hair, heard the words of murmuring love in her ear, and knew that nothing and no one could harm her within that protective circle of arms.

Ilchee spoke, and her low voice drew Ning Ho back immediately to the present. "You shall have the seed you seek," the old woman said. "It is floating on the waters within you even now, searching for its resting place. Raven has told me this."

Ning Ho sat up, her eyes wide. "When?"

Ilchee smiled. "You believe, then? You are not like the whites who say, 'Seeing is believing'? "

Ning Ho frowned in bewilderment. "They say this? In my land, we say that a man does not see a thing as it is, but as *he* is. This is true, ma?"

"And my people say a thing must be believed to be seen. Well, and we are not so different after all, small sister."

"But the child will come soon, you have seen it?" Ning Ho asked, her eagerness making her impatient.

The priestess rubbed her eyes tiredly. "That I cannot tell, so-journer." Her voice sounded suddenly troubled or vexed. "But you must keep from the whites, for they will bring evil to your people." She sighed wearily. "As they do to mine."

Ning Ho said, bewildered, "Yet your cabin is on their lands . . ."

"But my door faces the river," Ilchee said firmly. "I am here only to keep peace in my son's heart."

"Your son?"

"My son and my son's son."

Ning Ho's eyes widened further and her mouth opened in wonder. "The Old Master is your son? And the Young Master—?"

"My grandson. Few know this, sojourner, for few need to know. When my son married and crossed the river, he wanted his old mother near him. I would not live in the city of the whites, and I cannot leave my people. Here, they find me well enough, and I can still hear the gods over the rush of the waters."

"I have never seen your grandson follow the path to your cabin."

"He follows his own path," Ilchee said mildly. "He has heard the old tales of his father's people since his ears took root. But each must find his own stories. He has chosen his mother's people, and that is well enough."

Ning Ho scowled. "Still, he is son of your son, and it is only seemly that he—"

Ilchee laughed warmly and her sunken chest shook with delight. "I need no Celestial to defend me. But if you would like it, I will be your friend." The old woman fluttered a lined husk of a hand up and gently touched Ning Ho's shoulder. "The river can be a lonely place, neh?"

Ning Ho ducked her head in flustered pleasure. When she raised it again, the old woman had gone to the door and was holding it ajar. "Come often," she said softly, "whenever your ears grow tired of the words of men."

And so, Ning Ho found herself following the path to Ilchee's cabin frequently that season, and she came to know the old woman's words as wise, her heart deep as the river itself. Ah Fook noticed her detours and asked querulously, "What is it that my wife finds so important in an old siwash's ramblings, eh? Are you a child, that you need a lao-tai-tai, an old grandmother, to listen to your prattles? If you have need of things to keep you busy, there are work pants there that stink of fish oil, worse even than that old woman does, I am sure—"

"And they will be clean again before you need them," Ning Ho replied firmly. "Do the men taunt you because I speak to the si-wash?"

He sputtered with indignation. "Taunt me? They would not dare."

"Well then, never mind. It is well to care for the old ones, no matter whose people they are, ma? Perhaps the tangka people did not deem it necessary," she continued innocently, "but in the house of Ning, I was taught to show proper filial respect—"

"As was *I*, wife," Ah Fook bellowed. "Indeed, it is your duty to see after the old woman." He grumbled as he picked up his rice bowl to end the subject. "Just see that your *other* duties are not neglected."

Ning Ho bowed low, a silent smile of acquiescence on her lips.

In the spring of her second year at the cannery, she was weeding a rich patch of earth, readying it for the melon seeds she carried in her girdle. She had a neat pile of fish parts by her feet, meaning to feed each seed with a piece of the oily flesh to help it grow. In between bending and reaching, she became aware that she heard no birds call, and a great silence settled over the meadow.

Suddenly, as she bent over her hoe, she felt the ground begin to shudder, and she froze, staring wonderingly into space. She looked at the sprouts at her feet. They were quivering as though an erratic wind blew. The trees began to shake and hiss, and the roll of the earth grew stronger, knocking her to her knees. A huge rumble began beneath her, and she was instantly overwhelmed by the rising feel of dizzy nausea. She fell to her stomach, gripping the earth, clenching her eyes shut, moaning in fear.

The gods are surely afoot in this evil land, she thought in panic, and their great boots are stomping the ground in anger! The earth shook spasmodically, sickeningly, and she could no longer hear the river for the roar of the ground. It seemed to come from the sky as well, but she was too afraid to open her eyes and look about. Finally, she raised her head, and she heard the shouts of the men over the shriek of the earth.

They were pouring from the cannery, running in panic toward the open ground, stumbling and falling to their knees. She felt a quick surge of shame at being seen prostrate before the gods in such a way, and she tried to rise, but each time she did, a new roll tipped the earth in a wave of sliding chaos, and she gripped the weeds, the grass, the earth itself, trying to keep control.

Ah Fook was moving toward her, shouting something that she could not hear, and his knees were buckling under him as though he stood on a rocking ship. As she watched, her eyes widening in horror, a snakelike crack whipped across the ground right between them, opening a dark fissure in the earth. He dropped to his belly quickly, hiding his face in his hands. As she watched, the fissure swallowed up a whole corner of the field, one row of bean bushes, and then slid together with a grinding noise like a massive rusty gate swinging shut forever.

Behind her, she was dimly aware that a great tree shrieked, yawned, and crashed to the ground. She felt her mouth fill with liquid and her bile rose, but she fought down the vomit and willed herself to be still.

Finally, the tremors ceased, but as she began to rise, her trembling was so violent that it was as though the earth still shook. The rumbling moved away like distant thunder now, and the silence was heavy all about them. They waited, for what seemed ten ris of time. Hesitantly, a bird warbled across the silence, and Ning Ho looked down to see a small beetle crawl warily up a bean plant, waving its feelers to and fro as though to test the air. Her hands were wet with sweat. She pushed herself to her feet and looked about her.

Miraculously, the cannery, the China house, Ilchee's cabin, and her own yellow cabin still stood. Several buildings tilted slightly, and the tools she had leaned against the cabin wall were pitched about crazily. The cabin door sagged heavily to one side. As though from a great distance, she became aware that the river still coursed on, had kept moving even as the earth's roar muffled its usual rush. Somehow, that familiar sound gave her more comfort than any.

She hurried immediately to Ah Fook's side to help him stand, but he brushed her away, sensing that the men watched them. Isaac Demers called across the field from where he was crouching, dusting off his trousers. "Is everyone all right?" He looked directly at her.

She smiled, suddenly full of relief and a giddy joy at the passing of the terror. "Your land has strong gods!" she called, forgetting herself.

He laughed, again that boyish shout of pleasure that she had heard once before. "Aye, we got them hiding behind every mountain, I guess."

But Ah Fook scowled at her, and she turned away, confused by the flush which was creeping up her neck. To hide her dismay, she kneeled and brushed lightly at his trousers, casting her eyes down. He waited balefully while she cleaned him, and then strode away, back to work, the men following quietly.

She saw that the old sweeper went last behind them, slowly rising from his hands and knees. There was a dark stain at the seat of his trousers which he endeavored to cover with his jacket as he shuffled back to the cannery. She hurried to see that Ilchee was safe.

That night, the sky was filled with heavy dark clouds, edged with brown and black. The volcano that Ilchee called Loo-wit, Keeper of the Flame, had exploded across the river, sending billowing smoke and rusty-looking plumes high into the winds. The next morning when they awoke, the field was covered with thick gray ash, deep as Ning Ho's thumb. The ash clung to every surface like a light snow, powdering the trees, the rocks, the cabin, even sifting lightly over the surface of the shallows of the river.

She feared for her crops, wondering whether this was some new poison from the gods of the barbarians. But she kneeled in the dust and tasted it gingerly, letting it grit on her tongue. It was bland and cool, and when she rubbed it between her fingers, it seemed to disappear into her skin. Surely, this cannot harm the growing things, she thought to herself, or the mountains would not give birth to it. As much as the gods seem to delight in tormenting the fan-qui, they would not destroy this beautiful land.

She spent the day digging the ash into the soil and watering it thoroughly, until she was covered, quite happily, with a fine film of it all over her as well. "Earthquake," the barbarians called these tremors; "the shivers of the earth dragon," the men whispered behind their hands. Those who ignored the warnings of their own geomancers could expect little else, Ning Ho shrugged to herself. Whatever this violence was called, however, she vowed not to close her eyes next time the earth moved. She wanted to see just what was happening, no matter how it might terrify her to watch.

There grew a certain coolness between Ah Fook and Ning Ho after the great quake, as though he nursed a secret anger within his heart, yet he would not speak of it. She sensed that he had been shamed by her outspokenness to the white boss, and even her visits to Ilchee's cabin. She knew he thought he had lost face by her brashness.

In the private places of her mind, she grew impatient with his coldness. After all, she told herself, I did not speak first. Nor did I say anything unseemly. It was not my fault he spoke to me—to all of us, in fact—and would he have me blush and stammer like a stupid Hakka wench? I would not have spoken at all, she assured herself, except as a courtesy. The man can choke on his cursed pride.

When he continued to turn away from her in the bed at night, she felt her own pride harden against him. Well, for this was she keeping herself clean and fragrant and full of prayers to the goddess of mercy so that the old bone might get a son? She might as well come to his bed with her feet still stinking of fish oil, for all the mind he paid her, she muttered to herself. Who wants a son off such a man as he anyway, she frowned. Men were children their whole lives long, she sighed, for all their windy talk.

She recalled all the times she had pushed the sponge deep inside her to keep a seed from rooting in her womb, all the times Old Mother had warned her that if she found herself with child, she would be turned out to the street to beg or starve. She remembered the stark days of panic she had endured when her flux was late, certain that she would bear a bastard in this barbarian land. And now, the final irony: once she wanted a son, the gods were laughing up their sleeves at her despite Ilchee's reassurances, and her husband turned away in the night.

Sometimes she dreamed strange, hot visions of passion. She saw herself rolling in pleasure beneath a faceless man, arching her hips to meet him in a frenzy of desire, her black hair falling across their naked bodies, his hands gripping her surely and tenderly. When she awoke, she was wet and weary, but she harbored a secret joy inside her that carried her all through the day.

More bad news came upriver. At Hawk Creek, twenty fan-qui attacked a Chinese mining camp in the night. The whites wore cow heads on their shoulders, and leaped among the sleeping Chinese mooing and bellowing, waving pistols and clubs in the air. The Chinese scattered in fright, and the whites stole sixteen bags of gold, totaling nearly twenty thousand dollars in value.

When the men gathered to whisper the details, Ah Fook shouted angrily, "Aiya! You would not see me run in the night from bits of hide and horns, my friends. If the fan-qui want a fight, let them come to the China house one night, and we will give it to them, ma?"

Many of the men agreed with him, but several muttered behind his back that it was easy to bark of bravery in the night when one's master kept the leash tight. The men had no more than calmed themselves over this latest insult, when three men showed up at the cannery, demanding to see both the China boss and Isaac Demers. Isaac came out of his office glowering, for he had already heard of the men's visits to other canneries along the river.

"You know what we come for, Demers," the sheriff called to him.

"Aye, I heard," Demers said. "And I also heard you get a pretty piece of the action, Sheriff."

"Hell, what do you care?" The man grinned. "So we take twenty-four bucks out 'a each John's pay. So what? It ain't no skin off your hide, and I'm thinkin' you oughta sleep better nights, knowin' their money's goin' to pay for extry deputies to police their filthy shacks. We get more shootin's and rapes out at that Chinee slum than we get in the whole city put together. And more fires too, with their heathen rockets and their stinkin' incense. I'm damned if I mean to pay more taxes for 'em!"

"And *you* take more'n six dollars out of each tax, right?"

The sheriff rolled his eyes as though in silent supplication to an unseen god. "And *I'm* the one's got to collect it, ain't I? You think that's a pleasure, Demers? Now, line 'em up, or I'll do it for you. I got to read the law to 'em so's they know why their pockets are light come October."

Demers crossed his arms and didn't move. "They only make a dollar a day, man," he said quietly.

"Aw, come on, Demers," the old man whined. "Do I got to see your pa over such as this? Every boss on the river's cooperated, you want to be the only one called a Chinee lover? Hell, they don't do nobody no good, you know. They make a dollar a day, an' they spend ten cents an' send the rest back to some squatty ol' village in China. Lotsa folks'd like to run 'em out on a rail. I say let 'em stay, but they got to pay their way, is all. Now, line 'em up," he glared suddenly. "Or would you rather I haul 'em out myself?"

Isaac stood a long moment, staring at the ground. Then he turned slowly, said a few low words to Ah Fook, and walked back into his office. The men lined up in front of the sheriff, who read them the latest law from the territory. Few understood it, but six months later, each man had twenty-four dollars less in his hand than he'd expected for the season's work.

Ning Ho was beating Ah Fook's laundry on the wash rock, her most hated chore. Her own clothing could be cleaned in the large bucket, but her husband's coarse heavy trousers and jackets, stained with fish blood and oil, must be carried to the river, beaten on the flat stone, soaped and rinsed, soaped and rinsed again, and then carried, dripping wet and heavy, back to the cabin to be strung on stout cords pulled from tree to tree.

The first time, she remembered, her arms and feet had ached all through the night. The second time, she had nearly drowned, falling in the river. The third time, she lost two pairs of trousers to the current and came back to the cabin weeping and cursing the river gods as unholy demons with greedy bellies and sixty grabbing fingers. Now, she knew the river's tricks, she told herself wryly, and she could best the waters with a bit of luck. She was working over a soiled sleeve when Ilchee came behind her, chuckling softly.

"It is a strong green god, neh?" the old woman laughed.

"Ah ko," Ning Ho grunted impatiently. "It fights me for this fish blood like a mother for her own." She slapped the sleeve against the rock. "May all the gods bear witness, my husband must have wrestled the last catch to the vats with only his arms." She wiped the hair from her eyes and leaned back to rest for a moment. "I saw Young Master take the wagon to town this day. Does he never think to bring a wife back with him?" She dropped her head as she realized the impertinence of her question. "Sometimes, the men speak of this, yes?"

Ilchee shrugged. "He is young yet, for a man. The whites do not take a wife so soon as my people. Or yours."

Ning Ho shook her head gently. "He is son of your son, yet you speak of him as a stronger."

"I chose my own way, as did my son. Should I deny my grandson less? For him," she shrugged, "the old dreams do not speak."

"This is not the way of my people," Ning Ho said firmly. "The winds of change may whirl through the world, but a son must know where his rice bowl rests. Otherwise, all is chaos and destruction."

Ilchee smiled. "Good words. But my people say that a man should love his life, not endure it. I have learned one thing only in this life, I think, one thing which brings me peace, and that is, each age must find its own courage in its own time, neh? And also its own visions. No one wants to build his life on the dreams of another. My grandson is no different. Neither, when I come to think of it," she chuckled wryly, "was I."

Ning Ho sat thinking, staring into the water for a moment. "But your people have lost the river, ma? The whites have stolen it. Because your young ones would not dream the old dreams."

Ilchee groaned as she sat down heavily beside her. "They have not stolen it, small sister, they have only taken it for a time. But the river flows on, does it not?" She kicked her bare foot in the shallows. "It keeps its seasons and its storms, and reminds the whites of what they choose to forget. And someday, when it dies, they will remember too late. It will be too late for my people, as well, but perhaps some can find a way to bring life from death, neh? I have told my son. He listens. But when I tell my grandson, he only laughs and says I have eaten too many green berries again. His father should tell him, but the son does not wish to be as the father"—her voice dropped—"and so perhaps the old ways will end here, with him, for my son's grandson shall not hear the old dreams at all." She looked up and saw the confusion on Ning Ho's face and changed the subject amiably. "Well, and what does the China boss say of our talks, eh?"

Ning Ho giggled, her hand over her mouth. "He barked like a dog with a bone, and I had to break wind just to hide my laughter and save his face!"

"I remember how men are well enough," Ilchee said wryly. "My father told me that a woman has no need of dreams."

Ning Ho looked aghast. "What foolishness, ma? Wei, and it is women alone who keep dreams alive. It is good joss that you did not listen to him."

Ilchee smiled a secret smile and put her face to the sun. "It is fine by the river today," she said quietly.

The two women sat and splashed their feet together, and their laughter rose like clear bird calls over the rush of the water.

The following season, another delegation of whites arrived in camp. Two doctors, two assistants, and a policeman clustered in Demers' office. The boss came out, pulled Ah Fook aside, and spoke to him, and the men watched out of the corners of their eyes. Soon, all the workers were lined up outside the building with their jackets over their arms. As they had been ordered, they stood with their chests bared, shivering in the cool spring breeze.

"Men," Demers explained, "the doctors here have to check you all for leprosy."

The men were silent, for none understood his words.

"There's been an outbreak in the city," Demers went on, "And —well, it won't take long. I know you're all fit."

Ah Fook turned to the men solemnly, and they read bad news in his scowl. He quickly translated, using the Chinese word for the disease, ma feng, skin-gone-crazy. The crew began to whisper ominously, and one man hissed, "Do they check their own houses? We do not bring the ma feng to this land. *They* do!"

Ah Fook snapped a warning, and the men were silent. But they watched the white doctor warily as he moved from one man to another, probing, turning him round and round, and making him spread his fingers and toes.

Ning Ho had seen the white wagon pull up, and she watched from the cabin window. She saw the white doctor touch each man impersonally, and the men never met his eyes. Finally, he pinched each man's thumb, watching for one who would not wince.

"See?" Demers said impatiently. "I told you they're all clean. Now let them get back to work."

"What about that one there?" the doctor's assistant said, jerking a thumb towards Ah Fook.

"Oh, for Christ's sake, man," Demers said. "He's the China boss. Been China boss here for more'n five years."

"Well, that don't mean he can't get leprosy," the doctor said blandly. "Take your shirt off, John."

Ah Fook blanched painfully, and he stiffened with indignation, his anger like a woman's, impotent and proud. He looked to the white boss for rescue, but Demers merely shrugged and gestured to him to get in line with the others.

Ah Fook moved slowly into line, drawing his arms from his jacket as though he dragged them through something distasteful. He suffered the doctor's fingers stoically, staring straight ahead, a ferocious scowl on his face.

"Well, this one's clean, too," the doctor muttered, turning to pack up his bag.

Then the assistant said, "What about the one in the cabin?" He turned and pointed directly at Ning Ho's head, as she stood in the window. Her mouth opened in amazement.

Demers glanced at Ah Fook and then glared at the doctors. "Say now, this is getting out of hand. That's the China boss wife, see. And she doesn't have it, I can vouch for that. Just leave her be."

The doctor straightened up and followed his assistant's stare. "Won't take a minute, Demers. We got to check them all, you know. Call her out."

"You mean to tell me you won't take my word for it? Well, I won't do it. You can't drag her out here front of all these men," Demers said angrily. "If you want to check her, you better take her husband and go knock on her door."

The policeman spoke up wearily. "I ain't goin' in no Chink cabin,

Demers. 'Less you want these Johns to stand here all day, you best call her out here."

Demers cursed impotently under his breath and spoke quickly to Ah Fook. The China boss closed his eyes briefly, shut his lips in a grim line, and stalked across the meadow. In moments, he reappeared. Ning Ho hobbled along behind him, her head down, her hands hidden in the folds of her jacket. She stood mutely before the doctor with her head averted.

"Put out your hands," the doctor said gently.

She slowly extended two palms and then, trembling, turned them over. The doctor gasped and narrowed his eyes. Her hands were covered with small red nodules, some of them open and scabbed.

Ning Ho began to weep and stammer hurriedly, "It is berries. Every time, I get sores from berries. It is not the ma feng!"

Demers came to her side. "She's telling the truth, for God's sake. I've seen it myself. She works out in that damned field all day, and she gets a rash from the strawberries. Hell, I used to get it, too, when I was a kid, every spring."

Ning Ho looked quickly from Ah Fook to Demers to the doctor, still whispering, "It is berries. Not ma feng."

There was a long silence. Finally, the policeman said, "What do you say, Doc? Want to take her in?"

Ning Ho stared at his seven-pointed silver star. In China, such a badge would have been an omen of evil, for the points directed themselves to the corners of the earth where the demons lived, rather than in a circle to keep them out. She kept her head low, but she could not stop the tears from rolling slowly down her cheeks.

The doctor had been looking at Ning Ho intently all the while she wept, and he said slowly, "I got to see if it's just on your hands. Pull up your trouser legs for me, and roll up your sleeves."

Ning Ho forgot all modesty and shame and frantically yanked her pants legs up to her knees. Behind her, she sensed Ah Fook hiss like a shocked goose, but she barely heard him. When the doctor nodded, she pulled up her sleeves above her elbows and stood before him, legs and arms exposed, her eyes closed, her face turned up to the sky.

After what seemed forever, the doctor said mildly, "Well, that looks good enough, I guess."

"You sure, Doc?" the policeman said angrily. "Looks like scabs to me. We got to clean this town out, you know! Can't be takin' no chances!"

The doctor shrugged easily. "She's clean, far as I can tell." The policeman scowled and turned away, back to the wagon.

Demers met her eyes—a frank, open grin. "I could'a told you that," he said to the doctor, jauntily. "Fact, I did tell you that, you sonofabitch. Now, if it's all right with you, some of us has got work to do."

He waved the men back to the cannery, and Ning Ho walked weakly back to the cabin. When she was within a few steps, she broke into a run, raced inside, and slammed the door.

That night, Ning Ho was awakened by a distant shouting. She leaned up on one elbow and looked about the cabin. Nothing was amiss, and Ah Fook slept peacefully on his belly, his queue wound up snugly under his sleeping cap. But then she heard the shout again, this time more loud and clearly from across the meadow. She eased from the bed and went to the window.

There, across the field, a burst of flame licked from the cannery door up into the night sky. Men were beginning to pour from the China house, running about before the flaming building in confusion. She screamed and Ah Fook started up, immediately angry.

But she was already at the door, pulling on her clothes. "Fire!" she shouted, and raced across the meadow, her hoe in her hand.

When she reached the cannery, the flames were moving unerringly from the door, up the side of the building, and onto the roof. The wind blew from the river, forcing the fire up the walls and back into the open door, rather than out into the yard.

Men came rushing from their beds, pulling on trousers and jackets, shouting confused questions, hollering for water, buckets, and help, as the wooden walls began to be eaten away by the greedy yellow flames. The fire darted from the roof, leaping higher and higher into the sky with lightning swiftness. The windward side of the cannery began to glow like the coal of a cigar.

Ah Fook came from the cabin, shouting directions. The men ran for their water buckets, filled them at the pump, and ran at the flames, splashing the water at the fiery opening which had been the door. Billows of smoke rolled up wherever the water hissed into the fire, and Ning Ho could barely see. She heard Demers shout, "Bring blankets, tarps! Hurry, dammit!" and she ran for the cabin to get her oilcloth slicker to smother the flames.

She ran back and joined the line of men beating at the flaming walls. Tongues of fire jumped at them as if in battle, but they fought on with buckets and blankets and spades. From where she stood, Ning Ho could see through the window into the cannery. While half of the building was burning, the other half was almost untouched, save for smoke and embers. The oil pools from the salmon were burning freely, however, and the fire was edging closer to the piles of wood chips and sawdust that the men used to pack the boxes.

Several men ran past her, Ah Fook among them, into the untouched section of the building. She could see their bodies rise and fall as they slapped and beat at the flames, and then the smoke billowed out from the window so that she had to move back. The men were tinged with orange, and huge shadows of flame and dark danced around them, crackling evilly.

She joined the group at the pump, moving empty buckets to be filled and running back with them, sloshing the water on her bare feet and legs, her eyes smarting with the smoke. Ilchee appeared at her side, her blanket pulled tight across her shoulders, her eyes wide with fear—and something else which Ning Ho could not name. She grabbed the old woman and pulled her back from the sparks and the running men. Ilchee stared blindly up at the roof of the cannery, and she gave a low moan of terror. Ning Ho looked up and saw that Demers was on the roof, beating at the flames about his feet, slapping wet cloths, moving like a willow whipping in the wind. A roar was coming from the fire, a huge hungry maw, demanding to be fed.

"Raven!" Ilchee cried, her fists convulsing like claws. "Raven has come for me at last!"

Ning Ho held her, trying to calm her. "No, no, it is only Young Master, my friend, only your grandson—"

"No, it is Raven!" Ilchee screamed, writhing against Ning Ho's arms. "See his wings, his great black wings! Aiiyaa, he comes!" Ilchee suddenly remembered when she was a young girl, dancing before the whole lodge, naked and lithe and full of warm blood. She saw once more the white place in her mind that she had seen then, the light of wonder and peace, and she knew she was beautiful and powerful for the last time in her life.

Isaac Demers beat frantically at the flames round him rising and falling with the tarp, and for an instant, Ning Ho thought that indeed he did look like a great black bird flapping on the roof, with the evil yellow flames behind him. But she pulled Ilchee away, covering her head with her blanket, murmuring what words of comfort she could find. She sat the old woman down in the meadow grass, and turned when she heard Isaac's voice over the din.

"We got to keep it from the China house!" he shouted, and all eyes turned to look at the small stretch of open sky and trees that separated the two buildings. Each man instantly pictured his own belongings, his bedroll, his gambling money, his clothing, dissolved in flames. Sparks were flying with the breeze over the trees, in the direction of the wooden bathhouse. Ning Ho knew that the men kept cooking fuel packed tightly in the back of the shed, kindling, oil, and pork lard. If it caught, the whole camp would go.

Some of the men ran toward the bunkhouse, determined to save their belongings, leaving a gaping hole in the line of those beating the flames at the cannery door. Demers shouted at them to come back, but few listened. The fire had spread to the roof now, despite all his efforts, and the flames were moving in a circle toward the center of the building.

Suddenly, there was a shout of panic and a great rush of noise and smoke, and one edge of the cannery caved in, sending towering spears of flame and sparks into the sky. Ning Ho screamed and ran toward the door, shouting for Ah Fook to come out, but the heat and the smoke beat her back. She looked up in time to see Demers leap from the roof, fall heavily to the ground, and roll away from the flames, beating at his trouser legs as he twisted about.

Ilchee uttered a long piercing wail, her arms outstretched toward her grandson. "It is he, it is he!" she screamed. "Just as blinded as my father before him! Ah, Raven, Raven! Take me now, for I cannot see anymore!" She babbled, half in Chinook, half in English, her long white hair whipping in the wind from the fires. Ning Ho ran to her, took her in her arms, and felt a shuddering gasp move into her like cold steel. Her eyes rolled back to show white oblivion, and she was gone.

Then, with a great yawning shriek the cannery collapsed, sagging slowly, sickeningly, onto itself, the flames soaring into the air, the roar of the fire smothering the shouts of the men, the billows of smoke reaching high over their heads.

Ning Ho stood dressed all in white, slender as a pine, and gazed down at Ah Fook's grave. She knew that he would have prized his funeral, had he been able to see it for himself, for it gave him great face. "Ah Fook," she said quietly, "did you hear the firecrackers and the gongs? Many came from the city, bringing you road money and incense for your journey past the Yellow Springs. Surely, there was noise enough to scare away the most awful demon in this barbarian land."

Chin Fat, the grocer from Alder Street, had come all the way in his wagon, bearing heaping plates of fowl, vegetables, and rice for the funeral feast. The China crew had left six bottles of wine at each of the three victims' graves for the spirits to enjoy, one at every corner of the white coffins and one at each end, so no soul would have to reach far when it arose. Master Demers had brought a whole hog and large bowls of its flesh were even now lined in order about the three graves in case one of the wandering spirits was hungry before its long journey.

She had erected the customary sacred furnace near Ah Fook's grave, and friends had offered much spirit-money, paper clothing, paper servants, and tobacco pipes to be burned, so that he would have them to use in the spirit world. She sighed deeply. "You will be going home quite soon," she whispered to the ground. "Your ancestors must have been watching out for you, my husband, for your bones were nearly clean. Sooner than most, you will be able to go back to the Middle Kingdom."

The cedar trees rustled behind her, and she turned slowly to look. Ah Fook's spirit is probably moving about my shoulders, she thought. Naturally, he would be concerned about his final resting place, since he was a tangka. Boat people often were drowned at sea, and from the cradle, they feared that their bones would not find an eternal home. But even worse would have been to be left in the barbarian land. China was the land over which all spirits hovered, and only through a Chinese grave could a spirit enter eternity. Also, who would tend his grave, bring him full rice bowls at Tsing Ming, the feeding of the dead? Who would burn red money over his bones if he stayed in this fan-qui land?

No, the only proper way for a Chinese to end was in the Celestial Kingdom. Usually, the dead had to be buried and then disinterred after years. Then, the bones were cleaned and shipped back to China. But lately, the fan-qui police had arrested a Chinese herbalist who had a man's hands hanging in his window, drying for shipment. They accused him of murder. The poor man had to find the widow to testify on his behalf that he was only cleaning and drying her husband's body, piece by piece, until he could be sent back to his ancestral village.

But Ah Fook had good joss. His bones were almost ready to send right now. In a year, she could open the grave, scrape them of any remaining ashes, and pack them for shipment on the first boat to China. The only problem had been his queue. No Chinese man could be buried within China without his queue, of course, for this was the badge of his fealty to the Emperor. Moreover, the Buddhist priests often said that no man could return to this life if he was missing any of the parts of his body. Yet, Ah Fook's hair had been burned in the fire.

"You are lucky, my husband, that you have a wife to guard you while you ride the stork over this wretched land," she said to him now. "The others will rest in this place of demons forever." She pulled off the veil that covered her head from all eyes and leaned over the grave. Her head was shorn, shorter even than when she'd first arrived in the land of the golden mountains. "They will never know," she whispered. "When they bury your bones in the land of your ancestors, you will have beside your skull a full head of hair. No one will know it once sat on the head of a worthless sing-song girl from the House of Joyous Relief."

The cannery was ruined, of course, and the men soon were preparing to return to Chinatown. It was the beginning of the season, and few had hopes that they would find work, unless they were willing to travel many miles into the territory. Some talked of following the river up to the placer mines in the east. Tales were told of Chinese finding ample fortunes in the shafts the fan-qui had left behind. But most were loath to stray too far from what they knew.

Wheat prices were down, and the salmon runs were fewer this year than ever before. It was whispered that the whites were holding meetings in the city, demanding that the Celestials be shipped back to China. In fact, they said, they would pay any merchant five dollars if he would fire his Chink workers and hire white laborers instead. Let them go back to China on anything that floats, they threatened. To Hawaii or anyplace but here, where they lower the wages of decent white men in the territory. Besides, it was rumored that the men from the Demers cannery were more troublesome than most, possibly even diseased. The men left in the China house muttered that perhaps it was no accidental spark which had turned the cannery into a pile of smoldering ashes.

Ning Ho did not know what to do. Though Ah Fook had left some money in the pot buried under the bed, it was not enough for her to live on, nor to buy passage back to her village. She knew that few men in Chinatown would want to marry her, of course, because she was a widow, the worst of bad joss.

She was kneeling over Ilchee's grave by the river, carefully planting cedar seedlings. "These will protect you from the winds and the rain, my friend," she said quietly as she spaded the earth. "Did you hear what your son said before all his people? It gave you great face. The Old Master and the Young Master came together, and the Mistress rode up in the fine carriage, and when your son finished his talk, all wept good tears. Even the old sweeper bowed his head, old woman, and I know you smiled at that."

She brushed an errant windfall off the mounded dirt. "I did not tell them of your vision, never mind. Surely Young Master does not need more pain while he wrestles with his destiny. They think your old heart feared fire, not Raven riding on grandson's shoulders."

She heard a rustle of footsteps and looked up. Isaac Demers approached, and Ning Ho hurriedly got to her feet.

"It's good of you to tend her," he said quietly. "I wish Pa would have let me bring her to our own garden."

"She wants to sleep by river," Ning Ho said.

"Aye, but I hate to think of her alone out here."

Ning Ho shook her head gently at his lack of understanding. He was son of her son, her blood ran through his heart, but their lives touched no place that she could see. "Never alone in this land," she said finally. "Her people all around, yes? And her gods."

"Well, she lived a good life, anyway. She was a princess, did she tell you? But her time's passed now, and the land's got no more place for her people. The future's what matters."

Ning Ho's brow wrinkled in bewilderment. How strange these whites are to wish the past so quickly dead, buried, and forgotten. Indeed, this *is* a barbarian land. But she said nothing.

"I came to tell you," he went on, "we're just about ready, I guess. You got your gear packed up?"

She nodded sadly, looking over Ilchee's grave, across the meadow to the neat rows of vegetables just beginning to sprout. He stood and looked at her for a long moment. For an instant, she recalled the day she stood with him, gazing over his many acres—the look in his eyes was the same.

"Where'll you go?" he asked.

She shrugged silently. He bent down and pulled a green stalk of meadow grass and sucked gently on the sweet white root. "You've got no kin at all?"

"No," she said slowly, "but I find work."

"Doing what?"

She shrugged again, turning slightly away.

"Listen," he said suddenly, briskly, as though he'd just made up his mind, "my folks've got a big place in the city. A fine place. Hell," he laughed, "we're almost rich, you might say. We've got one other cannery upriver and five lumber mills and some leased land in the valley besides." He stopped, chewing thoughtfully on his grass spear. "My mother's looking for a good woman in the kitchen. Can you cook?"

Ning Ho's face blanched painfully with shame. She cursed herself silently for never thinking ahead to this moment. But she said honestly, "No. Not good." Then she lifted her head and added quickly, "But I am good in garden, yes? And I can do all other work. Wash clothes. Clean." She paused. "Keep babies, maybe?"

He chuckled, slapping his hands gently on his muscled thighs. "Well, not many babies at the Demers house these days, 'less you count my sisters' kids. But I think we can still find plenty for you to do. You want to come, then?"

She grinned, nodding quickly. "I come. I get my basket."

The Demers house stood on a hill back from the waterfront, and from the parlor, Ning Ho could see the great ships moving up and down the river as she ran her dust cloth gingerly over the tables. The house was two stories tall, flanked by wide circling staircases with dark pineheart floors which were waxed to a dull gleam. Gaslights sputtered and glowed at the end of long hallways, and tall white tapers added yet more light to the corners. Indeed, it was a house of light, Ning Ho thought, with leaded colored windows, flowers, and lace damask curtains which fluttered in the winds off the river, a place of many doors and cubbyholes and high-ceilinged rooms. The house seemed to have absorbed a life of its own, from Missee Demers' firm and capable hands.

Ning Ho had arrived one week after the cannery fire, and she felt the confusion of many changes made too quickly in her life. It seemed to her, as she stood waiting in the parlor for the fan-qui mistress, that it was only days since she had stepped from the red wedding sedan into the yellow cabin on the edge of the meadow.

Suzanna Demers swept into the room like a great white water-fowl, her yellow hair towering above a small, pointed chin and wrinkled, restless blue eyes. Isaac Demers sat in a corner chair, smiling his encouragement. "Sit, child!" the mistress said kindly. "My Lord, we don't stand on ceremony in this house."

Ning Ho eased gingerly into one of the velvet high-backed chairs, running her finger surreptitiously over the nap.

"Now," the woman said briskly, "my son tells me you're the widow of ol' Ah Fook, our China boss. Awful young to be left alone," she muttered almost to herself, "and he tells me you're a good hard worker. I like that. He also tells me you took care of my husband's mother with a good heart. I like that best of all." She eyed Ning Ho carefully up and down. Ning Ho sat a little straighter in the chair and met her gaze. Suddenly, the woman smiled, a warm grin that lifted up her whole mouth.

He is his mother's son, Ning Ho thought quickly.

"We can always find work for a pair of hands if they're willin' ones," the mistress went on. "Are yours, child? My son didn't drag you here 'gainst your will, did he? Promise you pie in the sky on a platter?"

Isaac laughed and rolled his eyes. "My God, Ma, you make me sound like a damned white slaver."

Ning Ho was shocked at this teasing between mother and son. In the Middle Kingdom, such indignities would never have been allowed. But she kept her face bland and did not show disapproval.

"Room and board and three dollars a week, cash," the mistress was saying. "Bridget's got Sundays off. You take Saturdays, and that should round out the week. Oh"—she stopped as if she just remembered—"I don't know much 'bout you Celestials, child. What day do you talk to your god, anyways?"

"Mother—" Isaac began.

"Hush, son. Let the girl speak up for her ownself. We got no room for a scaredy-puss in this house. Lordylord, that Bridget'll eat her up alive if she can't speak her mind, and she may's well find it out now, soon's later."

Ning Ho did not understand half of her words, but she heard

beneath them to her tones. This mistress was a rare woman of kindness and strength, common sense and softness, she thought. Somewhere, sometime in her life, someone had loved her very much, Ning Ho was sure of it. It showed in her eyes, her smile, the very tilt of her chin. Though she was past her middle age, she had a sense of youth about her, in the firm set of her shoulders.

She spoke up quietly, "We do not take one day to talk to our gods, missee. I call you that, yes? Saturday is good day as any. And this Bred-jit will not eat me up, never mind. I have plenty good teeth, also." She grinned, showing her open mouth as evidence.

Suzanna Demers giggled, a delighted, bubbling version of Isaac's own laugh. "I see you do, child. Well, good enough, then. It's settled, and that's all I'll say on't. I'll call you Ning. That's easy on the mind and right pretty, too." She stood and beckoned her upstairs, saying, "Come on up, and we'll get you settled." Isaac heard her voice float up to the second floor. "First thing, we got to get you some decent shoes. You run around barefoot on Bridget's floors, and she'll pitch a fit."

Again, Ning Ho did not understand all her words, but the next day, she learned what that particular phrase could mean. She had drawn several buckets of water from the deep, shaded well in the garden and carried them carefully to the kitchen, walking gingerly so as not to spill a drop. After five trips from well to washpan, she began to feel weary. The heavy leather shoes that the mistress had given her were unfamiliar and hard-edged to her skin. They were too large, and so they quickly rubbed two red and throbbing blisters on her heels.

She drew a last bucket of water and sat down in the shade to bathe her feet and to rub the backs of her elbows and her knees, the places where fatigue collects. Suddenly, Bridget erupted out of the kitchen, her face mottled and red, waving a wooden spoon. She was a huge woman with flaming red hair, flapping white arms, and a mouth wide as the Great Wall. Ning Ho steeled herself for battle, but she did not flinch. She continued to lave her aching feet in the cool bucket of water.

"Ach! Ye filthy divil, what's that yer doin' with the missus's water bucket!"

Ning Ho looked up blandly and gave Bridget her best look of total incomprehension.

"Holy Mother of God, will ye look at her? Now we can't drink nary a drop from it, ye little scut! Ye've had yer dirty, dusty feet in the bucket we take up the drinkin' water with. I ought to thrash ye good an' proper!"

Ning Ho stood and said quietly, "Water comes from ground, yes? I walk on same ground. There is nothing on feet not in water, same thing."

"Why, ye filthy Chink heathen, ye dare to answer back?" She stalked over to Ning Ho and snatched the bucket from her hand. "I'm tossin' this bucket on the dust heap! An' when the missus asks to know where it got to, ye can tell her yerself. Wash yer feet in the slop bowl in yer room like decent, Christian folk, or I'll see yer out o' here so fast, 'twill make yer pigtail curl!"

Ning Ho soon learned to avoid the slicing tongue of the red-haired demon and became adept at veiling her eyes, stopping up her ears, and slipping away into other rooms. The master of the house, Caleb Demers, had once come into the kitchen when Bridget was ranting at her for dropping a plate.

He was spry about the shoulders and the neck, moving gracefully for his years. His head had an odd slant to it, she noticed, as though his thoughts reached to the heavens, stretching his skull with them. He was shorter than his son, but everyone in the house looked up to him, nonetheless.

"Here, now," he said softly as he swung through the door. "What's all the row?"

"'Tis this dinnling dunce ye got to clutter up me kitchen, mister. She's got the clumsy paws of a hound at the end of her wrists."

He looked Ning Ho over carefully and said, "Hold them out, please."

She thrust out two slender hands, as smooth and unlined as though she'd never held a hoe.

"They don't look clumsy to me, Bridget. See if you can keep your screaming down to a level fit for human ears. You're making horses shy in the street."

Bridget gaped and gasped, but he just winked at Ning Ho and strode out the door. After that, Ning Ho took care to see that his plate was filled with those special bits of meat and sweets that he preferred, and in her heart, she began to think of him as Bak Ah, older uncle.

It was a special day when Isaac's two sisters came to the house, bringing in their arms their two sons. The mistress squeezed and fondled the two boys as though to warm herself on their young, ripe flesh, kissing and tickling them to make them laugh. She called Ning Ho into the parlor to meet her daughters. "Sarah, Elizabeth, this is Ning—she's the newest addition to our herd. Got a good hand with the dustcloth and can make a needle fly."

The two women greeted her cordially, and she made them her most dignified bow.

"Why, Mama, she's no bigger than a butter bean. Look at those tiny feet!" Elizabeth cried.

"Aye, but they move fast when they've a mind," the mistress said wryly. "Give over those two pups to her, and we'll set and rock a spell." Sarah put her son in Ning Ho's arms, watching her carefully. "His name's Caleb John, Ning, after his granddaddy. Keep ahold of him good and tight, 'cause he's a squirmer."

Elizabeth asked, "Are you sure you can manage both of them? Mine's a handful, all by himself."

Ning Ho nodded happily and took the second grandson into her arms.

"His name's Charles, Ning. We call him Charley, for short," Elizabeth said. "If he frets, you just give him this sugar-tit."

Ning Ho walked up to the nursery with the two fine, fat boys in her arms. "I carry 'Little Stupid' and 'Flea' up the stairs," she said loudly and clearly in Chinese. The white women took such chances with these precious sons! Best to fool the gods into thinking the boys unworthy, else they might trip up her feet, make them tumble down the stairs, and snatch them away for envy. She remembered her little brother had been called "Piece of Dust" for the whole first three years of his life, lest the gods steal him for their spirit world. She could do no less for these fine babes, sons of the house of Demers.

Isaac and his father went away each morning to offices in the city, and Ning Ho felt the house was quite empty until they returned for their evening meal. She passed the days in cleaning and washing and mending, but she tried, always, to end each afternoon outdoors in the garden.

There, out in the soil, she carefully tended the roses, plucking the dead blooms from the bushes, watching for mildew, and spading gently around their roots. She had snatched several fishheads from the chopping table when Bridget was not looking, and these she planted at the base of each shrub. Then, she worked her way to the rows of vegetables, weeding, watering, and hoeing them with pride. And always, she made sure that she stood near the gate when the men came home, for it was a pleasure to see them laugh, their heads together over some plan or another, their waves quick and their greetings warm.

The two of them found her one afternoon, planting cedar seedlings along the back of the vegetable garden. Suzanna Demers had come out to inspect her work, and she stood behind Ning Ho's bare heels, pointing out this weed or that tomato sprout that needed support.

"What in the world are you doing there, Ning? Aren't there enough pines around here without you adding to 'em?" Isaac teased her. "I wish you'd set the space to strawberries instead. *That's* what we need more of around here. Strawberry pie."

Ning Ho looked up, flustered to be the center of attention. Her spade stopped, and she looked at the three smiling faces above her.

"Here we are, paying men good money to cut trees down by the thousand-foot, and you're planting more," Caleb chuckled.

"For wind, yes?" Ning Ho stammered. "Trees will grow tall and keep wind off."

The two men laughed kindly. "Maybe when I'm in a rocking chair," Isaac said. "That's about how long those'll take to do any good. Put down some pole beans, if you want a windbreak, they'll come up to your shoulders before those squash even set blossoms."

But Suzanna Demers said calmly, "Oh, you two think you're so blamed smart, leave the poor gal alone. She knows what she's doing, I 'spect."

Ning Ho bowed her head and said quietly, "In my land, trees are sacred, yes? Once were forests, but now, not so many. To plant a tree is to hold the land from flying away to heaven, the sages say, and to make shade for unborn sons."

"Well, I think that's right nice," Suzanna said. "Shows good sense."

Isaac rolled his eyes. "Maybe in China, trees make good sense, where they're all jammed in elbow to elbow and there's not enough of anything to go around, but what makes sense in Portland is more of what we *ain't* got, and that's strawberries, not cedars. Right, Pa?" He grinned and winked at his mother.

Caleb Demers laughed softly. "Don't get *me* mixed in this, boy. Not with the ladies lining up on the other side—"

"You men think everything's gonna last forever." Suzanna grinned, pulling them away to the house. "We know better, don't we, Ning—you plant whatever pleasures you, child, and pay these two fools no mind at all." A thought occurred to her and she added, over her shoulder, "Just so long as you don't block the view, now!"

Ning Ho continued spading, her breath coming easier now that she was alone once more. Such strange people, these white barbarians! But then she recalled that even Ilchee had shown an odd unconcern for the land and the river, as though it would always be there, unchanged and inevitable as the sky. Wei! she thought scornfully, even the *sky* must be cared for, if it is to stand forever! Only Missee Demers seemed to understand that the trees, the river, even the earth itself might be gone tomorrow if it is not revered today, so spiteful are the gods of too much joss. She reached for another cedar seedling and pushed it firmly into the soft ground. Let them laugh, she smiled to herself, someday these trees shall shade the sons of the son of Demers, and then perhaps they will remember this foolish sojourner, ma?

The Demers family was often together, and Elizabeth and Sarah, the Demers daughters, enjoyed bringing their children to Ning Ho's arms. It was Ning Ho's first opportunity to observe the white demonesses up close, and for a long while in the house of Demers, she tallied up the things about them that were strange. They did not have pierced ears, for example, and they did not seem to care if they had boys or girls. In China, she remembered, the children were called "my little heart," or "my liver." In fact, the English word "sweetheart" was one of the easiest for the sojourners to learn and understand. But in the land of the golden mountains, children were often told to "run away and play" or "get down from there." And for creatures who were scolded so regularly, she thought, they showed little discipline.

She began to understand why America was called Wang hong, a country of crabs. These people did everything differently, often just for the sake of that difference. Like crabs, they walked sideways, rebelling against custom and tradition with almost childlike glee. They spoke in their whispering language, all hissing sounds and blowing, and their sentences all went up at the ends like interminable questions. She found if she spoke very slowly, she could be understood, but she never felt comfortable when they spoke to each other. She always wondered if they talked of her without her knowledge.

She wondered vaguely how two so different peoples could live in the same land. The Chinese put sugar on their food, for example. Just a pinch, to remind them, in a life of bitter struggle, of the sweetness of it all. And the first rule that a Chinese child learned was, "I am Chinese. I will do my duty."

The Americans, on the other hand, put salt on their food—the taste of the sea, the earth, human sweat and tears—as if always, in the midst of plenty, they looked for the pitfalls and the pain in life. And it seemed to Ning Ho that the first lesson that an American child learned was that he deserved all he could grasp.

They took no pains to hide their arrogance, either. It had taken her a long while to get accustomed to the barbarians' directness. Her people always gazed outward, as though they still saw vast masses of land across great seas of water. Even when they spoke to each other, their eyes rarely met. But the barbarians stared rudely into your face as they spoke, searching for lies. She had learned not to drop her head when they spoke, but she knew she would never get used to their ready laughter, their swift and unblushing inquisitions.

Indeed, there were too many differences between them for her to count. But they made beautiful children, that much was true. On warm days, Ning Ho liked to take the white sons out to the shaded garden. It was the coolest, most secret-seeming place in the city, and its quiet shadowed corners calmed her. The well stood at its center, low and narrow and edged with old bricks. She recalled that her mother had once held her over the village well, telling her to look deep into its black sparkling surface. "The eye of the world," she called it. Most believed that to look into the well made a child far-seeing and wise. Though Ning Ho did not truly accept such a custom—peasant superstition, she thought to herself—still, she took no chances. She held the two boys, one by one, over the well, turning their heads toward its dark depths.

She remembered, too, her mother warning her about a woman in the village who became pregnant out of marriage. She had been the most beautiful bride the village had ever seen, but her husband went to war, and she grew lonely. As her stomach swelled and grew, far past the time when it could have been a lawful child, the villagers were more and more indignant. Finally, as she was ready to give birth, they stormed her father's house, killed the chickens and the goats, smeared the walls with blood, and broke all the cooking pots. The next morning, her father found her body and that of her baby down the village well, where she had thrown herself in despair.

"Of course, the family had to leave their house forever," her mother had said solemnly. "Not only for the shame but because their daughter had forever ruined the drinking water for the whole village. They say that her mother died mad, wandering about the country, calling for her drowned daughter. Let that be a lesson to all beautiful girls to be able, capable, and to guard their virtue."

It seemed to Ning Ho, as she gazed into the well, that if she fell in, she would surely emerge in China, perhaps even in the well of her own village. If she dove in, head first, she could swim through the center of the earth and come up outside her father's walls. The hardest part, of course, would be to remain unafraid, she thought, during the long journey through the darkness.

One night, she could not sleep, and she crept down the stairs and out to the garden. She walked in the moonlight, in and out of the shadows cast by the cedars, running her hand absently along the high fence around the lawn. When she turned the corner, she saw Isaac Demers sitting on the stone bench, gazing out over the street to the river.

For an instant, she thought to turn back and go inside unseen, without disturbing his privacy. But then, she walked softly forward, wondering what trouble could have brought him out into the night. He looked up as she approached. "Ning," he said quietly. "What are you doing up?"

"I could not sleep," she said. A ghost of a smile traced her lips. "The moon called me."

"Me, too, I guess," he said, stretching languorously and gazing upwards. He slid over on the bench, making room for her, and she sat down on its corner.

For a long moment, she heard nothing but the sighing of the night breeze through the firs. The noise of the city seemed far away; the lights on the river danced like cold stars in the blackest skies. In the distance, a dog barked, and the groan of a foghorn throbbed downriver. It is a good omen, she thought, and she turned to look at him. He was watching her with a strange and quizzical smile. Their gazes locked, and then she turned her eyes back to the river, confused.

"Are you happy here, mei-mei?" he asked softly.

She nodded quickly. "Most happy."

His eyes moved over her face, her hair. It was longer now, and it swished over her shoulders when she turned her head, loose and silky in the sleeping style. "You know," he said, "you've changed some since you came."

Surprised, she looked up at him, her moth-brows arching up.

"You're more beautiful than you were."

She tensed slightly, casting her eyes away. She did not know what to say.

His voice was low, as though half to himself. "I remember when you came to the house that summer, carrying your vegetables like they were carved of gold. I used to watch you, you know. Or maybe you don't. Anyhow, I liked to watch the way you moved, so light and quick. But mostly, I just thought you were brave as brass. Lots of backbone. But now, you've gotten beautiful." He broke off and turned away, his voice more distant. "Anyway, I'm glad you're happy."

In the long silence that followed, she waited for him to go on. But when he said nothing more, she rose slowly—and he took her hand lightly. "You probably don't understand half I said, right?"

She shook her head delicately, her eyes on him.

"Well, I wish you spoke English better. But maybe, it's just as well you don't."

He released her hand and she walked, trembling slightly, back into the house. It was true, she did not understand all he said. But she did not need to know his words, to sense the lonely heat and the pain which rose off him like the morning steam off the river.

Ning Ho was serving the evening meal, carrying out plates to the mistress to pass down the table to her husband and son. The master was in a rare mood, more angry than she had seen him in nearly a year of service.

"Well, I don't see how they can invite them on the one hand and then run them out with the other!" he said firmly, as he set down the bowl of beans with a bang. "And they've got the gall to call themselves Christians. Bad as what they did to the tribes. It's disgraceful!"

Ning Ho set down the last dish and then stood at the kitchen door as was her custom, waiting for a signal to bring something else or carry it away.

"First, we get them over here by the thousands to do the work we won't touch. And they do a damn good job. And then, we tax them to death and tell them, move on!"

"It's worse down in California," Isaac said soberly. "They're pushing that new air tax to the limit. Mostly, against the Chinamen, of course. They say they got to have five hundred cubic feet of air to the man, and Lord help the ones packed in those shanties, five to the foot. They're burning them out just as quick as they can catch them. They're taxing them in the mines, the shrimp boats, and in the cigar factories. And the latest I heard is that no Chinese can even testify in court against a white man." He reached for another biscuit. "Which means, lots of them'll be moving up here, looking for a safe space to squat."

Caleb Demers shook his head in disgust. "Then we'll soon have even more trouble. I hear talk on the streets every day, getting uglier by the hour. Used to be, you only heard it from the men out of work. Now, they're all shouting, 'Chinks must go!' as if the Chinamen took their jobs right out from under their noses. But when I ask them if they want to work for a dollar a day, they curse me to my face! So, who the hell is going to work the salmon run next season? And the lumber and the new rail line up the coast? The bigwigs on Astoria Street?"

"I'd like to know do they plan to run the laundries, too, while they're at it," the mistress spoke up. "Nobody else'll do it. If I ask Bridget to do your shirts, she'll squall loud enough to wake the dead in Ireland."

The master suddenly turned to Ning Ho, standing silently in the corner. "What do you think of all this, Ning? What do your people say among themselves?"

She was startled to be asked such a question, any question, when all were listening. She looked about the table and every head was turned to her, waiting with interest for her answer.

She blushed furiously but spoke out, her voice calm. "It has been same forever," she shrugged. "I remember talk-story of my father. He tells of countrymen who go to Lu-sung, what you call Philippine Islands? They go to farm land. No one else would do it. But Spanish come soon and tell them they must pray to Spanish god. My people do not listen, and Spanish put them to death." She took a deep breath and bowed her head, wondering if she should go on. Finally, she said, "Twenty-five thousand Chinese killed. One hundred years

ago. But then there was no one to farm land. Natives would not do
it. Spanish would not do it. Everyone starve on islands. So then,
Spanish invite Chinese to come again. This time, pay big tax, and
stay to farm."

"Why in God's name would they go back a second time?" Isaac
asked wonderingly.

Ning Ho looked down at the floor, searching for the proper answer to give this man. "We say, things go in circle. Every thirty
years, small change. Every hundred years, big change. With every
change, new hunger comes, new mouths to feed, new rivers swallow
fields. That is why they call us 'sojourners,' yes? We are guest
people always, in many lands."

"So, where would you go then, Ning?" the master asked again
gently.

"I have no place to go," she said softly. "I do not know."

"Well, you needn't worry about it," he said heartily. "You have
a home here as long as you want one. I'll be damned if I let some
white, East-bred politician tell me how to run my mills or my house.
By the way, Ning, your English is getting better all the time.
Suzanna, please pass the butter."

The months slid by, one flowing into the other like river currents,
until summer came to Portland with damp days and warm, fragrant
nights. Ning Ho walked through the shadows of the garden every
evening now, and it was there, under the trellised arbor, where Isaac
found her. The air was heavy with impending rain, and Ning Ho's
skin felt restless and moist. She was sitting on the stone bench,
kneading the cool moss with her bare heels. She heard a step, looked
up, and his face loomed above her, pale as the moon. She said
nothing but only smiled and moved over, making room for him to
sit down.

"Can't sleep again?" he murmured, after a comfortable silence.

She nodded. "I do not wish to, never mind," she said quietly.
"The summer nights are so short."

She turned her face up to the sky, lighter patches behind the black
branches of the arbor, and he could see the reflections of a thousand
stars in her black liquid eyes, shimmering like the moon in well-
water. On an impulse, he took her chin in his fingers and drew her
gaze to meet his.

For an instant, he did not know what to say, now that he had touched her. "Your chin is strong," he finally whispered, his voice unsure.

She did not flinch or pull away, but met his eyes. "It is a sign of longevity," she said faintly.

He leaned forward to kiss her, but hesitated just enough to catch a quick flood of sorrow in her eyes, a naked and desolate acknowledgement of helplessness. He closed his eyes and kissed her gently, then more deeply, with a physical hunger that surprised him and smothered the warning voice he heard in his heart.

Ning Ho stiffened when he kissed her and then let her body arch into his. She felt a hot flame grow inside her, warm and throbbing as an underground pulse, a sweet fire licking at her spine, glowing in her loins, and kindling her belly. For an instant, she was intensely, gloriously, aware of every note of the night: the feel of the velvet air on her skin, the shift of the shadows in the breeze, the rustling of the leaves, the cool moss beneath her feet. She felt the stark exultation of her senses, painfully alive, in rhythmic harmony with every other living thing. She knew instinctively that Isaac felt none of these things. He was so intent on his body, so focused on the feel of her, that he was momentarily a blind man, deaf to everything save the pulse of his blood.

That is the difference between us then, she marveled, between men and women in their loving—and I have only just seen it. His hands began to roam over her breasts, his tongue became more probing, and a wave of liquid heat flooded her into oblivious passion. She felt only his strong legs, heavy on her, his arms gripping her, his searching mouth, as he pulled her down to the damp moss, into the deeper shadows.

The next night she waited at the stone bench for him, unsure why she was there but certain, somehow, that she must please him. She no longer knew who she was or what she was worth, except as the object of his desire. She had been lonely for a lifetime, it seemed, and now, though she felt she was being simultaneously created and destroyed, she could no more deny him than the gnarled wisteria over her head could deny the trellis about which it twined.

Love is a slow-growing tree, she thought—a live thing—and it is rooted in me now. She waited until the moon passed completely over the arbor, and then she padded back to the house alone.

Two more nights she waited and when finally he came on the

third night, he made no mention of his absence or the way his eyes had slid away from hers during the daylight hours. He only said, "I don't know what to say."

"Then it is well to say nothing," she said softly, and she gave herself up to the feeling of pleasuring them both.

After a week of shadowed meetings, he set her firmly on the stone bench one night and said, "We must talk, Ning. You know it, same as me."

She said nothing, but her eyes spoke all her peace, her admiration, her love.

"I was wrong to start this," he muttered quietly, taking her hands. "God knows, I'd never hurt you on purpose. You're a good gal, and I was raised better." He searched her face for a moment and then looked away. "Somehow, I guess I expected you to stop me before. But you . . ." he hesitated and grinned slightly. "You seemed to want it as much as I did. Anyways, I guess ol' Ah Fook was younger than he looked."

She furrowed her brow in confusion, momentarily bewildered. And then, at the moment that she realized he did not know her past, his eyes widened and his smile faded abruptly. "Ning . . ." he faltered, "What were you before you were the China boss wife?"

She lifted her chin and said quietly, "I was best sing-song girl in Portland. Best in whole territory, maybe. Men paid many taels of silver, just to see my face."

He laid her hands back gently in her lap and gazed out over the garden. Finally, he said, "I've got no call to judge you. And it's nobody's business, I guess. But don't wait for me again, Ning. I won't be coming."

For weeks, Ning Ho made herself invisible whenever her duties demanded that she be in the same room as Isaac. She never met his eyes, not even to see him turn away. She did not speak unless spoken to, and then only replied in a colorless voice, intended to remind no one of her presence. She succeeded so well in her disguise that no one noticed the change in her behavior.

At night, she had odd dreams, compelling in their deceptive reality. She dreamed that she was being born through a dark cold tunnel. The gods had pushed her out of heaven with a duty to perform, messages to deliver, tasks to accomplish—but she was trapped within an infant's body, helpless and feeble.

One dawn, she awoke with an aching sense of loss, and a young wind blew too hot through her body. She had been searching for someone half the night, it seemed, a small dark figure who was always half-seen, an elusive phantom who evaded her grasp. In the gray light of morning, she saw it for what it was . . . a son. And then she knew, with a deep shiver of dread, that her body was not simply fatigued or ill as she had hoped—she was with child. With child, as Ilchee had foretold.

She walked through her duties in a haze that day, holding out the promise of the shadowed garden as a reward where she might take refuge in its quiet peace, once her work was done. While all the house slept, she sat on the cold stone bench and gave herself up to silent despair. Though she had never carried life, she knew, unerringly, that his seed had taken root in her. And she knew, also with as deep a conviction, that such a thing could not be. Even if she left the house tonight, there was no place where she would be welcome.

A widow swollen with child would find no open gate in Chinatown, nor would a China boss wife with a barbarian child find refuge in his father's world. She imagined she could see through her smock to the blind parasite in her belly, sucking at her womb, gripping with tiny claws. She had ached for a child so often, and now—her mouth twisted with the sour irony of it—now, she felt only fear and hatred for that which grew within her.

She began to weep silently, rocking back and forth in an ancient rhythm, keeping her sobs low so as not to disturb the household. Finally, she was wearied with sorrow, and she stopped and gazed into the shadows. Her glance fell on a small violet under the pine tree. It had sprouted out of the layers of moss and needles, out of season and against all odds, jutting its pale head up as though to whisper frantically, "I will, I will make seed before I die."

She stiffened, straightened slightly, and gripped her belly. I am a comely girl, she thought, born in a suitable month, from a house with a high door. Always, the gods have smiled on me. I am unworthy to sit wailing with life growing in me. Wei, she cursed herself silently, does the earth hate the seed which roots in her, or weep and rend herself, saying the crop is not to her liking? Now is not the time to despair, she told herself. There are still paths of honor out of this shame. She stood and walked over to the violet, absently poked with one bare toe, brushing away some of the smothering debris.

The plot of ground on which the flower had rooted would never support it, she knew. It would grow and lift its head, only to die, shriveled in the heavy shade of the pine, its seeds smothered by inches of sterile needles. She knelt and dug gently around its base, lifting it from the earth. She looked around. The best place for it would be over by edge of the lawn, half-in, half-out of sun. There, it might live past one flowering. She took it to another spot, dug a small hole, and replanted the violet in the moist earth. She must remember, she told herself firmly, to water it well in the morning.

Then for no reason that she was aware, she recalled something that Ilchee had told her long ago. "Men rarely see farther than themselves, I think. Both men and women are tools, but only the woman knows she is a tool and give herself up to life to be used with joy. Men fight against life and so are often broken by it." What had she seen when she said this? What destiny had she visioned when she told me there was a seed floating within me? Keep from the whites, she said, but I walked into the very belly of the dragon with my arms outstretched. Yet I cannot find it in my heart to curse my destiny: Here is the joy of which she spoke, but it is a joy that can never survive.

On the following Saturday, Ning Ho made her way through the streets of Portland to the shop of Goon Dip, an herbalist known for his discretion. The old merchant greeted her from behind a huge desk. Behind him loomed a tall chest with a hundred small drawers, each one bearing the character of the herb or root within. He bowed deeply, gesturing to a carved turtle chair. "My wretched shop is honored, Ah Fook's widow," he smiled silkily, waving away his young apprentice to fetch fresh tea. "Please rest yourself and tell me how I may serve you."

She glanced about and lowered her voice. "I come for another, Venerable Goon."

"Many do," he nodded blandly.

"There is one in the house I serve—"

"The house of Demers," he added helpfully.

She hid her dismay. "You know it, then?"

He opened his arms expansively, "All know of the luck of Ah Fook's widow."

She hesitated and began again. "There is one there who carries life. An—unworthy Irish maidservant, only. But she is good, and I have promised to help her. She would rid herself of her burden."

He raised his eyebrows thoughtfully. "She does not go to her own people?"

She laughed desperately, "Aiya, Venerable Goon! A man with your eyes and ears knows that the black robes forbid such a thing." She calmed herself and shrugged casually. "I have said I would try to help her, but if you do not wish to involve yourself, I will tell her—"

"No, no," he interrupted her smoothly. "Of course, if you have given your promise, it is not my place to question it." He turned to the chest behind him and extracted a dried bundle, seating himself heavily at the desk. He moistened and inked his brush, labored slowly over the forming of each radical, and wrote out directions. Hurry, you old fool, she thought to herself, watching the back curtain for the apprentice, hiding her nervousness behind a placid smile. Finally, he weighed the herbs carefully, wrapped them in the paper, and handed it to her with a low bow.

Now that she was so close to salvation, she wanted nothing more than to be far away from this old man and his dusty herbs that smelled like shrouds. She returned his bow stiffly and slipped through the side streets back to the Demers house.

She willingly gagged down the foul-tasting cure twice each day for a week, checking her linen often for the first rusty stains. None appeared. And when a new nausea made it even more difficult to keep down the herbs, she knew in her soul that the treatment would not work. Isaac's seed was too deeply rooted to be dislodged. It was slowly taking possession of her mind and her body, as relentless as the force which planted it there.

Two nights later, Ning Ho stood at her accustomed station by the kitchen door, overseeing the evening meal. For the first time in months, she allowed herself to carefully watch Isaac from under lowered lids, wondering if perhaps she should tell him of her secret.

She had no idea how she could approach him or what he might say, but she stood silently, imagining various scenes between them, taking comfort from what she saw in her mind's eye. He might, after all, offer a plan or some advice. At the least, he might offer his regrets, giving her one last moment with which she might warm herself in the cold months to come. Suddenly, she was wrested out of her reverie by the words which floated over the table.

"She's a lovely woman, Isaac." The mistress was beaming. "Your father and I are so pleased you finally made your choice! After samplin' near every gal in the territory, I must say, it's about time at your age—"

"You say her family's Swedish?" the master asked as he ladled out the potatoes. "Any brothers looking to come west? I hear the Swedes are good with tall timber. Have you told her I want you to take over camp five? Hope that doesn't change her mind!"

Ning Ho realized that she must have uttered an unconscious and involuntary moan, for all heads swiveled toward her. Isaac glanced at her quickly, his face drawn and his lips tight. For one instant, their eyes met—and she thought she saw a flash of pity and shame —but then, his face closed, and he turned his attention to his plate.

"Are you feelin' poorly, Ning?" the mistress asked.

Ning Ho cleared her throat and shook her head slowly. "It is nothing," she said faintly and resumed her position. When all heads turned away once more, she delicately wiped her moist upper lip with her sleeve, closed her eyes briefly, and steeled herself to silence, her chin firm.

She went to the garden that night and sat beside the well, gazing into its black velvet depths. She felt a tightening in her head, like a flower planted in a too-small pot. How little I knew him, she thought, her mind weaving from memory to memory. How little he knows himself. Perhaps it is true, then, as the elders say, that plain women know more about men than beautiful ones do. Now, he will be married and begin a new life. Once more, I have imagined something that is not, that can never be. She watched the stars dance on the water deep below her, like a hundred bright eyes at the earth's core. She thought of her mother, her father, her home. Today, on the other side of the world, they are having a good day, she smiled. And my mother eats duck with sweet buns and plum sauce. She wondered if they remembered her, missed her, if they had ever discovered her fate.

Truly, she thought, the seas are not without purpose. The gods put them between peoples, and we break their will when we cross them. And I have spent a lifetime searching for the place where I belong. There is no such place. There never has been. It is memory which is the great betrayer, she smiled softly, and only necessity and duty are real—two high levees which have channeled my life. This is what comes of breaking all rules, all traditions. It is only justice.

A great peace settled over her, easing the tension in her neck and her shoulders. I have come through a land they will never know, she thought. She stood up and stared at the moon blinking through the trees. So then, she sighed. No gongs clash or trumpets sound when important decisions are made. Destiny comes silently, like the seasons. All I have to bear, I can bear. And the only hindrance is fear.

She stepped up on the cool bricks edging the well. The first step binds one to the second, she thought, her bare heels feeling the scrape of stone and damp. How blind I've been, she whispered, reaching her arms into the sky. I've been clutching at the ground, forgetting that earth is a star. And she arched her back and threw herself down into the depths of the cool black water, feeling the heaviness close over her head, her feet, a long descent into darkness. As she emptied her lungs for the last time, she cried, "Well then, let it be."

Ning Ho was buried beside Ah Fook in the meadow behind the little yellow cabin. From her resting place, she could see the lands across the Columbia, called Washington, lands which were clamoring to get a toehold in the Union, lands where the Demers logging camps came right down to the water. She could see, too, Ilchee's grave, already lost under new blackberry growth. If she listened, she could hear the surge of the river and the hiss of the wind in the firs.

Isaac stood and gazed out over the gravesites, to the meadow and the mountains beyond. The rows of vegetables Ning Ho had so carefully tended were now overgrown with wildflowers and weeds. He walked over to the edge of the field, his fists balled in his pockets. He was over the shock of finding her, at least. That moment had haunted him for days, and he'd feared it might follow him forever in the back of his mind. But who knew why the Chinese did what they did? It was possible she'd drowned herself because of him. But it was also possible—likely, he told himself—that she'd had other, private, reasons for her grief.

At any rate, she's gone. And though he felt a deep sorrow at her death, it did not have the sharp edge of pain that he'd half-expected. His boot brushed against something springy, and he looked down. There, at the edge of the meadow, a neat row of baby cedars had sprouted. When he looked closer, he saw that they were well spaced in the sun, with small hollows about their roots to catch and hold water.

She planted these, he thought, more damn seedlings, and his brow furrowed in bewilderment. Of all the things to plant. In a land

stiff with timber, she had saved the seeds, buried them, and nur-
tured them to life. Trees that she'd never see reach full growth even
if she'd lived another fifty years.

He shook his head dazedly. The Chinese have strange ideas, he
scowled, irritated at something which he could not name. And then
the memories flooded over him so powerfully that he swayed with
them. Ning Ho, pulled from the black waters, her hair streaming and
her eyes shut tight as though, at the last, she saw something too
terrible to bear. His mother weeping, the first time he had ever seen
her cry; Bridget's wails, her apron up over her face in horror; and
his father's white and rigid face sorrowfully directing a cast made
up of the gardener, two helpers, frightened boys, an undertaker, and
a half a dozen neighbors scurrying around, whispering behind
shocked hands. It seemed in that moment he could even hear the
sounds of the carpenter sawing and pounding for hours, building a
coffin that looked too small to hold anything but a child. He felt,
even now, the leaden somberness of the morning, and the morning
after that and after that.

His mother had faced him firmly the next day with the question
which had to be asked. "Now think, son," she said. "Do you have
any idea why she might have done such a thing?"

He could only shrug and turn his head away.

She stared at him for a long awful moment. "I see," she finally
said quietly. "Lord ha' mercy on her poor dear head. And on yours,
Isaac Demers." She paced before him, her face as white and rigid as
he could remember. "Well, it's a good thing the wedding will be
soon. You can take Margaret Polsen upriver to camp number five
and get on with your life." And she had walked from the room with
her shoulders stiff, never once touching him.

I am glad Ilchee is not alive to see this, he thought. My grandmother. He was vaguely aware that he rarely called her this in his
mind. It's all right for Pa, after all, since he's half-siwash. But I'm
only quarter-Chinook, and there's no reason to go round pressing
that fact on people. No reason to let it clutter up your life. She was
always talking about her visions, her dreams. Well, hasn't a man got
a right to find his *own* dreams, paddle his *own* damned canoe? What's
done is done and what's past is past, and it's time to get on with it.

All this he remembered as he stood over Ning Ho's neat line of
tiny cedars. Then he shook his head as though to release a burden
and walked quickly out of the meadow, away from the graves.

PART FIVE

The River Workers,
1880–1907

As I set down one evening in a timber town cafe,
A six-foot-seven waitress, to me these words did say.
"I see you are a logger, and not a common bum,
For no one but a logger stirs his coffee with his thumb.
My lover was a logger—there's none like him today—
If you'd sprinkle whiskey on it, he'd eat a bale of hay.
He never shaved his whiskers from off his horny hide,
But he'd pound 'em in with a hammer, then
      bite 'em off inside.
My lover came to see me one freezing winter day.
He held me in a fond embrace that broke three vertebrae.
He kissed me when we parted so hard he broke my jaw,
And I could not speak to tell him he'd forgot his
      mackinaw.
I watched my logger lover going through the snow,
A'sauntering gaily homeward at forty-eight below.
The weather tried to freeze him, it tried its level best—
At a hundred degrees below zero, he buttoned up his vest.
It froze clean down to China, it froze to the stars above.
At one thousand degrees below zero, it froze my logger
      love.
They tried in vain to thaw him, and if
      you'll believe me, sir,
They made him into ax blades, to chop the Douglas fir.
That's how I lost my lover, and to this cafe I come,
And here I wait till someone stirs his coffee with his
      thumb
And then I tell my story, of my love they could not thaw,
Who kissed me when we parted, so hard he broke my
      jaw."

—"The Frozen Logger," words and music by James Stevens

*A*nd the river ran broad and deep as the tides of memory and time, surging through dark canyons and white cascades, past the new orchards that sprawled up the sides of Mt. Hood, past the fertile fields, past the graves and the footsteps of each man who came to it, past the growing cliffs of the cities. The river was fresh with life and the dreams of those who hoped to tame it, smelling of snow and high winds and new plans, but now it begins to flow musty and darker in the lowlands, with the colors and odors of wood bark, wet needles, dead salmon, smoke and ashes.

Along its eastern bank, in a small stretch from Camas to White Salmon, a score of lumber mills, perching on huge piles of slabs and mill ends, spews out smoke and wealth. In the eighties, Portland is all muscled elbows and sprawling knees, young and loose-jointed, and Rudyard Kipling, passing through Tacoma, avows, "They are all mad here, all mad. A man nearly pulled a gun on me because I didn't agree with him that Tacoma was going to whip San Francisco on the strength of carrots and potatoes." One can sit in an acre of barroom in Portland, complete with electric light and a telephone, and in a half hour be deep in the thickest forests in the country. Vancouver's streets are quite likely to end abruptly in a fifteen-foot drop and a nest of blackberry brambles. In Oregon City, huge stumps stand at the very doors of her best hotels. In the crowded streets, ox drivers throng past eastern dudes, and everywhere is the raw new smell of fresh sawdust.

And past it all, the river rushes on to its own destiny, sweeping ships, moorings, bridges, and timber to the sea, in a maze of single currents melting into one another, twining together like roots of trees, and man is so far less disruptive to its inevitable tides than the movements of the waterstriders on its gleaming shallows.

DEMERS LOGGING CAMP WAS TWELVE MILES FROM THE COLUMBIA, DEEP IN a twenty-mile swatch of virgin fir, spruce, sugar pine, and red cedar. The mill site was five miles closer to the river, huddled on a sloping plateau, a small cluster of rough-hewn cabins near a pond and a stream, girdled by a blue haze of smoke.

After the wedding, Margaret and Isaac took the steamboat upriver and docked at Skamania, a little village set back from the mud flats. From there, they drove a wagon up a rutted path that diverted round huge stumps wide enough to accommodate a dozen dancers in a heel-and-toe. Isaac kept one eye on the mules and another on his bride.

It was at the opening of the Empire Hotel where he'd met her, a broad-shouldered Wisconsin Swede who drew his eye across the crowded ballroom and kept gazing at him until he finally asked her to dance. In his arms, she turned all light feet and bubbling laughter with eyes as blue as cold water and cheeks freckled like a guinea egg.

He certainly had no thought of marriage, he admitted ruefully, but there was something about her strong body and her even teeth and her blond hair that seemed so damned—so completely—*American* that he had overlooked the fact that she was probably the least beautiful woman he'd courted. But court her he did, and when his mother met her, she chuckled and said, "Isaac, I never thought I'd see the day when you'd take a gal whose eyes come near level with yours, but I guess every pot finds its own cover."

And so they were wed in a whirl of laughing relations, clinking champagne glasses, and pelting rice. She turned her head suddenly and caught him appraising her, and he clucked to the mules.

"Is it a good-sized camp?" she asked.

"Now, honey, I told you," he said, "it's nothing but a bunch of slapped-up shacks, so don't get your hopes up. Lumber camps got to be in the middle of high timber." He suddenly remembered their wedding night, when she had clung to him with wide white thighs, and he felt a flood of tenderness. "Remember, I warned you it's no life for a woman. I expect after one week with this cut-and-get-out bunch, you'll be heading back to Camas, where the other wives stay."

She mimicked the Swedish accent she knew made him smile. "Yu vill not get lost of me so easy, ja, Mister Demers? 'Vither thou goest,' by golly. Und dat goes for howling vilderness as vell."

They could hear the whine of the saw long before they reached the mill. At the top of a rise, they stopped and looked down at a rough wood cabin by a pond with a steam engine puffing at the back of the mill and another longer cabin, the bunkhouse. A cookhouse perched on the banks of a stream, and a squat little cabin with a sagging privy leaned against one huge cedar. From the mill uphill into the trees, a line of lumber lay side by side, forming a crude road —a skidroad, Isaac called it. The smoke pall that hung over the camp came from two chimneys, the steam engine, and a pile of smoldering sawdust in one corner of the clearing. All round, the dense woods crowded the little camp like heavy green curtains.

Isaac pulled up the team before the sawmill, and they walked around the side of the mill. It was an open porch with three sides, piled high with logs waiting to be cut into boards, railroad ties, bridge trestles, and shingles. The sawdust whirled through the air, and the din from the two saws was deafening. Isaac took her arm and walked her over to one of the men who worked a small saw.

"This is Ole!" Isaac shouted above the roar.

"Gud day, missus!" the man hollered, bobbing his head and touching his fingers to an invisible hat.

Margaret's mouth moved in a greeting, but he couldn't hear her. Her eyes widened as she watched Ole pull the great boards forward, his fingers feeding them surely and smoothly into the whirling jagged teeth of the saw. She smiled tentatively at him, and Isaac pointed to the other side of the cabin. Two men fed huge logs into a monstrous circular saw, two moons of steel, wide as a tree trunk and whirling in tandem, that split down the center of a giant cedar like knives through cheese. The men waved and grinned at her while their hands pushed wood, inches from the massive teeth. Isaac grinned back, mostly at her open-mouthed wonder.

He steered her outside, away from the smoke, dust, and din.

"Is it always so noisy?" Margaret hollered, cupping her hand over her ear to hear his reply.

"Should be!" he shouted back, "if they're cutting good! Once we get her fired up, we shouldn't stop 'til dark! But we don't always get the logs!"

Margaret nodded solemnly as he led her to the cookhouse. Inside, it was quieter, for the massive log walls helped deaden the squeals from the mill. It was a huge building, long as a train station, lined with rough benches and tables. In each place was a crockery plate, a large mug, and a knife and fork. At the back, a long sink and a great iron-bellied stove were cluttered with pans, pots, and cook tools. A grinning Chinaman hurried forward, nodding vigorously, and wiping his hands on a filthy apron.

"This is Chew Fat, camp boiler," Isaac said.

"Good name for a cook." Margaret smiled.

"Velly happy you come, missie!" Chew said, shaking his own hand and bowing. "I run best-dam camp on river! Chew's pigs never fat!"

Isaac caught her quizzical look. "He means, there's not enough table scraps to feed 'em, eh, Chew?" Isaac slapped the cook on the

shoulder. "He runs fifty men through here twice a day and packs
fifty pokes for their midday meal. You can float an ax on his coffee
and sleep on his doughnuts, and there's no more finicky eater than
a timber beast, I can tell you. We get more rumpus over a bad keg
of butter than we get in a whole season over wages. And if they
don't like his flapjacks, they might just nail them to the floor."

When they went outside again, Margaret asked, "How do you
know so much about this logging business, Isaac? I thought you
spent all your youth on the river."

He threw back his head and shouted, a single bark of laughter.
"My youth, eh? You think it's up and left me?" He bent his head
close to her and mock-whispered, "That's not what you said in
Portland, Missus."

She cuffed his arm lightly. "You know what I mean, you cad."

"Aye," he grinned. "Well, remember, the canneries closed down
three or four months a year, so I spent lots of winters at one camp
or another, and this one was my favorite. I was glad when Jack quit,
and Pa needed a new foreman."

The foreman's cabin was small but neat, with two glass windows,
a separate sleeping area, and solid chairs made of smooth cedar. "I'll
have the boys add a wing and put up some more shelves," Isaac said,
holding the door open for her. Suddenly, the place seemed impossible to him and he added, "I told you before, honey. This is no life
for a woman. And believe it or not, you're seeing it at its best. In
about five hours, a herd of men'll roar down that skidroad with their
mouths full of snoose, stomping through camp with spiked calk
boots and tin pants stiff enough to stand by themselves."

"Do you trust them? Around me, I mean?" Her voice was calm.

He flushed when he realized that he'd never even considered it.
"Well—'course I do. Hell, you could leave a ten-dollar bill on the
top of your bunk for a week, and no man'd touch it. They're mostly
honest, but they're not . . . refined, Margaret. Not by any stretch of
mind. You'll hear cussing that'd make bark smolder, curl, and fall
to the ground. I remember ol' Poots Woodland could cuss a man for
a full minute and not use the same word twice. Even awed the
buckers. But he—well, anyhow, he's gone. But there's still plenty
more who aim to fill his boots."

She thought for an instant. "Yet you brought me here when they
weren't around. At the best time, you said."

He ducked his head and shrugged.

"Isaac Demers," she laughed. "You're trying to glamorize this Babel so I'll stay, aren't you!" She put her hands on her hips and walked to the door, and for an instant, he thought she was headed for the wagon for good. But then she turned and said, "Before they start on the shelves, you might have them take a hand to the privy." She smiled. "I don't mean to sit on a slant for the rest of my married days."

Isaac was nailing together benches for the table when he heard a great bellowing from the path up into the woods. Margaret stuck her head out the door and they watched a team of oxen, six lumbering beasts, two black, two brown, and two piebald, dragging a log wide as the cabin down the hill. Behind them, punctuating their bellows with fierce shouts and flailing arms, strode the camp bullwhacker.

Isaac caught her look of amazement when the man bawled out, "Hump, you bitch! Move! Move! Move!" and he stabbed once more at the oxen's rump with an evil-looking goad.

The oxen strained reluctantly, grunting and lowing, plopping their heavy hooves into the mud between the huge timbers, and finally dragged the enormous log to the mill, rumbling it over the skidroad.

Isaac hollered, waved a greeting, and said to her, "Bill Nilson. He's the top puncher around these parts."

"That man's a menace," she said wonderingly, "especially to those poor brutes he's driving."

Her husband shrugged casually. " Bill's the best in the woods. He makes near a hundred bucks a month, three times what the buckers and the swampers make. He's responsible for every animal on his team, and those Durhams cost as much as three hundred a pair. Took him most of a month to teach them to move, stop, pull, or turn when he tells them. He feeds them every night, best hay and bran he can get, washes them down like babies, rubs their necks with liniment, and nurses them when they come up lame. In between, he cusses them and wacks them to make them move. When all else fails, I've seen him jump on their backs, walk the whole team, stomping with his calk boots, spikes and all, and bawling like a wounded grizzly."

"Do they ever just revolt and refuse to budge?"

"Never," he said. "He's their god."

Behind the team came the rest of the men, plodding down the

muddy path, their voices lifted over the whine of the saws. The trees seemed to bulge with them all of a sudden, Margaret thought, as though she'd brushed her hand through a dog's fur and found two dozen fleas all in a clump. A jack lifted up his beard and shouted,

> She boldly walked up and sat down on my knee,
> And says, "You're a pines-man as well I can see,"
> She says, "You're a logger right well do I know,
> For your muscle is hard from your head to your toe."

Isaac spied the log boss and lifted his hand again, but the man was hollering at the man alongside him. "You dumb Swede sonofabitch! You got to cut an' then get your ass the hell out of the way! When I'm movin', I'm lookin' for daylight!"

Kris, the faller, hollered back, "Ay tank ay don't need no more yur lip, boss, yu damn betcha! Ay go vork fur Benson downvater, ja?" Their exchange was lost in the milling crowd as they headed for the cookhouse, and Isaac took Margaret's arm and they walked down to meet his crew.

The room looked so much smaller, filled with the loggers, she thought. Every eye turned when she came in, and she ducked her head and smiled shyly. A few of the men wiped their mouths and slicked their hands through their unruly beards quickly, in a reflexive gesture.

Isaac grabbed a bench and stood on it, his hands on his hips. "Boys," he hollered, "you all heard I'm your new foreman," and his next words were lost in a thunderous yell of welcome. Isaac grinned. "Some of you bears've known me since I was no taller than this table. To those who don't, I'll just say this: Do a good piece of work for Demers camp number five, and this boss'll keep outa your way." He turned to Margaret and put a gentle hand on her shoulder. "This here's the missus," Isaac said firmly. "She'll be in camp, long's I'm here."

There was a short silence and then a voice from the back table shouted out, "Velcome to yu, flicka! Bossman be now better as new!" The men erupted in laughter, and more cries of "Welcome, missus!" came from a dozen mouths.

Margaret laughed softly. "Thank you, gentlemen. And *I'll* do my best to keep out of your way as well." She curtsied to them, turned,

and walked out of the door as they broke into raucous, back-slap-
ping applause.

"Maybe we should make *you* foreman," Isaac grinned. "You got
them eating out of your hand fast enough."

That night, Isaac lay beside his wife and listened to the sounds
of the woods. The camp was quiet, a minor miracle considering the
noise of the day. The wind through the firs was lulling and restful,
and he was almost asleep when, suddenly, a great howl went off
close to his head. It rose like a banshee's wail in the night and ended
with a long, rackingly mournful cough.

"Isaac!" Margaret said, shaking his shoulder. "Isaac, wake up!
There's a cougar on the roof!"

He could barely stifle his laughter, and he reached for her but she
stiffened. "Keep listening," she whispered, "he'll do it again."

Isaac sighed and put his hands behind his head, gazing wearily up
at the rafters. Once again, the howl echoed through the woods.

"See!" Margaret cried triumphantly. "Now, go up and shoot him
or something!"

"Margaret," he said quietly, "don't they have screech owls back
in Wisconsin?"

She slid back down under the covers and pulled the blanket up
over her ears. "Not in our beds," she replied firmly. "When I called
it the 'howling wilderness,' I had no idea how right I was."

Two years in the woods slipped away like snow under Chinook
winds, and in the summer of 1882, Margaret bore his first child, a
daughter. Katrin was eight months old when she caught pneumonia
in a winter storm. Isaac dug her grave by the frozen creek behind
the cabin.

He kneeled with Margaret in the snow, his arm around her shoulders while she sang a hymn over the tiny mound, her voice quavering up through the hissing firs. Finally, she stopped singing, and her
face took on a fierce, white peace. "Although the fig tree shall not
blossom," she murmured, "neither shall the fruit be in the vines, yet
I will rejoice in the Lord." She looked up at him steadily. "Say it
after me, Isaac."

And when he could not speak, she went on, her voice getting
more shrill. "Yea, I will joy in the God of my salvation, the Lord God
is my strength, and he will make me to walk upon mine high
places." Suddenly, she broke off and looked about bewildered, as

though for an instant she didn't know what she was about, where she was. "Oh . . . oh, my God," she groaned loudly.

Isaac took her in his arms, holding her tightly as she sobbed.

Three years later, Margaret bore a healthy son, William Caleb, and the sadness in Isaac's soul began to heal like a woods slash in the spring. Will looked like his mother when he turned his head a certain way, but his body was all Demers. When Isaac held his son in his arms, he felt a large piece of time slide by all in a moment, as if suddenly he could see all of the past and all of the future in one sweeping vista.

They made the trip downriver to introduce Will to his grandparents. Caleb sat in a chair with a heavy shawl over his shoulders, Suzanna standing behind him. Both of them looked smaller than when he'd left, Isaac thought, as though time sat on their shoulders, pressing them to the earth. Caleb's head was nearly bald now, skull-like in its angles and edges. The slope of his brow made by the ancient cradle board was never more plain, as though he returned to his roots as he grew closer to death.

"Pa, here's your namesake," Isaac said softly and put the child in his grandfather's lap.

Caleb looked up and Isaac saw in a blink of wonder that his father's eyes glistened. My God, he thought, he must be close to seventy. That makes me near middle-aged.

"We come full circle," Suzanna said gently, patting Caleb's shrunken shoulders. "Glad I lived to see it."

The old man gazed at the infant in his lap, his eyes clear and lucid. "Good stock," he said faintly. "Best on the river." He took the boy's right hand and held it up. "His Chinook name shall be Laplash, builder, for he has strength here."

Isaac frowned and reached for his son. "He doesn't need a siwash name, Pa—"

But Suzanna put her hand on his arm. "A boy can't have too many names from which to choose. Look, he answers to it. Long time ago, I remember a certain youngster had himself a Chinook gramma, and it didn't do him no harm." Her eyes welled up as she recalled the first time Ilchee had taken Isaac into her arms, calling him a "round-headed gull." She had said more, too, about a building and a tearing down, but the old woman's words were muffled in memory and dim.

Caleb enfolded the infant firmly in his arms as though the issue were settled.

Margaret spread her skirts at Caleb's feet and said, "I'm sorry I never got to meet your mother, Mister Demers. She must have had some marvelous tales to tell."

"She had more than tales to tell," Suzanna said quickly. "Tell about your papers, Caleb. I think it's high time."

Isaac glanced at his mother quizzically, but she only smiled. When Caleb did not speak, but only stroked the silken fuzz on Will's head softly, she went on, "Why, your pa's been keeping an account, a journal, like, of his recollections. Mostly about the tribes before they was scattered, mostly about your gramma and her predictions." When Caleb still did not speak, Suzanna said to Margaret, "Did you know, she was one of the first Indian women ever to own her own canoe? And marry a white man?"

Caleb raised his head. His voice seemed to come from far away, as if he saw old visions from the past, and he spoke in the old rhythms. "She went on the mountain, and Raven spoke to her there. No other women went on the Searching. And I wrote it down, so all will remember."

"I know, Pa," Isaac said quietly. "You told me what she said before, about the river drying up and the Chinooks dying off—"

"But you did not listen," Caleb said. "So I have put it down, for others who might wish to know. This round-headed gull, perhaps"—Suzanna glanced at her husband sharply, but he did not look up—"should know that the river will be tamed like a dog," Caleb added without pause, "and the land will float. She said it."

Margaret reached for her child, gently extricating him from Caleb's arms. "I think that's a wonderful thing, to write down the past for future generations, Mister Demers," she said calmly. "I'm sure that when Will is a man, he'll be very interested in it, to see who his great-grandmother was."

"Do not wait until he is a man to let him know who he is," Caleb said firmly, his voice suddenly loud.

The infant waved his fist, let out a healthy squall, and his father and grandfather gazed at each other over his head.

Will's first memories were of the lumber camp, the noise of the mill, and the trembling distant thunder of the earth when a mighty fir crashed to the ground several miles off. By the time he was six, he had explored the woods at least three miles in each direction from camp, wandering through thickets of trees so dense that the light barely dappled the mossy earth. He had a favorite perch on a hill where he could see all the way to the river, over the trees, which were thicker, Ole said, than the hairs on a dog's back and high as God's elbow. There, he often sat and read the books his mother had shipped up from Portland—when she would let him loose from his daily lessons, that is. Chew Fat was his ayah, every man in camp was his big brother, and the bunkhouse was his nursery, unless the men started up a draw poker game, and then his mother hustled him back to his own bed.

In the morning while it was still dark, Chew Fat rang the triangle or the "gut hammer" and hollered, "Loll up, loll out! Daylight in the swamp!" Of course, it wasn't. And sometimes, even after the men had eaten and trudged six miles up to the day's cut, the light was still too dim to work. But winter and summer, when four o'clock came round, they rousted out, working the woods for nine or ten months out of the year, unless the pond froze solid or it stormed too bad to climb the trees—and all for a dollar and a half a day.

To Will, Sundays were the best days in the camp. His father was close at hand, his mother sang church hymns under the cedars, and golden silence filtered through the woods, for the saws were stilled. The men sat around reading dime novels, writing letters, washing clothes, swapping tales, and playing cards.

Will and Isaac walked for miles together on those days, fishing, surprising deer, and hunting for tracks. "See," his father would say, picking up a cone, "this is a Douglas fir cone. Tallest tree in this part of the world. And this here," stooping to pick up a cluster of needles, "this is off a sugar pine. Pitch's so sweet, it draws bees and bears like honey. Good for shingles, because it won't warp."

They'd walk down the creek, and he'd squat and examine the mud for animal tracks, pointing out the signs of raccoon, beaver, deer, and rabbit. Sometimes, when the sun was warm and the noise of the camp far away, they splashed together in a hidden stream, naked as two otters, with the air around them like a tonic and the peace like unclaimed gold.

"What kind of fish you want me to catch?" Isaac would ask, crouching down over a riffle.

"A chinook!" Will would holler, meaning a salmon. "A *big* one!"

"Look out, look out! There he goes!" his father shouted, crashing through the shallows, falling face down and scrabbling for some invisible slippery prize, while Will laughed and laughed, throwing little pebbles at his father's dancing feet.

One day, Will was helping his mother hang washing on the line behind the cabin when they heard a team pulling into the mill yard. He dropped the basket and ran, for a wagon from town meant a new packet of drawing paper, maybe a brass whistle, and a handful of penny candy. To his surprise, the mill hands clustered around, showing more than their usual interest in this month's delivery.

"Yeah, I brung her, boys!" the wagonman called. "All the way from California, she come. Dolbeer's best model!"

From the wagon bed, the men carefully drew an endless, razor-toothed band of steel, three times the length of the wagon, coiled in on itself like a snake, and bound together by steel cables.

"Easy there!" the wagonman shouted. "That bitch gets loose, an' she'll cut through camp like a scythe through standin' wheat. Don't think I ain't thought o' that when I hit every godcursed bump in that godblamed road, too! Like ridin' with a rattler, that one is."

Will had never seen the men handle any piece of metal with so much respect, and he edged closer for a better look.

"Best keep back, kid," Hobbs, an old-time sawyer, called. "Boss'll be hot if you're the first thing cut round here with his new contraption."

"What is it?" he asked.

"A band saw, boy," he said gleefully. "Best damn cutter short of God. Your pa ordered it from Dolbeer in Eureka, man who invented it. They say she'll cut anythin' in the woods. But she's touchy, like any thoroughbred, an' apt to fly off the handle."

The men carried it gingerly into the mill and laid it down, coiled on the ground. Will stayed back watching as they cut first one steel band and then, so carefully, the other. Instantly, the saw uncoiled to a glittering ribbon of hungry steel, and began to whip about the floor. Will gasped and dodged behind a post; Ole cursed and dove behind the log carriage.

As the saw began to dance more rhythmically, moved faster and faster by the tension stored in its coils, Hobbs stood frozen near the center of the floor, staring at this monster of whipping steel. He was afraid to move for the door, no direction was safe, and he couldn't turn his back on the saw, like a giant clock spring, unwinding in all directions. The quivering blade hummed and whined, making serpent shapes in the sawdust, and Hobbs could only stand his ground, pale and ready to dodge. All of a sudden, the saw wedged itself in the corner of the mill, its coils caught on a snag or on each other, tightly rolled and ready to burst loose at a touch. The whining of the metal ceased, but a humming still came from the saw, as though it breathed restlessly.

The men let out their pent-up air in a collective sigh, and Will peered out from behind his post.

In the silence that followed, Ole piped up, "Go an' ask 'er to dance again, Hobbs. Ay tank meybe dis time, she take to yu, ja?"

The men laughed nervously, in a release from their fear.

"Yeah, Ole," Hobbs called. "You go over there an' tap her on the shoulder, eh? I ain't got the stomach for it."

But nobody would go near the band saw. In fact, it soon became obvious that no work at all could go on in the mill safely until the saw was caught and bound or destroyed.

"We could nail 'er down," Hobbs said.

"You want to be the man to try it?" another sawyer asked. But nobody did.

"We could shoot her dead," a man chuckled. But nobody would.

Finally, as Will watched in amazement, the men decided the only solution, without destroying it forever, was to box in the saw where it couldn't escape.

"She'll go right through wood," Hobbs said thoughtfully. "Got to be somethin' she can't chew up an' spit out."

By the end of the day, they had mortared up the saw behind a solid wall of concrete. And when Isaac returned from the woods, there was nothing to do but curse and order another, for no man would touch that particular band saw, "born of the goddamn devil!"

After Sunday chapel, Bill and Hobbs and a few of the men sat around swapping stories, and Will would sprawl in the moss at their feet. He knew the men liked best to talk of logs felled, comrades lost to falling timber or busted saws, and women. But for his ears, they spun tales of the mystical Sasquatch . . . and Paul Bunyan.

Most claimed to have actually seen the great logger—and big? "Why, boy, he was born in Maine, see. Same state that grew Hercules and Goliath. When he was just a tyke like you, he was such a lummox that he wallered round in his sleep and rolled down four square miles of standin' timber. Right to the ground. An' as he grew, his calk boots had to be delivered on two flatcars."

"Ja," Ole chimed in, "an' he tank meybe he like a tree to cut? He yust pinch a piece out wid his fingers, so to mark 'em.'"

"An' he were a tidy fella," Nilson said solemnly. "Had a head o' hair, all curly an' black. Like mine," as the men hooted, "an' his wife combed it with a crosscut saw an' parted it with a broadax. An' he combed his beard with a pine tree, for good measure.'"

"Tell him about Babe," a man would call.

"Well, he found ol' Babe in a lake, see," Hobbs began. "Jest a little fella, then. Lake was all froze up, but Paul, he could see them two little ears jest pokin' out. He waded a mile out, near up to his chest, grabbed those ears an' pulled this little ol' calf ashore. Nursed him back to life like a hound pup, an' the calf followed him everywhere after. But he always was blue, after that, even after he thawed out. Ol' Blue Babe, he was.'"

"How big was Babe?" Will giggled.

"Well . . ." Hobbs drawled, savoring the moment as long as he dared, "folks tell he was seven ax handles between the eyes.'"

"Nope," Ole said, shaking his head mournfully. "Yu got it hay-vire agin. Babe, his head vas seven ax handles an' a plug of snoose. On de money.'"

Hobbs said huffily, "Fact is, boy, Babe was big enough to pull anythin' with two ends to it, an' that's all any sensible man needs to know.'"

"Well," Will asked, "whatever happened to Paul Bunyan?"

"Why, nothin' happened to him, son," Hobbs said quickly. "Nothin' ever does to the best loggers. He just went off to some big green valley up north. And he's cuttin' there, still.'"

Will liked most to go with his mother when she hitched up the team and drove up the skidroad, following the sounds of the axes, to watch the men at work. They drove up the mountain for several miles, and the trees crowded in thick and dense all around them. The layers of life on both sides of the wagon seemed to push into his heart, and the woods hummed with movement and silence.

But he knew, because his father warned him often, that the land was as full of death as it was of life. He remembered Isaac's disgust at the new shipment of nails: two nights from Portland, bright and shiny, nickel-new, but somebody had left the top off the keg. Overnight, they were beginning to dull and rust; in a week, they'd be useless. And he recalled the time he was down by the stream bank and found a dead crow, sprawled blank-eyed and open-beaked, half-in and half-out of the water. He went back to the cabin to get a shovel to bury it. By the time he returned, snails had written glistening loops over it, and mushrooms had sprouted in the wet feathers, raising their umbrella edges to the sky.

In a clearing ahead, surrounded by stumps three times the height of any man, the crew was working, felling four huge trees. To the side, the oxen team waited. Off on the edge, the windfall bucker was sawing furiously at some fallen timber. Isaac shouted orders to the two men half-up a massive cedar.

Each had ahold of a long, double-edged saw and pulled it rhythmically back and forth, cutting deeply into the tree. They stood on springboards set twenty feet up the trunk, above the swelling at the base roots. Further back in the woods, other men sawed at different trees, and the noise and confusion seemed bewildering after the silence of the forest road.

The men looked like small beetles scurrying over a dead deer, a seemingly futile task far beyond their abilities, even working all together. But as Will watched, Isaac went and checked the farthest tree and proclaimed it nearly ready to fall. He shouted orders to the rest of the men, who moved to one side. The two fallers on the springboards shoved metal wedges into the deep cut and took out their axes, attacking the tree once more.

Finally, the tree gave its first slight shudder of death.

"Tiiimm—bbeerr!" hollered one of the fallers, and all eyes turned to the mighty cedar. Will looked to the top of the tree and saw it tremble, and his mother pulled him behind a huge fir, just in case. From the bowels of the tree came a rumbling, a dry tearing sound like a hundred sheets ripping, and the tree began to fall with a great swishing, as though a storm moved through the mountains. It hit with a thundering crash that made him flinch and the hair rise on the back of his neck. Through the hills, the thunder rumbled, as all the other trees groaned in sympathy.

Back at the stump, the fallers jumped to the ground, ready to move on to the next target. The smaller hemlocks and ferns at the giant's base seemed to tremble then, reaching quickly into the unaccustomed sun. The buckers moved to the felled tree to saw it into movable lengths, and an ox bawled, as if in anticipation of the coming load. The cutting crew moved on.

In 1895, the year Will was ten, news came upriver in a letter from Suzanna that Caleb Demers had taken to his bed. With Will and

Margaret at his side, Isaac went back to the white house which held
so many memories for him, to say goodbye to his father.

Will had seen his grandfather twice each year, in July when the
camp closed down for the Independence Day blow-in, and at
Christmas, when they took the ferry down to Portland. He remembered him fondly, but he was an old, old man and he spoke of old
people and old times which Will did not know.

He stood outside the deathroom door, hesitating. His father was
inside, his mother downstairs, having instructed him to go to see
Caleb Demers one last time. Down the long corridor, his grandmother came quietly, her long skirts swishing on the hardwood
floors.

"What are you waiting for, child?" she asked softly.

"Maybe I should stay out," he said, his head dropped.

She tilted his chin up and looked into his eyes. "You a'scared,
Will Demers? Scared of your own grampa?"

He shook his head slowly. But neither did he move toward the
door.

"You know what a duty is, boy?" his grandmother asked. "To do
for those who have done for us. Your grampa used to say that all
the time."

Will examined one shoe carefully. "He never said it to me," he
said finally, his voice low. "My father's in there, anyways."

Suzanna's eyes snapped steel, but her voice stayed light, amused.
"Never said it to you, eh? Why, Will Demers, you don't know the
half of it. You wouldn't even be here right now, scuffing up my good
floors, if it weren't for that man in there, you know that? Now, I'll
hear no more of this foolishness." She opened the door and gently
nudged him inside, closing it on his heels.

Will saw to his tingling horror that not only was his grandfather
laying still and white on the bed, but his father was standing over
him, his eyes wet and red, the first time he'd ever seen him weep
in his life. The back of his knees felt numb, but he stiffened his
shoulders and forced himself to go to the side of the bed and look
death in the face.

The old man's head swiveled slowly on the pillow, his eyes pinning Will and fastening somewhere in the space over his head.
"That Will?" he asked, his voice weak but calm.

Isaac cleared his throat. "Yes, Pa," he said. "Will, your grandfather wants to give you this." He reached among the bedclothes and
handed his son a bound book, small and much handled. Will turned

the slim volume over in his hands, his fear now ebbing as his
curiosity stirred.

"It's all there," Caleb said, his voice startling in the silence. Will
looked at his waxy yellow face and the way the skin was pinched
and sunken around his nose, and he knew his grandfather was
dying. He swallowed his panic and reached for the old man's hand.
It was chilled and dry as a wooden window sill in winter.

"He wrote down all he could remember of his mother, of your
great-grandmother, Will. There's a lot of history in those pages, a
lot of things of value . . ." Isaac faltered, and his voice thickened and
stopped.

Caleb spoke again, with a small squeeze of Will's hand. "I told
her that Raven didn't know everything, boy"—Will realized with
a start that his grandfather was mistaking him for his father, for he
had never called him this—"but I was wrong. It just took longer
than I thought. They all died! Every last one of them who didn't
listen to her! She came back and not a one of them was living on
the river. Some went to Portland, some went to hell—her own
father wouldn't hear her! Once, he commanded more canoes than
float the Willamette, and when he died, the whites buried him like
he was one of their own!" He faltered and plucked vaguely at the
blanket on his chest.

Will looked at his father, but Isaac had eyes only for the man on
the bed. "You told me, Pa. Now, don't excite yourself. Things
change, people change too, you know yourself—"

But Caleb wasn't hearing him. His voice went on, quaveringly.
"My village. Cathlamet, the whites called it. My grandfather's
lodge. The village of my mother—it's gone. There's only a cannery
standing where a hundred lodge fires once burned. She saw it, boy.
And those who followed her up the mountain, they lived, most of
them. And their seed, too. I reckon they went further north, up to
the islands, maybe clear into the Yukon. But she saw it, saw it all."
Caleb turned and looked directly at Will, seeing him clearly all at
once. "And you . . . your eyes are just like hers"—his voice faded
away hoarsely—"read it, boy, it's *your* destiny she saw . . ."

Isaac leaned over and peered at his father, and he said sharply,
"Run go get your grandmother, Will. Hurry!"

Will whirled from the room crying, "Gramma! Mother! Come
quick!" and waited, his face against the cool wall, as the two women
swept past him, holding their skirts to their sides, their faces grim

and full of sorrow. The door closed behind them and in a moment, his father came out. He put a hand on Will's shoulder.

"I never much understood the things he thought were important," Isaac said, his voice bewildered. "I guess that's the way it is with every father and son." He seemed to be speaking more to himself than aloud, and Will sensed that silence was all that was needed. He turned the book over and over in his hands.

"I don't know. All of a sudden, it seems like there was a hell of a lot I didn't get to tell him." Will looked up at his father's face and saw that it was wet with tears. His own throat closed suddenly, and he began to weep, great gasping sobs, for no reason that he could name. Isaac pulled him close against his chest, and Will could feel his father's heart beat hard and fast. His mother came out of the room then, and Isaac turned to her, sweeping a rough hand across his eyes. "He gone?"

She nodded and embraced him wordlessly. Will heard his father say, his voice hoarse and muffled on her neck, "Christ, I feel like somebody's stolen something from me. Like a piece of my life, a place where I fit, is gone. I never felt so old in my life."

Now, Isaac turned all his attention to managing the Demers camps. The Northwest was moving, changing, he said, and it was time they got bigger pieces of it. New machines were coming, and new men would run them.

"The old bindlestiffs are near through," his father said. "Like Ole, Hobbs, and the others. The rovers, the timber beasts who just drift in and out of the woods, cutting big trees with just their two arms and an axe—those times are done. You hear about that John Dolbeer? Got himself a hell of an engine, boy. Calls it the donkey, and it's gonna run these mountains one day, you watch."

When the first Dolbeer engine arrived in camp number five, the jacks sat around on stumps, spitting snoose and jeering. But after Isaac yanked two huge logs from the top of the hill and down to the mill in less time than it took to turn a bull team around, Ole said to the bullwhacker, "Nilson, ay tank yur finished, by damn!"

Bill Nilson snorted, "Well, I guess the blamed thing's good for the short haul, but how you gonna get 'em down off the mountain, huh? It'll take ol' Sampson an' Zeke here to pull 'em out then, an' they could pull Hell itself if it had a corner loose!"

But Will listened and watched, and he knew his father was right.

Change was coming to the woods. And the men had no more than hooked up two double engines and developed the ground logging and the lines to handle them, when the locomotive came as well.

As far back as Will could remember, the loggers always had to cut the trees so that they fell downhill, always down to the skidroad, down to the mill, and then down to the river. It was a grunt-and-get-'em-out sort of work, his father said, and it needed muscles, gravity, and a lot of luck. But now, the timber grew farther and farther up the hill, and the distance between the logger's axe and the sawyer's carriage stretched until it took more time to get the trees down to the saw than it did to get them down to the ground. Sometimes, Will knew, good timber was simply left to rot when it dropped, because it couldn't be dragged from where it fell.

The men tried skidroads and chutes and flumes; they floated them down on streams; they watered down the mud, waited for a hard frost, and slid the logs downhill, and they even put a rough saw mill way up the mountain. But eventually, something else was needed to get the logs to market.

That something else was invented by Ephraim Shay. "Shay's Folly," a geared steam engine locomotive that ran like a mountain goat, followed the jacks up the steepest hill, and rounded turns so sharp that the drivers swore the headlamp shone back into the firebox. Lumbermen laid down tracks in mud without realizing that it was impossible, dynamited out timber and brush, and shouldered through cedar stands to put trestles hanging in midair.

"You know," Isaac said, "this thing'll take three-tonners when she's up and running, jerry-built or no."

"It's going to be a lot more dangerous, isn't it?" Margaret asked.

"No doubt about it. A lokie jumped the track up at Johnson's camp and took out two jacks with it. They always got to be ready to ditch. But the machine age is coming to the woods and there's no stopping now."

In September of 1902, the woods were dry and hot all over the region. Searing, merciless winds blew in from the deserts east of the Cascades, swept over the mountains, and sucked all the moisture from the woods on their way to the Pacific.

Before nightfall, a dozen fires had started from Canada to California. Cinders from donkey engines or locomotives, broken oil lanterns, heat lightning, careless matches, sparks from stovepipes, no one knew how they started. But by noon of the next day, over one hundred blazes were sweeping thousands of acres.

Standing forests exploded like cannons as flames raged, towering into the sky. Driven by the wind and fueled by the driest needles in a decade, the fires crowned the treetops, speeding along the uppermost branches like waves of breaking surf in all directions.

In the Demers camp, watch was posted round the clock, and every eye searched for an errant spark. For two days, Isaac's nerves had been on a knife edge. Even if this camp survived the sweeping destruction, he said, odds were that half of the mills in the state would be torched.

The next morning, the sun was only a circle of sullen red, hidden by a smoky haze that drifted in from the north and hovered over the camp like a curtain. The loggers hurried through loads of timber, cutting as much as they could and sending it down the flumes out of harm's way. Stray flecks of embers floated in the air by noon. Isaac picked one up and rubbed it between his fingers. "Pine ashes," he muttered to Will. "Burning closer now."

Hobbs grumbled testily, "The dirtiest sky I seen in more'n forty years. There'll be a thousand more moose birds, come spring."

Will lifted his brows quizzically.

"Moose birds," Isaac explained, his voice low. "Camp robbers, the boys call them. They say, when a jack dies, he comes back as a blue jay, a camp robber. But don't let the rest of them hear Hobbs talk like that, or we'll have a stampede down to the water."

By nightfall, a ghastly light of yellow filled the sky to the north. Will stood outside the cabin, his hand shading his eyes. The woods around him looked unreal, ghostly, and the darkness had a menace that he had never known. The ferns shivered with a dry rustle, yet there was no wind. Not a crow scolded; not a bird called out a last, sleepy settling-in song.

Suddenly, he heard the whistle blast to the north. Ole and a small crew had been working a stand, keeping watch for fire. That whistle meant they'd spotted a blaze moving toward camp.

Isaac raced from the mill, shouting orders to the men, who gathered their bundles and tools and threw them in the wagons. Two teams sped down the mountain, and a third wagon stood by, waiting. Will shouted to his mother and she plucked up the packed satchel that held everything precious to her and ran outside.

"Move, damn you, move!" shouted Isaac, herding the teams into place. Suddenly, a wildcat sped through camp, its eyes wide and oblivious with terror, raced across the clearing and into a dark stand of timber.

Will looked behind him, wisps of hair blowing into his eyes with the first wind he'd felt all night. Isaac thrust a lantern into his hands. "Jesus Christ," he whispered, and his father turned around.

There, over the trees, billowing clouds of smoke were roiling through the sky, white at the bottom, black at the top. Tongues of fire reached up into the clouds, and a noise like a coming thunderstorm built steadily to a roar.

"Get to the water!" Isaac shouted, and he snatched Margaret's arm and began to run, Will right behind them. In seconds, the air was stifling, and wisps of dry grass were burning all around their feet. "Will!" his mother shouted, looking over her shoulder in terror for him, and he reached her, grabbed her other arm, and half-lifted her into the air, he was running so fast. The horses were screaming in panic; he heard an explosion, looked back, and saw their cabin in flames. His mother's hair fell down on her shoulders; Isaac turned, picked her up, and ran stumbling with her to the water. The full force of the racing fire was on them now with a deafening rush. He felt heat and flames all around, and trees were exploding, hurling burning branches in all directions; even the pond seemed to be on fire. Will dove in, Isaac jumped headlong into the water, and as Margaret felt it close over her head, already hot to the touch, she cried, "Oh God, don't let us die!"

They quickly buried themselves deeply as they could in a muddy overhang of roots, stumbling over each other's legs, and the fire passed over them in a searing, blasting lifetime.

When they finally crawled out, Margaret could scarcely stand. Her hair was singed short and frizzed all round her face. Isaac's skin was blistered where his hands and arms had been momentarily exposed, holding her, but Will was unscathed, and his mother sobbed on his shoulder. One by one, the men stumbled out of the blackened water, and no one spoke.

They gazed silently over complete desolation. Every structure was ashes; every tree was blackened and skeletal against the sky. The horses were twisted shapes of bone, melded to the smoking metal of the wagon. Most of the men had escaped, but two had not made it to the pond, and their bodies were unrecognizable charred heaps.

Isaac slowly sank to the ground, his hands clutching the hot smoking earth. "Hobbs?" he called out querulously. "Any you men seen him?"

One of the sawyers shook his head solemnly, his scorched face all screwed up in anguish. "I never seen him after the whistle. I don't think he made it."

Isaac looked over at the nearest lump of ashes, a burned body twisted in a flash of agony. His shoulders began to shake, and he put his hands to his face briefly. In the awful silence, Will could hear nothing but the hiss of burning wood.

For seven days, the fires burned over 700,000 acres, and the land was in darkness at all hours. Half an inch of ashes covered the Northwest from Seattle to Salem, and ships forty miles out to sea had to burn their lights all day to be seen through the smoke-haze. Steamboats on the Columbia used searchlights just to navigate the river at noon. Thousands of birds fell from the sky, suffocated by the smoke and ash. Salal and alder and fern leaves littered the scorched earth, gray and perfectly formed, but powder to the touch.

Finally, the wind shifted round to the west, clouds rolled in from the Pacific, and rain put out the fires. Over twelve billion board feet of timber were lost. It went down in history as the Yacolt Burn, a series of the most terrible forest fires that white men had seen west of the Rockies. Miraculously, Skamania was intact, and it was there that Isaac took his family to recoup.

Will read the paper aloud to his parents, his voice sobered by his own sense of loss. Hobbs had been like an uncle, and he could not believe he would no more hail him with a good-natured curse from the bunkhouse door. "Says here that over a hundred towns were burnt out. Most lumbermen have lost everything but the land under the ashes."

Isaac ran his hand through his thinning hair. "Well, we're luckier than most, I guess. We can move upriver to new plots."

"Such a waste of good timber," Margaret said quietly.

"The hell with the timber, it's the men it wasted that matters," Isaac said, his voice almost sharp. "And the time. It'll be two weeks or more before we can get those new saws up and running." He sighed and leaned back in his chair. "Now's the time to say so, honey, if you want to go back to Portland for good. Nobody'd blame you."

She put one hand on Isaac's shoulder and another on Will's arm. "And leave you two timber beasts here to go *completely* wild? Not a chance. I'm just getting you tamed down the way I want you.

Besides, I read where San Francisco is building up the side of the hills, running out of room. Looks to me like Demers lumber should go for a good price by spring. We need to be cutting fifty thousand board feet a day by then, and frankly, I doubt you can do it without me." She smiled softly, and Will thought he had never seen her look more lovely.

"Well, I surely wouldn't want to try," he said gently. "Would you, Pa?"

But Isaac was poring over the newspaper's figures on timber losses. "Huh?" he said, looking up. "Oh—no, indeed, son, no I wouldn't. You know, Johnson'll want to sell off that fifty acres above Beacon Rock, maybe we should make him an offer."

Margaret rolled her eyes at heaven and so didn't see Will's frown.

Skamania was no more than a cluster of shacks in a clearing, a place that catered to upriver travelers and roughhousing loggers, where Ben Miller's cows could be heard bawling from one end of town to the other. The single street down its center was muddy, full of potholes and stumps, and narrow as a Portland alley.

The best place in town was the Naked Truth Saloon, a shanty with a roughhewn cedar bar, spittoons, a sign reading NO CREDIT, gaslights, and four dismal rooms upstairs for Skamania's whores. There, the loggers could buy bustgut whiskey for a nickel a shot, but so urgent was their thirst after a season of cutting that they'd have downed grain alcohol or horse liniment if there'd been no other choice. They were long overdue and throbbing for either a frolic or a fight, whichever happened to mosey up first. It was here that Isaac brought Will, on his eighteenth birthday, to his first loggers' blow-in.

Margaret's lips had tightened in a thin line of disapproval when he'd first mentioned his plans, but Isaac reminded her, "Some of the boys are younger than him, honey, and up on the tallest timber from dawn to dusk."

"That's not what I have in mind for our son."

"I didn't say it was, but if we don't wean him soon, the rest of the crew'll never accept him, not as cutter nor as boss. There's nothing in Skamania he can't find on his own in Portland. I may as well be there when he does."

Some of the crew chose to make the trip to Skamania by riding the flume at the edge of the camp, a V-shaped trough of wood running six miles down to the river. Down the flume, they rode shingle bolts, cordwood, posts, and railroad ties on water, up to a mile a minute, hanging on for dear life and splashing into the Columbia. Once they hit the water, steel cords corralled the logs like so many plunging, bucking mustangs, and those riders who could still walk hobbled onto shore to make the twenty-mile hike to town.

"Are you going to let those men risk their necks like that?" Margaret asked one night over dinner. "Looks to me like a poor waste of fair loggers. Might as well try to ride a bullet."

Isaac shrugged. "They've done it since we've been in these woods. No word of mine'll stop them. Besides, six miles aren't so very far. There're flumes downriver twenty miles long or more, and the crazy fools ride those, too."

Margaret looked at Will sharply. He grinned at her delightedly, but her intense gaze made him drop his head. "I thank the Lord that both my men have more sense," she said softly. "May God have mercy on those who don't."

"Amen," said Will, chuckling. "But I aim to watch, at least."

Now, as Will and Isaac and most of the crew rode into Skamania, Ole, Pete, and two other flume-riders met them, eager to boast of their prowess and adventures.

"Ay 'bout tamed dat bitch!" Ole hollered to Isaac when he saw him. "She say she be back nex' spring fur 'nudder ride!"

Pete growled and cuffed him. "If you'd a been on mine, you'd be laughin' out of the other side o' yer mouth, you dumb Swede. Mine bucked like a nine-dollar whore! I swear by all that's holy, I ain't never had such a thrill!"

"No, und yu ain't gonna, needer," Ole yelped, " 'cause yu ain't got no nine bucks!"

The boys laughed and Isaac shouted over the din, "Anybody get stomped?"

Pete grinned ruefully. "Nothin' that a splint an' a few stitches cain't fix." He held up an arm and pulled up his sleeve to show a crude bandage wrapped from his wrist to his elbow.

"Or a cedar coffin," Ole said, rolling his eyes. "After Pete rode his missus-log, dat's all she's gud fur, ja?" They strode the streets in a bunch, shouldering each other aside and shouting for the sheer joy of it.

Homer, the barkeep, welcomed them with a wide grin and full

glasses, for he made enough money off the loggers in July to close up the rest of the summer, just in time to hit the salmon run. He'd done his best to encourage their trade, and Isaac complimented him on his latest decor. A new stuffed grizzly reared up in a shadowed corner, and faro tables ringed the edge of the room.

"Homer, I do believe you're trying to match Portland or Aberdeen," he said. "Christ, the boys scarcely need to go downriver at all."

Will crowded up to the bar next to him and leaned over, offering the barkeep his hand. "Will Demers, mister. Glad to meet you."

"Don't say!" Homer grinned. "Well, boys, we got to initiate him proper, right? A glass on the house, Mister Demers. And don't tell your ma where you come by it, eh?"

Will was lifting the glass to his lips when suddenly a huge beaver crawled from behind the bar and lumbered down its length, its flat gray tail yawing and swaying from side to side. "Good God!" he sputtered, spilling his drink.

The crew broke into laughter, clapping Will on the back. "That's ol' Duke," Homer chuckled. "He likes to welcome each new man in person. He's the meanest brute this side of the river. Whup any dog in the state and chase him hell to breakfast. But offer him a shot, an' he'll follow you anywhere, just like an ol' bluetick pup."

Will gingerly put down his half-full glass on the bar before the beaver. The sad-eyed creature sagged down on his webbed feet and delicately lapped at the glass, pulling his huge yellow incisors up and out of the way.

"Why, I'd purely hate to meet that booger coming round a dark corner," Pete grinned.

"Hell, he's so old, moss grows in his ears," Homer scoffed. "An' he's lazy as a Christmas pig. But the dogs don't know it."

Pete downed his glass and set it thump on the bar. "Damn, if it ain't time to get me teeth fixed," and he rolled his eyes upstairs.

"You got a toothache?" Will asked.

Pete slapped him on the back, "Yeah, kid! An' I know just where to get 'er plugged!" And he sauntered upstairs to the small rooms at the end of the hall, to the accompanying catcalls of the rest of the crew.

Isaac walked Will outside to show him around. Down Skamania's twisted street, saloons, restaurants, and lodging houses crowded each other's shoulders. Signs saying "The High-Lead" and "The Loggers' Waldorf" beckoned.

"First thing, we got to get some new duds," Isaac said, steering Will into I. S. Shay's shop under a sign that read, "Men's Furnishings." The window was full of cheap Sunday suits in a color resembling a day-old bruise.

Next door, Dr. Painless Parker had an outdoor dentist office going, and one logger already occupied his single chair, a bib around his neck. Down the block, a tattoo parlor and a barber shop completed Skamania's attractions. The town had no soldiers, no preachers of the gospel, and no schools. Speculators, timber beasts, and calk boots were its main currencies, and only those who catered to them were getting rich.

By dusk on the first day, Will and Isaac had been bathed, shaved, suited, and made soggy with drink. Just about the time the crew was wondering what else to do, another herd of jacks from up at Johnson's camp swarmed into Skamania, and within an hour, the fights had broken out. Since the town only boasted four whores, it was inevitable that eighty loggers would find the pickings skimpy.

Will and Isaac were strolling along the sidewalk back toward the Naked Truth when there was a splintering crash, and two loggers erupted through an upstairs window. Flailing and cursing, they landed with two distinct stomach-slapping thwacks in the muddy street below. Incredibly, they each staggered upright and began windmilling at each other again, kicking shins with calk boots, and generally making enough ruckus to shake a good-sized pine.

From the window, a half-naked woman leaned out and shouted, "And don't you two stiffs come back, ya hear? I ain't no roustabout! If you can't be no gentlemen, then take it down the hall, see!"

Isaac put his arm on Will's shoulders. "I was just about your age, son," he said softly, "when I had my first woman."

Will looked up, amazed and embarrassed, for his father had never spoken to him of such. He knew more about the female side of the species than most his age, he figured. No way to be on a logging crew and not hear it. He glanced up at the woman in the window, turned a darker shade of brown, and looked away.

Isaac smiled. "Your mother would keel over if she heard me, but I think, were I to wish one thing for you, son, it'd be that you have your first time with somebody like that lady, there. She's a fine woman, and she's got soft hands and a good heart."

Will said, "I don't know, Pa. . . ." He looked back at the upstairs window just as she looked down and smiled at him over two pink and creamy breasts. Without giving his mouth permission, it smiled right back. "I guess," he added, "it wouldn't hurt."

Isaac laughed, a loud bark of delight. "No, I daresay it won't. And those two boys already did half the job for you. The rest's easy." He whipped his hat off and grabbed Will's own off his head, stuffing it in his pocket. "Peg!" he yelled over the din.

She looked down and appraised the two of them warily.

"How'd you like to have the honor of properly breaking in our young buck here!" Isaac called. "There's not another lady who I'd trust him with. Shall I send him up?"

Peg leaned further out the window, her breasts mounding up on the sill, and smiled a slow velvet grin. "Well, I suppose," she said throatily. "He yours?"

"Best part of me, upright!" Isaac wheeled him on his heel, round the saloon, and through the door, Will half-heartedly pulling away at every step.

"Pa, leave me alone," he fumed, stumbling against the stairwell. "I guess I can find my way when I'm good and ready."

Suddenly, Peg appeared at the top of the stairs, and every eye at the bar swiveled upward. She was wearing a pink silk wrapper, tightly pulled around her plump body. In the dim gaslight of the hallway, her black hair seemed to curl in teasing, glowing tendrils down her throat, and her mouth looked red and wet. "Are you good an' ready *now*, honey?" she purred.

The loggers downstairs let out a ragged cheer. Nilson jumped up on the bar. "There's not a man here who's more deservin'!" he shouted. "An' all of camp five stands ready to see him first up an' first in!"

Incredibly, there was no argument, and five men joined Isaac in good-naturedly shoving Will up the stairs. As he reached the top, Peg put out a white, scented hand and led him to her room, her pink mule slippers making a soft slap, slap, slap, down the corridor. Even with the door closed behind him, Will heard the cheers and toasts continue.

She turned slowly, smiled over her shoulder, and let her wrapper slide to the floor with a silken rustle. She arched her back and turned her naked bottom to him. Slowly, she moved her hands to her buttocks and began caressing them softly. Her voice sent shivers to his belly as she asked, "What's your name, mister?"

Will blushed, grinned, and moved toward her, removed her hands, and replaced them with his own. "My name's Will, ma'am, and I think I'd just as soon do that myself, if it's all the same to you."

That night, Isaac walked along the river alone, listening to the sounds of the night. The noise of Skamania was far behind him, and he relished his solitude, his mind casting forward and back over his life. My son is having his first woman, he thought idly. That must be some sort of landmark for the both of us. He felt a twinge of guilt when he thought what Margaret would say if she ever found out. But a man's got to take his son in hand at some point, he reasoned, and help him to make his way. God knows, nobody else will, and I don't want him to get to be my age, knowing only his wife in his bed.

He sat on a river stone and wondered what Margaret was doing with her evening. Reading, perhaps. Was she thinking of him? Married forever. Like his parents, like every respectable couple he'd known. Always and forever, he would have another human being to think of, to provide for, to love. He looked down at his hands and wondered when they had got so lined. So old.

A feeling of pressure, of closeness came over him, and he took several deep breaths to try to ease the ache in his chest. I have no idea how I got here, he thought vaguely. And then, with an almost brutal sense of calm, he remembered Ning Ho and his feelings for her.

It seems a lifetime ago, he thought. Hell, it *is*. It was because of her that I married Margaret, he realized. To escape. To feel, at the end, that I had a choice, whether I did or not. He shook his head, laughing at himself inwardly. I'm sounding just like an old man now, he thought, acting like the past actually mattered.

Margaret is a good woman. Got sense and spirit and knows how to laugh. Talks to the Lord a lot, but you can't blame her for that, nobody else much to talk to, stuck way back where we are. She's not pretty, but she's sturdy enough, and hell, she made us a fine son, he thought. It sure wouldn't have worked with Ning Ho.

And then his thoughts turned to Will. Growing up fast and full of secrets. Can't seem to get him to take *hold* like he should. When I want him out with the buckers, he's off tinkering with an old tandem saw; when he should be up a tree, he's got his nose in that damn journal his grampa gave him. Always traipsing off to the river, and *still* hasn't learned to pick a bad-tagged pine from a good one, for all the times I've told him.

He sighed and closed his eyes, feeling the winds from the woods moving over his head. Every man's got dreams for his son, he thought. He could take hold and turn the Demers camps into a damned *empire*, if he wanted. No other reason I'm doing all this except for him. Well, maybe he's just a late-bloomer; God knows I was, too. I just want the best for him. His heart felt full of pride, pain, and memory all at once.

For an instant, he wanted to steal a canoe, slip it silently into the river, and row away to sea, never to return. But even as he pictured himself escaping, toying with thoughts of endless freedom, he knew he'd never do it. His parents had tried to distill the iron of self-control from his restlessness at an early age. He had faltered once, maybe twice in his life—the most monumental mistake being his brief affair with Ning Ho. He wondered if his parents ever really knew how far it had gone. He sometimes felt that the iron in his spine was corroding and poisoning him, and he felt a secret distance between himself and others. But then he threw off his mood with firm distaste.

Folks never said, "This is the truth, and I got to take it as it is," he thought. Instead, they said, "Well, *maybe* this is all I get for now." Only when they got old and doddery did they finally see the light and say, "Here it is and there's not going to be any better. Not for me. Not for anybody." He figured he was a step ahead for seeing it all the sooner.

He was happy, he knew it. And he was lucky. He had a fine wife, a good future, and a son who made him proud. If there was more to hope for, more to dream about, then he couldn't put a name to it or touch it with his finger. And if he couldn't see it or say it, then it must not be real.

Work picked up that fall, and a new crew was added to the old roster. One newcomer to Demers camp five was Sam Suckow, a shingle weaver.

"What in the world does a shingle weaver do? Stitch them together for a roof?" Margaret asked as she passed Will more potatoes.

Isaac chuckled and reached for another slice of ham. "Nope, not quite. He cuts the planks into shingles and bundles them for packing. Gets paid by the piece, so he's got to be fast and sharp-eyed."

And so Sam was. Will stood in the open doorway of the sawmill one afternoon, watching him. Suckow squinted appraisingly as the huge timber groaned up the carriage. He glanced up, twisted his wrist, and the log was captured by the bull chain. He shifted his weight, caught the lever, and the steam nigger—a piece of monster metal with teeth—turned the log over and slammed it down on the saw. The boards fairly flew through his hands and emerged, cut and planed, as square shields against the wind, rain, and snow for some hundred anonymous houses.

Will whistled softly under his breath, for he'd never seen a man cut a log so fast. It was the finished product that fascinated him the most, far more than the raw timber. The sheer *engineering* of it seemed a miracle, the way a single man could harness such power and make it over into something useful, something a man could hold in his hand. . . .

"You ever seen this done, boy?" Suckow asked suddenly.

Will shook his head.

"Want to hear what I saw last season?"

Will nodded, "Sure, I guess."

"Wal', this one ol' weaver sliced off three of his fingers in the saw, see, and blood was a' spurtin' all over the floor and the sawdust. He took off to get wrapped up, an' the foreman ran up, mad as a treed coon. 'How the hell did he do that?' he asked the second weaver." Here, Sam Suckow looked up and grinned at Will, his fingers still moving inches from the saw. " 'Like this,' the man said, and then he run his fingers right through the blade in the same way."

Will blinked and stared at Suckow's hand, certain he would see blood and flesh flying, but the log just kept coming, the saw kept whining, and the weaver laughed and shook his head, waving him away.

Sam Suckow was from Seattle, and Will found him later sitting among the boys after supper, telling about the new ideas from the north. He had a copy of the *Shingle Weaver Journal* under his arm, and he read from it, his voice rising and falling and sometimes catching fire.

"Boys, the name of the game is organize," he said firmly. "Says right here in black and white. 'Workers of the World, Unite.' You heard of Big Bill Haywood? Bull of a man with one eye, used to be president of the Western Federation of Miners. Well, he's workin' for you, boys. Workin' for all of us. Out to get us an eight-hour day an' three dollars minimum."

"I heard of that bunch," a logger muttered. "Buncha socialists, lookin' to take over the country. Wobblies, they call 'em."

Will stood in the background silently, wondering what his father would say to all this.

"Aye, they call 'em Wobblies," Sam grinned, "but there's nothin' wobbly about their balls, man. They mean what they say, an' they'll get it, too. An' them that joins 'em'll get the goods. Them that don't'll get a fistful of nothin'. Which is about what you got now."

Ole piped up. "Ay don't call a yob an' dree squares a day nothin'. An' moneys in my pocket, too."

"Well, I don't call it a livin'," Sam said, "an' I don't call it fuckin' square, neither. Not with the bosses makin' money hand over fist, on our backs. Workers are gonna be marchin' soon, you watch."

Will walked slowly away from the men, back to the cabin, his lower lip jutted out in thought. He sensed a menace in the man, like a tree bad-tagged, right before it fell. You couldn't say for sure which way or when, but you knew it was coming, and maybe in your direction.

A few nights later, Will was reading in the corner chair, his long legs draped awkwardly over the arm like jackstraws. His mother glanced over at him fondly. Newspapers, books, labels, anything he can find, he'll read it. And that journal his grandfather gave him is getting to be like a third hand, she thought. I'll have to rebind it for him, before it falls apart out on some trail someday. Four hours a day, she'd kept him inside the cabin, reading and figuring on the tablecloth, sending off for every text she could find.

Isaac said, "What's that you got your nose in?"

"This paper Suckow gave me," Will said. "You seen it, Pa?"

"Not more of that damn Wobbly crap," Isaac scowled. "I don't think much of any 'I won't work' stiff who just goes around stirring up trouble. If they don't like their jobs, they're plenty more who're waiting to put in an honest day's work for decent wages." He slapped his hand on the table, suddenly angry. " 'Organization!' Suckow can talk 'til his brains bleed, but it all comes down to the same thing. They're nothing but a pack of lazy bums looking for a handout!"

Will felt an unfamiliar stiffening up his spine, a cold distaste starting somewhere in his belly. Without warning, he blanched painfully and his voice lowered to a husky anger. "Well, I guess it's settled, then, eh? But I bet *you* never worked for a buck and a half a day in your life."

"Will!" Margaret warned him, glancing at his father. "Watch your tongue."

Isaac was shocked at Will's response, but he kept his temper. "Whose side are you on anyways, boy?" He tried out a sideways grin, but it wouldn't stay on his mouth. "Look, these are just a bunch of no-counts. You watch, it'll blow over, it always does. There's no way in hell a lumber camp's going to make any money passing out more'n three bucks a day to jacks for eight hours' work, and if you'd pay more attention to business around here, you'd see it for yourself. Mattresses and sheets, some of them want!" Now his smile came more easily, and he gave Will a comradely wink. "Can you imagine old Ole on sheets, for God's sake? Hell, he wouldn't know what to do with them if he got them."

"Sheets? In the bunkhouse?" Margaret looked bewildered.

Will waved her question aside. "That's not the issue, and you know it, Pa. They want better, safer working conditions. They want insurance for their families against cut-off arms and legs and broken backs and burnt-out bodies. They want decent wages and no more working from can't see to can't see. And frankly, I don't blame them. Doesn't seem like much of a life, to me."

"Oh, it doesn't, eh? Well, it's been a damned good life to *me*, boy, and to you, too, s'far as that goes! Families!" Isaac snorted. "They don't have families. They're just a bunch of rovers, most of them. Carrying their bindles on their backs, moving from job to job. And they're being led around by a bunch of fools! Trying to ruin this country and all it stands for, working from the inside!"

Isaac suddenly sighed, all the anger seeping from him. He spread his hands in an embracing gesture. "Look, son, you're young and you're full of beans, and you give a damn, and that's to your credit. I wish you gave a damn more for where we're going to lease enough timber next season, but what the hell. I care about the men too, you know. Hell, some of the best boys I ever met are right here in camp number five. But I owe them running this job the best way I know how. And that doesn't mean handing out all the profits to greedy bums, or wrapping them in clean sheets every night, or making some insurance company rich. I'm doing it all for you, boy, you might keep that in mind."

Will stood up and walked to the door, his back still stiff. "I'm going out for a chew. It's too stuffy in here."

Margaret waited until the door closed. "He's growing up," she said softly.

"I know it," his father said. "Just so he doesn't grow away."

When Will was twenty, Isaac closed the mill down for the July blow-in and took his family to Portland for a month. The Lewis and Clark Centennial Exposition had just opened, and visitors came from all over the country to see it. It was 1905, a hundred years since the two explorers had floated with a small band of Americans down the Columbia to the sea, and Portland was ready to show the world that the wilderness was tamed.

Business leaders, tired of hearing Portland referred to as "Stump Town," had wrested nearly half a million dollars from the state legislature to develop the show. With this amount in hand, they persuaded merchants all over Oregon to contribute another half, and the federal government chipped in almost two million more.

"Yessir!" Isaac said gleefully. "I sent them a hundred bucks myself! It's gonna be the greatest extravaganza since God created the world, and we're not gonna miss it!"

They took the streetcar to the Slabtown area, named for the sawmills and stacks of slabwood lined along the streets. There, over an almost four-hundred-acre tract, President Theodore Roosevelt had personally laid the exposition's cornerstone, and pushed the button that swung open the gates to surging crowds.

Will thought he had entered another world completely, of graceful buildings, glittering fountains, huge gardens, and stirring displays of modern technology. Isaac steered them down the midway, where Little Egypt danced the hootchy-kootchy merely by gyrating her hips, and where they tasted, for the first time, a confection of spun sugar called Fairy Floss, which stuck to Will's face and hair like a spiderweb.

As they strolled about the grounds, gaping at first one amazement and then another, they joined the edges of a small throng, listening to a woman speak about women's rights.

"You are forever a minor in the eyes of the law!" the woman shouted, her eyes flashing angrily at a knot of hectoring men in the corner. "Women of Oregon, unite! We pay taxes! We must have the vote!"

Will grinned. "So what would you vote for if we gave it to you, Mother?"

"I believe I'd vote out impertinent sons," she chuckled and took Isaac's arm. "And then I'd work my way up to husbands."

In a booth by the logging exposition, they joined a crowd to meet the Poet of the Sierras, Joaquin Miller. Next to him stood Ezra Meeker, the oldest pioneer in Oregon. He was planning to retrace his steps by oxcart back over the Oregon Trail, and people were lining up to contribute to his travel fund.

"It's hard to believe Gramma came out the same way, over all those miles," Will said.

"By God," Isaac laughed, "she's still tough enough to do it again!"

Over in the corner of the exposition grounds stood a building more massive than all the rest, visible from all points of the city. It was the Forestry Building. The great log house was over two hundred feet high, and its very walls were made of the tallest cedars that could be brought downriver.

As they walked about its huge corridors gazing upward at the massive trees all about them, Will whispered, "How in the world did they do this? Makes me feel so small, like a bug on the bark."

"They got them from all over the Northwest," Isaac said proudly. "They call it the Oregon Parthenon. Some came from our camps, others from Benson's downriver, lots more from Gray's Harbor and Port Townsend. But they're all the best the woods had to offer. And they took them down with nary a bruise."

"No, I mean, how did they get them to stand *up* like this, so straight? How did they put the thing together?"

Isaac shrugged. "Beats me. What matters is they did it, and folks who see it, know they got something to be proud of, something no other state in the country has—these giants." He patted a massive cedar fondly, as though he owned it.

A million people visited the fair that summer, and two million more came from all over the country before the gates finally swung shut for the last time. Portland was changing overnight, and Isaac looked in vain for old landmarks, only to find them hidden behind new buildings or gone completely. To his amazement, culture had come to the Northwest coast. Nancy Boyd still had her floating fancy house, though, hitched to first one dock, then another, always eluding the Portland police, the bright red smokestacks of her steamboat signaling all out-of-town loggers where pleasure might be found. And Erickson's, the largest saloon in the West, was still standing, Isaac noted with relief.

When he told Margaret he wanted to take Will to see Erickson's she frowned, but he said, "Why I'd rather see Erickson's with the lights on than the Grand Canyon herself!"

Erickson's sat sprawled in the center of Portland's North End, the liveliest skidroad in the Northwest. The bar alone was the longest in six states, six hundred and eighty-four feet, to be exact. The saloon itself took over a whole city block and had five entrances, each one a favorite with one logging group or another. One massive door closest to the docks was named "St. Petersburg" because the Russians and the Finns favored it over the other four.

Isaac and Will went through the revolving doors on the Third Street side and made their way to the bar. Grand chandeliers and mirrors sparkled round the room and laid out on a huge table was Erickson's famous free lunch, the mainstay of which was half a roast ox. Will filled a plate with sausage, cheese, and pickled herring and plunked down a nickel for a beer. He looked around and asked, "Who owns this acre of heaven, Pa?"

"August Erickson," Isaac grinned. "A Russian Finn. Made his fortune running salmon."

"And who's that mountain in the corner?" Will pointed to a massive giant, three hundred pounds or more, who lounged near the door.

Isaac laughed and slapped Will on the back, feeling closer to him than he had in months. "That's ol' Jumbo Reilly, the bouncer. I saw him toss a Swede jack out on his ear, Halfpint Halverson was his name. Halfpint went round the corner and came in another door, and Jumbo tossed him out again. He kept it up 'til he'd been thrown out of four of the five doors, right? Well, when he hit the fifth and last door, Jumbo met him head-on. 'Yesus!' Halfpint yelled. 'Iss yu bouncer in every damn place dis town?'"

Will laughed and groaned, "Pa, that's the worse Swede accent I've heard this side of Oshkosh."

That night they sat down to Suzanna Demers' table, spread with Isaac's favorites. Elizabeth and Sarah, Isaac's sisters, flanked Will on both sides. Suzanna's white hair was piled high over bright blue eyes.

"This town's changin', nearly overnight," Suzanna said mildly as she piled fresh green beans on Will's plate. "We got ourselves a regular flophouse district now, down by the docks. Lordylord, I never thought to see it in Portland!"

Elizabeth said, "It's a scandal. Seattle's full of bums, too, I hear, and Spokane, even down to San Francisco. Lots of them came out to work the railroads, and now that the lines're finished, they've got no place else to go. Hobos, immigrants, filling up the woods and loitering in the streets, I've seen them."

Sarah added, "Most of them can't even sign their names, but they got their stakes saved up from their last job, and they take what they can get off the soup lines and the skidroad mission houses. Why, the *Oregonian* says nearly five thousand of them will hit the streets by August. This town won't be fit for decent women to walk!"

"I don't know where we're going to put them," Elizabeth said.

"Well, I hope to heaven we put them to work," Suzanna said shortly. "Lord knows there's plenty to be done in this town. The streets are nigh to filthy and the roads're full of sumpholes. My pa used to call them ridge-runners and no-count, to boot."

"I'd hardly call a man no-count just because he's out of a job," Will said calmly. "Or looking for a better one."

"There's ways to look and ways to look, Will Demers," Suzanna said. "The best way I know to lose something, 'specially a job, is to go round with your hands open. Seems to me, that's what most of these boys is best at. Now, let's talk about something else. Tell us what you're planning for this strapping son o' yours, Isaac, he's growing taller than a back-lot cedar."

Will said no more, but Margaret noticed that his mouth tightened, and he ate little else that evening.

The next morning, Will went alone down to the skidroad district, walking the streets of the city. He passed small knots of men standing in the shelter of the alleyways, huddled around open fires in the early morning fog. Obviously, many had slept in the streets that night, for their clothes were rumpled and worn. They glanced at him as he passed.

I must look a swell to them, he thought, in my city clothes and my shined shoes. He had a sudden urge to go to them, take them by the arm, and say, "I'm one of you. Under these clothes, I'm just a working stiff, too." But he knew they'd pull away, alarmed, their faces hard with distrust. After an hour of wandering around the back streets down by the docks, past the flophouses, the burlesque theaters, and the fancy houses, he chanced upon an open door. Over the stoop, a small sign read, "Industrial Workers of the World." He went inside.

Right by the door stood a small rack full of pamphlets, recent issues of I.W.W. journals and newspapers, with a card attached that read, "Free for all Friends of the Working Man."

Well, I'm certainly that, Will thought to himself, and he took a newspaper, folding it under his arm. Inside the hall, a few men loitered around an old saloon piano. In a corner, one man sat at a roll-top desk, writing. Half-full spittoons cluttered up the corners. The smell of mulligan stew came from a squat-bellied stove in the back. One man poked and stirred at the pot while he argued heatedly with another cook.

"Read your Tom Paine," he said gruffly, "and then talk to me about the bourgeois conspiracy, man. He was a member of the master class if there ever was one, and he'd be on our side, fighting in the streets today if he was alive."

Another man plunked himself down at the piano and began to play, picking out the song slowly and singing unselfconsciously, half to himself, to the tune of the hymn, "Take It to the Lord in Prayer."

> Are you poor, forlorn, and hungry?
> Are there lots of things you lack?
> Is your life made up of misery?
> Then dump the bosses off your back.
> Are your clothes all patched and tattered?
> Are you living in a shack?
> Would you have your troubles scattered?
> Then dump the bosses off your back.

The man at the desk suddenly looked around and spied Will standing in the hall.

"Can I help you, brother?" he said, gesturing him inside.

Will instantly felt all eyes swivel to him, to his natty trousers and well-fitted coat, to his "town" shoes.

"I'm a jack," he said, pushing his voice past the dryness in his throat. "Just blew in town." He saw a few of the men exchange glances and sensed their wariness. "Demers camp, up to Skamania," he added.

The man at the desk stood up and over, briskly pumping his hand. "Glad to see you, come on in. See you got one of our papers under your arm, there. What'd you say your name was, friend?"

Will hesitated just a moment. "Hobbs. Ole Hobbs is the name." He felt out of place and wondered what in the world he was doing.

But then the man said, "A Swede, eh? We got lots of Swedes on the rolls, friend. You come to the right place. Step right up and pull up a chair—Hank, get the man a seat and a cup of joe—you're welcome, yessir. My name's Slim, and I'm a union man, just like my friends, here. Yessir, Ole, you come to the right place."

Within the hour, Will had paid his two dollars dues, signed the rolls of the Portland delegation of the I.W.W., and put his red union card in his pocket. He was finally a member of something, he said to himself, even if it was with a phony name. And when somebody said, "My Fellow Workers"—well, that man was talking to him.

In August when the men came back to work, Isaac noticed more and more of them clustered around Sam Suckow, swapping yarns and trading snoose. Once, he swore to Margaret that he'd fire the man in the morning.

"Just can his ass is what I oughta do," he fumed, "and send him on his way. Let him stir up his hornet nests in somebody else's yard."

Margaret pursed her lips and thought out loud. "I don't think you can do that, Isaac."

"What do you mean I can't do it? It's my camp! You just watch me!"

She wrapped her arms about his neck, soothing him. "Well, of course you *can* do it if you want to, I didn't mean that. But I wonder how it'll look, and all. The men'll say, those who want to beat a dog'll always find a stick, and that you were just laying for him. The men like him. He works good, you said so yourself."

Isaac sighed hugely and plopped down in his chair, rubbing his forehead. "Jesus, what ever happened to the days when a man did his licks, took his stake, drank himself a beer on the Fourth of July, and that was all he looked for outta life?"

Margaret grinned at him, and then lowered her voice in a good imitation of Ole. "Ay tank yur right, boss. A yob und dree squares a day shud be gut enuff fur any yack, ja?"

Will came in the cabin door in time to hear that last, threw his hat on the table, and said thoughtfully, "Even jacks got to feed something else besides their bellies. A dream, or something, just like any other man."

Isaac said shortly, "What we need around here is more damned dreams, all right. I can't keep the saws moving *now,* and when we're out of clear-cuts in that last lease, we're gonna be cutting thin air. It might help if you got your hind end *up* the mountain more, 'stead of *down* it. Every time I see you, you're either heading for the river or just coming back—"

Will interrupted him casually. "The river's where I'd rather be, Pa."

"Christ, you sound like an old siwash I used to know—my gramma was always rattling on about the river like she invented the damned thing. Time you figured it out, boy, there's no money in that river and never will be again. The salmon's petering out, and that only leaves water and a pretty view, and you can't sell what a man can have for free. Timber's the future of this country, not the blasted river, and I'm breaking my back here for *you,* goddammit!"

"I never asked you," Will said gently.

Isaac's face reddened in sudden incandescent fury, and Margaret moved to stand between them, wondering if the moment she'd dreaded, known was inevitable, was finally here. But no: Will went on quietly, "She never said *my* destiny was here, Pa, only yours."

"She? For Christ's sake!" Isaac exploded. "Is *that* what this is all about?"

"Now, that's enough," Margaret said firmly. "I won't have you two bickering like this, not when there's a common problem we've all got to face together. Will, your father needs you. There's trouble coming and when it hits, we've got to turn it aside as a family— that's all that matters right now." She went to Will and took his arm, looking up into his face. When did he get so tall? she wondered in the back of her mind; when did his jaw take on that edge, where did his freckles go? "Am I right?"

Will smiled ruefully, patting her shoulder. "Aren't you always?" He pulled up a chair, watching his father covertly.

Isaac walked over to where he sat and took a handful of Will's hair, tugging gently on it in a gesture he hadn't used since Will's head was too tall for him to reach. He looked down at his son, smiling tenderly, a little sadly, as though he had just created a magnificent snowman and the sun was coming out. Then he turned and walked out the door.

On December thirtieth of that year, an early snowfall blanketed the mountains clear into Idaho. At dusk, Frank Steunenberg, ex-governor of that state and resident of a little town called Caldwell, walked from his law office through the sleet to his house. When he opened the gate on his picket fence, a deafening explosion ripped him wide open and left him dying in the snow.

The blast was heard ten miles out of town, and the windows of the Steunenberg house were shattered into shards of glass which were later found embedded in homes a half-block away. The police picked up and arrested an itinerant Wobbly, Harry Orchard, who denied all knowledge of the bombing murder of the ex-governor. But under questioning by a Pinkerton detective, Orchard confessed to that and many other bombings that had killed at least thirty men. In his confession, he named two men who had paid him to do the jobs: Charles Moyer, president of the Western Federation of Miners, and Big Bill Haywood, president of the I.W.W.

The news rocked the Northwest, and the *Oregonian* led the headlines with the words "I.W.W. Bombers!" screaming across in banner print. Lumbermen up and down the river took sides, and fistfights erupted in Erickson's and other watering holes over Haywood's innocence. No less than Clarence Darrow defended Big Bill, and when he was found not guilty, many swore he'd bought off the judge and jury with union funds. Even President Theodore Roosevelt waded into the fray with a public letter stating that, guilty or not, Haywood was an "undesirable citizen."

Now, the Wobblies had an issue around which to rally their members, a blatant attack on the character of the working man, and a martyr—Big Bill Haywood. The week after Roosevelt's letter had been printed in the *Oregonian*, Sam Suckow came to camp wearing a button that read, "I am an Undesirable Citizen." Two days later, four of the men left camp to join a union parade in Portland, and before they left, they recruited two more members.

In March, word came downriver that the Wobblies had struck Portland. A dozen sawmills closed in the space of a week. Police arrested scores of strikers, throwing them in the city jail on charges of disorderly conduct, attempted arson, and disturbing the peace.

Two Demers yards were affected, and a shudder went through the whole industry, felt as far east as Spokane.

One week later, Isaac strode into the dinner hall while the men were eating, stood on a chair, and asked for their attention. "Boys, you've all heard 'bout the trouble downriver. There's some who say the logging business is going to hell in a handbasket. There's others who say that it's the jacks who're going to hell first. Well, I'm not here to make up your minds for you, but I won't have a bunch of troublemakers in Demers camp five."

There was a restless murmuring from the table where Sam Suckow sat, surrounded by his friends. Isaac raised his hand, asking for silence. "Times are changing. I know that and so do you. You're all good men, and I've known some of you since I wasn't tall enough to reach the cookstove. I'm offering you a ten-hour day and wages upped to two dollars for stiffs, two and a half for sawyers and weavers, and three for the foremen. Take it or leave it."

In the silence, Sam Suckow asked, almost thoughtfully, "Why the hell should we settle for your measly handouts, Demers, when we can shut down the whole operation, take it over ourselves, an' divvy up the profits fair an' square?"

Will looked up, shocked. He swiveled in his seat and stared at Isaac. From two benches down, he could see the veins stand out on his father's neck.

"You just try it," Isaac snapped. "I'll be waiting for you with a shotgun and the sheriff right behind me. Maybe back in Germany, a bunch of socialists can steal a man's land and business, but this is America, Suckow." He turned his back to the man and faced the rest of the crew. "How about it, men? My father ran this camp square, and so do I. Nobody here's ever had less than was coming to him in his pockets. Nobody's belly ever bitched at him that the boss was saving money by feeding him swill. I hear the talk same's you. I know they've struck in Portland, and more mills could be closing any time. When they do, I want Demers camp to be rolling out boards at a hundred thousand feet a day. I'm offering ten hours of steady work, better wages, and my hand on it. What do you say?"

"Don't fall for it, men!" Suckow shouted angrily. "Come with me, an' I can damn near guarantee you eight hours a day an' three bucks in your pockets! He can't run this mill by himself. He'll fold, right along with the rest of them!"

In the silence, Ole piped up, "Ja, und ve vill eat how, when he folds, eh? Yu vill feed us meybe pie in de sky?"

Suckow said, "Listen, old man. There's a new train comin' down the tracks, an' you fuckin' well better jump it or get mowed down. We're workin' for *your* rights, damn you!"

"Ay ain't never asked yu, ay tank," Old said blandly. He looked around the table to the men nearest him. "Yu can't chew wid some-body else's teet, ja? Yu vant to be bossman, meybe? Yu, Kris? Yu, Pete?" Both of the men shook their heads.

In the hush, Will stood, and all eyes swung to him. Isaac knew instantly, by the set of his shoulders, the tightness of his stance, that he was mad, but he could not tell in which direction his anger would flame. He sensed that the men waited for his word, and he won-dered, a tag-along thought that he scarcely noted, when this young man has assumed so much power in Demers camp number five.

"Men, you've each got a say here, and nobody's going to tell you what to do. That's for you to decide." Will shifted his feet and crossed his arms. "But I've got to say, this is the first I ever heard of taking a man's property from him. I'm for fair pay for a good day's work, you all know that, there're no secrets in this camp. But if Suckow wants to close down this camp and put you all on the Portland streets with a thousand other stiffs—and no jobs to be had —well"—he grinned suddenly, a hard rictus with nothing of laugh-ter in it—"he'll have to come through me, first."

Isaac's shoulders eased, and he took a deep breath. A man from the back called out, "Ten hours and two bucks sounds good to me, boss." And he rose, stomped the length of the cookhouse, and left. Two dozen others slowly got up and followed him.

"You damn fools!" Suckow shouted. "You're playin' right into his hands! He could pay you twice that an' still keep his wife in fancy lace curtains!"

Isaac whirled on him, his voice low and threatening. "Be off this land in the hour, Suckow. Or I'll have you arrested for trespassing. And if I see you in these woods again, I'll figure you for a torch and shoot you on sight."

Suckow stood up, letting his bench crash to the floor behind him. "I'm gone, Demers," he said. "But if you think you can run this camp like an army, you better damn well think again. These guys don't know what's comin'. When they hear that jacks up an' down the river are making twice what they got in their pockets for half the time, they'll rise up an' bring you down like a fuckin' brush fire." He strode from the room, three cronies at his side. "An' when they do, I'll be with 'em. Me an' a hell of a lot more just like me."

That night in bed, Isaac held Margaret tightly and tried to see into the future. He knew that he could afford to pay the men the extra wages for fewer hours so long as lumber prices held. But if they dropped, or if he had to pay higher wages for less wood, he couldn't lease that extra one hundred and forty acres of timber he'd scouted last season. And if he couldn't lease the timber, there'd soon be no wood to cut. No wood, no mill, no work at all.

He thought of Will's words about the men. It used to be so simple: A man did a job, a man got paid, somebody else got paid a little more, it all hinged together. There was enough for everybody. Now, it seemed, everything was changing, and too fast for him to grab ahold. There was a time when he felt things would last forever; now, he knew nothing would, even the earth, the trees, the river itself. But for now, it was all here, and he had to do the best he could to make it his own, for himself, for Margaret, for his son.

It seemed simple enough, lying in his own bed with Margaret sleeping softly, peacefully, at his side. Surely, the worst would not happen—he had often worried about it, but it never did. That knowledge was a talisman he carried with him, that the things he feared most never came to pass. This time, he vowed, it would be the same.

The Wobblies struck next in Spokane, and took to their soap-boxes by the hundreds. Word came downriver that when ten Wobbly spokesmen were arrested, striking hobos and migrant workers descended on Spokane by the thousands to protest the arrests. Two new fallers told of the most amazing addition to the I.W.W. ranks.

"Hey, I saw her myself, up close," Joe Stivick said. He was a burly jack from Montana, moving down the Columbia, cutting timber as he went. "Lizzie Flynn, her name is."

The men in the bunkhouse leaned closer, and his mate, Hal, added, "Could'a blowed me down with a feather. She ain't more'n five feet an' twenty years old if she's a day. Purty little thing with a cowboy hat an' a little ol' red tie round her throat."

"Is she married?" a jack asked, open-mouthed at this description.

"Naw," Joe snorted. "She's too busy makin' speeches. I heard her on Trent Avenue, shoutin' 'bout free speech an' all. Before I knew what was up, some copper hauled her off, hollerin' an' kickin', an' they threw her purty little ass in jail."

Ole glowered. "Yu ain't no gentleman, Yoe, to talk like dat. An' dey ain't no gentlemens needer, to drow a lady in de slammer. Ay don't care vhat she done."

Joe pulled a tattered newspaper out of his bundle and carefully unfolded it. "Well hey, I saved this paper to show you guys, anyways. Far's I know, she's still sittin' there." The Wobbly paper trumpeted in big black letters: TOOLS OF TIMBER BARONS JAIL REBEL GIRL, with a small line drawing of Elizabeth Gurley Flynn, skirts flying, hair falling about her slim shoulders, being dragged down the streets by no less than three huge policemen. Many of the jacks muttered angrily at that picture, wondering what sort of country they lived in, that would allow a young woman to be treated in that manner, simply for speaking out.

By morning, six men were missing—the ones who'd been most outspoken against such tactics. Will got the Wobbly paper the next week, and on the cover, more line drawings depicted stiffs and jacks marching the streets of Spokane, singing and brandishing tools, protesting such treatment of Beauty and Womanhood. Isaac heard that two camps downriver deserted in a body to go join the crowds.

The next Wobbly paper gloated that Miss Flynn had been released, along with all the rest of the arrested workers, and that now, "Spokane Streets Are Safe for Freedom!" Isaac wondered aloud over supper what the good people of that city must have thought when a thousand sets of calk boots chewed up their streets and a thousand jack voices caterwauled into the night.

When Margaret made a small joke to cheer him up, he snapped, "Well, you can laugh all you like, but it can happen in Portland just as easy. We're not out of this yet."

The next season, the I.W.W. convention in Chicago attracted loggers from all over the country. There, the boys voted to avoid politics and achieve their ends by means other than peaceful. Sabotage, strikes, and riots broke out in lumber camps up and down the Columbia.

One day, Isaac found a spike driven deep into a log so that the head rose above the wood—just high enough to shatter the teeth of the circular saw and send them flying all over the mill. He'd been inspecting the latest load from the crew in the top ten acres, counting up enough timber to keep the mill running for a week. It was a crew of ten men, four of them new hires from upriver.

He sat on the offending log and held his chin in his hands. It had only been luck that he'd seen it. There could easily be ten more spikes in this load alone, and he couldn't find them all, even if he were to search, he knew. There was no way that spike could have been an accident, and also, no way he'd ever be able to find out who put it there.

He thought of Ole, ducking wildly to avoid a saw gone mad, losing maybe an eye or a few more fingers before the teeth stopped whirling. For the rest of the day, he stationed himself at the loader, checking each log as it rolled through. He knew he could easily miss another spike; it could be driven just a little deeper, just under the bark, or could be mashed to invisibility when the log rolled. He knew he was wasting his time, but he had to stay there, nonetheless.

For the rest of the week, Isaac prowled the camp, searching for hidden sabotage, wondering which man was his enemy. He began to grind his teeth at night, and his food would not set well in his stomach. He sensed, though, for all his searching, where the disaster would most likely come—ol' Rotten. Two years earlier, when the locomotive was delivered to Demers camp number five, the crew had built a trestle spanning a canyon, two hundred feet up in the air. It sagged slightly in the middle, but the lokie was able to pull heavily-loaded logging cars up the grade, ease over the wooden bridge, across to the other side.

The engineer had dubbed the trestle "ol' Rotten," because he said it was slapped together with toothpicks and bean poles. The crew had worked up a rather grim way of dealing with their fear of the bridge: They put the lokie in motion at the top of the grade, leaped off, ran through the canyon on foot, and caught the hog on the other side before she started down again. The last man aboard had to walk back to camp.

Isaac had seen one railroad crash when he was working at camp number three, and he never forgot it. A car full of tall cedar was being winched down a seventy-percent grade, easing on down by a steel cable held to the steam donkey. Suddenly, the line snapped with a sound like one hundred whips. The loaded log car careened down the grade, crashed through the line below, and sailed across the canyon to blast into a sizzling, iron mess on the opposite side. No one was hurt, but no one slept well for several nights, either.

After a week of watching alone, Isaac decided it was time to tell Will. "Any of the new men been bitching more than usual?" he asked.

Will looked up from his book. "No," he said. "Not to me, at least. Why?"

Isaac shrugged. "I think we got ourselves a black cat in camp." The black cat was the sign of the I.W.W.; it stood for sabotage, strikes, and violent revolution.

Will's eyes widened. "You see something?"

"A spike set just so in a good-sized cedar. I figure, it wouldn't take much dynamite to take down ol' Rotten."

"Any sticks missing?"

"Enough to blow her to her knees," Isaac said calmly.

"Good Lord, Pa!" Will sat up, his voice taut. "Why didn't you tell me?"

"I just did. What do you think?"

Will shook his head slowly. "There's enough timber in that bridge to build a good-sized town, but a few well-set sticks'd take it down. It wasn't made to last much past the last train, anyway. You got somebody in mind?"

Isaac nodded. "Everybody. But I can't watch them all. I need another pair of eyes."

"You got 'em," Will said promptly. "I want a good deal for the working man, Pa, and I guess you know it." He looked his father straight in the eye. "I even signed their rolls and carry a card." He ignored his father's sudden gasp. "But I won't hold with violence. And every man here knows it."

Isaac scowled. "You got a damned union card? My own son? I suppose everybody in camp knew but me!"

"I'm still a Demers," Will said calmly, "and they all know that as well."

"I wish they didn't. Maybe then they'd let you in on what they're planning."

They sat over the fire until late, discussing the various vulnerable spots in the camp, in the woods, and in the mill. After listening for awhile, Margaret finally said woefully, "Good heavens, if I have to listen to any more ways for you boys to get yourselves cut up, burned to cinders, or smashed under something, I believe I'll go screaming out into the night! You better remember that those who fight fire with fire usually end up with ashes in their mouths."

So they said no more about it. But the next day, Will took a walk down the swaybacked old trestle and then to the canyon below, checking timbers for weak spots, danger points, and any suspicious tamperings. He said nothing to the crew, but he couldn't keep them from noting his actions.

Ivers, the engineer, called out to him playfully, "Hey, Demers, you looking for termites?"

"Yeah," Will said, kicking a timber lightly and then bending to check the base. "Termites with little red cards."

Ivers' grin faded faster than the flapjacks from a cookhouse platter, Will noticed, and by dusk, the whole camp was on guard. Old-timers eyed the new recruits with hooded, sideways glances.

Isaac was happy to have the help, not only from Will but from the rest of the camp as well, and he slept a little better, feeling himself not quite so alone. But he couldn't shake the melancholy that settled over him each time he thought of it.

The woods were different now, he knew, and so were the men who worked them. Used to be, the work was hard and dangerous and attracted men who wanted it so. Nobody gave a thought to comfort or wages or family or home; it was get in, cut, and get out. Now, the new boys talked politics as much as they talked timber, and they never seemed satisfied, not with the biggest log or the spot closest to the fire.

Three days later, Will was standing at the top of the grade, supervising the slow haul of a log car, watching from across the trestle as the engineer moved the lokie into position before he started it over the bridge. A movement at the side of his vision made him swivel on his heel, his heart pounding in his throat. A huge log was slowly sliding down the trestle, right toward the locomotive.

Jesus Christ, he breathed, running toward the log, this can't have been an accident. In the winter, the men sometimes slid the logs over frosted rails, using them as a skidroad. They usually didn't pick up much speed and were fairly easy to control. Isaac cursed because it played hell with the rails, but the logs got to camp in jig time. But they'd never used the trestle for such a slide, and never when a lokie was coming up in the opposite direction!

Will swore under his breath as he pounded down the slope, looked around, saw no one to help or blame, and without thinking further, grabbed a bucket of sand from the dump site and jumped astride the sliding cedar. The log was beginning to pick up speed now, in spite of the fact that the rails were warm. Thank God it's not winter, Will thought, as he frantically dumped sand in front of it, holding on with one hand and ladling out with the other. He dug his knees into the bark, slammed his calks into the log, and tried to force it to stop. The crunch of the log seemed a protest; the bark trembled as though it wanted to tear down the bridge and smash into the lokie, hell-bent for vengeance, but the friction kept it slow.

The log hit the swayback section of the trestle, and its snout began to point higher than its tail. Will hopped off the moving timber. It was slowing now, and he poured the rest of the sand directly in its path. With a groan and one final creak of complaint, the log slid to a halt.

Will looked up to see the engine crew leaning way out of the cab, gazing at him with slack-jawed wonder. They'd been ready to jump, when they saw that he'd made it unnecessary. "Come and get a hook into this bitch!" Will shouted, gesturing to them to hurry.

"How'd she get loose?" asked Ivers as he rushed up.

"You didn't see anybody?" Will glared at him.

"Not a soul."

"Well, it's for sure the damn thing didn't just fell herself, trot right over to the tracks, and lie down like a Skamania whore!" Will fumed. He whirled and walked back up the trestle, to the point where the log had started on its wild ride.

Two sets of calk boots were dug in right behind her skid tracks. Will could see it clearly. Two men had pushed the log on the trestle, aiming it toward the oncoming lokie. They hadn't thought it out very far, and their attempt had been clumsy, but they had deliberately tried to smash the train, the men inside, and maybe take down the bridge, besides. Will felt a cold shudder run through his belly, and he closed his eyes. Holy God, he whispered. Has it come to this? And for what?

That night, Isaac and Will huddled over the kitchen table, scowling into their coffee. "We can't watch sixty men every minute of the day and night," Isaac sighed. "Sooner or later, the bastards'll get what they're after, and somebody's gonna get killed, you watch."

Margaret sat down across from them. "Keeping secrets in this camp's like trying to grow corn on the ceiling. It can't be done. Somebody must've seen something."

Isaac stirred restlessly. "Sure, maybe somebody *did* see something. But they're not sure what they saw, and no man wants to be a fink, maybe rat on an innocent man."

"Not even to save their own lives?"

Will shook his head slowly. "Not these guys. They'd almost rather ride the train down into the canyon than point a finger at a friend, even if that friend's planting dynamite at the bottom of the trestle. If they did know, they'd likely try to talk him out of it or stop it. Solve it among themselves, you know. Anything rather than squeal to the boss."

"You're right," Isaac said firmly. "We got to catch the bastards in the act."

The kitchen was silent for an instant, and the fire snapped loudly, sending sparks up the flue.

"You could lay a trap for them," Margaret said quietly. When both men looked up, she continued. "I remember, my father used to say that the best way to catch a coon was to bait a trap with fishheads and honey. That old coon was smart enough to figure that even in coon heaven, he wasn't going to find fishheads and honey lying around right next to each other. It had to be a trap, but between the two of those scents, he just couldn't stay off. And so, he'd grab for the bait every time, sending up a little coon prayer that this time, he'd snatch them both and get away. A coon can resist anything but temptation, my father said."

"So," Will asked, "what do these coons want most of all?"

"To pull this camp down around our ears, and somehow, manage to make it my fault at the same time," Isaac said gloomily.

"And what would do that faster than anything?" Margaret wondered.

"Well, not a busted-up trestle," Isaac said. "Anybody can walk down and see that it's been blown on purpose. And even without the lokie, we can still cut timber. Hell, if we had to, we could slap together a skidroad overnight from the mountain to the mill, and call up the bulls again. Losing that bridge would slow us, sure, but it wouldn't shut us down. And everybody'd know it wasn't no accident."

"A fire in the mill would do it," Will offered. "A big one . . . melt down the saws, catch the rest of the buildings. Maybe even the woods."

"Not this time of year," Isaac said. "Not dry enough. But a mill fire sure would do it. Have to be a hot one, though. And the mill'd have to be empty so it could get a good start."

"Well, you can't exactly bring in kerosene and leave it laying about," Margaret said.

"No, but wait a minute!" Isaac whispered, slapping his hand on the table. "There's something else burns slower but just as hot—and makes us look like damn fools as well."

A week later, a wagon pulled up the road, bearing three great wooden kegs. Isaac was there to greet the driver and called over five more men to help him.

"What we got here, boss?" one of the men asked.

"Well, Sims, what we got here is the makings of the snortin'est, ugliest headache you ever had in your life," Isaac grinned. "The best rotgut whiskey Portland could spare. Hundred proof and rarin' to slide down your whistle slick as sap."

"Now I know you're prankin' me, boss," Sims said, his eyes wide with wonder. More men gathered round.

"Ain't no joke, men," Isaac smiled. "This next Saturday night, we're going to close this camp down for three days of the biggest, noisiest, drunkest blow-in you boys ever saw!"

"Holy Mother," breathed Sims, speaking for the others. "What's the occasion? 'Tain't the Fourth of July, is it?"

"Nope," Isaac said calmly. "This is in the way of a reward, boys. A way of saying thanks for a job well done." He faced them, suddenly serious. "I know some of you've been wondering about the strikes and the noise downriver about the union, higher wages, and all. And maybe some of you have even wondered what the hell you're doing working in this camp when you might be out carrying signs in the street and setting fire to every mill from here to the sea. But you didn't. You stuck here, and you got the job done. And by way of showing my appreciation, I'm blowing you all to a three-day bender with my compliments. Now, spread the word, boys, and tell the rest to save up their thirst for Sunday."

"You gonna ship in some whores, too?" one of the men hollered happily.

Isaac laughed and shook his head. "I ain't that brave a man, boys. 'Fraid you'll have to make do with this lot for entertainment," and he slapped the keg heartily. At the full, resounding music of the whiskey sloshing within, the men sent up a cheer.

By Saturday, Margaret had taken the wagon down to Skamania, and the men had moved the kegs to the middle of the yard. Sunday, they gathered up every loose bucket and tin cup in camp, and bellied up to the barrels like a troop of foraging ants. By noon, most were lolling about, sleeping in the shade, or arguing over a hot crap game in the bunkhouse.

Isaac and Will drank with the men, giving every impression of joining them in their celebration, but taking one sip for every three swigs they saw. By eight o'clock, the camp was quiet, and most of the men had crawled to their bunks, sodden and half-conscious. A small group still clustered around the kegs, singing and swapping tales.

"How're we doing, boys?" Will asked as he sauntered up, deliberately swaying back and forth unsteadily.

"Still got more'n two full kegs," mumbled a singer, breaking off his tune in mid-warble. "May take this lot more'n three days to get it all down . . ." He looked up hopefully at Will.

Will laughed gently. "Well, I guess they'll just have to swig it faster." He passed his own cup under the spigot, splashed out as much as he got in, and put it to his mouth. "Everybody find their bunk okay?"

"Yeah," burped one man, " 'cept for Ole and Ivers. They took themselves down to the river to catch a coon. Said they wanted to see the little sucker in the moonlight. Little fingers an' all."

Will was instantly alert. "A coon?" He made his voice as casual as he could. "What the hell they want a coon for?"

But the man was deep in his cup, and as Will waited for an answer, his head lolled back on his neck, his eyes closed, and he slumped to the ground.

Will found Isaac in the mill. He was leaning against a saw carriage, raising his glass with two of the sawyers. Will greeted the cutters and gracefully maneuvered Isaac outside, beyond earshot.

"Do Ivers or Ole know what's going on?" Will asked him quickly.

Isaac was instantly sober. "Hell, no," he whispered. "Nobody does."

"Well, I just heard they're going coon hunting down by the river. Sims said so."

Isaac's eyes narrowed. "Go find 'em, son. Even if there's nothing to it, I don't want them wandering around in the dark, with a gullet full of booze. Here." He leaned down behind a pile of logs and pulled a rifle from the shadows. "Take this with you, 'case you come on any trouble. And don't hesitate to use it."

Will crept from camp, stopped at the river, and splashed his face with cold water. His head was clear, but he felt unsteady, and the ground seemed to come up to his boots faster than usual. He followed the river, kneeling in the mud occasionally to track two sets of calk boots, heading down the mountain.

Meanwhile, Isaac herded the sawyers out of the mill, steering them toward their bunks. "You guys don't want to sleep in a pile of chips, do you?" he cajoled. "Hell, you stand in that stuff all day as it is. No sense in falling face down in it at night." He pushed them into the bunkhouse door. " 'Sides, you still got two days left on those kegs. Sleep it off, or you'll miss the best part."

Alone, he surveyed the camp. Two men were dozing by the kegs. Neither were new hires; both had been with Demers camps for more than ten years, altogether. When Isaac looked at them, sprawled and unaware, he was struck with a sense of tenderness for these men. They ask for damn little, he thought. He couldn't believe danger could come from that quarter. However, the shadows of the timber could have sheltered any number of Wobbly saboteurs, he knew. And so he walked back behind the shed, deliberately unsteady, with the strong feeling he was being watched from a distance. When he rounded a corner, he crept silently to a pile of logs at the back of the mill, crouched down out of sight, and waited in the darkness.

Will found Iver and Ole hiding behind a screen of fern and blackberry, overlooking the riverbank. He almost tripped over their crude wire trap, but he was alerted by their whisperings before he stumbled. He shook his head ruefully. A coon'd have to be deaf, dumb, and blind to get caught by these two. He hollered out, "Hey, Ole! Iver! Come on out, will ya?"

A volley of shushing noises came out of the brush. "By Gott," Ole cursed impotently, "yu vill scare de coons so far avay, ve never see dem a'tall, ay betcha."

"Go away," Ivers moaned drunkenly. "We almost had us one a minute ago. I heard him comin'. Now, you gone an' run him off."

Will chuckled, shouldering through the waist-high fern and hauling the two up by their collars. "That was me you heard, you fools. Come on back to camp before you freeze your asses off out here. What you hunting coon for, anyway?"

Ole looked sheepish and gazed away, over Will's shoulder. Ivers set his jaw stubbornly. "Don't tell him, Hansen. Else we'll have to share it with him."

"Share what, Ole?" Will asked. "Come on, ol'-timer, I won't butt into whatever you got cooking. But I tramped out here looking for you. Least you can do is tell me what's up."

"Ve got promise. Ten bucks if ve catch dis coon," Ole said reluctantly. "Ja, but has to be tonight, an' has to be least one mile from camp." He turned a mournful face to Will. "Now, ay betcha ve never catch him."

Will's hair rose slowly on the back of his neck, and his hand clenched on the rifle at his side. He had the quick urge to whirl around on his heel, sensing someone, something, behind him. "Who promised you?" he asked quietly.

"Suckow did," Ivers mumbled. "Suckow said we was to bring it to him, an' he'd pay up."

Oh God, Will thought, he figured one of us might follow them out here, leaving the other one alone. And if we didn't, two less loyal men around to stay their hand. So one of us here, the other back there, both of us more vulnerable to any "accident" they can pull off, and nobody to witness whatever happened to the one who followed but two drunken old men. He whirled without a word and crashed through the brush, holding his rifle high, jumping from boulder to boulder, making his way as fast as he could upriver, back the mile to camp, all the while praying silently, "Let me not be too late, oh God, hold on, Pa!"

Isaac was at the back of the mill, crouched down in a load of logs. He heard them coming before he saw them, calk boots clumping ungently over the bracken, hissing whispers in the moonlight. Finally, the moving shadows became two men standing at the side of the mill carrying four pails full of something that sloshed over their boots.

He eased his pistol out of his belt and sat up higher, the better to hear them.

"Lay that stuff down along the edge there," one man whispered. "Shit, I spilled so much on my boots, my toes'll be drunk."

Before the other shadow could answer, Isaac stood up suddenly, his heart lurching in his chest, and shouted, "Don't move! Put those pails down and turn around!" His voice sounded shockingly loud in the still forest, and he aimed his pistol right at the men.

Then he heard a mumble of bracken behind him. Before he could turn, a rifle snout poked his back.

"Put down the gun, Demers," a voice said confidently.

He started to turn.

"Drop it!" the voice said, more harsh.

Isaac tossed the pistol a few feet away, and turned slowly around to face Sam Suckow. Even in the dim light, he could see the man's bulky shoulders, could hear his nervous breathing. The rifle in his hands seemed endless, a long tube of metal death.

Isaac let his breath out slowly, feeling his fingertips throb with fear and helplessness. "I should have figured it was you," he breathed. "None of my own men would'a pulled this."

Suckow chuckled mirthlessly. "Wrong again, bossman. We never could'a done it without their help. An' when this mill goes up sky-high, not a one of them'll give a damn."

"You're full of crap," Isaac said.

"Who do you think told us of your little handout, eh, your piss-poor distraction from the real issue? Your own crew. You think by gettin' 'em drunk, they don't notice that you're payin' less than every camp on the river? You think a few kegs of cheap rotgut'll make up for the fact that this place is one of the last holdouts of the bossman's fuckin' *empire*?"

He nudged Isaac toward the mill with the rifle. "Get in there, Demers. Don't worry, we're not gonna kill you. We're just gonna let you start it up. I can see the headlines now: 'Drunken Boss Burns Down Own Mill; Workers Run Him Downriver.'" He laughed angrily. "An' then you can tell the rest of the bosses that the scabs weren't there when you needed 'em. The next mill that goes on this mountain'll be union!"

Isaac hesitated for an instant, mentally gauging the distance between himself and the rifle, his hand and the discarded pistol, his life and the lives of all the men unaware and sleeping around him. But then he looked in Suckow's eyes, and he saw a brief naked glimmer of sadness: He's gone too far, and he knows it. But he'd shoot me down if he had to, he's got no choice. He turned slowly toward the mill; anything rather than see Suckow's set, looming face.

Another voice rasped through the night, another pale face pushed through the brush, and Will shouted, "Drop the gun, Suckow!"

Isaac whirled in time to see Suckow lift his rifle to fire, a blast boomed through the silent woods, and Suckow dropped to his belly. Isaac turned, and the two men behind him dropped their pails and raced around the mill and out of sight. He went to Suckow.

The man was groaning deep in his throat, his hands were twitching as though to move to his wound. Isaac rolled him over gently. Will's shot had taken out both knees. Suckow was alive, but he'd never walk these woods again.

Will came up, his face ashen and twisted. "Jesus," he whispered. "I didn't think I'd shoot him. At the last minute, I still didn't think so. I don't even remember pulling the trigger."

Isaac looked up at Will quickly and it seemed to him that in that moment, he saw the youth in his son's face dissolve. Before him was a man, and Will would never be the same again. "Hey," he said huskily. "You had no choice. He was going to shoot one of us, sure." He stood and touched Will's arm briefly. "You did the right thing, son. The only thing."

"The right thing?" Suckow suddenly gasped harshly. "You think taking a man's sweat, his whole goddamned *life,* and tossing him a few bucks in exchange, that's the"—his face twisted in agony—"the right thing? You can't shoot us all, boss." And he fell back, his face shiny with sweat. Suckow was silent now, his eyes closed. But they could hear him breathing, and his face was ruddy. Will turned away and brushed his hand over his eyes. He strode a few paces away, took off his hat, put two fingers over the bridge of his nose, and began to weep silently.

"So this is what it all comes down to?" he mumbled. "Two guys shooting at each other over some damn mill? Bunch of lawless animals scrapping over—what?" His voice broke, and his shoulders heaved. "Oh God, I hate this, I hate it all, nothing here is worth this."

Isaac's eyes ached and he went to him. He put his arms around him and held him tightly, silently, until his son's back stopped quivering, taking comfort as he gave it. Finally, Will straightened, cleared his throat, and they dragged Suckow up to the cabin to tend his wounds, neither of them speaking of it again.

After Suckow was carried down the mountain back to Portland, the talk of strikes and shutdowns at Demers camp number five ceased. The Wobblies continued to make trouble at Port Townsend, Tacoma, and other mill centers, but by 1907, lumber was king. Since the virgin forests of the East were largely gone, the cutters of the upper Mississippi Valley and the Great Lakes region came west, eager to take jobs from strikers. Men like Pope, Talbot, Griggs, and

Weyerhaeuser were turning trees into gold, and they formed the Pacific Coast Association to combat labor problems, driving the struggling I.W.W. underground. But its roots continued to expand, taking sustenance from the new breed of jack who came to the Northwest, buckers and whistle punks and fallers who revered the trees more than the profits that came from them.

Demers camp was changing with the seasons. Production was up, two Dolbeers were pumping up the mountains, the sawmill was doubled in size, and a laundryman, two cooks, and a visiting nurse joined the crew. A minor change, but one which seemed to make a big difference in the mood at camp, was the addition of four women in the cookhouse to help serve and clean up.

A few of the old-timers groaned about it, wincing when they saw the women bustling around the camp, in and out of the kitchen. "Like a damn female seminary," a logger muttered, never taking his eyes off the skirts swishing between the tables. "Next thing you know, they'll be teachin' the boys embroidree after hours."

But Margaret loved the company, and Will seemed to find so many more reasons to loiter around the cookhouse that Chew Fat threatened to put him to work.

Isaac had been down at the river supervising the delivery of a new circular saw when the last woman was hired, a job he left to Chew Fat's discretion. That night, he strolled out of the cabin for a smoke, and he saw the new girl heading in the direction of the creek. She was young, younger even than Will, built sturdy about the arms and shoulders and hips. She wore a simple blue skirt and a white cotton blouse like the other kitchen help, but there was something about her that made him stop and watch.

Her hair was dark and thick, piled on her head, and she moved slowly, deliberately, with the sleek placidity of a grazing mare, as though she knew she was in exactly the right place at the right time, and there was no place she'd rather be.

On an impulse which he did not understand, he turned casually, went round the back of the cabin, and walked toward the creek so that he might encounter her, curious to see her closer. He picked his way down the slope toward the sound of running water, off the path now, and saw her sitting on a flat rock just out of the stream. Her legs were bare, and she was singing softly, splashing her feet in the water. Her voice was deep and slow-moving as a winter shadow melting before the sun.

He saw that she was even younger than he'd first thought, young enough to be his daughter, and he winced as though a gnat annoyed him. It was hard to believe he was fifty-seven. It seemed only a year or two ago that he was working the cannery, just six months ago that he was married, and yesterday that Will was learning to walk. Now, he's past twenty, and I can't see over his head, Isaac thought.

The girl didn't see him, or didn't seem to, and despite her work skirt, she looked a part of the woods and the river, as though she had just emerged from one or the other and could disappear at any moment, leaving not a ripple, not a fern waving with her passage. He walked up to her, deliberately making noise as he approached, just to see what she would do.

She looked up without a trace of surprise and said, "Evening, Mister Demers."

Knows her boss, he thought. "Evening," he said, and stood facing the creek, his hands in his pockets as though he came there every dusk. "You the new gal in the kitchen?"

"One of them," she said. "My name's Leona. It means 'light.' "

Certainly is that, Isaac thought quickly, skin as fair and smooth as cream. He wanted to hear her voice again. "Your first time in a logging camp?"

"First time away from home. My folks farm cherries up the Hood. You might remember my pa. Jack Cahill?"

Isaac's mouth dropped open. "Old BlackJack Cahill? Well, I guess so! Say, he cut for us for ten years or more—and you're his daughter? He never said he had a daughter, hell, never even mentioned a wife!"

She smiled. "Well, he's got one of each. And when it was time for me to get out on my own, Demers camp seemed the place to come. I heard the name enough, growing up, to feel like it was a second home."

"Old BlackJack. He was a helluva cutter, in his day. So he's up the Hood, eh?" He laughed nervously. "Up to his fool neck in cherries! What's he think about you following in his bootsteps?"

"Well," she said softly, "I guess they weren't too excited about the idea, all in all. They'd rather I did fancywork for the church or arranged the shelves over at the hardware store, but I wanted to do something with some memories to it, before I settle down." She smiled up at him as though she expected he would understand completely.

"Well," he said, clearing his voice, which had gone suddenly gravelly, "if I can give you a hand anytime . . . answer any questions, just let me know. You're pretty young to be stuck way up here . . . " His voice trailed off uncertainly.

She smiled again, brilliantly, and then turned back to watch her bare foot play in the water, as though in gentle dismissal.

That night he stood and gazed at himself in a mirror. "You think I'm getting a belly on me, honey?" he asked Margaret thoughtfully. "God, I got to get an ax in my hands more often. This standing around supervising will kill a man quick."

Isaac lay awake for over an hour, listening to the sounds of the moving water down the hill and the sibilant murmurs of the hemlocks. When he slept, he dreamed of a faceless child-woman who sat high on a log above his head. As he approached her, she parted her legs slightly and he could feel the heat of her, smell her sweetish, muskish scent. It mingled with the smell of the cedar sap and the sunshine, and she bent to him, drawing aside her long, black hair, letting him taste her dark, open mouth. He woke restlessly and turned to Margaret, lifting her cotton shift above her thighs. She awakened as he entered her, crying out in bewildered confusion at his unusual roughness. In the back of her sleepy fog, as he bucked and heaved in her, stubbornly silent, ferocious, she wondered who had angered him.

Problems in the mill occupied Isaac most of the next few months and also kept him close to camp. He saw Leona coming and going, carrying wood to the cookhouse, pails of water, throwing out slops, resting in the shade between meals, and talking with the others. He spoke to her from a distance only, nodding and tipping his hat. She did not attempt to shout across the yard, over the noise of the mill, but only smiled gently in his direction. Once, he heard her laugh at something Will said, and he turned his head suddenly toward her, grinning, wondering what made her sound so pleased. But she didn't notice his glance.

A month later, Isaac was out marking timber for falling, when he caught a glimmer of movement, a white flash among the trees. He knew instantly that it was Leona, and he came up on her quietly. She turned calmly and faced him across a patch of bramble, only her shoulders showing above the tangle of thorn and berry.

She lifted up her tin pail and called out gaily, "I found the best patch on the mountain!"

He laughed and pushed his way to her side. "Did Chew Fat run you way up here?"

"He says a woman'll find berries faster than a hungry bear," she chuckled. "I guess he's right, 'cause I've already got three pies' worth."

He methodically began to pick the berries and add them to her pail, reaching deep into the brambles for ones she couldn't easily pluck. After a moment of companionable silence she said, "What're you doing on this side of the slope? I thought the crew was up at the top ten today."

He nodded. "They are. But I got to find what they'll be felling tomorrow."

He watched her move out of the corner of his eye, watched the smooth pale arms reach, pick, and drop the berries, all in a single, fluid rhythm. Her arms were bare, her sleeves rolled to her elbows, and the light down on her arms shone in the sun. It seemed so natural to be with her. She was as young as a new day and just as fresh, nothing about her ruined, wasted, or getting older.

On a whim, he spoke his mind. "I can't see you spending much time in a logging camp," he said. "Even mine."

She looked up at him, amused. "Where can you see me, then?"

"I don't know," he hesitated. "Maybe teaching school. Maybe working in town doing something—better than this." He stopped and looked at her seriously. "You're too good for this kind of life." In a fluster, he reached away from her, high on a berry branch. "I wouldn't want any daughter of mine working in a camp cookhouse. Surprised your pa let you come."

She shrugged lightly. "It was my decision to make. I'm happy to get the work. Not lots of jobs open upriver, not for women, anyway."

He took the full pail from her. "Well, I'd like to help you if you'll let me. Get you some new clothes, maybe. Get you a better job. Maybe take you to Portland, where you could get something better, maybe get some schooling."

She drew back and gazed at him for a moment, and he felt her measuring him. "I'm too old for school," she said finally.

"Why, you're just a kid!" he said, almost reluctantly.

"Maybe on the outside, but not on the inside, where it counts," she said lightly. "I'm too old for book-learning, anyways."

"Well, you're not too old to make a better place for yourself. No one ever is. I'd do it for a daughter, did I have one," he added. "Let me do it for you, Leona."

"Why me?" she asked softly.

He shrugged hugely. "Oh, your pa was a good ol' guy. Worked for us since before I could stroke an ax. And any kin to him is sort of like one of the family, I guess." He didn't add that it was because her hair was black as a moonless night, her skin was ivory, and her smile made him feel young and restless as a buck in new velvet— and he would have fought the man who said it was so.

The next time he and Will went into Skamania for supplies, Leona rode in on the buckboard between them. She was eager as a child for the adventure and found pleasure in each new turn of the road, pointing out that wildflower or this bird song to Will, scolding him lightly when he couldn't supply her with the names for all she saw. Isaac took her to the dressmaker's, a new shop which had opened in the town since the fire. He waited in the saloon a decent interval and then loitered outside the shop, glancing at the dummied dresses in the window and fidgeting. Will came up with his arms full of packages just as she emerged, and Isaac's eyes watered at her beauty. The dressmaker had selected a pale gold lawn for her gown, stitched all around with small tucks and pleats to show off her breasts. It hugged her shoulders, clung to her waist, and fell in gentle swaths to her feet. Above the lace collar, her long neck rose elegantly, and the color set off her black hair like velvet against brass.

Leona was flushed and proud, searching their faces for a response. Isaac took both her hands and gently turned her around, grinning hugely. "Your pa wouldn't hardly recognize you," he said. "You look like a grand lady." And then he glanced at Will and saw that he was watching closely with a sad, knowing smile on his face.

He felt suddenly confused, so he tucked her hand in his arm, slapped Will on the shoulder, and steered them up the street, saying, "There's not a man on the river I'd trade places with today, by God," shivering at Leona's excited giggle.

The next month when Isaac took the family to Portland for the summer visit, he mentioned to Margaret he wanted to take Leona along, just to help her get started in a new job and settled.

Margaret was standing by the sink when he said it, and she made a strange noise in her throat. "Why?" she asked slowly.

He sat heavily down in the chair, twisting his shoulders away from her. "I want to get her out of here," he said. "She's a good gal, and she wants to make something of herself. I figure, in Portland, I can help her find a better job. Maybe learn a trade. Anyway," he grinned, "I liked her pa. He was a good man."

"If that's what you want," she said quietly, and went back to paring the apples. Every heart has its own secrets, she thought. What are his?

A week later, they all sat in his mother's parlor, exchanging news of the river. Sarah talked incessantly about the terrible problems "progress" had brought to Portland, and Elizabeth's voice rose in and out, telling of her son's latest accomplishments at the university. Isaac and Will talked of the profits they expected from the mills this year, and Suzanna prodded Will to talk to Elizabeth about the values of higher education.

Indeed, only Leona was mostly silent, and Isaac couldn't help but notice how lovely and serene she seemed, nodding and smiling when she was spoken to, letting them dominate the conversation, never intruding on what must seem to her to be an intimate family moment. A few times, he tried to draw her into the talk, but then Margaret or Sarah or Suzanna would begin again, and she would smile and listen once more.

Finally, Leona rose slowly and asked to be excused. She was tired, she said, and she was sure they would stay up all night, with or without her company. She thanked Suzanna Demers gracefully for her hospitality, turned, and went upstairs, her long skirts trailing behind her.

When she was out of earshot, Suzanna said, "That's nigh one of the handsomest gals I've seen at this table. Her daddy raised her right, you can tell."

Isaac snorted, amused, "Hell, her daddy didn't do a damn thing for her but send her to us, but by the time we get through with her, she'll forget she ever came from some ol' fruit farm upriver."

Will cocked his head at him curiously and Margaret wrinkled her brow, ready to register a mild protest. But before she could speak, Sarah began a long monologue on the evils of the federal government meddling in Portland affairs, and the moment passed.

Two nights later, as Will walked out in the garden, he found Leona sitting on a stone bench, looking at the moon. It was his favorite place in the Demers house, and he'd often come to the garden to think. Now, as he saw that she had usurped his place, he almost felt indignant. He started to turn around and go back to the house, for he did not feel like company. But on an impulse, he sat down beside her.

"I always wondered if I'd make it to Portland," she said quietly, as though she were not at all surprised to see him. "Up the Hood, you know, Portland's the big wicked city. Everything happens here, they say. And you can be anything."

Will laughed stiffly. "Hard for me to picture it that way. I come here twice a year, and it's just like any other place."

"Really?" she smiled. "Not to me. My momma used to tell me she could picture me here, doing whatever I wanted to do and being whatever I wanted to be. She'd say, 'I just close my eyes, Lou'—she called me Lou—'and I can see you plain as day, sitting in one of those fine houses down on the river, just watching the big ships come in from the sea.'"

"Could you see it, too?"

She nodded. "Oh, sure. I'd close my eyes right along with her, and there we'd sit, grinning like two newborn fools, not saying a word, with our eyes tight shut. Pa used to say the whole place could burn down around us, and there we'd sit, still grinning."

He tilted his head and looked into her eyes, all glassy with the moonlight. "So what *do* you want to do, now that you're here in the big wicked city?"

She giggled and put her hands up on her head, her chin to the sky. "I haven't figured it out yet. But I expect it's just around the corner."

"Well," he said, "your momma was right, you could do about anything you want. You're pretty enough."

She flushed and dropped her head. "Don't be silly, Will. Nobody's ever pretty enough."

He shrugged lightly and got up. "Guess I'll leave you to your dreams, Lou. Have good ones." And he walked back to the house.

Once he was out of sight, she let her shoulders sag, and a small crease appeared on her brow. The moon was still there but now, it was dimmer somehow.

Suddenly, Isaac stuck his head out of the upstairs window. "Leona!" he called. "Time to come in!"

A day later, Will mentioned he might take a stroll down into the city to check out the sights. "Leona," he said casually, "you want to come along? See what your momma was talking about?"

Isaac glanced up quickly, first at him, then at her. When he saw the eagerness in her smile, he said heartily, "That's a good idea, boy. Honey, get your shawl, we'll go along."

"Isaac," Margaret said quietly, "Will doesn't need a chaperon."

"Chaperon! Who's talking about a chaperon?" Isaac sputtered. "I'd like to take in the sights, too!" He turned to Will and grinned broadly. "That's okay with you, right?" He was getting up as he spoke.

Will shrugged blandly. "Sure, Pa, come on along if you like. God knows, it's a free country."

Isaac clapped him on the back. "You're damn right. Leona, you better get your warmer shawl, that wind down at the docks'll cut right through that light little thing you got there. Will doesn't know this city like I do, and he's apt to get lost, wandering around." He chuckled, drawing Margaret out of her chair.

As they left the house, Leona walked directly to Will's side and put out her gloved hand. "You better take my hand in yours, Will Demers." She smiled at him. "You may not get another chance like this one."

Margaret beamed as though she had just invented them both.

Soon, Will began to watch for Leona out in the garden at night, waiting for her to slip through the shadows and sit in the moonlight. He didn't feel quite brave enough to ask her to meet him, but he sensed that she knew what he was thinking.

Finally, she appeared in the garden, a white lace shawl over her shoulders as though she intended to stay awhile. He hurried down the path and then deliberately slowed, arriving under the shadowed lattice with a casual saunter. He leaned against the portico column, where he could see her plainly.

She looked up and smiled but said not a word.

"Beautiful night," he finally managed.

She nodded her head, and he could see the back hairs on her neck glisten in the light from the moon.

"I thought I'd come share it with you," he said.

She chuckled softly.

"You know," he started hesitantly, "I hardly know a thing about you, Leona."

"What would you like to know?"

Everything, he murmured somewhere inside him, but said aloud, "Oh . . . whatever you want to tell me. About your folks, maybe. What you'd like to do in Portland. What you think of logging."

"Why?"

He spread his hands helplessly. "I'd just like to know you better, is all. Do I have to have a reason?" And he watched as her mouth curved up deliciously in a smile.

"There's little I could tell you that'd help you get to know me, Will Demers. You had many a month in camp to ask me this, and you never did. Never said a word, hardly. And besides, the past doesn't matter much. I feel I'm just now coming to life, anyway."

He peered at her through the shadows. "Why's that?"

She laughed then, a silvery giggle of joy. "Well, I don't feel like shouting clear across the garden. If you come over here, I might just tell you."

He grinned sheepishly and sat beside her, gingerly putting his arm around her shoulder. He looked full into her face. She returned his gaze openly, with none of the usual discretion or disguise he had seen on the faces of other women. She liked him, it was as simple as that; she made no attempt to hide it. The knowledge gave him confidence, and he reached down and gently kissed her on the forehead, following the bridge of her nose and back again to her eyes, all slow and searching, as though he could not find her lips.

She murmured, "Kiss me, Will," almost with impatience, and took his face in her hands, covering his mouth with hers. She didn't move, didn't wrap her arms around his neck as another, more experienced woman might have done. She simply took his kiss and gave it back again, as she might have drunk deeply, joyously, at a well she had discovered in a dry land.

As he pulled away, he felt her lips curve up under his mouth, and she didn't turn away or flush or stammer. She just sat there, smiling proudly.

"I guess I've been trying to impress you," he said quietly.

"I know," she said.

"Has it worked?"

She chuckled softly. "It's starting to. Keep trying."

And he bent and kissed her again, this time pulling her into his body, feeling the buttons on her gown press into his chest, and her arms go up to his head and hold him fast.

They both heard the steps up the walk at the same instant and pulled away. Isaac loomed out of the shadows, his face pale as the moon. "What the hell's going on?" he asked, his voice low and irritable.

Will glanced quickly at Leona, but she said nothing.

"Not much," Will began. "We were just—"

"Yeah, I can see," Isaac said, in the same tone he might have used to a man caught stealing food from the camp larder. "It's late, and it's getting chilly. You best get to your room, Leona."

She stood, and Will saw the uncertainty in her. She opened her mouth to speak, and Isaac visibly tensed. He didn't say a word, just pointed one jutting finger toward the house.

As she passed him, she stopped and said quietly, "This time I go, Isaac. For you and all you've done. But it's the last time."

Will wanted to protest, but he sensed that there was more here than he understood. As soon as her back disappeared through the shadows, however, he crossed his arms and faced his father.

"What the hell was that all about? I think I'm old enough to pick my own company, 'specially when she's here in our own house. I thought you had this all figured out from the start."

"No," Isaac said. "Just keep the hell off. She's"—he struggled— "she's close enough to be your sister, for God's sake." His mouth twisted in a sour grimace. "I didn't bring her here so's you could ruin her and yourself in the bargain."

Will shook his head wonderingly. "I hadn't thought of ruining her, Pa, and she's no sister to me, that's for sure." He stepped past his father and then turned back. "And I'll court her if I want to and she'll have me."

Will walked toward the house, his hands shaking slightly with a feeling he couldn't name. He felt as if he'd been drinking what the crew called squirrel whiskey, a brew that made a man run up one side of a tree and then crazily down the other side. He hadn't intended to court her, hadn't intended anything that had happened. But now that he heard himself say it, he knew it was true.

Isaac slumped back to the bench, letting his thoughts wander and his eyes move restlessly over the garden. It seemed to him suddenly that the place was full of ominous shadows and loneliness, a place where he'd lost things before and would always lose. A place of sorrow, separation, and death. A place where he had lost Ning Ho and with her, his youth.

He felt a flush of shame move up his neck, and he bowed his head. Ning Ho. He had wanted her, taken her, and wronged her. But Leona was different—he could help her get a chance in life, if she'd let him. Let him what? Let him *do* for her. And all he asked in return, he thought, was just to have her around, just to hear her laugh and see her young, slender arms reaching up to pluck at things, things she should have, things he could give her . . . was that so bad?

He felt suddenly as though his life was slipping away, out of his grasp like water through cupped fingers. No matter how tightly he gripped, he knew that when he opened his fists, it would be gone. And he would be left an old, withered man. He turned and started toward the house, his jaw tight under his teeth.

He found Leona in her room, sitting quietly by the window, looking out at the night. Her door was open. He knocked gently and she looked up.

"Can I come in?" he asked.

She nodded, but her head turned back to the window.

He stood by the edge of the bed, facing her, his palms open. "Listen, Leona, I'm sorry about what happened out there. I guess I spoke out of line. But you got to see he's wrong for you. He's just a kid."

She turned to him with the calm ruthlessness of a woman who knows that she must only tell a man the truth to confuse him. "A kid?" she said softly. "When was the last time you took a good look at him, Mister Demers? He's a grown man. I'm a grown woman." She turned back to the window as if in dismissal. "To my mind, that makes us a good match." She looked back at him piercingly, and a sadness drew her features down. For just an instant, he saw what she would look like when she was old and bitter, but then it passed, and her eyes narrowed. "You think I'm not good enough for him?"

Her question startled him as he realized that, in fact, he had wondered if his own son was good enough for her. "Of course not," he began, faltering. "I just think you're too young, you should look for somebody who can give you everything, maybe an older man—"

"Like you, maybe?" she said softly.

Now that the words had been said, it was all clear to him. In fact, he was shocked, somewhere inside him, at how quickly he nodded, how much she had seen that he had missed. He flushed and looked away, wondering what else she had seen. "Yes," he said, as calm as he could manage. "Maybe some man like me. But in the meantime, I'm willing to take care of you, see that you get the best start, maybe help you get your own place, a job—" A soft knock shuddered through the room. Isaac froze, put up his hand in an effort to stop her, and before he could speak, she said, "Come in."

Will stood in the doorway. His eyes swept over Leona, who had not moved, to Isaac, by the bed. His face hardened with a cold disgust that made Isaac flame into anger.

"So this is it," Will said, a low contempt hollowing his voice.

Isaac lifted his chin and said, "Tell him, Leona. Tell him that it won't work."

"Wait," Will said with a slow deliberateness. "Maybe we should get my mother in on this. Want me to call her, Pa, or will you?"

Leona had been silent throughout, and now she stiffened and put one hand on Isaac. Will saw that he shivered like a mustang at her touch. "Both of you, be still," she said softly. "No one's calling anyone."

Will said, "I came here to ask to court you, Lou. I wanted to do it proper. But I wonder if I'm wasting my breath, worrying about what's right." His voice was soft, but severe as winter.

She bridled, and her eyes flashed. "I'm getting mighty tired of all this, gentlemen."

Before she could continue, Isaac said stiffly, "She's got other plans for her life, boy. They don't include you."

"That's enough," Leona snapped, and she stepped between them. She stood glaring back and forth, her arms crossed over her breasts. "Will, I don't know what you're thinking—no, that's not true. I *do* know, but I won't say it. What you're thinking's not so and never will be, not even in somebody's wildest dreams. But please leave us now."

Will glared once at Isaac and stalked from the room, closing the door softly behind him. That gentle, final shutting was somehow more final, she thought, more full of condemnation than a slam would have been.

She pushed Isaac gently down on the bed and stood before him. His face was sullen and closed to her, and she knew he was in pain, but she sensed that if she was ever to be honest with a man in her life, this was the time. "I don't know how this happened," she said softly.

Isaac shrugged wearily, unwilling to speak. He'd said all he could say. "You going to leave with him?" he finally asked.

She nodded, slowly first, as though she'd only now thought of it, then more firmly. "If he'll have me."

"He's too young for you," he said.

She took his head in her hands. "That's not for you to say, Isaac. Not anymore. Now, let's not speak of it again. I'll leave this house. If he wants to follow me, he will."

He got up and went for the door blindly, before she could see his eyes water with shame and confusion. Isaac hesitated in the hallway, uncertain where to go. He wanted to hide somewhere, but there was no place in the house he felt unexposed, not downstairs, not out in the garden, no place save his own bed, where Margaret slept. He moved like a sleepwalker to his room.

Margaret was awake, and she sat up and faced him. A thought flashed across her mind. It was easy enough to understand love at first sight. But it's when two people have been looking at each other for years that it's a miracle. And in that instant, she was reminded of all the reasons she had married him.

He suddenly was too exhausted to hide his feelings, and he pulled her to him, muffling his mouth in her neck.

She held him close, her grip stronger than he'd remembered. "Hush," she said quietly. "I know. I know."

"What do you know?" he said, dropping his eyes.

"Most everything, I expect," she said peacefully. "I know a drowning man will grab even an ax edge. I think I've known it longer than you have. You were getting old, you thought. She wasn't. Having a hand in her life, making her what you thought she should be, she was sort of your last chance, wasn't she?"

He nodded miserably, too ashamed even to try to dissemble.

"But you forgot that she could be Will's *first* chance. So now, she's leaving?"

He nodded again.

"Well, thank the Lord for that, at least," she said and hunkered down beside him, tucking her shift around her feet. She took his hand gently. "She's got more sense than I gave her credit for. Light's a precious thing, but too much'll blind a man."

"She's—"

But she interrupted him quickly. "Don't praise her to me, Isaac," she said, her voice low and smooth.

After a long silence, he said, "I wasn't going to. You know, I looked in her eyes and saw everything I was. And everything I couldn't be." He sighed hugely. "Christ, I feel like a sweenied horse. Nothing but sagging skin and old bones."

She hugged him fiercely, crawled under the covers, patted the pillow next to her, and when he got in, nestled closer to him. "Does he love her?" she asked softly.

He nodded. "Maybe. Anyway, he's fixing to find out."

"Good," she said firmly. "Then they'll be leaving. The sooner, the better."

He leaned up on one elbow, incredulous. "You don't mind your son taking off with her?"

A faint steel-edge of pride hardened her voice. "You think I don't see these things? You think, just because I've got a good sampler-thought for every crisis that comes along, I don't know what's going on around me? You think, just because I call on the Lord at times for help, I'm—simple? Isaac Demers, sometimes I swear you can see a cruiser's mark on a mile-off fir, but you can't see the flies on your own nose."

His mouth fell open, and he began to sputter, "By Christ, Margaret, I—!"

But she stopped him flat, her hand on his shoulder. "I'm not beautiful and I never was, but you married me for a lot of reasons, Isaac, and one of them was for my good sense, whether you knew it or not at the time. Now, I'm going to tell you what will happen here. It's time for Will to find a new way for himself. We never raised him to be a jack and if you'll look a little deeper than your pride, you'll see the truth of that. He needs more schooling than I can give him, and he needs space and sun to grow just like any other seedling in your woods, and he needs to make his own way, his *own* way, Isaac. He's *not* just some graft off your roots, you know. And if you had looked inside that book of your father's he's been carrying around since he was ten, you'd have seen it coming."

"Don't tell me you believe that old crazy crap about the river and the raven and the—"

"No," she said firmly, "but I *do* believe he wasn't made for the mountains, that he's got to find his path elsewhere. And if you had let yourself believe it, you'd have seen it, too." She smiled. "You know, it's not *all* crazy, Isaac. Your pa put it in your gramma's own words. You have to believe some things before you see them. He's all grown. Soon, he'll be gone. And if it weren't Leona, it might be some Skamania whore, and I couldn't stand that—no, don't talk of it, Isaac, I don't want to hear it," she said, her hand a warning in his face. "Just because I didn't take a peavey to you both when you brought him back doesn't mean I didn't know or care."

She smiled suddenly and patted him gently. "Now, don't fret on it anymore." She pulled the blanket up on her shoulder and made ready for sleep. "He's ready," she said, yawning, "It's time. Past time, if the truth be known. He's been following her for months now, even when he didn't know it, and she'll make him happy, I think, or she won't and some other flicka will. But he'll find his own way and it'll work out for the best. It always does." She closed her eyes.

Isaac lay awake in a confusion of feeling. He felt like a child, groping in the dark, shrieking with pain and laughter, while all the rest of the world looked on with amusement. In the space of one night, his son was grown to a man and his wife was grown to a— to a damned William Jennings Bryan! And the one thing he had counted on all his life to hold him up, the one thing he was secretly more proud of than any other—his physical vitality and strength, his manhood itself—now seemed the weakest link in his life. I wronged one woman, he thought, long ago, and I just about did it again. And worse, I just about wronged my own son in the bargain. Just as he was convinced he would probably never sleep again, a flood of relief cooled his body like a chill after fever. Thank God, he hadn't made even a worse fool of himself. It could have happened, he knew, older men than him did it all the time, and he was intensely grateful to whatever gods watched that he had not. He looked over at Margaret, sleeping on her side of the bed. Women, he thought. How was it that a man could stand up to just about any weakness but the lure of them?

Maybe you could never really know a woman, anyway, he thought. It was like trying to own the mountain, or a stretch of the river. Like going to a fancy woman. What you wanted was their softness and their laughing eyes and the tilt of their head and their youth—but what you got was a piece of flesh. Something was missing, even as you held it. Like when you pulled a bucket of water from the river. It was the stuff the river was made of, all right, but it sure wasn't the river itself. And as he tried to unravel these things, the merciful peace of weariness settled over him, and he slept.

Leona left the next day for a boarding house in the city. Will sat at the kitchen table, watching as the rain beaded up on the window.

He spoke to his father, but his eyes stayed on his mother's face. "I'm going to civil engineering school," he said. "Two years, and I can get a degree. And I'll be out of the woods. There's talk of building a dam on the Columbia some day. If they do, it'll be the biggest thing in one piece man has ever made, I guess. I want to see it go together." He looked now at his father. "And I want to have a hand in it."

"Dam the river?" Isaac said. "What for?"

"For the future, Pa, and to bring to life a million acres that're useless now. You've spent your life cutting trees to fill it up or fishing it for salmon. I just want to make the river work for us, instead of the other way around. And I'm not the only one. Guys in Spokane've been talking about it for awhile now. I think it could happen."

Isaac sputtered, "Well, if it does, it'll sure in hell kill off a lot of guys like me! We've got to have the river to get the logs down, and even if they *could* do it, which I sorely doubt, I can't imagine the people in this state *letting* them!"

Will laughed lightly. "They won't stop the river, Pa, only slow it down a little maybe. Anyway, you can't stop progress."

"Progress! Pretty word for an ugly business."

Will said, "Seems to me we've had this conversation before. But it was about Wobblies."

Isaac snorted.

"They'll be back, you know, Pa," Will said. "Sooner or later, the workers'll be organizing again, all over this country. I hope to hell they do a better job of it than the Wobblies did, but there's sure nothing we can do to stop them. Might even be a race between which goes first, the trees or the old-time jacks to cut them. Suckow was blind, but he wasn't a fool." He shrugged. "Anyway, the woods aren't where I belong anymore."

Isaac cleared his throat. "Listen, Will, if it's about Leona—"

"It's not," he said calmly. "She just made me see it clearer."

Isaac flushed with quick hurt, but he kept his voice under control. He glanced at Margaret cautiously and said, "I've been building it all for you, Will. It doesn't mean a thing if you don't pick up the reins."

Will shook his head gently and smiled. "You've been building it for yourself, Pa. And for Mother. And for every jack who ever set his boots under your mess table. But it's time for me to find something for myself." Will searched his mother's face for understanding and found it. He leaned across the table and took his father's hand, feeling him flinch at the unfamiliar embrace, but he did not let him go. "I've got my own wagon to drive, Pa," he said.

Margaret stood and walked to the window. Outside, the rain had stopped and the cedars dripped rhythmically. "You ever notice," she asked softly, "that the sun seems to shine brighter after it rains?"

Will went downriver from Demers camp to Fort Vancouver, where he could began his training as a civil engineer on federal lands. His first letter mentioned Leona only in passing. "We've decided to do what we need to do to make our lives what we want," he wrote. "She's going to train herself, and so am I. Then, we'll see how we feel."

When Isaac read those words, his body tensed for an instant as it had when he first saw her, and he recalled the way her haunches moved under her skirt, so innocent and yet so animal, the way his blood had surged like a warm tide, leaving him dizzy, pounding in his fingertips and the balls of his feet . . . yet he could scarcely remember her face at all, and nothing that she had said.

After Isaac and Margaret returned to the river, he hired a new foreman to take over Will's job, retiring himself to cruiser. Now, he spent the days walking stands of timber, estimating their value and the time it would take to cut them.

Margaret was especially gentle with him these days, he noticed, as though she knew how hard it was for him to quit the crew. For years, he'd been surrounded by noise and men all day; now he walked the mountains alone, marking trees and laying stakes for the fallers to come. In his mind, he pictured himself as one of the old mountain men, traipsing lonely ridges where no man's foot had been before.

At times, the woods were a deep, green refuge for him, shadowed and silent and eternal, and he realized for the first time how much he loved them. He wondered if Will had ever felt such a love. At other times, particularly when he came across a burned slash or a stand of fallen, wasted timber, the forest seemed to mumble a solemn rebuke, and unseen creatures slipped away into the brush, just out of his vision.

Sometimes, he came across a deserted logging camp and was

startled to see how quickly the woods came creeping back. Where once a mill stood on open ground, now ferns and grasses and fire-weed bunched hip-high. Small firs peered into the bunkhouse windows, jays scolded from their outposts in the mess chimney, and owls hooted at him from the cookhouse, flapping over his head in rage at his intrusion.

One day as he walked a deep stand of hemlock, he caught a glimmer of movement at the edge of his eyes. He froze. Silently, lifting each hoof like a cat in wet grass, a doe stepped carefully into the clearing. Her ears twitched toward him. Evidently she sensed no danger, for behind her a spotted fawn trotted eagerly, only a few weeks old. Suddenly, they stood still as the massive trees themselves, staring at him. She dropped her head and began to browse, keeping her body between him and the fawn.

Isaac moved slightly, unconsciously, and the doe swiveled her long head, facing him, her ears wide and trembling. Quickly, she bounded away into the brush and the fawn dropped flat to the moss. The doe stopped at the edge of the clearing and watched him.

Isaac stepped slowly toward the fawn. It didn't move and if he hadn't seen it go to its knees, he would have lost it in the bracken. Ten feet away from the creature, he could see its heart beating; still, it did not move. He moved so close he could reach out and touch it and then did touch its soft fur, ever so gently, and still, the fawn stayed frozen, only the hard pounding of its sides betraying its terror.

He glanced up at the doe, who watched him from behind the firs. In her eyes, he thought he saw a helpless resignation, a blend of fear and fascination so powerful that he was shaken to his soul. He had seen that look before somewhere, he knew, but where? And then, he remembered Ning Ho and the way she had looked when he first kissed her. The same helpless, inevitable giving up of something that no living creature should have to give up.

He turned slowly and walked far away from the fawn. From a distance, he watched silently as the doe called her baby to her side with some silent signal. The fawn tottered to its feet, glanced once in his direction, and trotted obediently after her into the woods.

That night he sat at the kitchen table, figuring for over an hour, scrawling numbers and sketches over paper.

"What are you up to?" Margaret asked, looking up from her mending.

"Look at this," he said pensively. "Tell me what you think."
She came and stood over him.

"See, I'm finding mostly hemlocks up there. All last week and this week, too. The Douglas firs are getting crowded out and so are the cedars."

"Why?"

He shrugged. "We go after the older trees—some of them are more'n five hundred years old, you know. And burns take down the rest. And then, the hemlock moves in and puts down seeds. It's a tough one. It'll grow under firs, but firs won't grow under hemlocks, they need too much light. So the hemlocks put down ten times more seed, take up ten times more land, and when Will's an old man like me"—he looked up and grinned to refute his words—"there won't be a fir on this mountain. Nothing but hemlock and salal and berries."

She eased into the chair next to him. "Is there anything to be done about it?"

He tapped the paper with his pencil. "I don't know for sure. Might be. But the boys'd laugh me out of the woods." He hunched over and pointed to a sketch he'd made. "We had some greenhorn foresters hanging around last year, calling trees 'conifers,' for God's sake, and we laughed them off. But I'm beginning to wonder if they didn't have something." He chuckled to himself, a private memory. "Like ol' Gramma said, maybe I just got to believe it first. See, we could plant as we cut, honey. We could gather up the fir cones, strip 'em of seed, and drop 'em as we go. Or better yet," he said, "we could set out seedlings. That'd give 'em an even better chance. And then a hundred years from now, there'd still be big timber on these hills."

Margaret beamed at him wondrously. "But where would you get the seedlings?"

"I don't know about that yet," he said softly. "I'm still thinking on it. But what do you think? It'd be a damn big job."

She took his hands. "Your share is to do the work, Isaac. God's share is to give you the heart and the strength to get the job done. Together, you can do it."

The next day, Isaac walked a tract of cut-over fir, bending and clumping the soil in his hands frequently. He sat on a stump and gazed over the land. It was ugly, he grimaced. Rough and scarred by machines and men, stumps hacked everywhere to the ground,

and salal and berries running roughshod over it all. He turned and
looked in another direction. There, just over the hill, were the
scorched edges of the last burn. That land was even more desolate,
with its charred ruins of timber cast about like corpses.

He had always leased the land: Cut it and get out, his father
always used to say, and that was the best way then. Just let the
farmers come in and plant it to truck gardens or orchards. And some
of them tried. He'd seen the little abandoned cabins where families
had labored long to burn, dynamite, and grub out the stumps and
boulders. Once they got the land cleared, though, they discovered
the soil wasn't good for anything but high timber, and they moved
on.

He stood and stubbed his boot at a struggling seedling. A hemlock. About the only thing that'd take root here, he thought. But the
hemlock doesn't build the best woods, not for man, anyhow. He
bent and touched the little tree, feeling the creak in his back and his
knees. He recalled, as if it were a dozen lifetimes ago, the way Ning
Ho had planted a line of cedars at the edge of her meadow. And in
his own backyard. Suzanna called them her "back-lot cedars," a
blessing for the cool shade they provided in the summer and a
shelter from the river winds in the winter. Ning Ho had seen something, even then, that he was only just discovering now. That the
woods, the trees, even the mountain itself had a life, a soul, a place
in things, and he held some responsibility for their survival, just as
he did for his own. He shook his head ruefully. They'd laugh at him,
all of them. Put the men to work gathering seeds from cones, holding on to leases just to put the seeds in the ground, nursing an acre
of seedlings and paying good wages to get them planted. Aye, the
men would say he was crazier than an old woman on a hot day. He
grinned suddenly. He always wanted to live so he could tell them
all to go to hell, and now he could. Let them laugh. Someday,
Demers land would have the only Douglas fir and red cedar on these
mountains.

Will is gone, he thought, off to find his own life, his own
dreams. And that's as it should be. There is a proper order to
things, a time for growing and changing and losing and gaining
again, and Ning Ho taught me that, as well. He dropped his head
in wonder. For an instant, it was as though he could see her eyes,
feel her slight body against his, hear her voice even in the whispering of the trees.

He remembered suddenly, as though it was yesterday, a talk he had had with his mother shortly after Caleb had died.

"Isaac," she had said, looking intently into his eyes, "I often think on that little slip of a Celestial, Ning Ho was her name, wasn't it? Pert little gal. You ever think on her much?"

Surprised that his mother would bring up such a memory, he had said, "No, not much. Why speak of her now?"

His mother had smiled sadly. "Did you ever wonder why she did such a thing?"

He shrugged, uncomfortable under her gaze.

"I never knew a gal to take her own life that way, save to protect something else," Suzanna continued, almost as though she was talking to herself alone.

He had changed the subject then, but now the conversation came back to him with a shock, for he suddenly understood what his mother had been trying to tell him. My God, my God, Ning Ho was carrying my child. Carrying a piece of me under her heart, as she plunged to her death. And now, almost thirty years later, he realized that he carried a piece of her as well, a part of her soul which only now could be heard, a counsel as old as the land itself, and an understanding of her tough Chinese reverence for the land, a peasant respect for all those things which he had spent his life taking, taking, and never giving back. He looked up at the trees around him, his eyes watering in the sunlight. She's been gone for so long—yet she's still a part of me. And a part of the future, if I can learn her lesson. I owe her that much, at least.

A year later, Isaac and Margaret stood at the edge of a clearing in the sunshine. Before them stretched row after row of five-inch cedars, reaching their fringed fingers to the blue sky. Margaret linked her arm through his and smiled up at him. "I must say, I never thought I married a planter, Mister Demers. What're you going to call this, anyway?"

"I'm calling it a tree farm," he said cheerfully. " 'Bout time we jacks learned the truth about these woods. It's a crop, just like corn or cotton. It takes a longer time to grow, is all." He bent and poked the soil more firmly around a seedling. "Someday, maybe in a hundred years, these mountains'll have more timber than they had when we first logged 'em. You and I won't see it, honey. Neither will our son. But somebody will."

She leaned over and touched his shoulder, feeling the warmth of the sun on his shirt, leaning into his body for the pleasure it gave her. "Well, you've stirred the soil up with your plough, my dear. And now, it'll never be the same again." She laughed as the thought struck her. "And neither will you."

PART SIX

The River Movers,
1915–1942

Green Douglas firs where the waters cut through,
Down her wild mountains and canyons she flew.
Canadian Northwest to the ocean so blue,
It's roll on, Columbia, roll on.
Roll on, Columbia, roll on,
Roll on, Columbia, roll on.
Your power is turning our darkness to dawn,
So roll on, Columbia, roll on.

Other great rivers add power to you,
Yakima, Snake and the Klickitat too,
Sandy Willamette and Hood River too,
Roll on, Columbia, roll on . . .

Tom Jefferson's vision would not let him rest,
An empire he saw in the Pacific Northwest.
Sent Lewis and Clark and they did the rest,
Roll on, Columbia, roll on . . .

At Bonneville now there are ships in the locks,
The waters have risen and cleared all the rocks,
Shiploads of plenty will steam past the docks,
So roll on, Columbia, roll on . . .

And on up the river is Grand Coulee Dam,
The mightiest thing ever built by a man,
To run the great factories and water the land,
It's roll on, Columbia, roll on . . .

These mighty men labored by day and by night,
Matching their strength 'gainst the river's wild flight,
Through rapids and falls they won the hard fight,
Roll on, Columbia, roll on . . .

—"Roll on, Columbia" by Woody Guthrie

*S*o finally, the river began to move aside for man, to eddy into smaller pockets of wharfs and cities, to grow more sluggish under man's wastes, more dark with his stains, weltering around the crustings of his buildings, his bridges, his dumpings. The power of the river that had drawn so many to its shores now lured new dreamers, men who had bigger hungers, who searched out anything that promised new energies and profits, even if it meant the river, the source itself, was altered forever.

High up at the Canadian border where its waters were new, the river paused, with a great attentiveness, slowing for a moment to feel a different generation of man's intrusive fingers. Down at Carson, between the Wind and the Hood rivers, men were building a series of canals and locks at the Cascades to admit great ships farther up the Columbia. Then the engineers moved to The Dalles, where the river boiled and roared for more than ten miles of rapids. There, they blasted and drilled a path, an eight-mile ditch at Celilo, to allow steamships to bypass its treacheries and advance deeper and deeper into the upper river. Finally, they built a paved highway on the river's south bank from Portland to the headlands of Celilo. Past Crownpoint, past the many little creeks tumbling straight down the canyon walls, past the falls of Latourell, Multnomah, and Horsetail, they poured their concrete ribbon, and at Mitchell's Point, they built a daylight tunnel that was the rival of any in Switzerland. The Columbia Gorge Highway was one of the most spectacular in the nation, and imaginative men stood on it and gazed down at the river, at the surging power that came hurrying from the high backbone of the continent, and wondered how this immensity could be further controlled.

Proud and glittering, the river waited, biding its time.

LEONA DEMERS LAY GASPING IN THE LAST STAGES OF A LONG LABOR, HER belly taut, her arms and legs wet with sweat. She was dimly aware that Margaret, her mother-in-law, was ministering to her, vaguely conscious that Suzanna Demers hovered somewhere at the edges of her vision, murmuring ancient words of comfort. But she could take little comfort, find no refuge from the gripping pains that shuddered through her back, her abdomen, her legs, as Will Demers' first child struggled to be born.

"Take some water, dear," Margaret said soothingly, dribbling cool liquid from a cloth between Leona's clenched lips.

"How long has it been now?" Suzanna asked faintly, fanning herself in a corner chair. The old woman was wizened and white with age; still she sat up and watched patiently as though she waited for something other than this birth. "Isaac took nearly this long to come, I recollect, nigh ten hours or more."

"So did Will," Margaret said, laying the damp cloth on Leona's brow. "Try to breathe slowly," she added. "Save your strength."

My strength! Leona thought, as she closed her eyes, her mind, to the pain. Little does she know I would lie here forever to birth this child, I've a bottomless well of strength if I need it, I've waited too long to give up now.

Her mind whirled back to the past, anything to divert her from the wrenching agony of her body, back to a time when this child was only an empty ache in her heart and its father a space in her arms.

Will had taken forever with his marriage proposal, as hesitant as he'd been with their first kiss. For a man who had bold visions and wide dreams, he certainly was a cautious courter, she thought wryly.

At first, there were only letters after she left, sparse and carefully worded to avoid any mention of their mutual memories of the Demers house, the garden, Isaac, or her departure. Written as friend to friend, they came regularly for a year, and she answered each promptly. She waited patiently for his early warmth to return while she worked at the woolen mill in Washougal upriver, daydreaming of Will as she stitched together lengths of soft cloth, feeling his last kiss each time she closed her eyes.

But at the end of the year, her patience ebbed, and her letters to him became more familiar, more friendly, more—firm. Well, I certainly wouldn't call it *fast* to let a man know you like him, she thought as she panted shallowly, after all that had already happened between us. The pain was building to a new plateau now, and Leona gripped the sheets with clenched fists, willing her mind elsewhere. After he finished his engineering school, he got work on the Cascade locks. Out of sight, out of mind, she knew, so she invited him to visit her in Washougal before he left for farther upriver. Thank God, I did, she thought, or he might *never* have spoken up. He kissed her again, that trip, kissed her while they sat on the banks of the river, throwing pebbles and watching the crayfish scurry.

"Can you push?" Margaret said, leaning over her. "It's time, I think, if you can—"

Go away, go away, Leona thought, her mind clenched as tight as her fists, let me stay here in this memory—Will's mouth had dropped lightly on hers, then more insistently, his arm round her waist, pullling her closer, and she felt the grass crinkle under her skirts. After that kiss, the letters came more often, while he worked on the canal, and for another year, she sewed woolen cloth, wondering when her life would start. He loved me, even then, she thought, and I knew it, but oh to get *him* to know it, to *own* it, to cross that distance between himself and others, to believe in some other future than just the one he could make with his own hands!

"Ahh-urrgh!" she shouted, amazed at the force and the violence of her cry, wondering someplace inside who was making that awful clamor and knowing that it was herself. Her back arched of its own volition, and she felt that a knife was cutting her in two, sawing up between her legs with a terrible inevitability.

"Push now! Push!" she heard Margaret cry from some high distant peak.

And then the war in Europe was coming, was coming for certain, and it was on everyone's lips, in everyone's mind, and she was getting older, so was he, and the dangers seemed to press on them from without, more ominous than any they felt within, and she knew she must have him or be forever empty! And would she ever be empty again, oh God! She pushed, her feet shoving and writhing, her hips twisting, and finally, *finally,* he came to her with that question in his eyes, on his lips, and they were married, and now—

"I see the head!" Margaret cried, her hands moving in a flurry over Leona's body, pressing and pulling at her legs. "Push now again!"

And then they moved farther upriver, where he wanted to build the canal at Celilo, more company shacks, more company settlements, and nothing more permanent than a geranium in a pot and flour-sack curtains. Married, married, forever and at last, the first step and now the second, a child, and if they could ever settle down in one place long enough, a home, a real home with a cherry tree in the yard. She screamed again and pushed as hard as she could, yanking her knees up to her breasts with all her strength. A blackness welled up from her belly and threatened to engulf her, a veil over her eyes, but she fought it away and clearly felt a jolt, a catch of tearing and heat, and the child slipped away from her into life.

"It's a girl, dear," Margaret said gently, "a lovely baby girl with lots of beautiful black hair like yours."

Leona could barely hear her for the roaring in her ears. She struggled to sit up, reaching frantically for her child. Black hair, dark eyes, she examined the infant quickly, carefully, and then fell back on the sodden bed in exhausted relief.

Suzanna Demers laughed from the corner, her voice sounding as weak as Leona felt. "You needn't worry, child," she said. "A Demers don't make nothing but good stock!"

Leona smiled, her lips quivering. Thank God, she thought, she's all Demers and me, not a bit of my mother in her.

As though she read her mind, Margaret said, "It's a shame your mother couldn't have lived to see this day, Leona. It's always a happy time when babies come, and even though we never got a chance to meet Mary, I know she'd have been proud of you both."

"Thank you," Leona said weakly, silently thanking whatever gods watched that Margaret would never know the truth. At least, not from *this* birth. From her own light skin, from her own slender face and form, no Demers would ever need know that Jack Cahill had taken himself a Klickitat squaw named Mary for a wife. She knew that Will was part Indian, way back in the past, but he rarely spoke of it, certainly not with pride, and even if he had, part Indian was a lot different than half. "Light," her mother had named her, light enough to pass in school, in the lumber cookhouse, all her life, just as her daughter would now. She put the infant to her breast, watching as she opened her mouth soundlessly, her tiny fists clenched in some private dream.

"What're you going to call her?" Suzanna asked, leaning over them both with tired eyes.

Leona said, "I think I'll let her father name her."

"Smart idea," the old woman nodded. "I did that when both of my gals come."

"Shall I go tell him you're ready to see him?" Margaret asked. "They've been waiting out there since breakfast. By now, Isaac's probably got him so riled, he'll be *relieved* it's a soft, pretty girl instead of another ornery male."

The two women went out, and Leona pulled the child close to her, staring into her eyes. Dark eyes, like her own, stared back, unfocused, opaque. She began to croon to the infant, tucking her under one arm, nestling her close to her breast. You are wanted, oh so wanted, she thought, and loved more than you'll know. Three years it took me to get him to make a space in our lives for you, to look up from his plans and his picks and his river to see the future, *our* future in your soft, dark eyes.

Will and Isaac had been awaiting the birth, sitting out on the porch of the little company shack, rocking in the shade.

"It's good that wife of yours had the sense to commence on a Sunday," Isaac said idly. "You don't even have to take a day off."

Isaac and Margaret had taken the ferry upriver from Skamania, since Leona had no female kin to help her. At the last moment, Suzanna had announced she was coming along. When Isaac had reminded her that it was a long trip for a woman near eighty-five, she'd only scoffed and shook her small white head. "Lordylord, you think I got something better to do than watch another Demers come into the world? I guess I can make it, son, if you can."

Will's cabin was just a stone's toss from the river, and the sound of the moving water made all their words this afternoon seem no more important than the murmuring of the trees. Will tried to remember this last, as he listened to Isaac continue.

"Yessir, I recall the day you came, made quite a to-do about it, too. They had to come and get me clear off the timber line, almost, and I was scared you'd get there before I did and I'd have to hear about it the rest of my married days."

Isaac's words didn't seem to need an answer. After a long moment of silence, his father said, "So you figure to be finished here soon, you say? And then where're you off to next? Camp three could use a good foreman, you know." He paused, glancing at Will out of the corner of his eye. "And the woods aren't a bad place to raise a sprout, as you might recall."

Will smiled sadly and shook his head, his eyes closed, his chair tilted back on two legs. "You don't give up, do you, Pa."

Isaac said mildly, "Just a thought. I know it would certainly please your mother."

It had been a long day, and it might be longer still. Will decided to let that one lie where it was thrown.

Isaac was silent as long as he could stand it. Finally he asked again, "So, what *are* your plans? Now you got a family to tend for, you need something steady."

Something steady. Will rocked forward and let the two front legs of his chair bang firmly on the porch. "They're going to be starting up the first dam on the river soon. I'll be working on that. I guess that's steady enough."

Isaac rolled his eyes. "You've been talking about that dam for ten years, boy, and nobody's done nothing to slow down this river yet, so far as I can see. They've been digging ditches *around* it fast enough, but like I told you, nobody's going to dam this river, not in my lifetime. And not in yours either, I bet. Why don't you hitch your wagon to a sure thing for a change?"

"Nothing's more sure in this whole state than the river, Pa," Will said quietly. "And nothing's more sure than the fact that man's going to use it to his own ends, one way or the other."

"Christ, the only things that's sure in this world is birth and death and war, boy. *War's* here, or haven't you heard? The damned Germans are going around sinking ships right and left, and if you don't get yourself something steady, you might as well just go sign up, ship out, and get yourself blown to bits on some French beach or another. Of course, you figure to come into a damned healthy inheritance when me and your ma pass, but if timber prices don't pick up, it won't be enough, not the way the world's turning these days."

Will laughed softly and shook his head. "Pa, you and I aren't ever going to see eye to eye on this. I've told you over and over, I want to make my own fortune and find my own way. You've already had to sell off three camps just to keep the last two going, so don't tell me how 'healthy' timber is. Anyway, even if it was a damned gold mine, it wouldn't be for me. You know what I want to do with my life, I've said it often enough, so why do you keep asking me, if you don't like the answer? You think a dam shouldn't happen, I think it should and it will, and I'm going to be a part of it. Now, let's talk about something else." He picked the one subject he knew would divert his father's ire. "You able to keep full crews on, what with the war and all? Any labor problems this season?"

Isaac snorted like an old crotchety bull and began a long tirade on the swift dissolution of the American working man, and Will leaned back once more, two chair legs teetering, listening with one ear for some telltale cry from the house.

Margaret appeared on the stoop, her eyes dancing with pleasure. "Go see your wife and your new daughter. And don't forget to tell her she's beautiful, son. She'll never need to hear it more."

The chair banged down loudly, and Will was past her before she finished speaking.

Leona watched Will open the door and hesitate, as though its threshold was the gate to a suddenly strange land, and the only familiar landmark was the bed on which she lay, which they had shared.

Leona summoned up more strength and grinned at him. "Well, come on in, Mister Demers," she laughed softly. "We ladies don't bite, you know."

He smiled—she wondered how a man who was normally so in control, both of himself and his surroundings, could suddenly look so sheepish—and sat down gingerly on the side of the bed.

"You okay?" he asked softly. His eyes were fixed on the top of the infant's head, as though he could scarcely believe her presence.

Leona reached out with an effort and patted his arm. "We're both fine." She pulled the child further out of her swaddling and held up one tiny fist to her father. "Your daughter's quite a fighter, sir. I reckon she takes after her pa." When he didn't move to touch her, Leona took the infant's hand and touched his arm with the little fingers; the child squirmed and wrinkled up her face, disturbed. He tentatively touched her hand.

"I thought it'd be bigger," he said wonderingly.

"This is a 'she,' Will Demers." The infant suddenly squawled loud and fiercely, and all three of them started at the noise. Leona laughed. "And I have a feeling she's not going to let you forget it anytime soon. What would you like to call her?"

He looked surprised, as though it hadn't even occurred to him. Then he said hesitantly, "How would you feel about naming her after my grandmother? Suzanna Blue Demers. It would certainly please her."

Leona smiled, for this was exactly what she had hoped for, that he would begin to make these connections. "I think it's very fitting. Miss Suzanna Blue Demers. Now, may I have a kiss for all my hard work?"

He smiled shyly and leaned over, careful not to press the baby, and kissed her softly on the cheek, resting his face for an instant against hers.

Leona woke late that night, alone in the great bed. Will had made a pallet on the porch so that she might sleep undisturbed, but where was the baby? Then her eyes made out the shape in the dim light: Someone was sitting in the corner chair, a white bundle in her arms. It was Suzanna Demers, holding her namesake. The old woman was wrapped in a yellow shawl, rocking gently back and forth, the baby in her lap.

Leona raised up on one elbow.

"Sorry, honey," Suzanna whispered. "I didn't mean to wake you. Just wanted to make this gal's acquaintance a mite."

Leona settled back under the covers. "Couldn't you sleep?"

"Plenty of time for that." Suzanna picked up the baby and held her close under her neck. "We've been having ourselves a nice little visit. She's got more hair than I had when I was ten, black and shiny as a wet rock."

"Yes," Leona said carefully. "My mother had dark hair, and mine's been dark since I was tiny."

"And dark eyes," Suzanna said lightly, "just like woods eyes, eh?" She paused, stroking the infant's head gently. "We got ourselves a little maverick here, I think."

Leona stiffened. "What do you mean?"

Suzanna smiled, her eyes gentle. "I mean, missy, that I've seen too many siwash an' part siwash in my day not to know another little papoose when I see one. Margaret and Isaac, Will, now they haven't, but don't forget, I *married* me one. This little mite's got some river blood in her, as we used to call it. So do you, if it comes to that. But don't think for a minute I give a damn, one way or t'other. And if you aim to keep it close, why that's none o' my affair. But I got to ask you . . . why?"

Leona was silent.

Suzanna pursed her lips appraisingly. "You think Will'd love you any less, did he know?"

Leona cast about for the proper words of denial, but there was nothing to say. Finally, she said, "Demers was a big name in my house, growing up. When I first met Will, I loved him. Loved him before I even knew his name, before I knew he was a Demers, the first time I saw him coming round the corner of the cookhouse." She sighed and leaned back on the pillows. "But it's taken him a long time to love me back. I'm still working on that, if you want to know." She added reluctantly, "I thought he didn't need any excuse to love me less."

Suzanna thought this over for a moment in silence. "Might could be, he loves you all he's able. Some men are like that, just not the giving sort. His father wasn't."

"What about *your* man, Will's grandfather? Was he the giving sort?" She fumbled in her confusion. "What I mean is, how did you make him love you?"

The old woman laughed. "I didn't, child. It don't work that way. Making a good marriage isn't finding the right person, you know, it's *being* the right person. I was just so blamed lovable, he couldn't help himself." She grinned and waved her hand in dismissal. "Oh, they're all like that, I think, every man jack of 'em, not wanting to love any more than they have to, to get by. Just as like one another as minnows, men are, and it's when you discover it that you're free of frettin' over 'em. You're doing just fine. You got a good heart, you're good to look on, and you love him. That should be enough for any man, Demers or no."

Leona got out of bed and came to stand beside Suzanna, gazing down on her daughter. "How did you guess? Was it her eyes, gave her away?"

"Nothing gave her away. Now, you get back in that bed and rest up. Let me sit and rock a spell with this little fawn."

Leona slipped back under the covers, suddenly and irresistibly weary. The last thing she heard before sleep claimed her again was a soft lullaby coming from the shadowed corner.

> Rise up my dearest dear
> And present to me your hand,
> And we'll march you in succession
> To some far and distant land,
> To some far off distant land.
> There the boys will plow and hoe,
> And the girls will spin and sew,
> We'll travel through the cane-break,
> And shoot the buffalo,
> Oh, shoot the buffalo!

Dawn woke Leona early, and she rose up and looked over at Suzanna. The old woman had fallen asleep, her head back, the baby nestled securely in her lap. Leona went over to gently extricate her child and saw that Suzanna Demers' eyes were open. Sometime in the night, perhaps in the middle of a lullaby, she had died. Leona took the baby from her stiffening hands and sat on the edge of the bed, gazing into the withered face, a face filled with white peace and the quiet joy of a life well lived, well loved.

Five years passed, the First World War came and ended, and Will went to work on the Columbia Gorge Highway. His daughter had a baby brother now, a boy as light as she was dark, and Leona had carried the potted geranium and the flour-sack curtains from one company house to another, this one farther upriver at Wishram. The little town sat on the site of the old Indian place of trade, and Will's son, Jack, spent most of his time squatting on his heels, digging with a small stick for arrowheads and trade beads.

Will was assistant to the roadmaster, and as such, he spent a lot of time driving up and down the gorge in his Model T, inspecting the great concrete highway as it grew. But now he was on another errand, almost two hundred miles north and out of sight of the river.

Will pulled the Model T to a shuddering stop outside the barbed wire fence, put on the hand brake, and stepped out into the dust. He opened the gate, brushing a half-inch of silt off the crossbar. Just up the rutted road, he could see the farm. Or what was left of it. The wind was already beginning to pick up, though it was still early afternoon.

Christ, he thought, licking his dry lips. In another two hours, this place'll be an inferno, and it's not even July yet. He fingered the real estate pamphlet he'd carried in his pocket from Spokane. Some boomers with big ideas were offering "bargain tracts" out here in the Big Bend country, promising water and a regular Eden, complete with apples. Another Yakima in three years, they said, all for the grand sum of fifty bucks an acre. The Evergreen State.

He squinted and looked over the fields. A far cry from paradise, he thought, but a man had to start somewhere. The Ford gave a final resigned hiccup, as though to remind him that it was still there, and settled on its frame with a faint wheeze. Will's mouth twisted in a wry grin. That old hulk was about the only thing on the horizon that smacked of the twentieth century. To look at the parched land, the flat, treeless, barren fields, the sagging farmhouse in the distance, you'd never know it was 1920. Back in Spokane, chicken dinners were seventy-five cents and the Dusty Rhoades Orchestra thrown in for good measure, but out here on the plateau, time stood still. He got back in the car and trundled up the road, throwing up dust clouds a hundred feet into the air. On the porch sat an old-timer, leaning his hardbacked chair up against the rail. Behind him, a big Nehi thermometer edged up over eighty-five degrees. Will got out and hailed him.

"Will Demers, Mister Gibbs, I sent a wire?" He stepped up the porch, hearing the sand grit under his boots.

The old man stood and extended his hand. "I seen you comin', Mister Demers." He chuckled, a sound like a snorting mule. "That's one good thing 'bout all this damned dust. Nobody kin sneak up on a man." He gestured to another cane chair. "Pull up a seat."

He peered at Will from under a creased felt hat, the same color as the dust. "You look a mite younger than I figured," he said.

Will grinned amiably. "I'm thirty-five. Old enough, I guess. You out here by yourself?"

"Yep," the old man said, slapping his thigh. "Just me an' a hundred an' sixty acres of the best land in Grant County. My wife's buried out back, 'longside one of my sons. It like to swaller me up, too, but I ain't gonna let it. Damn dirt'll take me soon enough, I reckon, but it won't be this lot. I give it enough."

"How long you been here?"

The old man leaned over, spat off the porch, and shifted a wad of Copenhagen to the other cheek. "Twenty years, comin' up. Me an' the missus moved out after our second was in short pants. Weren't nothin' but sage an' bunchgrass, then. But we got some rains an' the soil was good, an' we got near eighteen bushels of hard wheat to the acre. For a few years, it was real tolerable. Then, the wind came up an' the rains quit, an' the blasted dust commenced to blow. We lost the wheat the first year. Planted again, an' the same damn thing happened. Verna was took that winter, nursin' our boy through the influenza. He went, too." He leaned back, crossed his arms, and his eyes blazed briefly. "You can't tie down topsoil, boy. I tried it. I know. A damned howlin' Sahara's all it is, an' welcome to it."

Will frowned slightly. "You're a hell of a salesman, Mister Gibbs. You tell this to all prospective buyers?"

"Yep." Gibbs grinned mischievously. "An' it runs 'em off right reg-a-lar."

"But you figure, the man who sticks around must want it bad. Or he must know something you don't. And so, he'll likely pay your price. And in the meantime, the bank won't take it, long as it's for sale, and you might just be here when the water comes, after all."

Gibbs snorted again. "Yer a fast one, Demers. Yessir. I read the papers, too. I see where those fellas in Spokane is still jawin' 'bout putting a plug in Grand Coulee and sending us some o' that river. I figure I can live on cornflakes an' tea awhile longer, if I got to. I'm patient as a rattler. Got to be."

"I see," Will said, letting his eyes roam casually over the fields. "I'll tell you what, Mister Gibbs, I may be a grand champion chump, but I think I'll call your bluff. Forty dollars an acre, your agent said. I'll give you ten, and you can live out here long's your cornflakes hold out. I won't need the place for a few more years, and I figure to be tied up elsewhere for awhile. In five years or so, I'll be back. If you're still here, the house is yours, and I'll build across the field."

The old man pulled at his lower lip in fierce concentration. "Thirty," he said finally.

"Fifteen," Will said patiently. "And after you're gone, I'll bury you next to your wife and boy and plant shade trees round all three of you. That's the best deal you're gonna get, four ways from the jack."

Gibbs sighed hugely. "You got yerself a deal, boy. An' good riddance, too. You youngins think you can fix near anythin' with spit an' Wrigley's gum. Go to 'er. But where you gonna be for the next five years?"

Will stood and stuck out his hand, already anxious to be on the road. "I hope to be building a dam, Mister Gibbs. Sooner or later, I figure all this talk's going to turn into something solid, and I mean to be there."

As Will drove back to Spokane, he allowed himself a rare and intoxicating mouthful of victory from the bootleg bottle he had wedged in the seat. That land would be, he felt, one of the most satisfying bargains of his life. The dam would be built, he knew it. As deeply as he felt the movement of the blood through his veins and the strength of his own body, he knew the dam would rise above the river, *someday*. And when it did, these dry acres in the Big Bend of the Columbia would be worth ten times what they were now, a fine place to raise a family, to make a wife happy, finally, with a home of her own. Did she think he didn't know what she wanted, think he didn't notice the way her face sagged a little in on itself when he mentioned moving on to another project, one after the other, through the last eight years? She was no longer the little gal who'd switched her skirts between tables in the cookhouse, he thought, but the spark she'd showed standing up to both Pa and me had certainly flamed into a steady fire, one a man could warm his hands at all his life.

He recalled with a warm pleasure one of his favorite memories, the time he'd taken her on a picnic down on the Washougal. They'd been to the river once before—I kissed her there, I recall, he thought —so it all started there, really. And then that second time. . . . The day was warm, and even the dust seemed golden as it settled on the ferns. They hiked down to the water, carrying a picnic basket and a blanket. She had slipped behind a rock and into her bathing clothes while he stood stoically, facing the river. After a brief interval while she giggled and teased him unmercifully, never letting him turn around, she emerged from behind a boulder, tripping lightly over the sandy beach in a sleek costume of cobalt blue.

She was beautiful. All white and gleaming, black hair streaming down her back, more a thing of the woods and the water than a woman. She watched him, suddenly shy as he rolled up his trouser legs and his sleeves. Then she stood and gently touched his shoulder. When he reached for her, she turned and raced to the water, diving in with barely a splash. He followed her in and when he reached her side, he wanted to touch her, didn't know how, so he grabbed her round the waist and tossed her high in the air, watching as her black hair whipped across her face, catching the sun and flashing, then disappearing in a froth of water and light. She bobbed to the surface, gasping and giggling, cuffing water at him, fighting and thrashing. They had ducked and bubbled like two young otters, he smiled to himself, until they'd exhausted themselves.

I guess it was inevitable, he thought. When he came out of the water, she was already on the blanket. He lay down beside her carefully, closed his eyes, and listened to the river tell its tale. I remember, I watched her, he thought, through slitted eyes while she dozed next to me. The sun made refractions, rainbows and discs of color about the edges of her, and it almost hurt his eyes to open them fully. He could see the goosebumps on her flesh, the small creases in her neck and shoulder, the movement of her ribs under her skin as she breathed.

He reached out and gently stroked her arm, and she took his caress as her due, like a contented cat by the fire. She was so alive in that instant, such an integral part of the sun, the sand, and the water, that he felt by touching her he touched all of life, something elemental and eternal and full of joy.

She reached over and touched his chest, laughing softly. He rolled on his side and took her in his arms, covering her mouth with his, tasting salt, sun, and something dark, cool, and mossy, which he supposed was the actual flavor of the river itself. Her arms went about him, and he pulled her body to his with a hunger that roused them both instantly, making them tremble. He had made love to her there, that day by the river, with only a blanket between them and the world.

He shifted on the Ford's leather seat now as he remembered the feel of her body eight years ago. I knew that day that I was in love with her, he thought, but I couldn't say it. Twice, in the sun, in the water, he wanted to tell her so, but some instinct made him hold back. There was something about her, even then, some mysterious allure that was at once old and also the newest, most rare and womanly accomplishment, which made him mistrust her, want to hide himself from her. He grinned again, suddenly proud and grateful for something he couldn't even name. After eight years of marriage and two kids, it's still there, I still want her, and sometimes, when I hold her, she still trembles in that old way.

He let his mind roam over old memories, back to when he'd finally seen in print, for the first time, what he'd been hearing about for years: the dam. When the idea of damming the Columbia was first proposed, he remembered, it had touched off a controversy that threatened to split the whole state. Rufus Woods, editor and publisher of the *Wenatchee World,* and his two friends, Billy Clapp and Jim O'Sullivan, were the core proponents of the plan to block the river and use the stored water to irrigate almost two million acres of arid land. Their first editorial had come out two years before, and the state *still* hadn't simmered down, he thought. In fact, once congressmen and the private-power men got lined up, the fury spread over a six-state region.

And it'll still be a few years before it goes up, he thought. But it *will* happen, I know it. It's my destiny—my great-grandma knew it, somehow, my granddad knew it, else why did he put that book in *my* hands, and even if he hadn't, *I* know it, have known it all along. All the years I could have been up a cedar with an ax, I was down at the river, watching the way the currents changed, the sandbars shifted, the tides moved up and down its belly. I was getting ready, though I didn't know it then. But you don't always get to do your life's work right out of the blocks. In the meantime, a man's got to feed himself and his family, so he took what came along, waiting for his destiny to begin.

He turned the Model T off the road from Odessa and headed south, dust roiling behind him. A year ago, he'd come up this same road, scouting for land: land he could buy now and use to hold Leona at bay with the promise of a better tomorrow. Then, he had driven all the way to the lip of the Grand Coulee Canyon itself, just to see what all the talk was about.

He stood and looked over the vast, mile-deep trench that the ancient waters had ploughed, two miles wide and fifty miles long, before the river had switched course. He knew its history, of course, how the glaciers had plugged the river, forcing it down the canyon, over Dry Falls to Soap Lake, how it had channeled its way through lands which were once green and fertile as the Willamette Valley was today. And then, the glaciers melted, the river assumed its old course, and the land took on its present bleak and arid face. All because the river moved. But if a glacier could do it, he had wondered, why not man? The canyon was nothing but a waiting trough for a giant reservoir, if they could just get the water into it and hold it there. And the lands which were desert would bloom again like a second Eden.

The only real argument against that dam, against *any* dam, he thought, was that it was just too big a job. He shook his head unconsciously. Almost un-American, that kind of thinking. He turned west to Yakima and headed the Model T toward home.

It was 1927 before the first dam rose on the river, and it was not the Grand Coulee, as Will had dreamed. Below Wenatchee, the Puget Sound Light and Power Company began surveying for the Rock Island Dam, and Will found a place on the crew. Here, in the flatlands between Mission Peak and Whiskey Dick Mountain, there were no company houses, only tarpaper cabins, and Leona set her potted geranium in the one shady spot between the privy and the back porch, under a leaning pine.

She was out hanging washing when the back door banged. Three children tumbled out: Suzanna, twelve and already proud of her thick black hair in two plaits down her back; Jack, a quiet and thoughtful nine, and Anna, her lastborn, a sturdy seven-year-old, the image of her gramma, Margaret.

"Mama, Mama!" Anna hollered before the rest could reach her, "We caught a fish, we caught a fish!"

Jack was carrying a large silver fish in his arms carefully, his eyes glued to the ground so he would not fall.

"*I* caught it, Mother," Suzanna said quickly, "anyways, I baited the hook and picked out the spot."

Jack brought the fish to Leona and presented it to her shyly. "What kind is it, Mama?"

Leona bent and took the fish from his arms, laying it gently on a dishtowel. "Why, it's the best fish in all the world, honey. You caught a salmon."

"I helped!" Anna said, tugging at her apron.

Leona pulled the three around her and they squatted together, staring at the big silver fish.

"See, it's a coho salmon," she said, lifting up the edge of one gill. "You just never know what the river will bring, do you? This one looks young and strong. What did you take him with?"

"Cheese!" Suzanna said triumphantly. "I knew he'd like it."

"Well, next time, do what the Indians do. They only catch the weak fish, the ones who can't jump the falls. That way, the ones who are left make stronger fish next year."

"How do you know it's a coho?" her son asked.

"Because it's silver. Also, the time of year. Chinook salmon come in the spring, the steelhead come in November. Silvers come in the middle, like now. But this is more than just a fish, you know. Do you know what else this is?"

All three children shook their heads solemnly.

"This is the spirit of the river itself. That's what the Indians think. This big fish is born in the river, swims downstream and grows and struggles and runs away from everything that wants to eat him, and finally he makes it all the way to the ocean. And there, he grows some more and *everything* wants to eat him, sharks and whales and men with nets, but he fights and runs and finally, when he's ready, he comes back up the river, all those miles up the white water, until he gets back to where he was born. And then do you know what he does?"

Their eyes were huge with wonder as they pictured the salmon's long struggle.

"Then, with his last bit of strength, and this is one strong fish, let me tell you, he finds a mate and makes his babies, and then, he dies."

Anna's face puckered up woefully. "Did we get him before he made his babies?"

Leona pulled her close in a hug. "Maybe. But you can make it up to him. We'll have this big strong fish for dinner tonight, and you can take his strength in your stomach and so can your pa, and in that way, we'll all be stronger and his life and his death won't be for nothing."

Suzanna thought this over carefully. "How come you said he was the spirit of the river? He's just a fish."

"Because," Leona smiled, "he's just like the river, going on against all odds, renewing itself, choosing its own path. Anyway, that's what the Indians say."

Jack picked up the fish resolutely. "I'm going to take him back," he said, his little voice low and quavery.

"Don't be stupid," Suzanna said. "He's *dead*."

"It's not stupid, Suzanna," her mother said firmly. "Not stupid at all, but maybe a better idea would be just to remember, while we're eating him, to give thanks for what we're getting. Now"—and she took the fish from Jack and headed toward the kitchen—"tell me how you caught this big river monster!"

That night in bed, Leona said to Will, "And you should have seen Anna's face when she asked about the salmon babies. You'd have thought I told her the world was coming to an end tomorrow morning. You know, we'll have to take them up to the hatchery on Sunday. I know it's not finished yet, but I bet they have some tanks and maybe some fingerlings the kids can see up close. Give them an idea what I was talking about today."

Will pulled her closer in his favorite position, her backside wedged securely into his stomach, her ankles interwoven with his. "Well, I was going to tell you this later, but I've got to work Sunday. I'm afraid you'll have to take them without me."

She reared back and stared at him over her shoulder. "What? You don't work on Sundays; you *never* work on Sundays."

"It's only eight miles into Wenatchee," he said patiently. "The road to the hatchery's this side of it and clearly marked. You've driven farther than that before by yourself."

She sat up now and pulled the blankets up under her breasts. "That's not the point, Will, and you know it. I'm doing a *lot* of things by myself, these days, me and the kids. Lately, it seems we're doing *without* you more than with. What in the world's so important that you got to do it on your one day off in seven?"

He looked away, his face closed. "A union meeting."

Her jaw fell open and her brows lifted. He turned and glanced at her, then away again, and she closed her mouth firmly. Then she said, "Well, I can hardly believe it. Wobblies on this site? You never said a word about this, Will, you just sprung it on me, and to take our Sunday, our one day together as a family—"

"I just heard, myself," he said. "Not two days ago, a few of the boys came and told me. Said they heard I was on the rolls."

"But that was years ago!"

"I told them that, but they said it didn't matter, they're starting up again out here and they want me in."

Leona crossed her arms. "Well, tell them no, Will, and good riddance."

He smiled at her in the darkness, and she felt her lips turning up in the corners as though they had a secret pact with his, unbeknown to her mind. He took her hand and asked, "Since when are you so riled against labor, eh? Your pa was a working man; *you* put in a good day's worth yourself, as I recall."

She frowned and clenched herself tighter. "I know, I know, but that doesn't mean I hold with strikes and fighting in the streets and getting hauled off to jail. And I *certainly* don't hold with a man giving up his Sundays!"

Now, he laughed softly. "I don't hold with any of that either, honey, but I feel I got to go to this first meeting. I'm not a boss now, just a working stiff, and not far up the ladder at that. I can't afford to be the only man on my shift that doesn't at least poke his head in the door, and me with a red card in my pocket at that. I got to work with these guys next week, and the week after."

She sighed hugely and let him pull her back down under the covers.

After a long moment of silence, she said, "Well, I guess you won't stay long, anyway. The kids can tell you all about it when we get back."

He began to stroke her flank rhythmically.

"But Will, I want you to hear me on this. We're hardly a part of your life at all anymore. You come and go and drop off your clothes and sit down at the table for a few minutes, and you're gone again."

He slid her nightgown up her leg and pulled her closer.

"And I don't want you getting involved with those Wobblies. Don't sign anything and don't promise anything, just listen to be polite and come on home."

He moved his mouth slowly down her neck to the place where the pulse beat rapidly at her throat. "Anything else, ma'am?" he asked, his voice husky in her ear.

Without a word, she turned into him fiercely and met his mouth with her own. His hands slipped down to her breasts, cupped them, lightly pinched her brown nipples until they hardened like raisins, and then moved down to her belly. As he always did, he felt her slowly, sliding his hands over her skin as deliberately as though he was blind and was discovering her for the first time. She held her breath, as if he had commanded her to be still, to wait for his touch. With infinite patience, a delicacy that must be unusual in such a large man, she thought, he ran his fingers over the nooks and crannies of her body, along each crease where her legs met her body, where her stomach folded, under each breast, at the curve of her waist, lightly trailing over her most tender flesh, parting the hair with his fingers, never tangling, always pressing and exposing and exploring. He never quite touched her long enough, never quite deep enough, for her expectations to be filled, and so each time his fingers moved, she waited for them to return. Finally, the heat rose off of her with a palpable steaminess, a moist warmth that seemed to fill the space between them, bind them, and she reached out and gripped his hardness, pulling him between her legs. He throbbed, almost winced with the pleasure, and rose up to cover her body with his own. Urgent and eager as ever, her mind registered, past forty, the both of us, three kids, and still, he comes to me like a boy with his first woman, makes me feel it, too, and then he was moving relentlessly in her, filling her, and her mind whirled away in the ritual of their love, which was at once old and practiced and yet newly birthed as life itself.

Later as he slept in her arms, she tried to peel back the places in her heart that were still wounded, tender to the touch, like something ripe and bruised. For all their loving, fine as it was, fine as it *always* was, there was still an empty hollow within her. I am lonely, she thought, with a certain wry amazement. A good husband, three kids, enough to keep *two* women busy, and I am lonely. A piece of me is still hidden, missing, unpartnered. Why? Because he is not, as his grandmother said, a giving, a loving man? Because his mind and heart, most of it at least, goes to his work? She closed her eyes, willing herself to rest. Because, a final voice hectored, you have a secret, because you do not *trust* him to love you if he knew, because you have created your loneliness? Because, at bottom, you cannot believe he loves you as you want to be loved, because to believe would be to accept that a Demers, a hero from childhood, could love such as you, and so could not be a hero? There were no answers, none that she could grasp or command in her weariness, so she slid into sleep.

On Sunday, Leona herded the children into the Model T and started up the river road toward Wenatchee. Suzanna was chattering away, half to herself as she often did, about a dream she'd had the night before.

"So then this big bird came at me in the sky, Mama, and I woke up. But just before I woke up, I thought he was going to fly away with me, and I wanted him to, I really did. I wanted to fly. Do you think dreams ever come true?"

"Anna, sit down now, like I told you. Sometimes, I guess. But neither one, good dreams or bad, ever come to you complete, so I wouldn't worry much on it, Suzanna."

The eight miles stretched long, for the road was pocked and bumpy, amd the car's narrow tires slid in and out of the ruts as though they were greased. Leona remembered the old joke Will told her about the Model T. It didn't have a speedometer, but it didn't need one, he said, because you could always tell how fast you were going. At fifteen miles per hour, the windshield rattled; at twenty, the fenders rattled; at twenty-five, your teeth rattled, and at thirty, your fillings dropped out. She'd never gone that fast in her life, of course, and could scarcely imagine it. It was enough to be driving alone at all. Why, before the war, she recalled, it was against the *law* for a woman to drive alone. Or to wear trousers or to curse or to smoke in public. Well, I've never wanted to do two of those, but right now, she winced as she pulled the car back onto the road with difficulty, I might try a good dammittohell, like Pa used to say. Now that she thought of it, most every man she knew growing up could curse like an ore-car pusher. Every one but Will.

The river was always on their right, smooth and glistening in the sun, and they passed places where the crews had been working, piles of rock and sand mute testimony to their efforts. The children grew quiet, watching the water move beneath them, as though hypnotized by its silent promises.

They came to a road that veered off to the left, away from the water, and they followed it to a cluster of small white buildings, set back from a stream. The children piled out of the car, and Leona stood, her hand to her eyes, wondering why in the world she had come at all. There was nothing to see, really, except a fish pond, a big wooden tank, and an old man hobbling over to greet them.

"Hey, missus, keep that 'un back from the water!" he said by way of greeting. Anna was teetering precariously on the bank of the pond, balancing herself on her toes, peering into its depths.

"Anna, Jack, come here," Leona said. "Hello, mister."

He nodded, touching his hat. "What can I do for you? It's Sunday, you know, and ain't nobody here but me."

She gave him her most brilliant smile. "Why, I know it's Sunday, and such a fine day for an outing. We come up from Rock Island. My children here wanted to see the hatchery, and I wonder if you could just let us look around?"

He shook his head. "Can't do it. Nobody here but me. Not a blamed thing to see, anyways."

"Mama, Mama, there's fish *babies* in here!" Anna clamored, pulling at Leona's skirts in the direction of the pond.

"Wal o' course, there's fingerlings, an' all, but we're not ready to plant yet, so there's no yearlings," the caretaker said reluctantly. "Not much to see, really."

"Oh, we didn't expect much," Leona assured him, "but you must know all about what they're doing here, maybe you could just explain a little bit?" She gestured to the tank. "What're they doing over there, for example?"

With very little coaxing, the caretaker explained how once the dam at Rock Island was up, no salmon could get up to spawning grounds in the upper Columbia, not until they finished the fish ladders—

"Fish ladders?" Jack asked, his eyes wide. "They climb up ladders?"

"Sure they do!" the old man said, warming to his audience. "Those blamed fish can jump higher than your head, boy! They'll put them ladders right up the sides of the dam and the fish'll climb up like they got cleats on their boots, right up one side and down the other. And for those who maybe can't make it, we got other ideas."

He went on to tell how some of the fish would be collected at the base of the dam and brought to the hatchery. Here, they would be stripped of eggs and milt and then released. The fingerlings pro- duced from this harvest would be reared in large pools, then planted downriver from the dam in streams where they weren't plentiful now. That way, they hoped to make up for those that inevitably would be lost trying to make it over the Rock Island Dam and upriver.

"How do you *plant* fish?" Suzanna asked skeptically.

"Wal', not headfirst, missy!" the caretaker chuckled. "We'll take 'em by truck in buckets up to where we want them. Then ol' Mother Nature'll do the rest. They'll swim downstream, get fat, and come back to increase and multiply, like the Good Book told us. 'Course, we're just getting started, it's all just experimentin' at this stage, and not much to work with, neither. So far, they haven't figured out what makes these red fish run, but when they do, they hope to fool 'em into running harder and faster than they ever did before. Mister Coolidge'd rather pass out the greenbacks to widows and orphans, and I can't say I blame him for that, but we got a lot of work to do before that dam goes up."

Leona and the children followed the old man around the grounds while he pointed out pumps and pools and ponds which would one day help to fill the river with new life.

When they got back in the car, headed for home, Leona said cheerfully, "Well, I just never realized such a thing was going on, right under our noses, did you? Pulling the fish out of the river, making baby fish, and then putting them back in, right where they're needed! It's a scientific miracle, is what it is."

Jack spoke up from the back seat. "That's what I'm going to do when I grow up. I'm going to work at a hatchery."

"Then we'll call you fish-boy! fish-boy! stinky ol' fish-boy!" Suzanna giggled, poking Anna, who joined in merrily in her high squeaky voice, "Fish-boy!"

Leona shushed the girls. "You know, that's not so silly as you might think, Miss Smart-Annies. The Indians used to believe that there was one man in a hundred who was meant to call the salmon."

"Call salmon!" Suzanna collapsed with laughter. "Here, fishies!" Jack glared ferociously at her.

"No, I mean it," Leona went on. "One man in a hundred who the fish could hear, who was sort of like a salmon spirit, who could call the fish up the river and protect them and bring them back from the ocean each season. And if it weren't for that man, the tribes would starve. So I think it's a wonderful thing to think about, Jack. Maybe some day, you'd like to learn more about the hatchery business. I daresay, it's going to be a growing one."

"Mother," Suzanna asked, suddenly serious. "How did you learn so much about the Indians? You're always talking about them."

"I am?" Leona laughed. "Seems to me I talk about a lot of things. But you need to remember, I was born on the river. And you can't be born on the river without learning something about the tribes. I guess I just picked it up when I was small."

Suzanna searched her mother's face intently, but she said nothing more. With a small frown, she turned her head out the window and watched the river roll by.

Meanwhile, Will sat on a rickety bench in a shack back from the water, listening to Tom, a drayman, harangue the small crowd. It was a sleepy Sunday, he thought, one of those warm days when a man wants only to wander slowly from shady porch to sunny riverbank, with no more direction than a meandering dragonfly. But direction was what they were getting now, in spades.

"I tell you, men, this is the first dam on the river, but it won't be the last!" Tom shouted from the makeshift podium. "If we're going to make a stand, take some position that *matters* to the working man in this state, it's got to be here and now! Once they run over us here, they'll do it on every damn site up and down the river! We've seen it happen at Townsend, Gray's Harbor, in Seattle, Tacoma—you think it'll be different here? I say, let 'em know we're united!"

Will sighed wearily. He had picked a seat at the back, hoping that he could avoid visibility. Damn it, I'm an *engineer,* he thought, not a mucker or a pickman or a drayman or a surveyor, but that's what I've been doing for nearly ten years, waiting to do what I trained for: concrete engineering. He straightened his long legs and looked down at his boots. He was not a big man, in the sense that some of these guys were, he knew, not one for bulging muscles and brute strength. Yet he felt trim and hard as he ever would, and he knew that he could take rain and cold and discomfort well as any man here, so long as there was a purpose to it. I've been waiting for that purpose long enough, he thought.

Jackson Lake, Wyoming, Arrowrock, and Deadwood dams in Idaho, Flathead in Montana—dams built in other states, by other men. The Columbia's just sitting here, waiting for us—for me— making all the rest of those rivers look like spring creeks. In engineering school, they used to say a man's got only one good dam in him in his lifetime, the rest were all practice or a prelude to retirement. The Grand Coulee's going to be mine, he thought, but I'd sure in hell like to get in some practice first. And if these boys get their way, the Rock Island won't get built 'til I'm too old to work it.

Tom had quit speaking and another man took the podium, a shovelman from one of the upriver crews. "We've 'bout got the stage work done," he was saying, "and now's when the money's gonna roll in for the real construction. Now's when they need men, skilled men, to do the job. Any fool can man a shovel or a pick, but when the pouring starts for this baby, that's when we got clout! I say, we tell them we walk unless we get two a day!"

Will shook his head silently. Two dollars a day would break this project fast. It was ten cents above the national average, and thirty cents over what was being paid in Oregon for the same work. The private-power boys didn't have the juice that a government project might—it'll be a *small* dam, just a first toe in the river, as it were, and if it stops here, it'll be the *last* one for awhile.

A man sat down next to Will, a carpenter he recognized from the Columbia Gorge job. "You in?" he asked mildly, keeping his eyes on the man up front.

Will hesitated a moment. "I haven't heard them say how they're going to do it, yet. I haven't seen the budget sheets, but I can't figure how this job can support a thousand men at two a day—and we'll be up to two thousand when we start the pour."

"You're on the rolls, though," the man said.

"Yeah, I carry a card. But that's no passport to heaven."

A vote was being called for up front, and from the murmur moving through the fifty men on the benches, Will sensed that they were going to press their luck. White flutters through the crowd, copies of the *Industrial Worker*, were being passed hand to hand.

"So?" the man asked again. His shoulder was pressing gently

against Will's, a feeling of subtle pressure. "They won't take kindly to scabs, even if it's you. The men like you. We need you in the front ranks."

Will made his decision and stood up suddenly. "I'm not interested."

The man stood too, his hand on Will's shoulder. "What's more important, all these guys looking for a decent wage, working together, or some damn mud plug in the river? They can't build it without us! It's the men or the dam."

Will pulled his red union card out of his pocket and handed it to the carpenter. "Then I guess I choose the dam," Will said quietly, and he walked out of the shack.

He walked up the river until he found a flat stone for a bench and sat watching the water move by with a life of its own that awed him. So, he had come to another crossroads, made another choice, for good or ill. It might mean his job—hell, it might mean his job no matter which side he chose. He remembered Leona's words as she asked him not to get involved, the way she held him like a spring, live and poised and trusting him to do the right thing for them all. She'll be glad, I guess, and so will Pa, when he hears. Strange that he doesn't want the dam, doesn't want the union; I want the dam and want the union, too, yet by walking out today, I might have lost both. But somehow, I can't watch while they draw a toe-line in the sand, working men on one side, the dam on the other. I can't stand on the opposite side. This dam's got to go up, and I won't do anything that might slow it down, even if it means I won't be there to see it finished.

He recalled something one of his professors once told them in engineering school. The man stood before the class, his hands making large gestures in the air, a man who clearly had big visions to match his movements. "One thing you'll learn, *must* learn as an engineer, is that there's always going to be a problem to solve. You may not see it right at first, huddled over your T squares and your rulers and your plans, but it's there, waiting for you every time. And if you do not see it, it will beat you. *First* find the problem, then solve it."

So what is the problem? he asked himself. A divided heart. And a man with such division can't know what he should be doing, where he should be doing it, or who he is. He put two fingers to the bridge of his nose and closed his eyes. I *know* the goddamned problem, he thought. But I don't know how to solve it.

For two years, construction continued on Rock Island, and Will did his best to avoid confrontation with anybody carrying a red card. He'd heard that they'd applied to the I.W.W. chapter in Spokane for recognition, but no word came. He sensed a growing frustration in many of the men: As the winter came on and wages stayed low, the tunnels were almost completed. Once the dirt was moved and the concrete crew came on, muckers and draymen and carpenters would be a dime a dozen, and they knew it. Will had been promoted to tunnel supervisor, whether because of his antiunion stance or his skills, he never knew, and so he took less pleasure in the new challenge than he might have.

One night, he came home and tossed a paper on the table. "What's that?" Leona asked, laying the plates down.

"The subject of this week's supervisors' meeting. Take a look."

She opened the *Wenatchee World* and read:

We demand to be treated like men instead of beasts of burden. We want wages of two dollars a day, eight-hour shifts, four safety men per crew, per shift, or we'll close down the project. We've got the men to do it—five hundred on our rolls already and more joining every day, and the spirit of all true Americans behind us! We will be heard!

The letter was addressed to the editor and it was signed, "Oscar Gold, I.W.W. organizer."

"Five hundred men!" Leona gasped. "Is that true?"

"Not even close," Will said. "And as for the spirit of all true Americans, I doubt it. Since the I.W.W. came out against the war before it even started, they lost a lot of sympathy. And then when we won it, they looked like fools, or worse."

"Can they close it down?"

"That's what we're meeting about tonight. We've had slowdowns on a couple of crews, sand in the tractor engines, blown tires, ruptured hoses, but we can't tell where it's coming from or who's behind it, not for sure. Sometimes we fire a few, or separate them, move them to different shifts, keep them guessing. But this is the first time they've come right out and said what they want. And what they'll do if they don't get it."

"I notice it's 'we' and 'them' now," she said with a small smile. "That's good."

"Well, I don't really like it," he said. "I know them all and like most of them. Hell, I'm no better than they are. But I like the alternative even less. This dam's too big to stop now, and so are all the other ones coming after it." He sat down at the table and picked up his fork, leaning into his plate with the hunger of a man who has made a decision and now is no longer haunted by the alternatives.

That winter, the barometer began to fall impetuously, as though it had a presentiment of doom. A storm came whipping up the canyon, the worst they'd seen in years. It began by battering the dam site, halting all construction, and tearing some of the tarpaper roofs off the shacks. It then unleashed a steady rain that increased to a torrent. As tunnel supervisor, Will's job was to keep the half-finished corridors in the canyon walls open, free of muck, and ready for the concrete. Any cave-ins now meant months of delay, many more dollars, and possibly, his job.

Will raced out of the house after gulping a hot cup of coffee. He yanked on his rain gear as he called out instructions to Leona. "Keep the coffee on, honey," he said, cursing at a flickering flashlight, "and keep the phone open. God knows what'll come tonight!"

"Are you expecting trouble?"

"I'm *always* expecting trouble. If somebody wanted to do some real damage down there, this would be the night to pull it off!" And the door slammed behind him.

He drove up to the plant in time to see Hutchins, the foreman, hurrying out to meet him. "She's out!" the man hollered over the wind.

Will clambered out of the company truck, his rain gear whipping around his legs. The lights were dark all over the dam.

"Damn thing blew with the first real gusts!" Hutchins shouted in disgust. "I'd hate to see it in a *real* storm!"

The Puget Sound powerhouse had been designed to take the brunt of stronger winds than those now buffeting the wires. Will could see workers dragging emergency generators into place, shoveling out wires covered with mud, shoring up walls, and digging levees around the plant. If the river rose, they had to be ready. The site was at one of its most vulnerable stages: tunnels open but the river still not under control, steel girders for the dam foundation still not cemented in concrete, and a hundred machines standing ready to pour just as soon as they could get the river turned.

Will was moving fast to the bottom of the canyon, calling out orders and encouragement, leaning way out of the truck in the slanting rain. He almost ran over one mucker who was bent to pick up a bucket in the darkness, and had to swerve violently, scraping the truck against the canyon wall. A shivering began up his spine, part from cold, part apprehension, but he fought it down and tightened his hands on the wheel. The dam site was in blackness, even the light from the generators didn't pierce the gloom of rain and the canyon depths. He could barely make out the entrance to tunnel two, fifty feet upriver, and he heard nothing but the roar of the wind on the rushing waters.

He looked around, saw no other supervisors in the canyon yet, and called to those men he could reach to begin sandbagging the bank. The flicker and jump of flashlights, moving shadows, and lanterns gave the whole place an unearthly, unfamiliar rhythm, and he almost felt he had to check his footing each time he took a step.

He grabbed a light and two men and checked the first tunnel. It was clear and dry, little seepage, wondrously quiet without the drum of the rain on their hardhats. The next two tunnels upriver were the same. But when he came up to the fourth, the farthest from the site, he heard voices echoing out through the darkness, over the hiss of the rain. He motioned the men behind him, tucked his light under his coat, and rounded the corner of tunnel four.

Three, maybe four shadows moved in the darkness. The tunnel was black as the bottom of a well, but he sensed strangers, dimly felt them clustered together in a group against the mud wall. Will felt the hair prickle up the back of his neck and his arms like seaweed shifting in a tide change. There was a hiss, a flare of a match, and he saw that there were four of them now, only two with hardhats. The crate at their feet had black stenciling on the side: DANGER! DYNAMITE! TO BE USED BY AUTHORIZED PERSONNEL ONLY!

He knew there was no time to do anything but act, no time to get help. It was three against four, and his three had no weapons on them at all. "What're you doing there, boys?" he asked softly, his voice as startling as a shout in darkness.

All four heads and a flashlight beam whirled to him, counted the two bulks to either side of him, and turned to one man, evidently their leader. "Nothing that concerns you, Demers," the tallest said. "Get out of here."

"Everything on this dam concerns me, mister," Will said calmly.

"Especially what you got in that box concerns me. Put it down and come on out. Now." A strong whirl of *deja vu* moved over him.

"Or you'll what?" the man asked, an angry sneer rising up through the darkness. "He ain't seen your faces, boys. He don't know you from Adam, and he ain't got a gun or he would'a used it. Mister Supervisor!" he called out. "You turn tail and get the fuck back, or we'll set this box off like the Fourth of July! You hear me? Stand back!" The leader held one stick aloft, a match in his other hand.

Will felt the men on either side of him shift weight, like a wind through birches, but he didn't move. "Go ahead," he said smoothly. "Set her off. I figure you mean to anyhow. But just tell me one thing, you bastard. Where do you figure to run to when it's lit? The back entrance is blocked by a slide. Didn't know that, did you? And you got to come through us to get out, once you light that fuse. And we maybe won't get all of you, but I can damn well guarantee, we'll get two, maybe three. You can bring it down, all right. But you'll be digging your own grave. You've got my word on it."

The leader hesitated a moment and then snarled at him, "You lying sonofabitch, it ain't either blocked!"

"Go ahead and light it and run see, mister. It's just a half-mile or so. We'll wait right here." Run, run, his mind chattered.

"He's bluffing, boys!" the man shouted, his voice ricocheting off the walls. "He's not going to die for this damned tunnel! The minute we light these suckers, he'll run like a scared rabbit!"

"We got a lot more invested here than you do, Mister Union-man." Will's voice was cool, sober, and seemed to come from every corner of the tunnel at once. "We've got our wives and kids back home living off this dam, and every piece of mud's got a drip of our sweat in it, too. You think you want it down more than we want it up? Light it and see."

Suddenly, another man spoke up, his voice wavering. "And what if we give up, hey? What'll they do to us?"

"You crawling coward," the leader spat. "They'll hang you by your balls, that's what they'll do! You think you'll get any mercy out of those blood-sucking power boys?"

Will's mind flashed back to the scene before the mill when he held a gun on Suckow, and he almost turned and walked away without another word. But then he remembered the men behind him, the hundreds more waiting for work, and he said smoothly,

"It's not the power company's say-so. We've got laws in this state to protect people who commit a crime, and the company has to go by them, too. And it seems to me, they're not nearly so hard on the guys who start to go bad and then change their minds. Put it down and come on out. But hurry up before they send a search party out for us. Then, you'll have no choice."

Three shadows began to move toward the entrance unhesitatingly.

"You stupid bastards!" the leader shouted. "You're playing right into his bluff! I'll show you how to take this fucker down"—and he fumbled for his match, the stick of dynamite still in his hand.

Will shouted "Wait!" and started to go for him, but before he could move, a curse splintered the darkness, a flash of flame, the crash and echo of a shot, and the leader fell forward, motionless.

Will yanked out his lantern and ran to him. He was dead. Oh Lord, he thought, and time stopped as memory flooded him, a memory of a shotgun in his hands and Suckow on the ground, writhing. Back at the entrance, one of the crew members was pinning a man's arms, taking the gun from him. He was a worker Will dimly recognized, a young boy from the day shift.

"He told us to come unarmed, but I'm glad I didn't pay him no mind," the worker said blankly. "What you said about a wife and kids. I got them, too."

"Why did you listen to him in the first place?" Will asked, bewildered. Part of him wanted to weep as he had a lifetime ago. This boy's life was essentially over—and all for a job.

"I'm a driller, mister. Ain't no more work for me, here. Man said he'd pay me a hundred for this job an' put me on the union payroll. An' even if he was lyin', one tunnel down'd mean more drillin'." He bowed his head.

Will looked at the other men. "The rest of you drillers, too?"

But they just looked away, their faces closed and silent.

"Take them up top, boys," he said quietly. "Make sure everybody on the job knows and post guards on all tunnels, all entrances."

One of the captured men turned to gaze at him. "So there wasn't no slide?"

Will shook his head and walked away.

As the concrete was poured and the dam rose foot by foot, another crew worked furiously to complete the fish ladders, so that this year's salmon spawn could be saved. There were three fishways, one at each end of the spillway, and one across the face of the powerhouse itself. Each fishway had three parts: the collecting pool, a fish ladder, and a pair of fish locks. The ladders were like huge flumes, thirty feet wide, with a series of weirs. Under each weir was a pool, each a foot higher than the next one downstream. Fish-counting stations were set at each ladder, and it was here that Will brought Leona and the kids one Sunday to watch the salmon migrating up the Columbia.

Jack had been pestering him for weeks to see the ladders, soon as there was enough there to see. His son asked for little, showed small fascination with any other part of the dam, so as soon as he had the time, Will escorted them to the fishways.

They stood in the darkened counting house, gazing through thick glass windows. All three kids had their noses pressed against the glass, their eyes huge. The floor of the gate through which the salmon swam was painted white for easier identification. Suddenly Jack gasped and pointed silently, as though the fish could hear him.

Three fish, two big, one small, moved across the patch of white paint, heading for home waters, separated from them by only a sheet of glass.

"That one's a chinook," Jack said, never taking his eyes off the swimming fish.

"How do you know?" Will asked.

"A Royal Chinook," he said, as though he hadn't heard the question. "Look how deep he is from the top of his back to the bottom of his belly. Downriver, they call them June hogs. It only takes one slice of him to fill a whole can, and he goes out to sea farther than any other salmon, more than a thousand miles. That other guy's a silverside. Mom calls them cohos."

"My God, the boy's a regular Fish and Game man. How did you learn all that?" Will asked, grinning.

"I've been reading up on them. Also, some of the guys on the ladder crews told me."

"Where will these fish swim to?" Anna asked, trying to peer around the corner of the glass.

"Upriver, of course," Suzanna said. "They'll lay their eggs and die."

"I *know* that," Anna said loftily. There was little her older sister could say anymore to ruffle her nine-year-old composure. "But what stream do they go to?"

"Nobody knows," Will said. "Wherever they were born, I guess."

"How do the fingerlings get back down?" Leona asked. "Otherwise, all this effort's wasted."

Jack spoke up quickly. "Lots of them can get through the turbines when they're finished, the guys said, or go over the spillways. But in case those two ways don't work, they're going to build some bypasses around the ends of the dam, so that they won't lose too many."

"Why, what a clever system!" Leona smiled. "You've really learned a lot about it, Jack, I had no idea."

"Look, here come two more!" Jack said. "Yeah, it's really smart, but the fish are even smarter. You know Ned? That old guy who drives the truck for the foreman? He used to be a big fisherman down at Astoria and he told me the fish are smarter than the men who catch them. They wait, see, outside the channel for some big steamship to go upriver. They know that when the steamships go up, the fishermen have to pull in their gillnets. So they follow the steamship into the river, right behind it, and they get past the gillnetters at the mouth."

A moment of pause and then Will said, "Well, this was really interesting, Jack. I'm glad you suggested it. But now, come on, I want to show you the new compartment they're pouring next week, you can see all the electrical stuff packed in it before it goes in place," and he turned from the glass. Suzanna, Anna, and Leona followed obediently, but Jack stayed at the window, unmoving.

"Hey, Jack, come on!" Will laughed. "Those fish'll be there forever, this compartment won't."

"In a minute," his son said.

"You take the girls up," Leona said smoothly. "I'll stay with him for a bit more and we'll join you all on top."

Will looked at Jack with his whole body pressed against the glass as though he wanted to swim alongside the fish, and he shrugged. "Okay. But don't be long, I've got things I've got to do today." He took the girls up the stairs out into the sunlight.

Leona stood behind her son, her hand on his shoulder. This is the first time I've seen him so absorbed in anything, she thought.

"Imagine what it must be like for them," Jack said quietly, his eyes still following the fish as they came into and then left his field of vision. "They make it all this way, and then they got to find the bottom of the ladder. Maybe they follow their friends, or maybe they're the first ones here, but they finally make it to the first jump. Then, they've got to figure out what to do. They jump from pool to pool, maybe thinking they're right back in their old stream, remembering boulders, or maybe knowing that something's different, but they don't know what it is. And then they get to this white place—and it's too bright! So they turn and run back into the darkness. But then, little by little, they get up their nerve again, they've come so far, they can't turn back, and they have no choice. So they come out here slowly, investigating. And they see or sense human eyes staring at them, and it scares them, but they keep going, faster now, down the ladder on the other side and out into the slough. Imagine how relieved they must be to have it over, even if they have to die when they get there."

Leona was startled into silence. She had rarely heard Jack speak so long on anything in his life, with so much intensity. Something about his words and their tone made her very proud . . . and rather sad. He understood so much for his age, yet said so little.

She squeezed his shoulder gently. "You about ready? We can come back again, you know. Like your pa said, these fish'll be here forever."

He said, "I guess," and turned reluctantly from the window, following her up the stairs.

When spring came to the river, Isaac and Margaret made one of their infrequent trips to see their grandchildren.

"It's such a hard journey for your father anymore," Margaret told Will privately. "He would come more often, but I won't let him."

Will was startled by the change in his father, picturing him always as he'd seen him last. Now, he was eighty, and his skin seemed almost translucent, a thin parchment of gray and yellow and browns, the blue veins visibly stretched over every knob of his skull.

His mother was old and withered as well, but her mind was still clear, and her eyes as alert as ever. When Leona discovered that Isaac would be celebrating his birthday during their visit, she arranged for the *Wenatchee World* to send out a reporter.

"After all," she said to Isaac as she settled him in a chair on the porch, "it's not every day a man turns eighty." She set all three

children on a blanket at his feet and wrapped a robe around the old
man's knees. "You're a regular pioneer, you know, and people want
to know all about you. What you remember, how you got to live
so long, that sort of thing. When Will comes home, we'll have three
generations of Demerses on this porch. Won't that be fine?"

Isaac gazed at her and then out into the distance. "A newspaper
man come to see me?"

She nodded heartily.

"Not Margaret? Just me?"

"Well, you're the oldest, the patriarch, the man said. They'll take
your picture and write up everything you say for the newspaper.
Margaret can help you remember, if you want."

"Nope," he said quickly, firmly. "I can remember myself. I'll tell
about the cannery fire 'cross the river. And Bill Nilson and the
bulls."

"That'll be wonderful. You just answer the man's questions, and
take your time."

"Where will Margaret be?"

"Right beside you, I guess, Isaac. And so will the kids and me."

"Are you cold, grampa?" Suzanna asked softly, pulling the blanket up closer about Isaac's feet.

He focused on her dark head, his eyes gentling for a moment. She
was the one he always seemed to remember, even if he couldn't
keep the other two straight in his mind. He reached out and cupped
her head with one hand, as he used to do when she was small. Not
a pat, really, just a cupping gesture, as though she were too fragile
to accept more.

"Getting to look more like your ma every day," he said, his voice
hoarse. "Worse things than that in this world, I'll tell you."

Jack said, "Grampa, did you ever catch a Royal Chinook?"

Isaac said, "Hell, boy, I caught more chinook than you could
count, more than you could *eat* too!"

"Jack can eat a *lot*," Anna said loyally.

The old man settled back in the rocker and began to tell the three
his memories. "It's a good thing when folks remember us pioneers,"
he said. "I got a lot to remember. Yessir, I can call to mind when
Portland wasn't nothing but a stump-town. Stump-town! That's
what they called it, boy." He chuckled softly. "And I can remember
when Pa first put up the cannery on the river; that season the run
was good, and we built another one the next year. Yessir. And the

trees came thick down to the water, then." Isaac turned to the boy at his feet. "Remember ol' Sam Suckow, Will? Now, there was a double-dipped sonofabitch . . . " But Will looked confused.

"Isaac, that's *Jack,* Will's boy, you remember?" Margaret said softly from behind him.

Isaac said, " 'Course I do, woman! I remember everything!" He talked on for awhile, his voice getting softer and softer until soon, his head drooped on his chest, and he slept.

Isaac was awakened when Will touched his shoulder softly. "Pa, the man from the paper's here. You ready?"

Isaac looked around, startled. The three children gazed up at him expectantly, and he sat up straighter, smoothed the robe over his knees, and said, "Bring 'em on."

Margaret and Leona brought a young man forward, a man with a jaunty straw hat. "Happy birthday, Mister Demers," the man said cheerfully. "I'm Davis from the paper. Understand you're a whopping eighty years old today, is that so?"

Isaac turned his head around slowly, a frown of bewilderment. "This him?" he asked Will.

"Yes, Pa. He's come to see you, special."

Isaac bobbed his head quickly and gripped the arms of the rocker. "I'll tell about the fire," he said loudly.

Leona and Margaret exchanged a glance over his head, but before they could speak, Davis said smoothly, "That's fine, Mister Demers. Just fine. But first, why don't you tell me how it feels to be eighty years old! I understand you were a pioneer, one of the oldest living lumbermen in Washington, and folks want to hear what it feels like to live so long."

"Feels old," Isaac snapped. "Why, I can remember . . . fire started in the shed . . . jacks with buckets . . . I was on the roof, an' it caved in . . ." He struggled through the story, leaning forward eagerly, his eyes misting over, until he faltered, and his voice died off, glancing over to Margaret, who sat beaming at him with pride.

"Well, that's really interesting, Mister Demers," Davis said, making a few perfunctory notes on his pad. "What was Portland like when you moved there—let's see, your son says you were born there in 1850, is that right? What do you remember about the town then?"

"Buncha damn stumps, is all," Isaac said. "And cow pastures. Say, I'll tell about Bill Nilson and the bull-team," and he was off wandering through memory again. The children followed every word, their faces open and enthralled.

"Well, I guess we'll take that picture now, Mister Demers," Davis said heartily. "Don't want to take up too much of your time on this special day, eh?"

He motioned the rest of the family around and waited patiently while Leona arranged the kids at Isaac's feet so that each face showed clearly.

"Everybody say 'Wenatchee'!" he called, and Isaac's eyes watered from the flash.

"Any last piece of advice you'd like to give our young people, Mister Demers?" he said as he edged off the porch.

"Yeah," Isaac said slowly. "Don't walk under a dead snag and vote Republican."

They all laughed, and Leona showed the reporter to the door.

In June of 1929, President Herbert Hoover had issued a proclamation stating that the Bureau of Reclamation was to begin irrigation projects all over the Northwest. Hoover was an engineer himself, and that one quality captured Will's vote over any other: The man meant to build, and build big. But five months later, the stock market crash scuttled those hopes along with the hopes of most of the nation.

The Northwest was more vulnerable in the Depression than most other regions because of its agricultural base. Lumber exports dropped to less than half of what they had been during the war; rail shipments of forest products to less than one-third. Wheat farmers sold their tractors and went back to their horses and still couldn't make a living. Apple growers, no longer able to export shipments to Europe, pulled up and burned their trees rather than maintain them. Nobody bought salmon, nobody built houses, and people left the region in droves.

But these changes were not to come overnight, and in at least one part of the Northwest were scarcely to be felt at all. Work on Rock Island Dam went on as scheduled, employing thousands of men out of Wenatchee, Spokane, Ellensburg, and Yakima. As the dam neared completion, Will got a telegram from his mother. Isaac Demers had died peacefully in his bed, with the whispering, hissing sounds of Ning Ho's back-lot cedars round him at the last.

"Don't grieve for him past what's proper, son," his mother wrote.

"He had a good life, more years than most men see. He was real proud of what you were doing, Will, even though he never told you. After he came home that last time, he sat down and wrote to you, special."

A small note was enclosed with his mother's letter, carefully folded and tied. Will unrolled it and read,

To My Son, William Caleb Demers:
You were a Good Son, Will, and always were for all these years. I wanted you to work in Lumber, but you couldn't see your way clear. Now, I know you did what was the best thing for you. For your own Life. That Dam will be a good thing, if they ever get it done, because Lumber is hardly profitable no more for a good Businessman. I want you to know that I am real proud of my Only Son.

signed,
Isaac Demers, Your Father

When Leona found Will, he was at his desk, his face on his arms. She touched him softly, and when he raised his head, she saw that he had been weeping. Silently, she embraced him.

"I think your ma should come and live with us when we move to Spokane, don't you?" she asked gently. "She can be a big help with the kids, and she's getting on, herself. She shouldn't be alone. Shall I write and ask her to come when we get settled?"

He said nothing, but only reached up and squeezed her hand. Together, they read Isaac's note again.

As the dam rose higher and higher, Will was promoted again, to foreman of the concrete crew. Finally, he was doing what he'd been trained to do. He'd anticipated a groundswell of rebellion or adjustment when he took over the new men, since they thought him to be unsympathetic to their labor grievances. But to his surprise, they accepted his leadership easily. He learned that two things had stopped the union's progress from a small discontented group to a destructive force: First, they assembled their members to discover that no one was listening. While a few wildcat strikes continued over the state, the I.W.W. had been largely swallowed up by the emerging American Federation of Labor, carpenters' guild. The A.F. of L. stayed out of politics, at least publicly, and supported no

unplanned walkouts, tactics which had been the mainstay of the
I.W.W. Second, the union failed because the dam provided jobs, and
when men could look to Spokane, Seattle, and Tacoma and see an
ominously growing unemployment rate, they had no stomach for
strikes.

Will saw the first turbines growl into action at Rock Island in
1931, and finally, oh finally, it seemed all eyes were turning west.
Hoover authorized the federal Corps of Engineers to produce an
overall survey of American rivers. The engineers' study was called
the "308 Reports" and included the largest survey of the Columbia
River that had ever been completed. The papers were full of the
news that the Army Engineers and the Reclamation Bureau had
come to agreement on the Grand Coulee project, and the dam was
to begin. At the same time, the Bonneville Dam downriver was
starting, but there was never any question in Will's mind where he
belonged. Since he first stood on the cliff above the Grand Coulee
Canyon, he had known that someday, his hands would help control
its destiny. At forty-six, after fifteen years of hewing his skills on
lesser dreams, he was ready. He and Leona packed the kids into the
new Chevy and turned north to Spokane.

Mason-Hangar, the biggest construction company in the state,
was based in Spokane. The town's *Spokesman-Review* claimed that if
any one company was big enough to build such a dam, than the
Mason-Hangar boys were the ones to try. But there was far from
unanimous agreement on that point, not to mention whether the
dam should be built at all.

In Portland, an editor called the idea of the Grand Coulee "social-
istic, impractical, dam-foolishness," and the private power companies echoed his cry. In Congress, one senator stood before his
colleagues to demand:

> What do we want of this vast, worthless area, this region of
> savages and wild beasts, of shifting sands and whirlwinds of
> dust, of cactus and prairie dogs? Mister President, I will never
> vote one cent from the public treasury to place the Pacific
> Coast one inch nearer Boston than it is now.

Interest groups in Bellingham, Seattle, Tacoma, and Yakima fought
the Grand Coulee project, but through the furor, Will never
doubted that it would be built.

Leona read the papers as the controversy grew and said, "Well, *you're* the engineer in the family. They say it'll be bigger than Boulder with ten times the runoff. Can it be done?"

"Hell, yes," Will had laughed, "but it's going to take an *imagineer* to see it. You remember what my grandpa called me when I was born—"

Leona smiled. She had heard this story so many times before.

"Laplash, the Builder, he called me," Will went on. "And I don't think he meant roads and canals, either."

The Mason-Hangar mud yards sat on the outskirts of Spokane, and Will had to drive through the downtown district to reach them. For the first time, he saw evidence of the Depression all around him. Men and women stood at the doors of the Salvation Army and the United Presbyterian Church, some of them looked as if they'd been there for days, waiting for a bowl of hot soup and a small loaf of bread. Will had seen vagrants and hobos panhandling before, but nothing like this silent file of people, most of them healthy and neatly dressed, waiting patiently for food.

He had passed more and more cars on the road to Spokane with out-of-state plates, from Montana, Idaho, Oklahoma, and Texas. Before he settled Leona and the kids in a small boarding house, he had taken them on a tour of the city. On the fringes, out by the river, they drove past sprawling tent cities, filled with women and children—but not a man in sight.

"Where are all the fathers?" Anna had asked. She was almost twelve now, and like Jack in that nothing escaped her attention. Unlike Jack, however, nothing escaped her comment, either.

"Working, of course," Suzanna said loftily. "Anybody knows that." At sixteen, there seemed little Suzanna didn't know.

"Or trying to," Leona added. "When the dam starts, I guess there'll be enough work for everybody. Won't there?"

Will shrugged. "Not if the whole state fills with outsiders."

He took his family back into town and headed back toward Mason-Hangar, stopping into the nearby cafe to test the waters. Men in hardhats and work boots clustered around the tables, hovering over cups of coffee. Nobody was ordering from the menu, Will saw immediately. He took a seat at the counter. He suddenly realized the tension in the room was so palpable he could have twanged it like a guitar string.

"You from out of state?" the man next to him quickly asked.

"Nope," Will said calmly. "I was born and raised here."

"Where?" The man's voice had a hard edge of suspicion.

"Skamania, downriver. Worked on the Celilo canal, the Gorge Highway, and just finished up the Rock Island." He turned and faced him. "Any other questions?"

The man turned back to his coffee cup. "No hard feelings, mister. I've lived here all my life, is all, and I'm tired of moving over."

Will looked around the room. Most of the men were listening. "How bad is it? I thought they were putting them on soon."

"Soon isn't now," another man spoke up. "They're coming in like flies to a carcass. Something's got to be done, by God."

"Aw, they're just foreigners," another man muttered. "We let too damn many of them in the country, and this is what it gets us. They're taking jobs from the working man across the boards like a plague of damn locusts."

The man next to Will spoke up. "No, I seen 'em," he said wonderingly. "They ain't no different from you or me. They speak English good, an' they ain't no krauts nor micks. They's just yer average joe, tryin' to make it."

Will examined his menu carefully, wondering how lumber prices were holding up. Isaac had waited too long to sell, he knew, and hadn't got near what the camps were worth, prices as bad as they were after the war. There was plenty for his mother to live on, live well, in fact, and probably some left over when she went, but there sure wasn't enough to put them on easy street, not on a bet.

The winter came to Spokane with a vengeance that year, and the bread lines grew. Hoover was no longer a savior, but Satan incarnate. The jobless sleeping on park benches called the newspapers they used to keep off the cold "Hoover blankets," their lines of ramshackle tents and tar paper huts were "Hoovervilles," and they wore their empty pockets inside out as "Hoover flags."

When the Spokane bank folded, huge crowds gathered in the street outside. Will and Leona watched from the upstairs window of the small flat they'd rented, clutching each other with relief. Margaret stood at their side, shaking her head in disbelief. Her own savings were still in Portland. Hundreds of men, women, and children milled about in the pouring rain. Many were crying unashamedly, beating their fists in frustration at the cold walls of the bank building, cursing the bankers, the government, the gods, and each other in despair. Will thought of the strongbox under the bed, the one that held all their savings from the last three jobs, savings he had not had time to put in the bank. For now, he vowed, it can stay there.

Later that evening, Will read that one Mr. Jesse Gillis, a night-watchman, had taken more drastic measures. The *Spokesman-Review* account told in somber tones how Mr. Gillis had carefully saved over two thousand dollars in forty years of work. He had planned to buy a chicken farm, his wife said, so that he might be his own boss in his old age. After waiting all night outside the Spokane bank, he came home wet, exhausted, and delirious. While she thought he was upstairs sleeping, her husband hung himself from a steam pipe in the basement. The paper asked that all contributions to his widow be sent to Box 457, in care of the editor.

There were now four breadlines in the city, but little food to be handed out, for few could afford to donate any surplus. Cheese sandwiches and coffee rewarded a man for six hours in line at the church; oatmeal and milk filled the bowls at the Salvation Army.

Some women begged for their children; others couldn't bring themselves to join the long lines of men, and it became somewhat less of a shock for Will to round a corner and come upon a young woman who had fainted in the street. Once, he helped a girl to her feet and took her home for supper. When Leona questioned her, she admitted that she'd been shut up in her room for a week living on crackers, allowing herself one cracker a day. When her crackers gave out, she went to the library, for she heard they served hot coffee on rainy nights. Will gave her three dollars and sent her home, and no one felt hungry that night round the little table.

Prices for wheat and corn were down to eighteen and twelve cents, respectively, and Yakima apples were piling up in the ware-houses. The farmers couldn't afford to ship them, merchants couldn't afford to buy them, but the trees kept producing. Finally, the Apple Growers' Association hit on an idea. They offered to give each unemployed man a crate of apples, on a credit of $1.75 against his signature, so that he could sell them on the streets for five cents apiece.

For the rest of his life, Will would remember the apple sellers, standing in the dead of winter, some of them squabbling over the choicest corners, hawking their apples loudly. Most carried home-made signs imploring passersby to "buy an apple, feed a child," or "give a good man a break." Everyone knew that even though the apples were bought and sold, it was thinly disguised begging, and the fruit was bitter.

The other sight he could not erase from his memory was the garbage truck that trundled down the road from his job site. Each morning, it unloaded the refuse from the day before, collected at the restaurants and hotels in the city. Crowds greeted the truck, cheering, and men and women, small children and grown boys, started rifling through the dumps eagerly, digging with sticks, cramming things in bags, grabbing bits of food and vegetables and shoving them in their mouths and their pockets.

In the spring, the weather broke, winter receded, and the farmers waited for rain. April came and went, and then May. Week after week passed, and scarcely a shower was seen over the whole state. News came in from the East that no rain was in sight across the width of the continent.

In the Basin, streams dried up and rivers shrank, exposing cracked, lifeless mudflats. The long, hopeful green of corn slowly shriveled, turned pale, and curled in on itself. As the summer winds came up with still no rain, the corn rustled mournfully, waiting for relief. Calves were slaughtered, for their mothers had no milk. Prize bulls, driven mad by winds, dust, and thirst, ran crazily from fence to fence until they had to be shot.

It was the worse drought in American history, the papers said, smothering most of Kentucky, Illinois, Missouri, Virginia, Ohio, Tennessee, Mississippi, Louisiana, and the whole state of Arkansas. Nevada became a dust bowl; so did some of California, Oregon, and Washington. It lasted more than a year, covered an area the size of Europe, and sent two million people away from their farms, looking for relief somewhere, anywhere.

In the Columbia Basin, the drought drove off those few who had been homesteading, waiting for water. The succeeding dust storms had taken the topsoil; now, even the sage and bunchgrass lay parched and lifeless. Will drove out to his farm and found the place abandoned. Mr. Gibbs had deserted his shack, and the winds rolled over the graves of his wife and son, unshaded by any tree.

In 1932, Roosevelt was elected by a screaming landslide, and everyone in Spokane held their breath. But as one of the first pillars of his New Deal, he gave the go-ahead on the Columbia dam project. News flashed into the Northwest with the speed of a hungry man gulping gruel: The Grand Coulee Dam would begin construction, with no more delay.

Immediately, the state put up close to four hundred thousand dollars to begin work. Crews started to move loose rock and gravel from the dam site, opened up sand and gravel pits nearby, built roads from the nearby towns to the site, and laid the foundations for the company town on the Coulee, where construction crews would live. The Northern Pacific Railway began surveys for a new line that would run from Spokane to the site, and construction companies all over the Northwest hurried to submit bids.

In June, the contract submitted by the Mason-Hangar/Atkinson-Kier group was the lowest: just under thirty million dollars. And this represented only half the cost of the project, because the Bureau of Reclamation, with federal monies, was to furnish all materials. M.H.A.K., hereafter known all over the Northwest as "the Company," was awarded the honor of building the Grand Coulee Dam.

On a warm day in July, 1933, a crowd of close to seven thousand gathered to see Governor Martin drive the first stake and Senator Dill turn the first shovel of gravel. Indians from the Colville Reservation came down out of the hills and wandered among the white folks, wearing their blankets loosely draped over their heads, for the temperature topped one hundred degrees.

Leona stood by Will, Margaret and the children before them, watching the crowds of people, edging close as he showed them, with expansive gestures, where the dam would block and hold the river. "I've asked for the position of concrete engineer," he said. "And even if they don't give it to me, they're bound to put me on staff. I've got a degree and ten years of experience pouring mud," he grinned, "and nobody else in Spokane can touch that."

Two days later, Will got his promotion: He was now a concrete engineer, one of three men in charge of the first piece of the dam —a dam which would eventually require ten million yards of concrete, according to the Bureau's plans, the biggest thing in one piece that man had ever built. But before a single bucket of concrete could be poured, the dam site itself had to be prepared.

"It's like filling a tooth," he showed the children over supper, picking up a black pencil to draw a sketch on the tablecloth.

"Don't do that!" Leona reached out to stop him. But he pulled away.

"Let's leave it," he said. "It'll be good to look at it every night for the next few years. Maybe by the time it's built, I'll draw the whole thing for you, and we'll have the damn cloth framed. See," he went back to his drawing, "first we've got to drill some probes to see just what we've got under there. The first surveyors found good bedrock, solid granite. But we've got to know how deep it goes and how wide. Then, we'll do some excavation, to dig out a hole for the dam to sit in, sort of like the dentist drilling. We'll get her all cleaned up and polished, and then, we'll plug up the holes with concrete."

"And that's where you come in?" Jack asked.

"Officially, yes," Will nodded. "But I've got to be on the job all the time, because they'll need to know the concrete mix, how much, and where we want to put it. Besides," he grinned eagerly, "there's a hell of a lot of other things to do in the meantime. We've got to build a whole city to house the crew."

"I heard it's going to be a government town," Margaret said. "No gin allowed."

"Where'd you hear that?" he asked quickly. "The details for the town are supposed to be a secret."

Leona chuckled wryly. "You think you men can keep this sort of thing quiet? Every wife picks up a handful of details, and sooner or later, word spreads all over town. They're saying it's going to be a strict company town, no one house better than another, no liquor, no clip joints, and no dancehalls."

"That's right," he said. "Which means the roads into Wenatchee and Spokane'll be well worn."

Suzanna said, "Well, it'll be good to get out of this town, anyway. It's so *depressing*. As soon as jobs open up, I'm going to apply for something myself."

Will and Leona glanced at each other over her head. They'd been expecting this declaration for the past year, knowing that it probably would have come sooner but for the unemployment in the region. "I guess that wouldn't hurt," Leona said slowly. "So long as it's the *right* job. And just until you decide what else you want to do. Maybe you could go to college or a training school of some sort. Would you like that?"

Suzanna smiled happily. "I'd *love* it." But then her face fell. "Do we have enough money for that, though?"

Margaret chuckled wryly, "Don't you worry about that, missy. Just worry about whether or not you've got what it takes to get the job done."

"I do!" Suzanna said staunchly.

"Well, then." Margaret turned to the other two and diverted them with a lively story about the time she heard a cougar on her roof.

Leona said quietly, "Now, it really starts, doesn't it, Will? You finally get to begin what you've been waiting for." She leaned forward and absently traced his dam drawing on the tablecloth.

He gripped her hands and she felt some of his excitment. "I'm glad you understand, honey. For the first time, I feel like I'm getting on with the job I was meant to do. I've got you, I've got my family, and now I've got my dam."

"I like the order you put those things," she said. "I know you're going to be pretty busy these days, but I hope you won't forget that we came first."

He hugged her hard and went back to detailing his drawing on the linen, showing her projections for core drillings, bedrock excavation, and honeycomb pours.

The months went by, the dam began, but still the houses out on the plateau weren't ready. Even though it would be her seventh move, Leona was anxious to get out of the little rented flat in Spokane and closer to the site, if only to save Will driving back and forth. They had considered moving out to the farm on the Basin. The wind was blowing cold the day they drove the family out there, with only a hint of the warmth to come on the edges of the air. Dead brown sage rolled across the road just in front of their Chevy. All the way out, Will talked about what had been happening down on the site, glancing in the mirror back at Jack.

"We've got the core drills done now," he said, grinning at Leona to be sure she was listening. She smiled and waited for him to go on. "We're just about ready to pour."

"The dam?" asked Suzanna.

"No," he said, a little impatiently, "the fills. Remember, I told you all we had to drill the holes in the rock first, and then fill them with concrete."

Suzanna nodded absently.

"Well, we finished her up—six miles of holes in the bedrock, drills a yard wide or more in some places. Now, we've got to fill them." He glanced back at Jack, who was staring out the window over the land, absorbed in some private vision.

Anna piped, "If you were just going to fill them up, why did you drill them in the first place?"

Will chuckled, enjoying the audience. "Granite's full of fissures and joints and cracks, honey. Even the best bedrock has got to be jacked up to hold a couple of million tons of dam. We bore the holes, then we force concrete in them at six hundred pounds per square inch until every crack and cranny is crammed full. When that's done, we really get down to brass tacks on the dam proper."

"Oh," Anna said. Margaret pulled her closer and gave her a small hug.

When they reached the old farm, Will hopped out of the car and opened the gate, throwing his arms wide in an expansive gesture. "Here it is! Someday, this place'll be greener than Olympia, thanks to our dam!"

They pulled up to the deserted farmhouse and Leona got out, stretching a kink from her shoulders. She had heard so much about this place, she had imagined it so often in her dreams, that now she could find little to say. Will scuffed at the ground, grinning at them all. "The topsoil's still good, what's here anyway. Just needs a little water, and this place'll outproduce half of California."

Suzanna eased out of the car, her face a picture of despair. "You don't expect us to *live* here, do you?"

Margaret put an arm around her shoulders and said quietly, "Hush, miss, and let your folks talk this out." She herded the three children around the back of the house, ostensibly looking for the well.

Leona stepped up on the porch. It sagged and creaked under her feet, and the door hung slightly ajar, mute testimony that there was nothing inside worth protecting. Or that no barricade could keep the outside from coming in. She peered through a window, rubbing a small square clean with the palm of her hand. Dust mounded in little rivulets and hills all along each corner, and the stark wooden walls were the same color as the dirt. She could see no spider webs. Likely, even *they* couldn't make a living here, she sighed. But she turned and smiled at Will softly. "It won't be bad at all, when the water comes."

"Hell, I know the house isn't much," he said easily, "but I never figured on living in it. We might stay awhile just until we get our own built, but even then, it'll only be temporary. It's the land that's really something. Gives a man a solid feeling just to stand on it. To see it stretching out before him, all his, just waiting for his hand on it."

The family rounded the corner of the house, and Jack asked, "You want to move out here someday, Pa? Permanently?"

Suzanna was hugging herself hard, scowling at the wind and the dust.

"Oh, not for a good while, yet," Will said firmly. "Maybe long after you three are grown and gone, five years or more at least. Take that long to get the dam up, get some water out here, get crops in. A couple of good horses, some hunting dogs, maybe. It'll feel good to take a living off our own land, won't it?" He turned to Leona and asked her, more quietly, "Is this what you've been wanting?"

Part of her wanted to weep with disappointment, but it was a home, land, that belonged to them. It was a start, anyway. She said, "For a long time."

"Well," Margaret said cheerfully, "I'm certainly glad I got to see it."

"And *I'm* certainly glad I don't have to sweep this porch!" Anna said briskly.

Will laughed. "This porch might not look like much to you, but it's land we don't owe a dollar for, that nobody can take from us. By the time we get out here, the whole place'll look so different, you won't even recognize it. I wouldn't be surprised if there was a town or two close by, and neighbors on all sides. Be years, yet."

Thank God, Leona thought silently. In five years, a lot can happen, even to this . . . wasteland. She put her hand in his and followed him around while he showed her where the barn would go, where the creek would run, and where he'd build her a tall, white house, shaded by maples and pines.

Finally, the Company town of Mason City was sprouting on the plateau above the river. Unfortunately, Margaret did not live to see the move. Toward the end of that winter she caught a cold that moved into her chest, and despite the doctor's best efforts, she slipped away from them.

"She lived a good, long life," Leona said softly, as she sat up with Will before Margaret's coffin. Will's mother was to be buried in the new cemetery overlooking the dam site, one of the first funerals in Mason City. "Nearly eighty-one and healthy almost to the last. No one could wish for more."

Will was silent, staring down at his mother's face.

This is the way it always is, Leona thought. Always a time of regrets, of memories, of things unsaid, love unspoken. Flickerings of Margaret's gestures, the way she held her head when she listened, the softness of her touch . . . Leona recalled so many moments. Imagine how many *he* recalls, she sighed. Her mouth twisted in a wry smile as she suddenly remembered when Suzanna brought her hair ribbon to her grandma for tying, and kept twisting and turning to see it until she'd worked herself into a small hissy, and her grandma had only said calmly, "God loves you, child. And I'm trying." Another time, when Anna had asked her hundredth question for an evening, she had sighed and said, "That's the way of the world, I guess. The old forget, and the young don't know."

"I'll miss her," she said, half aloud, half to herself.

Will shifted in his seat as though he had just awakened. "There was so much I wanted her to see," he said. "Now, it's too late. I took too long to get started, and she'll never see what I wanted her to see me accomplish."

"You mean the dam?"

He nodded. "She never saw me do one thing I set out to do."

Leona's eyes widened with alarm. "Why, Will, that's just not so! You did *everything* that came along, and did it well! You built canals and roads and the first dam on the river, you have three fine children, a good life—"

"But that's not what I set out to do," he said softly. "And now that I'm doing it, I'm not even sure why it drew me so hard."

She saw quickly that his grief was corroding his spirit, making him say things he didn't actually feel but might come to believe, once he heard them. She said firmly, "Will, you're just tired and sad, is all, and that's natural, but it's no reason to question your whole life. Has anything happened down at the site? Has anything changed?"

He shrugged and looked away, and for an instant, Leona saw Isaac in him clearly. "No. I guess not. It just doesn't seem to mean as much as I thought it would, now that I'm actually here, building what I've been wanting to build all my life." He chuckled mirthlessly. "I kind of wonder if this is all there is, you know?"

She went to him and held him. "That's the way it is with everybody, I expect, honey. Life's like the river you're always battling. Both of them choose their own paths finally, no matter what you do."

He pulled back and looked at her strangely. "If I believed that, nothing would make sense at all. I got a destiny; so does this river."

She saw immediately that she had taken the wrong tack. She said soothingly, "You're just naturally disappointed that your mother won't be alive to see you finish what you've started. But that doesn't make it any less important or worthwhile."

"I feel—I don't know . . . empty."

"Do you remember what your mama always used to say so often? Why, I must have heard her tell the kids this a hundred times. She used to say that it was only with the heart that a person can see rightly. What's really important is usually invisible to the eye alone. Once you start seeing the dam with your heart again, instead of just with your eyes, it'll fill you up, soon enough."

He smiled sadly. "Some things must be believed to be seen."

"Why, that's right," she said, a little surprised. "Did she say that too?"

"Nope," he said, rising at last. "Somebody else did." He leaned over and put one large hand on his mother's small white ones for a long moment, but his eyes were far away.

The Company would move their furniture, Will said, so they drove out to their new house on the plateau on a Sunday, with only Suzanna's box of hats in the back seat. When they pulled up the rise and stopped, Leona leaned out of the car window in astonishment. It was as though a mirage had suddenly come to life before her eyes. Where before the land had been flat, empty, a lifeless extension of the canyon below, now it was swarming with men and machines, and in the distance, a small town squatted out in the middle, as if in defiance of the land all around.

"Are those trees?" Suzanna pointed, her mouth ajar.

Will said, "I knew you'd like it, honey. We planted shade trees all up and down the streets, we're putting in parks every five blocks, and we're seeding grass just as soon as the weather breaks."

"Even the roofs are green," Anna said wonderingly.

The thirty completed houses, all identical and in a line, had green shiny roofs, like an artificial lake in the middle of the desert. They drove to the edge of the canyon, where Will pointed out the men dotting the canyon floor, moving like a colony of desert ants, hundreds of them, crawling over the sand in twos and threes, controlling machines and dirt, and all in silence. The river was wide and gray green beneath them, sliding away unconcerned.

A person could sink down there, just jump off and plummet, Leona thought, and disappear without a trace. They'd fill in the hole, move the river, and never find her.

Their house sat on the end of the street, a flat-roofed, white, one-story building without grace or apparent design. A precise, rectangular square was roped off in front and behind, imaginary markers where grass would be sodded. Two small elms were staked at the edges of the would-be lawn; two pines listed at the corners of the house. Everything was exact and raw in its sameness. The tenth house in a row of identical boxes.

"I know it doesn't look like much," Will offered. "But it beats driving so damned many miles a day to work. And when those trees get some heft on them, it won't look so much like a new haircut." He glanced toward Suzanna. "Honey, there's a library opening in town soon, and I've got you down on the list for a job there, if you want it."

She walked cautiously towards the house, like a cat in wet grass. "Okay. But if it doesn't pay very well, I might want to go back to Spokane instead."

Leona took her arm firmly, leading her to the door. "That's not even an option, miss, so let's think very good thoughts about libraries." She hesitated on the stoop. For an instant, she wished Will would take her in his arms and carry her over the threshold. She knew he never would, wasn't the type to think of it, and certainly not with the children right there, but she couldn't help wishing.

Inside, the little house was clean and expectant, as though even the walls waited for their approval. There were three small bedrooms down a long hall, and the kitchen was the largest room in the house. Jack said, "It's just fine."

"Naturally," Anna said tiredly. "You get a room to yourself."

Will said, "We can do a lot with this, really. We're not supposed to paper or paint or make any changes, but since I'm a supervisor, I don't think they'd care if you want to slap on some color here and there."

"How much do we pay for it?" Leona asked.

"About a dollar a day. The boys who eat at the mess hall and also take company housing'll pay about two a day."

"You make almost six a day," she said, thinking out loud. "We should be able to save a pile. That way, we can use your mama's money for the kids' education. Anna, you think you can be happy here, going to school out here with the rest of the company kids?"

At thirteen, Anna still had not discovered she was growing into a young woman. Leona was in no hurry for her to learn it, either. "Sure," she said calmly. "But make Suz leave me at least two drawers in the chifforobe."

"Suz just may give you the whole thing," Suzanna said coolly, "if she can't find work in this place."

Leona ignored her eldest and asked Jack, fifteen, "You think there's enough to keep you busy out here?"

His face lit up eagerly. "I'll say—anytime we're closer to the river, it's okay with me."

In the days that followed, Leona watched from behind her new curtains as neighbors began to fill the houses on either side. Suzanna discovered the library was the cleanest place on the plateau and attracted many single young people in the evening, so she happily accepted a job as assistant librarian. Jack had found a nearby hatchery to explore and had already made friends of any Fish and Game men he could find. Anna was gone from early morning to dusk, running wildly over the newly greened lawns with a pack of youngsters, and now that Will was home before eight every evening, Leona had every reason to feel content. And yet, she was not. It seems, she thought, that I am always waiting for something, some alteration or event which will suddenly change things, make things better, happier, make us closer—and it never comes. And what's worse, I'm not even sure what I'm waiting for . . . all I know is, it hasn't come to me yet. I had thought with Will working so close to home and the kids growing older, we might create something new for ourselves—something I could warm myself on forever. But I can't create it alone. Maybe when the pouring's finished . . .

Finally, one day, Leona strolled out to the backyard to hang some laundry, purposefully timing her trip to introduce herself to the woman next door.

The woman leaned out the window and bellowed, "Well, my Lord, I wondered when you'd show yourself! Come on in and have a cup of coffee!" She waved Leona inside. "I'm Gabby Binns, short for Gabriel, because I'm such an angel." Leona opened her mouth, but the woman cut her off and gestured to a chair. "I know, I know, you're Leona Demers. Your man bosses the concrete, mine does the drilling, so we've got something in common right off. Sit down!"

Leona nudged a huge calico cat off a chair to take a seat in the cluttered kitchen. Children's toys and blocks littered the floor, and she felt sugar and cornflakes crunching under her shoe.

Gabby never apologized for the mess, never even referred to it at all, and for that, Leona instantly admired her, as though, somehow, details such as a fastidious kitchen and a clean floor were for lesser minds and lives.

She bustled at the stove for a minute, all her movements quick and sure, her mouth never stopping, and poured two cups of coffee. Without asking, she ladled a teaspoon of sugar in each and plopped them down on the table. "So I told him," she was saying, "if it's a damn company town, it'll be like all the rest, dull as yesterday's dishwater, and out on that plateau, why the summers'll be as hot as Saturday night in Jerusalem. But all Mac can think of is the change in his pocket come payday, so me and the kids can go whistle. We're here for the duration."

"How many children do you have?" Leona asked, figuring at least five, by the litter at her feet and the girth of Gabby's waist.

"Just two little pup-squeaks," she said, "and both of them were a mistake. I put it off as long as I could, hell, it took me 'til I was an old spinster lady to find my Mac! Damned if I'll have another, though. Too much bother and noise, and it ruins my figure every time." She sat down and smoothed her hands over an expansive lap. "I know, you got three, nearly grown. That eldest of yours is a real sight for sore eyes, and the way they're looking at her, I'd say every man under twenty in town's got sore eyes!" She laughed and rocked with pleasure at her wit.

"Is this your first dam?" Leona asked.

"Hell, no!" Gabby laughed. "I've followed Mac from one state to another putting up the blasted things. Last, we were in Nevada, plugging up the Colorado, so I've seen my share of company towns and heard my fill of core drills and tunnels and coffers. There's not much difference between one site and another. They like to hire Mac because he's so tight with a nickel he can give the buffalo the nosebleed, and his men follow him like drag-belly pups."

Suddenly, two small boys raced into the kitchen, slamming the door. Gabby bounced to her feet with surprising agility and shouted, "Out! Out! You got the whole damned Basin to play in, and I don't want to see you 'til suppertime!"

The boys whirled on their heels and exited, laughing and cuffing each other, obviously used to such banishment.

Leona took a big gulp of the coffee, remarkably good and rich. "This is our second dam, but to hear Will talk, it's the only one in the world."

"They all say that 'bout this one," Gabby nodded.

"Well, I sure look forward to its finish," she said. "It'd be nice to have a home of our own one of these days." To her surprise, tears welled up in her eyes. She blinked them away and made a studied exploration of the bottom of her coffee cup with her spoon.

Gabby peered at her sharply and then reached across and patted her hand awkwardly. "I know what you mean, honey. The slapped-up towns and the long hours and the dust and the dirt. And the loneliness."

Leona looked up and cleared her throat, calm now. "I certainly don't have any reason to complain." She laughed weakly. "Must be the strong coffee."

Gabby chuckled. "Oh, I know what you mean, it chokes me up regular. I tell you what I do when it does, though. I call Mac a worthless old warthog, slap my kids, and make a big to-do over a ratty piece of embroidery or two. Remind me to show you the ones I've dragged from site to site, make your hair curl. But after I do all that, I just make do. Sometimes, it's like trying to sew a button on a custard pie, but you do it. Because there's nothing else to do."

"I don't like to think we're here because there's nothing else to do. My Will is doing what he was born to do, he thinks." She looked away for a moment. "I guess I just want to feel the same way."

" 'Course you do! I can't tell you how many times I've near walked all the way back to Spokane, and we've been here only five days! It's that way, every company town I come to, but we make things to do, each place we go, and build it up, and underneath, I got to admit, if you aren't here 'cause you want to be, 'cause there's no place else for you, given the way you feel about all things considered, then you're no good to anybody. Not to yourself, your man, or even the job. The worst sin of all, I guess, is sitting on your ass, wishing your life away. And now, if I haven't shocked you into spavins, I'll pour you another cup of coffee and you can tell me all about yourself, and give my jaw a rest."

Leona soon was giggling over Gabby's description of the fore-man's wife, and they huddled over their cups until the laundry had dried and it was time to think about some supper in both identical, little white houses.

After a month in Mason City, Leona began to feel more at home —indeed, she smiled wryly when she thought of it, it's getting to be that wherever I lay down my head for more than two nights, I'm already measuring for curtains. Now, whenever she wanted to, she could stroll to the edge of the canyon, peer down to the site, and see the men carving away tons of earth, moving machines, setting up conveyor belts and hoops of steel.

The excavation was going well, no major problems that kept Will awake at nights. The drilling, probing, and filling were almost through. Soon, they'd have a solid base for the ten million yards of concrete he'd be pouring, and Leona smiled when she heard his enthusiasm each night. He was like a small boy with a huge mud pie before him, itching to get at it.

"This'll be my territory," he told them, sketching more details on his pencil diagram of the dam. "All the mud and everything that happens with it. Of course, Mike and Wilson'll be there to help out, but basically, that's my baby. At least for the first course. It'll be tough work, and guys'll be hanging on the side of the cliff pouring mud in a real sweat box, cherry pickers, we call them. That canyon'll be a hundred and twenty this summer."

"And not much cooler up here," Suzanna snapped.

Will pulled back, a little hurt, and Leona frowned at her. He went on showing the other two his plans, a little of the eagerness gone from his voice. Suzanna was changing overnight, it seemed. Tall and lovely, with straight black hair, she had grown into a woman, Leona thought, while they were looking elsewhere. Lately, she had been troubled by sleeplessness and nightmares. When Leona went to her bed, called there by her moans and sharp cries, she trembled and held her mother as though she was a child again. "Birds," she whimpered. "Always, big birds in my dreams."

Leona soothed and quieted her back to sleep. Too much happening inside her body too soon, she guessed, and not enough to keep her busy and moving during the day. She always did have more imagination than the other two.

Will came home for supper one night with what looked to be an extra furrow in his brow. "We've got problems brewing," he said.

"If it's not one damned thing it's another. The Wobs are gone, but now the Indians are acting up!"

Leona stiffened infinitesimally. "What Indians?"

"The ones that live out on the other side of the river. The Colvilles and the Nespelem, and for all I know, the Spokane tribes, too. We got an Indian agent on the site who's supposed to keep them quiet, but he can't handle it, I guess, and now it looks like all hell might break loose."

"But lots of them are working, you said. I remember, you hired whole crews of Indians a few months back."

He nodded. "And I was glad to do it, too. Most of them are damned good workers. But there's a few bad apples who are pulling them off the job, yanking them back to the reservation to hear an earful."

"About what?"

Jack walked into the kitchen then and said, "About the fact that their whole territory's about to get flooded out, that's what. About the fact that they were promised fishing rights so long as the river flowed, and now the river's not going to flow and there won't be any fishing left for *anybody,* much less the mouths that depend on it." He sat down calmly and faced his father. "And frankly, I don't blame them much."

Will glowered at his fork as though it had somehow offended him. "It's not that easy, son. It never is. I can remember my father sweating blood over these guys, or guys just like them, anyhow, and there was a time when I was sympathetic. But now they're going way out in left field. They want more and more every day. The Wobs just wanted a bigger slice of the pie; the Indians don't want the pie baked at *all.* It gets so that the job doesn't matter at all, only some group's 'rights,' and then the whole damn thing comes to a screaming halt and *nobody* gets paid." He grinned wryly. "It's come full circle. I'm sounding more and more like my old man every day. Nothing like being a boss to put things in perspective."

"Or an Indian," Jack said quietly. "What they're saying is that they'd rather *not* get paid than see the river destroyed."

Now Will ran his fingers through his hair in a gesture of exasperation so like Isaac that Leona was startled. "I'm not destroying the river, for God's sake, I'm building it up. When we're through, this river is going to be bigger and better than ever, and everybody in this state is going to benefit from it. Including the Indians."

Jack shrugged and rose. "They don't see it that way." He walked out of the room.

Leona said, "He reminds me of you more every day. Except you wouldn't have been so calm. What about hiring more Indians on the site? Give them more of an investment in the thing?"

"We probably will, just to try to quiet them down. But you know, it's not just the guys on the job. It's the ones who didn't get the call, couldn't do the work even if we gave them the chance, the ones who're sitting in Spokane or Ephrata or up on the reservations, drinking all day, sore as boiled owls for a hundred things I can't do anything about. They'll take orders from any chief who promises them a big settlement from the mean ol' white man."

Leona felt deeply offended by this last, when she thought of her mother, her uncles, her grandfather who had been an important man in the Klickitat tribe, but she kept her face bland.

Will slumped with fatigue. "They're good men, really. But it only takes one or two angry bastards to screw it up for the rest of us. We've got muckers and cablemen, and mudders and oilers and water boys and carpenters, plumbers, crane operators, high-scalers, common laborers, you name it, and we got it. And in the bunch, there's a lot of greenhorns, a few reds, some Indians, and just plain punk kids." He lowered his chin on his arms. "You know, I've got no quarrel with a man who wants a decent wage, but to want to stop anybody from having any wages at all! Seems like they just want to ruin it for the rest of us, because they didn't get a slice. Or a big enough one."

Leona could no longer hold her tongue. "I think," she said carefully, "that you and the other supervisors might be making a big mistake, thinking the Indians are just one more labor problem, Will. This is their land, by treaty. Did they sell it legally? Did anybody ask them if they minded if it was flooded?"

"Of course," he said patiently. "The chiefs knew this would happen, just like everybody else. Any fool can figure this dam is going to change things for a hundred miles upstream once it's done. Anything lower than thirteen hundred feet's going to be covered, and that includes eleven different towns! Why, Boyds, Peach, Lincoln, Daisy, Gerome, they're all going to have to move or be abandoned. The government's going to buy the land, just like they'll buy the Indian land. They gave them an indemnity. It was all worked out before."

"But who's going to pay them for the salmon? And for a whole way of life lost forever?"

"No one, of course. No one can put a price on that. But that's what progress is all about. Things change."

"Jack says that there's going to be no provisions at all made for the salmon, is that right? No ladders, no locks, no canals for the fish to get around the dam?"

"I don't think so. But then, I don't really know. The Fish and Game guys are working on it. I've got my *own* job to do, and it keeps me plenty busy," he said coolly. "In case you hadn't noticed."

She pushed herself back from the table and stood up. "I've noticed, all right." She felt the anger rise in her like a spring flood, and she turned away from him to the stove, her voice quavering with a sudden intensity that surprised her. "You can bet I've noticed, Will Demers. It's *you* who hasn't noticed!" Before he could answer her, she slammed out of the house, her face flaming.

Thank God, Mac's crew is working late, Leona thought as she burst in Gabby's back door. Her friend turned, surprised, with a spatula in her hand. "Well! Come on in," she said when she saw the look on Leona's face. "You're puffing and blowing like a bull with a red rag."

Leona sat down heavily.

"Is it the kids or Will?" Gabby finally asked as Leona fumed silently.

"It's everything!" she exploded.

"Everything. My. Well, that's going to take a heap of talking," Gabby said calmly, reaching for a second cup.

"Has Mac told you that the Indians are making trouble now?" Leona said, forcing her voice to steady.

"Hell, yes," Gabby said. "So what else is new? Everybody's got to get their own private beef in before it goes up. It's been that way with every dam we ever worked. Is that what's got you so riled?"

Leona shook her head vehemently. "It's Will. It's his—his damned *disrespect*!" She stopped abruptly. It was the first time in her life she could recall using such a tone to describe her husband.

But Gabby didn't seem to notice. "Disrespect? To you?"

"No, to the Indians, to the people who were here first, to all those

poor people who're going to be flooded out by his precious dam, and
he can't see anything but what's right in front of him, won't hear
a word about anything he can't see or touch!" She paused for breath.
"Even Jack has more sympathy for them than Will does, and he's
just a boy."

Gabby looked bewildered. "Sympathy for what? They were
paid, just like everybody else was, for the land. And as for not
having much use for things he can't see or touch, hell, *all* men are
like that, honey. Dam men are the worst of all. They're so *fixed* on
themselves, on hanging onto whatever they got in their hands,
whatever they can possess, that they can't see much else. You
know that, you've been married long as I have. Hell, longer.
Women are different. But that's no reason to get in such an up-
roar. The dam's going up lickety-split, and you should be just as
proud of that as he is." She leaned back and crossed her arms as
though barring any further discussion. "Indians, bah! If it's not
one damn thing, it's another."

"That's just what Will said! You're as disrespectful as he is!"

"What's there to respect?"

"Just a whole way of life."

"A way of life that died a hundred years ago and never was much
good to start with? What do you want the Company to do about
it?"

Leona sat silently, her face wooden.

"You want them to shut the damned thing down, is that what you
want? 'Cause if you do, you're sitting in the wrong kitchen."

Leona closed her eyes, her mind in a whirl of confusion. The
feelings she had were so mixed, so many raveled loyalties. There
was no way for Will or Gabby or *anyone* to know how she felt, unless
they knew the truth about her . . . knew her heritage, the tales her
mother told her about her people, the cradlesongs she sang at night,
felt the growing shame she had felt as she learned more about the
world, the shame that her mother's people had allowed to come to
them through the whites, the fear that others would judge her as
weak or lazy or useless, as they judged her mother's people. She had
kept the secret all of her life. And now, when only its telling could
help those she loved understand her anger, there could be only
silence between them. Tears of frustration welled in her eyes. She
had never felt so alone.

Gabby said, "There, that's the best thing, I think. You just cry it out, honey. What soap is for the body, tears are for the soul, my ma used to say." She watched her carefully. "You get yourself together and then go tell your man you pick him and his dam over some ol' pesty Indians, any day."

Leona smudged her hand across her eyes. "I don't think he's seen me so mad in a long time."

Gabby laughed, "Hell, honey, he'll get over it. Just go give him some loving, and he'll forget all about it. So will you."

Leona shook her head. "No, that won't work. When something's wrong between us, he just gets cold. He seems to forget he ever loved me . . . if he ever did." She sat back, her eyes dry now, so dry they seemed to burn. "I don't think he's ever loved me, like I do him. I'm always trying to get him closer to me and the kids, but he's always looking away, it seems, at something out in the distance, that doesn't have much to do with our real lives."

"Like the dam? You mean, you don't think the dam has much to do with your 'real lives'?" Gabby leaned forward earnestly. "Did you ever stop to think, maybe you don't like his work because you think it steals him from you? Maybe you're just jealous, eh? Maybe you think he loves that dam more than he loves you."

Leona stood up abruptly. "No, that's not it, Gabby. I guess I can't explain it so you'll understand." She turned and walked out, letting the door slam behind her.

For a time, the tribes demanded meetings that mostly excluded labor supervisors, and so there was no more talk of salmon and treaties in the Demers house. It was a moment of rare excitement on the site, for the tunnels were completed at last, and it was time to turn the river into them. Leona gathered with most of the wives on the canyon cliff to watch what she had heard was one of the thrills of building the dam.

There, several hundred feet below them, at least a thousand men were working. A steady line of tractors and trucks moved down the road, kicking up dust and gravel; a train of tankers took water to the workers below. Leona looked up at the ropes and cables stretching across the canyon. High-scalers clung to the cables, perched in little boxes over the canyon walls. In the distance, through the dust, she could see the cement plant where Will supervised the mixing of the mud.

The men below looked so tiny, so vulnerable, dwarfed not only by the massive cranes and the power shovels, but also by the huge walls of the canyon itself. From this height, each looked like a hard-shelled beetle, naked to the waist, all with identical carapaces —the green hardhat of Mason-Hangar. They pulled levers of giant machines, straining together to lay a section of pipe, a ribbon of steel, a bucket of mud.

Leona thought of the men who had died so far on this dam: seventy-two of them, Will said, some in blasts, some in cave-ins, some in stupid accidents with machines. Many times, she had heard the high-pitched wail of the noon whistle blowing like a wind from the north, at some ungodly time like nine at night or eight in the morning, unsettling everyone who heard it. It was the common signal for a fatal accident. When it happened, women poured out of their houses, calling to each other and their children, drying their hands on their aprons, peering anxiously down the road that led to the site. Then the men came home, and often enough, she had had to go with Gabby and other supervisors' wives to console a new widow.

She remembered so clearly the time Will lost four men in a tunnel blast. She had embraced him, full of sorrow for those lost and those left behind. When she asked him how such a thing could happen, he had said, "I'm not the blaster. They'll figure it out soon enough." But then he had wiped the back of his hand across his eyes and added, "I hope to God those poor bastards never see darkness again."

Now, the river drew her eyes. It was swollen and placid, deceptively smooth, a constant gray green mass moving as though it had all the time in the world, completely unconscious of the men working to change it forever.

"There are the tunnels," Gabby pointed from behind her. Leona turned and smiled pleasantly. Neither had spoken of their last disagreement, hoping that with time, it would be forgotten. And it will, Leona thought, but in the meantime, I miss her.

"That's where they'll move her," Gabby was saying to one of the younger wives, "so they can build the rest of the dam. They'll drive about a thousand trucks up that road," gesturing to another graveled scar across the canyon, "and they'll dump tons of rocks on her back 'til they push her where they want her to go. Then, they'll build the cofferdams."

Leona knew that the cofferdams were little boxes built on the bedrock, watertight areas where the men could work, laying the foundation of the main dam.

"If the river's turned," the young wife asked, "why do they need the cofferdams? Why can't the men just build the foundation directly on the granite?" She laughed charmingly. "I guess you all think I'm stupid, but my husband doesn't explain these things very well."

"None of them do, honey," Gabby said, to the sympathetic smiles of the whole group. "Anyway, they build the cofferdams because once they turn the river, they'll have three thousand men on the floor, sixty feet below her level, and if something goes wrong—say, a tunnel collapses or floods—the river's on them so fast, they're dead men. So they build four coffers, like big, safe shells, and then when they turn the river back and the lake rises, the coffers'll be covered up forever. Who knows?" she laughed. "Maybe they'll name one of them after your husband, sister!"

She blushed. "Do they really name them? He'd like that."

Gabby went on, "See, a dam's not just a matter of dumping mud down on some river and plugging it up. Most of a dam is moving earth around. First, they got to dig the tunnels and put the rock someplace where they'll be able to get at it later. Then, they've got to dig the bed for the dam itself. And in the meantime, they're digging roads, storage for water, foundations for your houses, sewage, gravel pits, water lines, you name it. And even while they're laying concrete in one place, somebody else is digging up a hole for them to fill someplace else." She laughed loudly. "It's a hell of a way to run a river!"

There were two hundred trucks lined up at the gravel pits, loading every rock and boulder the crews had dug and piled, especially for this moment. At the signal, they began to trundle forward, each in line, waiting to dump their loads into the water. Will stood on the bridge, directing traffic. This wasn't his arena now. The engineers had planned the site, they supervised the turning, and he was a little regretful that he couldn't wear two or three hats at once.

Slowly the rock pile grew, and at first, the Columbia ignored the boulders dumped on her edge, as the men ignored the women and children watching from the plateau. They knew they were there, but they were too busy to look up. Finally, the rock pile grew one foot above the surface of the water, and still the line of trucks kept coming, backing up, sliding off the rocks, and driving back up the road for another load. By the end of the day, the rock pile was four feet above the water surface, but the river just bulged over it, unperturbed, coursing down the canyon as though it already could picture the sea. The women went back to their houses.

The trucks kept rolling all night, for if they stopped, the river might somehow shove all their hard work aside. Wives kept plates hot and ready and then lay awake most of the night, hearing the grinding of gears, the splash of huge boulders, and the distant shouts of men. By dawn the barrier was twelve feet high, and the river was beginning to hesitate. In some parts, the waters still surged and breached the rocks, but in others, the river smashed against them, eddied back in confusion, and went around. Again the trucks rolled all day, and Leona wondered that there could be that many boulders in the state. Finally, at four o'clock, they heard the news coming up the line. The river was taking tunnel two. The trucks kept coming, and the barrier went to fifteen, sixteen feet high, and suddenly, the men at the bottom shouted and cheered. She was taking it at all four tunnels, moving placidly through as though this diversion had been her intention all along.

Will stood and looked down at the great green tide. The water hit the rocks, swerved, and moved sideways right where they wanted it. He could hear the yells and the yahoos clear up the canyon, and he knew men were heading for Grand Coulee, the boom town across the river, to celebrate. But just for a moment, he had to stand and watch it happen. A hundred million horses of power, and they had shouldered it aside. His throat ached with pride and something more . . . a secret sadness that he did not understand. He took off his hardhat, wiped his eyes, and jumped in the nearest truck for town.

Now that the river was turned, it was time to buld the cofferdams and dig to bedrock. To accomplish this, the crews were up to a total of over seven thousand men working two shifts, a massive fleet of trucks, tractors, trailers, dozers, and power-plants running on both sides of the river. Meanwhile, inside the canyon walls the engineers were blasting out the penstock tunnels that would be used to carry water for power once the turbines and generators were in place. Upriver, the men built the intake towers; downriver, they put up storage facilities for more power. "It's like a battle site," Will told

Leona. "It's us against the river, and we've got the armies, but she's got the power. And the minute we forget it, she reminds us."

Each worker had a job he did over and over again: a run from the gravel pit to the mud plant, drop off the load and go again; or maneuver the concrete bucket in place, load it up, and open the hatch; or drive a tractor through tons of rubble, pick up the pieces, and come back for more. Seven thousand men, seven thousand tasks, each one a thread in a huge, colorful tapestry of action, and it took only one man forgetting, ignoring, or simply being careless with that task to bring it all down like a stack of cards.

By early spring of 1937, the cofferdams were almost all in place. The biggest one in block 55 had been operating for two months. A huge shielding box over seventy-five feet high, it sat in the middle of the river holding back the waters. It had been built solid, pumped dry, and two crews worked inside, laying the bridge foundations. The river outside crested at about sixty feet.

On March 17 at eight o'clock in the morning, the main cofferdam sprang a leak. Immediately, sirens went off at all corners of the dam site, and most crews were called off their assignments to lend a hand. Two thousand men rolled trucks in an assembly line past the dam, dumping rocks and gravel, frantically trying to divert the river. Signalmen stood on the cofferdam walls, ready to give the sign to abandon the site if their efforts failed, and every available man jumped into battle.

Will stood on the bed of a truck, directing the workers, and he had a quick presentiment that something awful was about to happen. He was breathing hard, and the blood was hammering in his temples; the cold canyon air prickled his throat like cut hay.

Suddenly, a cell burst in the cofferdam with a roar and the river was in. "Get out! Get out!" he shouted, waving the men off the signalposts, watching with his fists clenched as they jumped aside to avoid the mass of dirt and rocks that crashed down into the pit. Two men plunged into the water and fought the currents to shore, pulled up on the bank by comrades. Six more were buried below.

Quickly, the engineers called in every available pump, and men fought to get them in place. The trucks began to roll again, and the dike grew slowly, thousands of tons of earth and rock poured into the angry swirls of water. The shifts changed, and the trucks rolled all night. Crews went out to gather sandbags, sacks of cement, tumbleweed, even mattresses from the bunkhouses, anything which could be wedged between the river and the dam. The pumps were making no headway, and the water was still rising slowly in the cofferdam, when a nine-thousand-gallon pump blew.

"Jesus, if we don't get this thing plugged, we're back to base one!" Will hollered to one of his foremen, an Indian he had hired in the last month. "We got to dump some granite in there, something that'll stick and hold!"

The foreman said calmly, "It won't work, boss. This river is out to get us, I think. Anything you put in, got to come out. We'll be back to base one, anyway."

"If we *don't* do it," Will shouted angrily, "we got no bases at all! Get them moving!"

And so the trucks began to dump granite blocks into the river just ahead of the cofferdam. Three huge electrical shovels fed a line of trucks over a mile long, ten seconds per load. Another crew fought to get the pump back in operation. By dawn the news came down the line that the pumps had gained ten inches on the waters; it was pathetic, but it was a beginning. The next day, the trucks rolled continually. Men raced home, bolted down a few bites, and hurried back. Workers staggered out of the pit, collapsing from the strain, only to be replaced by a new crew. Will had not eaten or slept for two full shifts.

Finally, at dawn of the third day, the water was pumped out, and the dam was saved. When the investigation crew went down to see what had caused the disaster, they found an unlocked manhole cover at the end of the outlet tube. The water had slowly seeped, then poured in, so the switches could not close the gate control mechanism. A single mistake, and it had almost pulled the whole thing down around their ears. Two men were fired . . . and eight more were dead.

Will went to bed, intending to sleep round the clock. His body was exhausted, but his mind was incredibly alert, and when he finally fell asleep, a strange leaden numbness crept over him. In the night, he dreamed of a huge black bird flapping slowly toward him, coming relentlessly, soundlessly closer. He was standing on the edge of the canyon, looking down at the bowels of the construction site. He could see the men scurrying about, and from this height, their movements seemed so trivial, so ineffective. A constant roar washed over his ears, the sound of the river, and the bird flew closer and closer. Now he could see that behind the bird hovered great dark clouds. The clouds moved faster over the river, and he could hear death wails from some distant unseen Indian village. The bird was almost upon him now, and he stood rooted with fear. It was a giant black raven, and on its back an old woman perched, clutching a carved stick in her outstretched hands. The death wails grew louder, came from *her*, he saw now, and her eyes gleamed like coals. He dropped to his knees, every hair standing up on his head, as the bird swooped over him, raucously shrieking in rage.

And then he woke in a panic, his legs and belly wet with sweat. Curled next to him, Leona slept peacefully. He got up, his hands shaking, and sat by the window. Such a fierce nightmare! He could not recall ever dreaming such horror. And yet, as he went over and over the dream, there was nothing there that should have scared him so badly—no murders, no blood, no death, no real threat at all —only that giant bird coming closer and closer with some ancient banshee riding its back. He crept back to bed exhausted, resolving to dream no more.

The Indian agitation over the dam grew apace with the construction itself, and finally, Will was nominated to be part of a committee to visit the tribal elders.

"Why you?" Leona asked. "You didn't show much interest before—"

"Because my job's largely done," he said briskly. "Once we get that last cell poured, I'll be about finished with this crew. And it doesn't have anything to do with interest, so get that out of your head. It has to do with getting an order and doing what I'm told. You can come along, if you like. Maybe the kids would like to see a reservation up close."

It was two hours driving up a winding bumpy road to the Colville Indian reservation. It sat on the Nespelem River, a cluster of small wooden shacks leaning in the dust. Old gray trailers, pickup trucks, and smokehouses crowded together along the waterline. Mongrel dogs ran loose ahead of their car, barking and leaping as high as the windows.

Four supervisors pulled up in two cars right behind Will. "Missus Demers," they nodded politely. "Not much to see, is there?" one man asked jovially. "I guess your kids'll be disappointed."

Suzanna and Anna stood nervously by the car. Jack had walked to the edge of the river, followed by most of the dogs.

"I think we're supposed to go to that building over there," another supervisor said, gesturing to a large square lodge with a tin roof. "Not much of a meeting place, but I think they're expecting us."

Anna came up to Leona and whispered, "It looks like a ghost town, Mama. Should we wait in the car?"

"Jack?" Leona called. "Come on with us. No, honey, I think we better stay with your father. We've come this far, we might as well see what we came to see." She glanced at Suzanna, who, surprisingly, showed none of her usual disdain. They followed the men into the largest lodge in the village.

Two Indian men greeted them solemnly and led the supervisors to the front of a circle of waiting elders. Three old woman quickly got up off their benches to make room for Leona and her family; eyes followed Suzanna's every movement as she carefully arranged her skirts over her knees and smoothed her long black hair.

The lodge was shadowed and smoky from the single fire that burned on the ground in its center. Leona looked around and realized with a start that close to a hundred Indians were packed in, shoulder to shoulder. No wonder the place looked like a ghost town, she thought. Some of these people must have traveled for miles. Many were dressed in what appeared to be ancient ritual costume, shimmering with beads and feathers, bits of ribbon and medals. Others wore only shabby work trousers and boots, as though they'd just come off their fields not a moment before.

One of the elders at the center of the circle was speaking in careful English. "And so we welcome our white brothers in a spirit of peace and mutual understanding. We have come together this day to try to find a solution to our common problem. As you know, we have met many times before with your representatives," he said, now turning to the white men about him. "We have explained to them that most of the land now bordering the river is Indian land, given to us by treaty. We Colvilles share our borders with the Nespelem and the Spokane tribes, three large nations that have, for centuries, shared also the river. Now, much of our land will be lost. Though we are not content, we are resigned to this loss."

One supervisor spoke up courteously, "Chief, it's our understanding that you have been paid by the government for your lands, is that true?"

Another elder answered him, "This is so. We were paid same as the white farmers. The Bureau gave three thousand five hundred for the average farm and two thousand for each homestead. But it is not enough."

"Well, I'm afraid there's nothing we can do about that," a supervisor began, "that's up to those government boys, you know—"

"We are not here to bargain," the first elder said firmly. "I have said, we are resigned to the loss of the land. But we are not resigned to the loss of the river and all it brings us."

A murmur went through the listening crowd, and Leona was startled to realize how still they had been up to this moment.

The elder took from behind a bench a map mounted on an easel. Gesturing with a pointer, he said, "Here, you can see the river as it comes down from the Canadian border. Here, further down, it joins the Kettle River, passing through Nez Perce and San Poil lands. Here," and he made a circle on the map with red, "is Kettle Falls, where the two rivers come together to form the Columbia. On this spot, for many centuries, the San Poil, the Colville, the Spokane, the Nespelem, the Nez Perce, the Okanogan tribes, and many others have come together at the twin falls to spear and net enough salmon to last the next year."

The murmuring grew louder in the lodge, and Will looked once, uneasily, at Leona. Jack and Anna were listening intently. Suzanna stirred restlessly in her seat.

"But all this will soon change forever," the elder went on. "When the dam is complete, the falls will be covered by the lake waters."

"But that's more than a hundred and fifty miles from the dam site!" one supervisor said.

"This is true. Nevertheless, our surveyors tell us it will happen. And even if it does not, the salmon cannot make it past the dam itself."

Will gazed at the map in wonder. To think that the dam would affect such a huge territory—he had never really pictured it. Almost all the way to the Canadian border, the river would be altered forever. Hell, it wouldn't even *be* a river anymore, he thought. It'll be a lake, if their surveyors are right. An old memory suddenly came into his mind, when he was just a boy, playing hooky away from the timber camp, standing knee-deep in the river fishing. The salmon were running, and he could feel them bump against his knees, they were so thick. He had dropped a line in the water, and he'd snagged a fish almost before the line touched the surface. A sadness welled up in him.

The old chief was saying, "We know that we cannot stop the dam. We are not content, but we are resigned. We ask you here today to bring our message back to those who can act. Our right to fish the falls was guaranteed by treaty. There have been many systems built at other dams to save the spawnings. We want these systems built at Grand Coulee. We will give up the land, but we will not give up our way of life."

"I understand that President Roosevelt has authorized a special indemnity for those lost fishing rights, isn't that so?" a supervisor asked casually. "I think this issue has already been settled."

With that, the murmuring crowd broke into individual voices. One man behind Leona called out, "A man should not make himself a dog, just for the sake of a bone!"

Another man stood and shouted, "Birds build, and yet the tree is as it was before. Why can't the white man do this?"

The elder chief gestured for silence.

Leona looked down at Jack, surprised to see tears standing in his eyes. Suzanna had shifted her body away from the other two subtly. A young Indian man two rows away was trying to catch her eye, smiling steadily at her as though she were the sun itself. A blush crept up her cheeks, even as she looked away.

"This solves nothing," the old chief was saying. "It is an old truth that everywhere the white man touches the earth, it is sore. But we are not here today to speak of this. We are here to offer solutions. We ask that you take our demands back to your supervisors."

"But this isn't really a construction issue," a man said, looking around at Will and the rest of his collegues. "It's a Fish and Game problem. *They're* the ones you should be talking to."

While they spoke, Leona looked around the room, overwhelmed by the sheer physical sensation of being in this lodge. She was acutely aware of the new smells on all sides, the odor of dust and smoke and sweat—and something else that she could barely remember, some smell she associated with an old memory: the green-grass herbal smell of her mother. There, an old man looked just like her uncle. There, an old woman resembled a long-forgotten aunt. And there, over in that corner, was a young woman suckling a brown baby—it could have been her own mother. A deep sense of shame flooded her. These are the people I have forsaken, she thought. These, the memories I have denied. She bowed her head, and her heart was full of a hundred feelings she could not name.

"Always, this is the way it is," the elder was saying calmly. "No man will take responsibility, each says it is not his job. But we tell you now that this responsibility belongs to everyone. You must save the salmon in the upper river, not only for those seated around you, but for those in the centuries to follow. It has been done elsewhere. It must be done here, as well."

On the way back home, they were quiet, each lost in separate thoughts. When they had left the lodge, the young man followed Suzanna almost to the car, saying nothing, but only smiling shyly when he caught her eye. Will had glared at him, glared at them both, and tucked his daughter swiftly in the Chevy. Suzanna's eyes swiveled to the young man once, twice, and then she settled into a fine pout in the back seat. Jack was sober, his eyes sad. Even Anna had little to say.

That night, the raven came to Will again in his dreams, looming larger and more horrifying than before. This time, Will stood at the edge of the cliff, once more looking down at the men below him, gazing at the swollen river, and the bird came from the east, flying low over the water. As before, the old woman rode his back; as before, she held a carved stick—a totem stick, he could see it now clearly—and whipped it over her head as she screamed. The shadows moved over the land and the river, and the death wails rose from the distant villages, and Will shivered violently in his sleep. The bird was coming closer and closer and then it became an eagle, bound and tied on his wrist. He felt the claws clutch at his arm, the soft underfeathers brush his skin, and he was above himself, watching. As he watched, the eagle grew larger, blacker, once more a raven, and it turned and plucked out his eye—his own eye!—swallowing it like a berry, leaving him blind and gasping. From somewhere, he heard the old woman calling, and then the bird rose solemnly, flapping away with great dignity, the woman perched securely between its wings.

As before, he woke in a sweat, crawling from the covers as though death hunted for him there. He sat in the chair, waiting for dawn. What could such a vision mean? Once, it is only a dream, he thought, but twice? My eye! Blinded by the bird, while that old woman screamed something at him, at me.

He glanced at Leona, sleeping. He yearned to go to her and hold her, for his own comfort. But there had been a distance between them lately, growing slowly since—since when? He searched his mind carefully. For a long time, perhaps, but certainly since they'd come to Grand Coulee—and even more, since the Indian issue. She was so damned *pious* about them, all of a sudden, about their *rights,* like some kind of sociological Carrie Nation, for God's sake.

Clearly, this vision is related in some way to the dam, to the Indians, probably brought on by that trip to the reservation, he thought. But it's so *familiar.* As though I've heard it before. And then he remembered the old book his grandfather had given him, the book he had read so often as a child and not opened since he grew up: the book of Ilchee. He rose and rummaged through the dresser quietly until his fingers brushed bound leather. From behind his sweaters, way in the back, he drew the old journal of Caleb Demers. He sat down again and began to read.

The next morning at breakfast, Will made a rare appearance. Usually, he was gone to work before all the family assembled, but now, he sat waiting for them. On the table before him was the old book.

Leona came in, tying back her hair. "Haven't you gone yet?" she asked. "It's late, isn't it?"

"I'm not going in until I've had a chance to talk to you. To everybody. Something's happened, and I think we should—"

"Hi, Papa," Suzanna said, breezing in and kissing him lightly. "You playing hooky today?" She had on a new dress, ready to go to work.

"No, I wanted to call a family conference," he said.

Her eyes widened and she sat down suddenly. Jack and Anna trailed in, glanced at both parents warily, and slid into their seats. "What's that book?" Anna asked. "Aren't we gonna have breakfast?"

"In a minute," Will said. "I want to tell you all something that happened to me last night." He began to relate his dream, making it as large and as ominous as he had felt it to be, describing the bird, the shadowed clouds moving up the river, and the view from the cliff. When he got to the part about the death wails, he noticed Suzanna shiver and close her eyes.

"What is it?" he asked.

"I've had a dream just like that," she said softly. "For years now,

I've been dreaming of a bird, sometimes lots of birds, coming right at me, wanting to carry me away."

"Why didn't you tell me?" he asked, amazed.

She shrugged. "It was just a dream. Mama knew."

He glanced at Leona and went on, telling of the old woman who rode the back of the raven, and finally, told them how his eye had been plucked and swallowed, leaving him blind.

Anna shuddered. "What a horrible dream!"

"It wasn't just a dream," Will said. "It was a vision. I know that now." He held out the book. "It's all right here, and it concerns all of us." He turned the pages reverently. "This is a book written by my grandfather, Caleb Demers. It's about my great-grandmother, Ilchee, who was shaman of the Chinook tribe."

"Wow!" Jack said. "Our great-great-grandmother! I knew we had a little Indian blood, but I didn't know she was a shaman."

"What's a shaman?" Anna asked.

"A priestess," Suzanna said with dignity. "But what's all this got to do with us, Papa? I'm going to be late."

"This vision that I had—and I guess you've had pieces of it, too, Suzanna—is the same vision *she* had a century ago. Listen to this." And he read, " 'And Raven told her that the river would be tamed like a dog, the people would die, the land will float, and the red fish will come no more.' "

"It's coming true," Jack said. "The people aren't dying, but everything else is coming true."

"That's right. Raven was her spirit partner. She went on a Searching and he came to her in a vision. A vision just like mine."

"What's a spirit partner? What's a searching?" Anna screwed up her face in frustration. "I don't understand *any* of this!"

Leona sat down heavily, her face pale. "There is a great deal to understand, honey. More even than you know." She glanced at Suzanna, who was staring at her intently, her eyes deep and searching. She turned to Will, and her voice took on a tenderness he had not heard in awhile. "There is something I must tell you. Tell all of you." But her eyes never left his. "You are more than just part-Indian. And it is no accident that Raven comes to you now. In Ilchee's vision, she said the people would die, and they are—or will, once the salmon are gone forever. *Her* people will be no more. But those tribes you visited are not just 'her' people." She hesitated, faltering, and Will could feel the pain pour off of her like heat. "I should have told you so many years ago, but I thought—I thought it didn't matter, not really, and I was ashamed. Not of the secret, but that I hadn't told you before." She raised her head and her eyes flashed, almost with a defiant release. "But now is as good a time as any to tell you. My mother, Mary, was a Klickitat squaw, full-blood." She touched Will's hand once, lightly, and then withdrew it. She said no more.

There was a long moment of silence. Jack was the first one to speak. "That explains a lot," he said gently.

"Well, it still doesn't explain what a spirit partner is or a searching," Anna said impatiently. "So, we've got Indian blood in us, that isn't so bad, is it? None of us *look* like Indians, anyway."

Suzanna was pale, the edges of her face like stone. "One of us does." She turned on her mother in a fury. "How dare you keep such a secret! How *dare* you! *It wasn't yours to keep!*" Her voice ended with a scream that made Leona flinch and close her eyes.

"Stop it," Will said, the ice of command in his voice. "Sit down at once, Suzanna." She sat, the air whistling out of her like a pricked balloon.

Leona opened her eyes, but she couldn't look at him. The coldness in his voice!

"Well, Jack is right," Will said wryly. "This certainly does explain a few things. It explains why, for example, I've got a son who is drawn to the river like a bear to honey, why he fiddles away all his time with the Fish and Game guys. It explains why I've got a daughter who dreams about Raven, and now Raven is coming to me with a vengeance. It explains why my wife has turned against this dam, against my work." The unspoken "and against me" hung in the air.

"And it explains," Suzanna said coldly, "why Mother always seemed to know so much about the Indians. I asked you that once, I remember, but you changed the subject. Why tell us now, after all these years?"

Leona said, "Because you're all adults now, or almost. Suzanna, you'll be twenty-two soon; Jack, you're almost nineteen, and Anna, you're almost finished high school. It's time you know who you are. And besides," she sighed wearily, "I just got tired of keeping it to myself."

Will said nothing.

"So is this Raven going to come to all of us, now?" Anna asked. "Am I going to have nightmares, too?"

Will shook his head. "There's nothing for you to worry about, honey. Raven is a spirit partner. That means, he came to my great-grandmother and told her the future. He didn't come to my grandfather, though, or to my father either. I don't know why he's suddenly decided to show up to me—and I guess to Suzanna, once in awhile—but he's not going to come bothering you, I don't think."

Jack asked, "But why did he pluck out your eye?"

Will shrugged with a calmness he did not feel. "Maybe to get my attention, who knows."

"I think he's trying to tell you something," Jack said. "If it's true, like Mother says, that the salmon is the spirit of the river, and the dam is going to kill off the salmon, then it makes sense. You always said you loved the river. But you can't claim to love the river and also be helping to kill off its spirit. Maybe Raven is trying to tell you that you're more blind than you know."

"I doubt it," Will said easily. "Anyway, I guess I've said about all I wanted to say on the subject. If you're interested, you can read this old book of Granddad's. It's all here."

"It's such a *sad* book, though," Anna said.

"Not as sad as real life," Suzanna snapped and went for the door.

Will watched her leave, got up slowly, gathered up his clipboard and his keys, and left as well. Not once did he look in Leona's direction.

That night, Leona waited for Will to come to bed. Dammit, she thought, this is exactly why I didn't tell him in the first place, I *knew* he'd respond like this, and what did it really matter, after all? Aren't I still *me*; aren't I still his *wife,* for God's sake? But she felt a flash of guilt—I should have told him anyway. This is what happens when you keep secrets.

He came into the room and looked at her, the first time he had met her eyes since breakfast. Without a word, he undressed and got into bed.

She couldn't stand it another moment. "Will, if you're going to freeze me out of your life forever, I might just as well get up and go live somewhere else."

He didn't speak.

"Will, for heaven's sake, *talk* to me!"

"Like you did to me?" he said quietly. "*Now* you want talking? You should have thought of that twenty-five years ago."

"I was scared to tell you," she said. "Scared you wouldn't marry me, if you knew. Scared you wouldn't love me." She touched his back. "And I wanted you to love me, Will."

He turned, almost reluctantly, to face her. "What made you think I wouldn't?"

"Are you kidding? A Demers? King of the Timber Beasts? Why, my father put the name of Demers and God in one sentence so often, I grew up thinking they were the same thing. And then when I saw you, I fell in love with you right away, without thinking. For awhile I thought maybe Isaac had guessed, because he tried to keep us away from each other, but then I knew it was just because—I don't know, just because I was young and pretty and something in him wanted me for himself." Whew, she thought in a panic, another thing said that never has been before. She rushed on, "But then we got past that, and you came to Washougal and I almost told you, but my mother died, and I saw that maybe it didn't matter. I didn't *want it* to matter, Will! Don't you see? I was afraid of losing you."

"So instead, you kept your secret all these years."

"I was so relieved," she whispered, "when our children looked like you, like us, and not like throwbacks to some siwash chief somewhere."

"But you knew *I* had Indian blood—"

"Oh, a *little* maybe, but everybody's got some out here, whether they know it or not. A Klickitat squaw, full-blood, is another story. Will . . . " she breathed out a huge sigh, "I am so glad you finally know. No matter what happens, I couldn't keep it in any longer."

"I'm not surprised," he said mildly. "I kept wondering if you'd ever get around to it."

For an instant, she didn't hear him. Then, she thought she hadn't heard him right. But her eyes widened, and her jaw fell slack. She caught her breath. "What did you say?" she whispered.

He smiled wryly, as though it was forced from him. "You should see the look on your face."

She closed her mouth. "You knew?"

He sighed and moved a little closer to her. "Well, not really *knew* for sure, but I guessed a long time ago, way before I ever asked you to marry me, that you had some river blood on one side or the other. Your hair was so beautiful," he said, and he stroked it lightly. "I guessed, but it didn't matter. It might have mattered to my parents, I don't know. I never brought the subject up."

"All these years?"

He frowned. "What matters is that you kept this a secret, kept it between us for so long. By keeping such a thing silent, especially when I guessed it all along, you kept a piece of yourself from me, Leona. It's like a lie—an unspoken one, at least. And *that's* what I find hard to forgive. I don't give a damn about the other."

"My God," she said weakly, falling back against the pillows.

"And also, it's not fair to the kids. If you were going to keep it a secret, you should have kept it forever. If not, then you should have told them long ago. The way you did it was . . . cruel, I think."

This wounded her deeply, and she began to weep. "I just wanted you to love me," she sobbed. "That's all I've ever really wanted. And you always seemed so distant, somehow. You never loved me as much as I loved you—"

"You mean, I never loved you *enough*." His voice took on a note of impatience now, and she heard it jar warningly in her head, cutting through her tears. "Leona, I *always* loved you. You're the one who created this thing between us, who didn't trust me enough to *let* me love you. You didn't give me a chance to love you enough, don't you see?"

"But Will—"

"It looks to me, honey," he finished, his voice gentle now, "as though *you're* the one lacking in trust and love, if anybody is."

Now she was weeping softly on his chest, tears of relief, of pain, of a great weariness. "Oh God, oh God," she said softly, "maybe you're right. Gabby said I was jealous of your work, maybe she was right, too . . ."

He held her closely, murmuring in her ear. "Sshh, honey, no reason to cry. Let's not talk about this any more tonight. We've got the rest of our lives to sort it all out."

He fell asleep holding her while she lay awake in his arms, thinking over twenty-five years of a secrecy with no purpose.

Will walked out over the plateau to the edge of Mason City, out to where the little cemetery perched on the cliff. It was almost vacant, but some considerate soul had planted pine trees along the wind line. The wildflowers Leona had put round his mother's headstone were blooming in the sun.

He almost said, "Hello, Mother," out loud, so strong was the feeling of her presence. He sat down in the dry weeds and stared at the tombstone.

Margaret Polsen Demers, Beloved of Isaac Demers
1853–1934
"A Faithful Heart Which Never Faltered"

It had been Leona's idea to put that last, and it gave Will comfort now to read it again. A faithful heart. She always believed in God, in my father, too, so far as I know, he thought. Always had a good word at the right time, usually some homey phrase or another that she thought fitting. And usually, it was. So here I sit, fifty-two years old, and what does it all mean?

He remembered vividly the advice from his engineering professor once more: Find the problem first, then solve it. So what was the problem? I used to feel the problem was that I had a divided heart. I guess that's still the problem, but divided over what? The dam's almost done, at least my part in it. When the Wobs said choose the dam or the men, I chose the dam. I've never been sorry, but was it the right choice? And if it was, why does this vision come to *me*? An old memory floated up: the voice of his grandmother saying, "Miracles happen only to those who believe in them." The words written in the book, Ilchee's words, "Some things must be believed to be seen." His mother's words, echoed by Leona, "It's only with the heart we can see rightly. What is most true is often invisible to the eye." All the same message, really, from so many women in his life. Somehow, it is all linked with my vision, he thought. Raven plucked out my eye, leaving me blind. Yet before he came, I thought I could see. And now, I feel more blind than before.

What should I be doing with my life? Have I taken the wrong course? Is *that* why I feel empty . . . or is it only my age talking, old bones beginning to rattle aimlessly to a divided heart? I did not have to take my family to the reservation that day, yet I did. Leona did not have to tell her secret, but she has. The book was placed in *my* hands, the dream comes in *my* sleep . . . it is all a pattern, but I can't make sense of it.

Ah, Mother, he thought, rising with a clenched fist, it would be possible to shrug all this off, to blame the vision on a bad meatloaf, my emptiness on old age, but then what will they write on *my* tombstone, eh? "He Never Learned Who He Was or What He Was to Do"?

But there was no answer from the silent grave, only the steady hiss of the wind in the pines as it swept across the plateau.

It was February, and a cold layer of frost made the ground crunch under the car. It was snowing just east in the Kaniksu Mountains, but by the water, the roads were still passable. Will was taking the family up to Kettle Falls to attend the ceremonies there. The Indians called it "The Ceremony of Tears," and the ritual was timed to take place on the day the lake waters finally drowned the falls completely. Though the dam was not quite complete, the river was already backing up as high as the Indian surveyors had predicted.

They walked to the riverbank and looked over the water. Where once a set of rapids and falls had carved out the stones, leaping and thrashing waters around huge boulders, now a placid pool was rising. Will could remember seeing the Indians fishing at Celilo before they built the canal. They stood on rocks with nets and spears and poles, their hats pulled down over their black hair, their women, long skirts and scarves around their fat, brown faces, waiting on the banks to club the fish. The salmon had jumped and leaped in the water, ignoring the men who called to each other, boasting of their prowess. Each man had his own rock, his own riffle to watch, and most seemed to spear those fish who couldn't make the leaps properly, who fell bruised and gasping to the rocks below. Piles of salmon had lain on the beach that day, and Will saw children poking at the dying fish, waving away the dogs with their sticks, hoisting pretend-spears over tidal pools.

Now, over a thousand Indians gathered by the river, clustered together shoulder to shoulder, their blankets covering their heads. From far back in the crowd where Will stood, a wailing began, a soft dirge of loss, a song of irrevocable sadness. Women at the front took up the notes, and soon the whole crowd was singing. Even the canyon walls seemed to shiver with despair.

There were a few whites in the crowd, mostly at the back. Will recognized men of the Fish and Game crew off to one side. Jack had moved over to join them. Will touched Leona's shoulder and was surprised to see tears standing in her eyes.

"I feel so ashamed," she said softly. "This didn't have to happen."

There were a series of speakers who addressed the crowd, some in the old Chinook trade jargon, others in English, but they kept their words short. For the most part, the ceremony seemed to consist of simply coming together and sharing this moment. A few children, dressed in native costume, carefully laid salmon on the riverbank. Grown men came out before the crowd and danced, pretending to throw spears in the water and nets at invisible fish.

That young man who had smiled at Suzanna before had edged closer in the crowd. They were talking together quietly. She kept her eyes on the river; he kept his eyes on her, but their bodies leaned closer, and Will felt a tug at his heart as he watched them. She is grown now, he thought. Perhaps she is falling in love. Another time, he might have scowled at them both and pulled her away, but somehow, such an action seemed inappropriate in this place, at this time. He could only feel a sadness, a resignation, a peace.

An old man came before the crowd now, and he spoke in English. "For generations, our people have had a legend," he called out over the water. "That one day, the white man would come and with him would come the death of the river. Then, the Old Ones said, the land would float and the red fish would come no more. We have seen all this come to pass. Where there is sorrow, there is holy ground. This spot shall be sacred to the people." He pulled back a gaunt arm and threw a single spear into the lake. It must have been weighted with stone, for it sank soundlessly beneath the smooth water.

Will was rocked with a sudden realization, and for an instant, his eyes swam and blurred. The exact words of Ilchee's vision! Perhaps she was not the only one to see Raven, to hear his warning! Other shamans, in other tribes, must have seen the same vision; not a vision, but a prophecy—and one that I have helped to bring to life!

He bowed his head. My God, my God, this is what it all means, then. He plucked my eye out, blinded me, that I might see, finally, with my heart; and not with a divided heart, but one that at long last knows its true path. Some things must be believed to be seen —yes, I believed, because of the book placed in my hands as a child —and so he came to me. Raven comes to those who have not found their path, cannot see their way clearly, and by exposing blindness, shows the way. *This* is the true power of such a spirit partner, a spirit partner which must have been with my family all along, as each of us has built our separate dreams: a vision of the heart. Once, with a divided heart, I chose the dam over the people. The choice was not wrong, in fact, it was prophesied . . . but now, I must make a new choice. And these—these blanketed, leaderless, despairing souls— are my people. It was Ilchee who came to me herself, on the back of Raven. *She* said her seed would be shaman. Her son was not; her grandson was not; but perhaps, just perhaps, her great-grandson can help repay the debt. This is, after all, who I am; this is what I was meant to do.

He felt so suddenly sure, so whole, that he was startled as out of a dream when Jack touched his arm. "I'm going home with the crew," he said, his eyes cold.

"But—but, don't you want to come home with us?" Will faltered. "Jack, I have some things I want to tell you—"

"Not particularly," he said stiffly. "I don't feel very good about riding in the Demerses' car right now." And he turned on his heel.

It took days for Will to sort out how he felt, what he wanted to do, and what words would be best to tell his family about his new plans. Before he could explain, however, Jack made his own decision. He had gone to work at the small hatchery and sent word back that he would be joining the WPA crew. His letter read:

> Some of us are going to be working to move Colville, Nes- pelem, and Spokane graves to higher ground. The government is sending out crews to a base camp at Crown Point, and the first grave we're to move is Chief Joseph's.

He signed it simply, "Jack."

When the letter came, Will said, "Well, I've got two ideas, and I want to know what you all think. First, I've finally got an idea about what I'd like to do with my mother's inheritance."

Anna said, "I thought it was going to go for school."

Will nodded. "That was the original plan, but here's another. See what you think. I want to give the money to the hatchery. They've been asking for donations to get their experimental planting off the ground. I'd like this family to be a part of that. But I didn't want to make the decision without you girls having a say."

There was a long silence. Leona said, "What about Jack?"

"I think Jack's already decided what he wants to do," Will said. "He's never mentioned college. But if he wants to go, he could always work his way through. Lots of kids do."

"So could we, I guess," Anna said. "And the money really is yours, Pa."

"I doubt I'll be going to college," Suzanna said quietly.

All heads turned to her. "But honey, you always said you wanted to—" Leona protested.

"No," she shook her head firmly. "Everybody else always said I wanted to. And anyway, I've got a right to change. Everybody else is."

"Then what else will you do with your life?" Leona asked.

To their surprise, Suzanna blushed and said softly, "I'm not quite ready to talk about that yet."

Another long silence. Anna said, "You said you had two ideas?"

Will smiled. "You know my work's done here on Grand Coulee. The rest is up to the power boys. I'm proud of what I've done, but I'd be a lot prouder if I could do something else now. Maybe work with people, for a change, instead of concrete."

"What did you have in mind?" Leona asked.

Will looked a little sheepish. "They called me Laplash, the Builder, remember? But they also said I would be shaman. Maybe those elders out at Colville could use some direction."

Suzanna laughed, but kindly. "Papa, you might not have noticed it, but they've got a lot of leaders already. They've got a council, an elected government of their own, a whole raft of engineers, surveyors, lawyers, accountants. This isn't the old days anymore."

"But if you want to work, they can always use another pair of hands," Leona added. "Why don't you go join Jack in the WPA crew? I don't think you're ready for retirement yet, are you?"

"No." Will frowned. "But I don't know if I'm ready to work with Jack, either. He and I haven't exactly seen eye to eye lately."

"Did you ever hear the story of the old king and his son, the prince?" Leona asked. "They had a falling out, and the king commanded his son to return to the palace. The prince sent back a message that he could not. So the king sent another message and it said, 'Come as far as you can, then, and I will come the rest of the way.'"

Anna laughed, "Looks like it's your move, Pa."

Over three thousand WPA workers were assembled at Crown Point, forming six base camps. Will found Jack directing the removal of two shallow graves in Nespelem Canyon. His son looked far older than when he had seen him last, taller too, even against the sheer Canyon walls. Will came up carrying his shovel and said, "Put me to work, boss."

Jack turned around and gestured to a group working to coffin a shrouded figure. "I think they need some help over there." And then he recognized his father. A slow smile broke over his features like sunshine. "How did you find me?" he asked, almost shyly.

"It wasn't too hard," Will said. "I just looked for the man who looked like he knew what he was doing." He put out his hand. "Can you use me?"

"Are you serious?"

Will nodded. "I figure, I had a hand in these rising waters. I'd like to have a hand in their . . . reconciliation."

"Then we can use you," Jack said, taking his father's hand. "In fact, I doubt we could get the job done without you."

Leona went to see Gabby, the first visit she had made since the day she'd slammed her kitchen door.

Gabby greeted her as though she'd only been gone for the weekend, clapped her down at the kitchen table, and said, "So! I hear your eldest is thinking of getting spliced!"

"What?" Leona sputtered, almost spilling her coffee.

"Getting married! I hear she's been seeing that young buck Sam Cato; he's been taking out so many library books, he's either got to go blind or marry her, one." She peered at Leona's face. "You didn't know? Well, my God, I'm sure sorry, honey, I just figured you'd have heard it from her. But maybe she doesn't know it herself, yet. Some gals are like that, secretive as cats with kittens."

"Well, she comes by it honest," Leona said wryly. "No, she hasn't said a thing. Or rather, she said she wasn't *ready* to say a thing."

Gabby laughed. "Well, she *did* tell you then, but you weren't listening. And come to think of it, you're not smiling, now that you've heard. What's the matter?"

Leona frowned. "Sam Cato? I don't even know the man. And I know her father won't like the idea."

"Why not? He's a good one, from all reports. A surveyor for the Colvilles, full-blooded Spokane, got a house in Grand Coulee. I hear his mama was some kind of Indian princess, and you couldn't ask for a better-looking son-in-law." She cocked her head and grinned.

"Don't tell me you've got something against Indians, Missus Demers?"

Leona laughed in spite of herself. "You're enjoying the hell out of this, aren't you, Gabby?"

Gabby chuckled. "Wonderfully. Last time you were here, you were so sodden with sympathy for those 'poor souls,' you about flooded my kitchen. And when I had the gall to wonder why, you called me disrespectful."

"Glad you're not going to rub my nose in it," Leona said. She leaned back and thought for a moment. "Well. So, that's the way the wind blows, eh? I suppose I should be more upset about it, but somehow, I can't muster up too much outrage. She's over twenty-one, after all, and if he's as good as you say, I guess it'll work out." She grinned. "But he better come around and meet her father, because he'll certainly have a thing or two to say about it. I guess if I had to hear if from anybody but her, I'm glad it was you."

Gabby just reached around her and grabbed the coffee pot in a practiced motion that needed no words.

On March 22, 1941, the Grand Coulee Dam was officially completed. Will stood at the head of the commencement platform, shoulder to shoulder with the rest of the foremen and the supervisors. Next to them were other officials from the Company, the men from the Bureau, politicians from four states, and President Roosevelt himself.

Will's thoughts flowed from one thing to the next as swiftly as the water at his feet. He surveyed the crowd and noted the farmers standing with their wives, wearing dusty hats, patched overalls, and faded cloth coats. Some of them were old men, and they had waited for water and prayed for water and some had even hired a Nez Perce medicine man to conjure water, yet the only moisture which wet their lands was snow, and that melted in the constant winds. But now the water was coming. They cheered lustily as each speaker rose to tell them of their future. A few of them ducked their heads and wept.

He thought of the white house, surrounded by maples and pines, that he and Leona had lived in for the last two years. It had taken a long time, a *life* time, but she finally had her home. And on one wall was a framed tablecloth, rather frazzled at the edges, showing a crude but detailed drawing of the dam, the drawing he'd added to for the last eight years.

He remembered the eighty men who had died on this dam, eighty men who were buried in some portion of it, and for an instant, he could almost see their faces, hear their voices in the swirl of the water. Other graves too: those he'd helped move with Jack. Well, Jack was working for the Fish and Game full-time now. Only twenty-three, and already, he'd found his rightful path.

"Enough concrete to lay a highway from Seattle to New York and back again by way of Los Angeles!" one speaker shouted, and Will thought of Ned Wilson, pouring bucket after bucket of the stuff.

"Seventy-seven million pounds of steel!" a senator told them, and he saw Fred Nevins waving that huge crane in place, picking up girders and putting them down.

One thing they're not saying, Will thought, and it matters more —no, not more—but just as much. The Wenatchee, Entiat, Methow, and Okanogan rivers are now full of salmon, fifty percent of which were raised in hatcheries below the dam, hatcheries that Margaret and Isaac Demers helped to build, though they'll never know it. Jack says they expect to triple the spawning runs in ten years. Though there's no more red fish *above* the dam, there's more below it than Ilchee could ever have dreamed. I guess once a man finds out who *he* is, he can see who his father was, too. I thought I pushed away everything my father stood for, all his choices, but I was really only standing on his shoulders, building my own future. My helping to save the salmon is just another version of his tree farms. Each of them, Ilchee, Suzanna, Caleb, Isaac, Margaret, and probably a few I don't know who influenced *them,* they're all a part of me, a foundation I've built on. Maybe that's why Ilchee's book seemed so sad. She couldn't see where her vision would lead, but I can. I wonder if I would have had her courage, to have that "faithful heart," to follow it, blind, no matter where it would take me.

The band played and the speeches went on. Leona sat at the front of the crowd, gazing up at Will. He stood at attention as though he faced an army, and his face shone with pleasure. In that instant, the years fell away, and he looked just like the young man she'd first seen in his father's mill, arguing about the Wobblies, full of eager ambition, with the light of pride and idealism in his eyes. Fifty-six, and that light's still there, she thought. Now, both of us are doing what we were born to do. The past eight years seemed no more than the motes of dust which rose on the canyon breeze, gleaming in the sun.

Suzanna's gone and married now, she thought, happy, I hope.

Anna's off to college; I'm glad one of them made it. And Will and
I finally have a home on those acres he picked out so many years
ago. It's not much yet, but it will be when the water comes. At least
the white house is sound, and I've finally got a cherry tree I can call
my own. We're both setting down solid roots, at last. Life *is* like the
river, they both *do* choose their own paths, I was right. But Will was
right, too. Because the act of trying to alter the path, either life's or
the river's, is part of the plan itself. Life's plan.

Chief Jim James of the Nez Perce stepped before the control panel
in the twenty-story powerhouse at the foot of the dam.

"We red Americans are glad to join the white Americans to celebrate the beginning of generation of power at the largest plant in
the world," he said, and his voice was almost lost in the cheers.

People crowded to the edge of the viewing area to see the dam
come to life. A huge eight-hundred-ton rotor was lifted into place
by a giant jack, the penstock gates opened an inch, and water from
two hundred and fifty feet below the surface rushed into the power
tubes. As the crowd shouted, the blades of the water wheel in the
control room began to roar, and the man at the switch gave a thumbs
up sign. The gates were opened all the way now, and a head of water
three hundred feet long furled over the top.

A giant whir filled the air, and two ten-thousand-kilowatt generators started up, sending electricity pulsing over lines to the Colville
Indian Reservation. Everyone had read that the first house to receive
the power would be that of Mrs. Ernestine Nanamkin, a full-
blooded Spokane. The *Grand Coulee Courier* had reported that she'd
bought a new electric washing machine, especially for this day.

The Grand Coulee Dam was at work.

PART SEVEN

Today

Rivers are the true highways of life. They transport the ancient tears of disappeared races, they propel the foams that will impregnate the millennium. In flood or in sullen repose, the river's power cannot be overestimated, and only men modernized to the point of moronity will be surprised when rivers eventually take their revenge on those who dam and defile them. River gods, some muddy, others transparent, ride those highways singing the world's inexhaustible song.

—*Tom Robbins*

*T*he river knows what man does not, in its rude strength and almost-captured beauty: that the reality of life is a maze of single currents melting into one another, twining together like the roots of trees, but at heart, unarrangeable as the sea waves themselves. Each current is unique and separate, swirling with others temporarily, as if it never expected to know another solitary moment, or loneliness, confusion, or restlessness again. And then the flood comes, the bank gives way, and each is released to move away from the other, slowly or swiftly, seeking new channels, inescapably and without distraction or remorse, as continents drift apart and hearts split asunder. The river, like life, cannot abide such changeless, perfect patterns. And each generation must learn its own games, forge its own courage, and make its own heroes.

"DOCTOR SING, DOCTOR SING!" THE VOICE BLEW UP ON A CANYON WIND from the dry bed below. Lisa Sing sighed heavily and sat back on her heels, frowning at the heat, the stubborn clay beneath her fingers, but most of all at the intrusion. She stood wearily, wiped her thick black hair back under her visor, and noticed the cramping in her knees. Clearly, the ability to squat Chinese-style for long hours was a learned one, not genetic, she noted subconsciously. *I'll remember that the next time the head of the department tells me how "aptly suited" I am for field work.* She turned to face the aide below.

"He's here!" the young man called out, his voice wavering up in the still summer air. He pointed to a jeep pulling up to a shuddering stop before the small collection of tents in the dry bed.

Doctor Sing bent and deliberately took her time gathering her brushes, probes, camera, and field forms from the floor of the cave. *Let him wait,* she grumbled to herself. *It's bad enough I have to lose half a day playing tour guide to a reporter. I don't have to act eager for the privilege.*

The cave in which she worked was set back in the canyon wall, sixty feet above the dry bed below. It was little more than a temporary shelter, she knew, and she scarcely hoped it would ever become a major find like the Marmes dig in '64. Still, the two assistant professors and twelve graduate students under her direction had worked diligently for over a month now. They'd uncovered several promising strata, and the Folsom points they'd found were well formed for basalt tools. The nomad tribe that had made this rock shelter its camp boasted some fine hunters, from the looks of their weapons.

She brushed off her khaki shorts and strode outside the cool walls of the cave. As always, the heat of the Grand Coulee Canyon smote her like the flat of an iron, and she paused to orient herself before climbing down the narrow path cut into the canyon wall. Hurrying is what makes for mistakes, she told herself again; accidents happen when you let down your guard. And out here, forty miles from Electric City, twelve miles from Ephrata, and over two hundred from her book-paneled office at the University of Washington, she could ill afford for anyone to have an accident. Even herself.

She took hold of the handropes set into the basalt walls and eased herself down carefully, once more marveling at the difference in the landscape. Twenty years before, in the early fifties, when the first team of archaeologists came to this canyon, they'd found it dry and dusty, a seemingly lifeless land that could support only sage, bunchgrass, rattlers, and jackrabbits. Radiocarbon dating confirmed the dig at 8,700 years, plus or minus 400. Though the tools they'd found were relatively sophisticated for the region, the team was still puzzled, and a host of scholarly papers had addressed the question they'd raised. Why did early man live in the canyon at all? Later tribes considered the Grand Coulee a place of ghosts, and few native hunters had ventured within the six-hundred-foot walls. And yet clearly, prehistoric man had found something in the Coulee worthwhile.

Now they had a piece of the answer. When Lisa Sing first saw the canyon, she could scarcely believe she was seeing the same site described in the earlier team's field notes. Where once the Coulee was dry, barren, and forbidding, now it was green and lushly tropical. Though the dry bed below still showed its gaunt sides, evidence of the river's early power, water now flowed slowly down its center. The Grand Coulee Canyon was steadily reverting to the same conditions that must have existed nine thousand years before. The Columbia Basin irrigation project was not only nourishing wheat, orchards, and factories for over a thousand miles, it was also reversing geological time.

She glanced at her watch. Time—and running out of it, too. They'd been here nearly a month, and in less than one month more the river that now flowed quietly at her feet would fill its old banks, then creep up the walls and swamp the canyon completely, stopped by the Dry Falls Dam when they finally closed its completed gates. Less than two months to save the past, before it was swallowed up forever by the future. And she had to spend part of it playing P.R. for a Spokane reporter. That's the problem with federal grants, she grimaced, you have to justify each dime to the public. Everybody wants to be sure they get their money's worth.

She briskly threw back the flap of the visitors' tent, tossed her visor on the table, and stuck out her hand to the young man before her.

"Doctor Lisa Sing. Project director. And you are . . . ?"

The reporter grinned slowly at her, taken aback by her no-nonsense greeting. "Nelson Demers, Doctor Sing. The *Spokesman-Review,* Spokane's largest."

Lisa willed her face into her blandest, most courteous smile, "And no doubt its finest. Well, shall we take the grand tour?" She was halfway out the tent before he stopped her.

"Hey, wait a minute, Doc." He deliberately eased down in the canvas sling chair, plucked out a notepad, and stretched out his long khakis with the posture of a man who wasn't used to being hurried.

No doubt brand new, Lisa scoffed to herself. Not a crease or a smudge from the belt to the knees.

"Don't you think you oughta give me just a little background first? Tell me what I'm going to see before I see it?"

She sat on the edge of her desk, poised for defense. Or attack. "You mean, you didn't do your homework. Do you know what we're doing here at all, Mister Demers?"

"Nelson. Sure I know what you're up to out here, more or less. But I need a little local color first, just to get the full flavor of the thing. People want to know a little about you, too, you know. The human interest angle."

She grinned evilly. "You mean, what's a nice girl like me doing in a place like this?"

He chuckled, unperturbed. "Yeah, sort of. Can I call you Lisa?"

She was unsettled by his easy manner. She nodded curtly. "So ask."

He scribbled a few quick notes to himself.

He was tall, she saw that right away, with a skin well suited to the sun. His brown hair fell down over one eye when he bent his head to his pad, his hand moving swiftly over the paper. He looked good, hard, healthy—older than most of the graduate students under her wing but no less robust. Not like a man who spent hours at a typewriter.

He glanced up at her, and she saw the swift, frank appreciation in his eyes.

She shrugged a small dismissal. Yes, she was beautiful, she knew that. Her body was slim, her cheekbones high and finely hewn, and her hair fell down her back like a black waterfall. She'd heard it before. She was beautiful. So was he, in his way. And now that they had both noticed that much, she hoped they could get on to it with a minimum of clutter and wasted motion. She had neither the time nor the inclination for anything else, she reminded herself.

"How'd you get picked for this particular dig?" he asked finally.

"Merit."

"Naturally," he said smoothly. "But what I meant is, what previous experience did you bring to the project? Is this your first as director?"

She hesitated for an instant. "Yes," she said firmly, as though she'd just made a decision about something. "But I've been on every dig the university's sponsored in the last three years, I'm a full professor of archaeology, with a minor in geology, and a specialty in the Cochrane glacial period and the later anathermal, altithermal, and medithermal postglacial climatic periods. I'm fully qualified to handle two assistants and a dozen graduate students. I'm unmarried, twenty-eight, and compulsive about my work." She paused for breath. "And I highly doubt that your readers would be interested in this sort of detail."

"On the contrary," he said. "It's just the sort of thing they like to know. Especially the last part."

She glared at him. "Because I'm a woman or because I'm Chinese?"

"Both," he said cheerfully. "If this project merits it, I suspect I'll be out here quite a bit, poking around and generally getting in the way. News is slow in the summer, and folks like to hear what's going on in their own backyards. The more they're on your side, the better for both of us. We sell papers, you sell credibility, and everybody's happy."

Her face turned glum, and she sighed, closing her eyes briefly as if in pain.

He chuckled, shaking his head. "You're in fashion, now, Lisa. Don't you know that? Archaeology is chic."

She laughed ruefully, in spite of her exasperation. "Just my luck."

"Yeah, isn't it? And mine, too."

An hour later, however, she was showing him over the site, caught up in her own enthusiasm, and forgetting the inconvenience of his presence. "What we do know," she said as she showed him the graded layers of gravel from the canyon wall, "is that this nomad tribe was relatively well developed for nearly nine thousand years ago."

"How can you tell?"

"Because of what we *have* found, and what we guess is still up there to find. We know they were a small band, nowhere near so numerous as the pit-house people around the Spokane area, but they were every bit as sophisticated. See"—she bent and pointed to a small dull rock, carefully scraped on one side—"they used red hematite, probably yellow limonite, too, for ornamentation. Only bands that are getting enough to eat spend time decorating themselves."

"How did they paint themselves with that?" he asked, bewildered.

"By mixing the powder with oil or grease, probably," she said. "And we also know they gathered seeds and roots, berries, and other vegetable foods. Which means they probably had at least some rudimentary skill in storage. Baskets, hide pouches, the like."

"Did you find any?"

She shook her head, absorbed in what she was saying. "No, of course not. That stuff deteriorates too quickly, even under the best of conditions."

"So what *don't* you know about these people?" he asked.

"The main thing we don't know is what they hunted," she said. "We can guess they hunted ducks, geese, small mammals, that sort of thing. But we don't know what larger game they might have found here. Mostly because we're not sure yet what it was like in the canyon before the glacial lobe melted and the river went to its later channel. It probably wasn't bison, because there likely wasn't enough grassland to support them. But it could be. We just don't know yet."

"How do you know how old the site is?"

"Carbon-14," she said.

"How does that work?"

She spoke quickly, with some irritation. "Didn't you take a geology course in college? Every living thing takes in an unstable isotope called carbon-14. Takes it in each time it breathes, eats, or moves. At the same time, the carbon-14 is breaking down inside the organism. At the moment when the creature dies, it stops taking it in, obviously, but the breakdown process goes on. We know how fast it breaks down, and we know how much should have been there in the first place, so all we do is measure what's left and that tells us when the death took place."

"Sounds simple enough," he said with a bemused look.

"It is," she answered briskly. "The best things always are. Now, take a look at this, this is really exciting." And she moved him over to several sheets of canvas stretched out in the shade. "These are the implements we've uncovered so far. As soon as we're done sketching them and taking their pictures, we'll ship them to the university." She bent and gently touched a sliver of bone. "It's a needle," she said quietly, almost reverentially. "A needle of bone. We found it in the cave up the canyon."

He bent to look at it closer.

"Don't move it," she said quickly. "It's been under a layer of clay on the floor of the cave for nine thousand years. Out in the air, it's too fragile."

He stared at the tiny splinter of bone, from some animal long before extinct, used by hands long since dead. It was sharp at the end, with a broken tip, and stained with lime deposits. Up the shaft was a neat round hole for ancient thread.

"That's incredible," he said solemnly, catching her mood.

She beamed at him. "Isn't it? They've found a few at the Lind Coulee and the Marmes sites, but never this far up the canyon. It's the first evidence we've found that a tribe actually lived here, at least for a time, rather than just passed through."

"How do you know that from this needle?"

"Because we didn't just find it on the ground, along the path or something. We found it carefully buried against the wall of the cave, as though the owner prized it highly and meant to save it. Intended either to use it or come back for it later."

"Is there any chance it's just a natural form? Maybe carved out by the river or something?" He guessed the answer before she spoke, but he had to ask anyway, just to see her catch fire with the pleasure of telling him.

"No. Even if the hole wasn't so perfectly formed, we'd know it was a tool. The bone's lacking periostium, the outer layer's scraped off, which always happens when bone's used as a tool, but not in simple aging."

"How did you find something so small?" he asked. "I'd have thought it would be broken just in the digging."

"We used a screen—it *would* have been broken by normal tools. We put each shovelful through a one-sixteenth nylon mesh. That way, we also found some fossil seeds and small bones and teeth." She frowned in thought for an instant.

"What?" he asked.

"Well." She shrugged. "We found something else in the screening, too, and we can't figure it out yet. We found a couple of rattlesnake fangs buried along with the needle, as though they were being saved or something. I don't know if the band *ate* the snakes, or what. We'll just have to keep digging for the answer. It's strange, though. I don't remember any mention of fangs in the literature."

"What's your theory?"

She grinned at him suddenly. "I try not to have theories, Mister Demers. They get in the way of the facts. Check with me later, same time, same station, and we'll see where we are then."

"Will you take me up to the cave?"

She cocked her head pensively. "I guess so. If you promise not to write so rhapsodically about it that I've got all of Spokane in my lap."

"You have my hand on it," he said and he put out a palm for her to clasp.

She hesitated for a moment, wondering if he was just looking for an excuse to touch her or if he wanted to start fresh. She decided to give him the benefit of the doubt and took his hand, gave it a firm pump, and then let it go. "The cave's up this path," she said loudly. "Watch yourself on the ropes. We want to disturb the surface as little as possible."

He pulled himself up the path after her, stumbling occasionally on the loose gravel. She moved ahead of him, sure as a mountain goat, intent on what lay just over the lip of the ridge.

Finally, Nelson stood within the mouth of the cave. The cool air, seemingly centuries old, wafted out and fingered his face. The floor of the cave had been dug out in layers, and the crew had carefully placed all the finds on the canvas sheets in the corner.

"We're finding more at the back than at the entrance," she said, her voice low. "That's typical for these rock shelters. The fires usually were closer to the front, but the life of the tribe went on behind them, nearer the walls." She gestured to the objects laid out and marked. "We've found some grinding stones—choppers, scrapers, drills, knives—mostly larger projectiles. Too early for bows and arrows. And look at this." She squatted on the hard-packed clay and pointed to an object set apart from the others.

"What is it?" he asked, moving closer.

She picked it up gingerly and placed it in his palm. He turned it over—an owl's claw, pierced with a single hole.

"What did they use this for?"

"Magic," she grinned. "An amulet. Just another piece of evidence that this tribe was well fed, well organized, and relatively stable. They may have had elaborate caste systems like the Spokane tribes or the Chinooks, or they may have had only primitive healers. At any rate, they certainly believed some objects had spiritual power." She held the claw up and turned it slowly. "This hung around the neck of someone fairly important, I'd guess."

"Thought you didn't believe in theories," he chuckled.

"I don't," she said. "But I can't help imagining."

He stood and looked about the dim corners of the cave. It wasn't very large, maybe forty feet from front to back and about fifteen feet at the opening. But in the cool silence, he thought he sensed the whispers of the past sliding back and forth before him, the comings and goings of whole generations, hunters and fishermen, women and children, lighting fires, eating, pounding seeds and scraping furs, telling stories and listening to the sounds of the night outside.

The wind lifted the hairs on the back of his neck, and he shivered slightly. Seeing this cave is like experiencing time as God knows it, he thought. And to realize that man is nothing more than the whispering of the breeze along the canyon walls.

The sun outside felt suddenly warm and amiable rather than uncomfortable, and he wondered how such a woman could spend her days fingering skeletons, dust, and secrets long forgotten.

Three days later, Nelson Demers found himself back at his desk at the *Spokesman-Review.* He'd thought he had plenty of notes for a fine article, could even picture himself handing it in and receiving the well-earned congratulations of his editor and peers. But as he began to type, he realized that the angle was missing.

Every piece needed an angle—he knew that as well as he knew that the "t" key lay over the "g." But for some reason, he couldn't summon one up. He could have rattled off the usual corn about Beauty Against the Wilderness, but he knew that wasn't nearly good enough. There were other possibilities: the urgency of her task, the threat of the rising waters, the heartbreak of dealing with ponderous bureaucracy, the usual cliches. But none of them seemed worthy of the project. Or of her.

He realized he had to go out to the dig once more, to nail this thing down. It was clear he didn't know enough yet to do it justice. This could be a big story, and a big chance, as well.

When he pulled his jeep up in the dry bed, he saw her working on the floor of the canyon, up against the sheer rock wall. She had cleared away some reeds and brush from the clay and was hefting a pickax over her head. He felt a quick irritation that none of the graduate students was doing the heavy work for her, but as he looked around, he saw that they were all occupied at one task or another.

She looked up as he walked closer. "No time for a tour today, Nelson," she panted, clearing rubble from the canyon wall.

"That's fine," he said heartily. "Just had a few more questions, and then I'll get out of your way." He squatted down on his heels and watched her.

She had thrown aside the pick and was kneeling in the gravel, plucking away refuse with gloved hands and a trowel. Now that he was closer, he could see what she was doing. She had painted over a section of the canyon wall with a thick layer of resin, which had hardened and fixed the rock with an amber shield. After cutting a long column in the rock, she poured more resin along the sides, placed a long two-by-four against the vertical shaft, and cut the column free from the wall. Now, she gingerly laid the pillar down on the dry bed and was probing the resin, gently brushing away the loose gravel.

"What questions did you have?" she muttered while she worked, never looking up.

"Well, to start," he said, "what's that for?"

"Vinylite resin soil column," she said, leaning back for a moment.

"It's kind of like a thermometer. Or more accurately, a barometer."
She pointed to the different-colored strata of soil and rock that
striped the column across its whole length. "We've had some luck,
Nelson. Found something fairly rare—maybe a clue to some of our
bigger questions. And we found it right here." She patted the column fondly.

"In the rock?" he asked, bewildered. "What was it?"

She stood and walked quickly over to one of the crew, a student
hunched over a shiny black spear point. He was carefully cleansing
the projectile with some solution, as gently as a mother wiped a
newborn child.

"It's obsidian," she said happily. "There's no place in the whole
state it occurs naturally. Closest place is either Oregon or British
Columbia. Once in a great while, we run across a piece, but not out
here. And never so fine a specimen."

"How did it get here?" he asked.

The young man spoke up quickly, almost with disdain. "Trade,
of course. These guys were movers."

Nelson ignored him and peered closer at the spear blade. "Looks
sharp as hell. So what's its significance for the project?"

She led him away a distance, and he wondered briefly if she was
being sensitive to his feelings or to those of her student. "The
significance is that these obsidian points are so rare, they must have
been quite valuable to whichever tribes owned them. They only
used them for big game, important kills, kills with a spiritual meaning, even. That this tribe had obsidian means they were relatively
rich, as Plateau cultures went. That we found it on the canyon floor,
under several strata of soil, means that the river has covered something under itself that we want to find."

"More obsidian?"

"Maybe. But more likely, whatever they were cutting up with it.
It could be the answer to what drew this band into the canyon and
kept them here long enough to fill the cave with tools and the needle
and all the rest."

"Why was the obsidian so valuable?" he asked as they walked
back over to the soil column.

She squatted and began sketching as she talked. "Because it's
sharper than any other tool, many times sharper than our best
surgical scalpels. It can be flaked in any direction easily; it's got an
edge no thicker than a molecule, and it's strong and light. One of
my colleagues had to have surgery twice—once, for a cancerous

lung—and he talked the surgeon into using obsidian flints for the operation." She looked up, her face shining. "You should see him. His incision's nearly a foot long, and the only scars are from the stitches themselves. You can't even see where the obsidian cut him. It's so sharp, it almost goes between the cells."

"Jesus, that's a great story," Nelson said. "It's so ironic, isn't it? I wonder how the A.M.A. feels about taking lessons from prehistoric savages."

"Some would scoff, I'm sure," she said. "But the ones who were meant to be surgeons in the first place, and good ones, would welcome the challenge, wherever it came from." She stood up and dusted off her shorts. "Now, did you get the answers you wanted, Mister Demers? I've got to get back to work."

"Wait," he said, standing up to face her. "I've got just one more." He hesitated for an instant and then cocked his head at her, grinning. "Do you see yourself as a heroine, Doctor Sing?"

To his surprise, she didn't flare up. She stood and gazed into the depths of the canyon, thinking of her answer. "No," she said finally, thoughtfully. "Not really. You see, we—" She stopped and chuckled to herself. "I almost said, 'we Chinese believe . . . ' I believe in a certain inevitability, Mister Demers." She smiled softly at him. "Nelson. I believe that this nation, every nation, tends to call up what it needs when it needs it. If it doesn't, it perishes. There was a time when we needed 'men to match our mountains,' and we got them. Then, we needed farmers to stick on a plot of ground and till it, never knowing if it would ever pay off. Then we needed dreamers and prophets, and when we did, they came forth. And builders and movers and shakers, and when the time was right for them, we looked around, and there they were. None of these men were heroes, in my opinion. But they had the type of courage that they needed at the moment. They were there, doing a job that needed to be done at the right time in history. I'm doing the same thing." She glanced at her watch. "And now, I've got to get back to it."

Nelson no longer made any pretense of it—he returned to the dig because he wanted to be there, found it fascinating, and didn't care who in the office knew it. He'd written one article, was working on a sequel, and had badgered his editor into using the project as the subject of a weekly column. Two more assignments languished on his desk as he once more drove out to the Grand Coulee.

This time, he found Lisa in a pit nearly over her head, surrounded

by two assistants and every spare hand. Several columns of strat-
ified soil lay in rows by the tents, ready for shipping, and the
riverbed had been scoured with pockmarks and trenches half
the length of the dig. He noticed, with an ominous hollowness, that
the river had risen steadily since his last visit. It now lapped gently
up the canyon, edging closer to its original banks.

He stood and looked down at the team in the pit. Lisa had her
head bent to some soil samples, probing, brushing, and frowning in
concentration.

"We've missed it, haven't we?" one of the assistants muttered. He
was a wiry-thin guy with huge glasses, pale skin, and a wide-
brimmed hat. No threat, Nelson thought, unaware that he'd even
catalogued him.

"I'm afraid so," Lisa said, standing erect. "Judging by these ash
samples, we're looking at vulcanism at least ten thousand years
old." She looked up and saw him but said nothing. "Well, we'll have
to move upstream. It's a fifty-fifty shot, but I'm guessing up rather
than down." She accepted the boot-up the assistant offered and
clambered to the top of the pit.

"Problems?" Nelson asked.

"Just delays," she sighed. "But the way the river's rising, that's
a problem. The answer's here, we're all sure of it. But finding the
spot to dig is something else again."

She turned and walked aimlessly up the riverbed, kicking at loose
gravel. He said nothing but only walked at her side. They rounded
a small bend in the river and were out of sight of the camp, though
only a hundred feet away. She was silent, brooding, stubbing along
with her head down. She scuffed a rock aside and then stopped
suddenly, looking intently at the dry bed. She squatted, pulled her
trowel from her back pocket, and began to gently scoop away the
gravel.

"What is it?" he asked.

"I don't know for sure," she said, moving gradually on her knees
toward the canyon wall, pushing aside small gravel and into a
thicket of reeds. "Something is buried here, see the water marks?
But I can't tell—"

Abruptly, with no warning, a harsh, loud rattling startled her to
silence. She gasped and froze, one hand outstretched, her trowel
parting the reeds. On a hidden pile of rubble, a huge rattlesnake
coiled, inches from Lisa's trembling hand.

It was a fat, mottled snake, tan with wide gray blotches; its head hovered motionless above its roped body. The rattling had ceased, but its flat, opaque eyes followed Lisa's every subtle movement; its tongue flickered in and out, scenting her fear. She was close enough to gaze into its eyes and count the lighter underscales of its jaws. She could have reached out and traced the lines of its head, felt the coolness of its leathery skin.

"Oh my God, don't move," Nelson whispered.

Lisa was an alabaster statue, pale and stiff, her eyes glazing over helplessly. "Crotalus viridis," she whimpered low in her throat. "At least six feet."

"I'll go get help," he said.

"Don't move!" she hissed. "The vibrations alone may make him strike. He can't hear you speak, but he'll certainly hear you run." She began to straighten imperceptibly, each muscle fluidly moving her more upright, inch by inch. Nelson held his breath, and all he could hear was the pounding of his heart in his throat. Now, her arm was still deathly close to the reptile's head, but she was no longer crouching over, off balance.

"I'm going to move back slowly," she whispered.

"He'll strike!"

"No choice. If you move, he may anyway. And even if you can find a tool big enough to kill him with one blow, there's nobody quick enough to get him. I'm too close."

She slowly swiveled the trowel so that it was upright in her hand, the movement so gradual Nelson had to watch constantly to see it happen. The snake followed the trowel with his eyes, but he did not move. When she had positioned the trowel between the snake's head and her wrist, she gradually slid one knee backward in the gravel. Instantly, the snake reared up, alert, and began to rattle ominously. She froze, one knee slightly forward, one back.

My God, if she falls or tilts or loses her balance, it's all over, Nelson thought, his mind a whirl of panic. And it may be anyway. But Lisa steadied herself and waited patiently. Gradually, the rattling ebbed and then died. The snake hovered motionless again.

Once more, she eased her forward knee back. This time, despite the slight scrape of gravel, the snake did not rattle. Inch by inch, she shifted her body farther away. Nelson felt the sun beat down on his head, and he yearned to wipe the sweat from his eyes, but he dared not move. Flies buzzed around Lisa's face. She ignored them but only kept moving, ever so slowly, never taking her eyes from the snake, murmuring something low in her throat that Nelson could not hear.

After what seemed an eternity, she was three feet from the snake, then four, then finally five feet or more, still kneeling, her hand outstretched, the shielding trowel in place. Suddenly, as if it had tired of the game, the snake fluidly uncoiled, lengthened out, and slid away, disappearing into some hidden crevice in the canyon wall.

Nelson took her in his arms, felt her resolve drain away, and held her while she calmed herself. He eased her down to the sand and they sat silently, his arm about her shoulders. Finally, he said, "That was one of the bravest things I've ever seen. What were you telling him?"

She smiled, a trembling version of relief. "That I knew he could bite me if he wanted, but that I hoped he wouldn't, and that I'd be forever in his debt if he'd just let me go."

"You said he couldn't hear what we said."

"He can't," she said. "But *I* could. Now, we need to see where his hiding place is."

"You're kidding! Let's not push our luck!"

"That was a Northern Pacific rattler, Nelson," she said patiently. "They're famous for denning up. This whole canyon may be pocked with subterranean caverns, or his may be the only one. But if what we're looking for isn't in that hole, it may at least give us a clue where else to dig. If we drop fifty pounds of ice down it, it'll drive him out or freeze him into dormancy. Either way, now that we know he's there, he's not such a threat."

The next day, Nelson drove back to the dig with as much ice as he could carry, packed in huge aluminum coolers, and antivenin serum from Spokane General. He stood by with a sharp-edged ax while the crew cleared the reeds and brush from around the canyon wall and scraped away half a foot of rubble.

"There're too many crevices and holes here to know which one he's in, if any," Lisa said. "We'll cool the whole area and hope to drive him off. Then we can dig." They shoveled the ice all around the base of the canyon, covered it with wet burlap and reeds, and waited.

At dawn, Nelson walked outside his tent and looked up the

canyon. It was his first time overnight in the Grand Coulee. He'd bunked with the crew, and the beauty and fierce silence of the canyon at night had dispelled his irritation at having to share a tent with strangers. He was determined to witness the events of this morning.

Lisa poked her head out of her tent and smiled impishly at him. "Thought I heard somebody up. But I didn't think it'd be our star reporter. Are you beginning to catch the fever?"

He grinned ruefully. "After the excitement of day before yesterday, anything you pull out of your hat today has got to be an anticlimax."

"Don't be so sure," she chuckled. "Now's when it all pays off. I hope."

After breakfast, the crew moved the equipment upriver and dragged away the burlap and the reeds. There was no sign of snakes, not even any furrows in the mud where they might have slid away. The floor of the canyon was damp, cool, and empty. They began to dig, two students to a three-foot plot, carefully sectioning out the dirt, sifting through it, troweling over the rubble, and making endless notes in their field pads. Lisa went from pair to pair, discussing, directing, and supervising their progress.

Finally, after more than two hours of digging, one of the assistants hollered, "Over here! I think we got something!"

Lisa hurried to look, Nelson at her side. She squatted in the dirt for long moments, carefully cleaning away dust and small bits of debris with her camelhair brush from the surface of a limestone-covered object. She gestured for some water and gently hosed off the surface, probing all around its sides as she did so.

She sat back on her haunches. "This is it, gentlemen," she said, and the crew sent up a raucous cheer.

"What! What is it!" Nelson shouted.

"This is a rib bone," she grinned. "And it's from a big animal. We know that because here's one of its teeth, buried right next to it. But the best news is right here." She pointed to some pale fragments splintered out of the brown bone, jutting up at an angle. "This is a spear point, broken off in the rib. Man killed this creature, at least nine thousand years ago, I'm guessing, and that's what drew this band into the canyon. They hunted the biggest prey in their world —Mammut americanum. The mastodon."

"How can you tell it's a mastodon?" Nelson asked, amazed.

"By this tooth. Mammoth teeth were for shearing, mastodons' for grinding, and so they look completely different. This molar is worn to the gum line. The animal was old, maybe one of the last of its species. Until now, we had no evidence of mastodons in this area. Whoever killed it would have had quite a battle, though. And if he did it alone, it took a lot of guts. Mastodons had tusks over eight feet, sometimes."

In the silence, Nelson stood and gazed at the ancient rib bone, the jutting spear, and in his mind, he pictured the battle that might have taken place right where he stood. He was awed by the weight of the past that flowed over him like a cool tide, and his throat ached with emotion. "So this is what you were looking for?" he finally managed

She nodded. "We didn't know what we were looking for. But we found it, nonetheless. I guess the truest answers come in that way."

That night, Lisa and Nelson sat by the fire, each lost in separate thoughts. The camp was quiet; the river flowed just beyond their vision.

"Well, I'm going to write an article that'll save this canyon," Nelson finally said. "I can't just stand by and see your find covered with water. I don't care if I lose my job, you can bet I'll do my best to bring this dig to the attention of the world."

He had expected gratitude, but to his surprise, she chuckled softly and threw another log on the fire. "That's a good thought, but first of all, it's not *my* find. It's nobody's. Belongs to nothing but the past. Second of all, it wouldn't be right, even if we could, to try to hold onto it, to try to block the building of the dam. The land needs the water; the people need the land." She shrugged eloquently. "Priorities."

"What do you mean? Don't you want to save it?"

"For what?" she asked. "We have what we need, now. We know more than we knew. It's time to let it go."

"I can't believe you'd give it up so easily," he said. "Where's the spirit I saw two days ago? You wouldn't give in to a rattler, but you'll give in to public opinion?"

"I *did* give in to the rattler. I didn't try to overpower him, I simply moved aside. And then when it was time, I came back to get what I wanted. Remember, I said there were all kinds of courage? Well, one kind surely must be the courage to see that there are things we cannot change, must not change. Sometimes, we have to have the strength *not* to need to know what's going to happen next, the courage to accept that we're *smaller* than something, rather than being always in control, and to not be paralyzed by that knowledge. To let it be, even if it inconveniences us."

"But this find could mean big inroads, couldn't it? What about the future of archaeology in this state? Do we just go about dumping the past for the future, over and over?"

"Look, I'd be the last one to argue a preference for the future, Nelson. I've spent all my life looking backward, to the past. Because I believe that's the only direction we can learn from. My father used to say that we're born of our mothers, but earth bred us first." Her voice fell away in memory. "He was a farmer, and he loved the land. So do I. But the dam is here, like it or not."

He frowned and muttered, "There're lots of people, even today, who say the dams should never have been built. None of them. My grandfather helped build the Grand Coulee, the biggest of them all, and I was always real proud of him for that. But now, when I see how they're killing off the salmon, polluting the river, and ruining the last piece of wilderness left in this state, I'm not so sure. And all for big business."

She gazed into the fire. "It was right to build them then. Just because we see more problems now doesn't mean it wasn't right then. And what we do to salvage the salmon or clean up the river is right for now. It's not for one generation to judge the vision or the courage of those who went before. Oh, we all do it, but we forget that while we push aside the hard-won choices of our fathers, we're building on them all the time, finding our own way like little streams pushing questing fingers into what seems to be new soil. And so the future, just like the river, is built finally of a thousand different streams."

She stood and stretched, gazing up the shadowed canyons to the caves. "Nine thousand years ago, a tribe lived along this riverbed, looking to survive the best way they could. Somebody, maybe a hunter, maybe a young warrior, found an old mastodon, one of the first they'd seen—and one of the last to ever walk this canyon. And with little more than his bare hands, a few prized tools, and native cunning, he brought the great beast down. He was probably the biggest hero of his day. Whatever gods he worshiped must have been mighty ones."

She lifted her hair off the back of her neck, feeling the cool canyon breezes, the whispers of the past. "But he's dust now, and so is the mastodon, and so are over four hundred generations that came after him. What lives on is his courage—and maybe just a little piece of his dream, passed on from soul to soul, like a million tiny currents forming a powerful river that is as eternal as the earth itself. That's what we must preserve, that river of dreams and courage and hope. Not a handful of old bones and tools and magic snake fangs. Nothing really changes, Nelson, and it'll still be here nine thousand years from now. The bones of the past are still in the earth."

He sighed hugely and walked to the river, looking out over its swift currents, feeling, even as he couldn't see, that it was growing at his feet. "Well, okay, then. I guess I can buy that."

She stood and walked to his side.

"It's one hell of a strong river, isn't it?" he whispered.

She slipped her arm through his, her face full of peace, "It's a god," she said.

And they stood together, listening to the waters rush down the canyon in the darkness.

Afterword

This is a work of fiction, and as such, has occasionally had to subvert historical accuracy for thematic and plot purposes. Those who are expert in Northwestern history may notice minor alterations in dates and places; however, the bulk of this project is as historically true as smooth fiction could allow.

My mother and my grandmother were both born along the Columbia, and I spent most of my childhood summers in Washougal, a town where people still greet each other by first names on its single main street. As a long-time lover of the Northwest and her peoples, I would hope that I might be forgiven some liberties with the dry facts of her lineage. History, someone said, belongs to those who write it. *Columbia* is my version of the past. The Doppler effect describes the physical phenomenon that the sound of something, anything, coming at you—say, a train, or the future—is always louder than that same thing going away. I do not have perfect pitch, but I can hear the past going away, and like all falling bodies, it constantly accelerates.

I believe that *Columbia* is one way it sounded as it passed.

References and Acknowledgments

PART ONE—NINE THOUSAND YEARS BEFORE PRESENT

Clark, Ella, *Indian Legends of the Pacific Northwest* (page 141, quoted by permission). Berkeley: University of California Press, 1953.

Daugherty, Richard D., Information Circular #32, State of Washington, Department of Conservation, Division of Minerals and Geology, Marshall T. Huntting, Supervisior, Olympia, Wa., 1959. (Information on Grand Coulee geology.)

Kirk, Ruth, with Richard D. Daugherty, *Exploring Washington Archeology.* Seattle: University of Washington Press, 1978. (Basic information on mastodons, early tribes, tools, and geological formations of the Pacific Northwest.)

PART TWO—THE RIVER PEOPLE

Armstrong, Virginia I. (ed.), *I Have Spoken.* Chicago: Swallow Press, 1971.

Boas, Franz, *Chinook Texts.* U.S. Bureau of American Ethnology, Bulletin #20, 1894.

Brown, Vinson, *Peoples of the Sea Wind.* New York: Collier Books, 1977.

Colbert, Mildred, *Kutkos, Chinook Tyee.* Boston: D. C. Heath & Co., 1942.

Collins, June McCormick, *Valley of the Spirits.* Seattle: University of Washington Press, 1974.

Coombs, Samuel F., *Dictionary of the Chinook Jargon.* Seattle, 1891.

Cox, Ross, *Adventures on the Columbia River* (two volumes). London: J & J Harper, 1831.

Demers, Modeste, *Chinook Dictionary: Catechism, Prayers, and Hymns.* Montreal, 1871.

Drucker, Philip, *Cultures of the North Pacific Coast.* San Francisco: Chamdler Publishing Co., 1965.

Gunther, Erna, *Indian Life of the Northwest Coast of North America.* Chicago: University of Chicago Press, 1972.

Haeberlin, Herman, and Erna Gunther, *The Indians of Puget Sound.* Seattle: University of Washington Press, 1930.

Haines, Francis, *The Nez Perce: Tribesmen of the Columbia Plateau.* Norman, Ok.: University of Oklahoma Press, 1958.

Hays, H. R., *Children of the Raven.* New York: McGraw-Hill, 1975.

Hines, Gustavus, *History of the Pacific Northwest: Oregon and Washington.* Portland: Hurst & Co., 1889.

Holbrook, Stewart, *The Columbia.* New York: Holt, Rinehart & Winston, 1956, 1974.

Hosner, James K. (ed.), *Captains Lewis and Clark to the Sources of the Mississippi* (two volumes). New York: A. C. McClurg, 1902.

Jacobs, Melville, *The People Are Coming Soon.* Seattle: University of Washington Press, 1960.

Johansen, Dorothy O., and Charles M. Gates, *Empire of the Columbia: A History of the Pacific Northwest.* New York: J & J Harper, 1957.

Jones, Roy Franklin, *Wappato Indians of the Lower Columbia River Valley.* Vancouver, Wa., 1972.

Lockley, Fred, *History of the Columbia River Valley From the Dalles to the Sea* (two volumes). Chicago: S. J. Clarke Publishing Co., 1928.

MacInnes, Tom, *Chinook Days.* British Columbia: Sun Publishing Co., 1926.

Neithammer, Carolyn, *Daughters of the Earth.* New York: Collier Books, 1977.

Ramsey, Jarold, *Coyote Was Going There.* Seattle: University of Washington Press, 1971.

Ruby, Robert H., and John A. Brown, *The Chinook Indians: Traders of the Lower Columbia.* Norman, Ok.: University of Oklahoma Press, 1976.

Stern, Bernhard J., *The Lummi Indians of Northwest Washington.* New York: Ames Press, 1934, 1969.

Strong, Thomas Nelson, *Cathlamet on the Columbia.* Portland: Binsford and Mort, 1906.

Williams, Chuck, *Bridge of the Gods, Mountains of Fire: A Return to the Columbia Gorge.* Portland: Friends of the Earth, Elegant Mountain Arts Publishing, 1980.

*   *   *

Special thanks to Jeri Inabnit and John McDonald of the Chelan County Historical Society Museum, Cashmere, Washington, for answers to difficult, sometimes obvious, questions, always with good humor and a rare enthusiasm for their region.

Thanks also to the fine staffs at Suzzallo Library, University of Washington, Seattle; the Oregon Historical Society, Portland, Thomas Vaughan, Executive Director; the Seattle Public Library; and the Pacific County Historical Society, Raymond, Washington, particularly Mrs. Ruth Dixon.

PART THREE—THE RIVER SETTLERS

Attwell, Jim, *Columbia River Gorge History* (Vol. 1). Skamania, Wa.: Tahlkie Books, 1974.

Case, Robert Ormand, *The Empire Builders.* Portland: Binsford and Mort, 1949. (Permission to paraphrase from Case's history of Elizabeth Smith and her family.)

Clark, Malcolm Jr., *Eden Seekers: The Settlement of Oregon, 1818–1862.* Boston: Houghton Mifflin, 1981.

Drury, Clifford H. (ed.), *First White Women Over the Rockies: Diaries, Letters, and Bibliographical Sketches of the Six White Women Who Made the Overland Journey in 1836 and 1838* (three volumes). Glendale, Ca.: A. H. Clark Co., 1963.

Faragher, John Mock, *Women and Men on the Oregon Trail.* New Haven and London: Yale University Press, 1979.
    Two songs quoted from this source. Details of Suzanna's quilting come from a letter by "Aunt Jane of Kentucky," page 56 of the Faragher work, quoted from Elizabeth Wells Robertson's *American Quilts,* New York, Stucco Publications, 1948; Suzanna's song on men comes from Vance Randolph's *Ozark Folksongs,* Columbia, Missouri State Historical Society, 1946–1950, Vol. 1, page 217.

Fogdall, Alberta Brooks, *Royal Family of the Columbia.* Portland: Binsford and Mort, 1984.

Gray, William A., *A History of Oregon.* Portland: Harris & Holman, 1870.

Johnson, Robert C., *John McLoughlin: Father of Oregon.* Portland: Binsford and Mort, 1935, 1958.

Myres, Sandra L., *Westering Women and the Frontier Experience, 1800–1915.* Albuquerque: University of New Mexico Press, 1982.

Schlissil, Lillian, *Women's Diaries of the Westward Journey.* New York: Schocken Books, 1982.

Stratton, Joanna L., *Pioneer Women.* New York: Simon and Schuster, 1982.

Victor, Frances Fuller, *River of the West.* Hartford: R. W. Bliss & Co., 1870.

*   *   *

Perhaps one of the most valuable (and fascinating) of sources is the Locksley Files, by Fred Locksley, *Conversations With Pioneer Women*, compiled and edited by Mike Helm, Rainy Day Press, 1981. A compilation of actual diary extracts and letters, it allows the reader to hear the words of the pioneers themselves. Katie's remark that "The gun killed my ears!" is a paraphrase of Laura C. Caldwell's memory of a child saying, "I am shot through the ears." Philura's complaint of the rough trail; Mrs. Ketcham's setting fire to the wagon; the kidnaping of a child by the Indians—all were actual anecdotes recorded in the Locksley Files.

Thanks also to the staff at the Whitman Museum, Walla Walla, Washington, and the staff at Fort Vancouver, National Historical Site, Vancouver, Washington.

PART FOUR—THE RIVER SOJOURNERS

Barth, Gunther, *Bitter Strength: A History of the Chinese in the U.S.* A Publication of the Center for the Study of the History of Liberty in America. Cambridge, Ma.: Harvard University Press, 1964.

Binns, Archie, *This Roaring Land.* New York: McBride & Co., 1942.

Chin, Art, *Golden Tassels: A History of the Chinese in Washington.* Seattle: University of Washington Press, 1977.

Hildebrand, Lorraine Barker, *Straw Hats, Sandals, and Steel.* Tacoma, Wa.: State Bicentennial Commission, 1977.

Kingston, Maxine Hong, *China Men.* New York: Ballantine, 1977.
————*Woman Warrior.* New York: Vintage, 1977.
    Two excellent studies of what it is to be a Chinese-American today.

Lee, C. Y., *Days of the Tong Wars.* New York: Comstock, Ballantine, 1974.

Maddux, Percy, *City on the Williamette: The Story of Portland.* Portland: Binsford and Mort, 1952.

Martin, Mildred Crowl, *Chinatown's Angry Angel: The Story of Donaldina Cameron.* Palo Alto, Ca.: Pacific Books, 1971.

McLeod, Alexander, *Pigtails and Golddust.* Idaho: Caxton Printers, 1947.

Seufert, Frances, *Wheels of Fortune.* Edited by Thomas Vaughan. Portland: Oregon Historical Society, 1980.

Sung, Betty Lee, *The Story of the Chinese in America.* New York: Collier, 1967.

*   *   *

Special thanks to the staff of the Clatsop Museum for information on the Chinese in Astoria.

I would like to thank my mother-in-law, Juanita E. Koons, for traveling with me for three arduous weeks to China for the resources necessary for this section of the book. Her patience, unfailing good humor, and enthusiasm for all things unknown, all details undug, made the writing of Ning Ho's story a pleasure—indeed, made it possible. Special thanks to the Chinese guides, both national and local, and to the CITS for their cooperation and interest in this project.

PART FIVE—THE RIVER WORKERS

Brissenden, Paul F., *The I.W.W.* New York: Columbia University Press, 1919.

Churchill, Sam. *Big Sam*. Sausalito, Ca.: Comstock Books, 1965.
———*Don't Call Me Ma*. New York: Doubleday & Co., 1977.

Holbrook, Stewart, *Far Corners*. New York: Macmillan, 1952.
———*Holy Old Mackinaw*. Sausalito, Ca.: Comstock Books, 1938, 1956, 1980.
For those readers interested in the logging era (indeed, in anything at all about the Northwest), Stewart Holbrook's books are most highly recommended. They are always factual, entertaining, and legendary in their understanding of the region.

Jensen, Vernon A., *Lumber and Labor*. New York: Farrar and Rinehart, 1945.

Kastrup, Allan, *Swedish Heritage in America*. Swedish Council of America, 1975.

Kinsey, Darius, and Ralph W. Andrews, *This Was Logging*. Seattle: Superior Publishing Co., 1954.

Lucia, Ellis, *The Big Woods*. New York: Doubleday & Co., 1975.

Morgan, Murray, *The Columbia: Powerhouse of the West*. Seattle: Superior Publishing Co., 1949.

Tyler, Robert L., *Rebels of the Woods: The I.W.W. in the Pacific Northwest*. Eugene, Or.: University of Oregon Press, 1967.

*   *   *

Song of the lumberman comes from *Rainy Day Songbook*, Linda Allen (ed.). Bellingham, Wa.: Whatcom Museum of History and Art, 1978, 1980.

PART SIX—THE RIVER MOVERS

Goldston, Robert, *The Great Depression: The United States in the Thirties*. New York: Fawcett Premier Books, 1968.

Horan, James D., *The Desperate Years.* New York: Bonanza Books, 1962.

Lowitt, Richard, and Maurine Beasley (eds.), *One Third of a Nation: Lorena Hickock Reports on the Great Depression.* Dekalb, Ill.: University of Illinois Press, 1981.

Morgan, Murray, *The Dam.* New York: Viking Press, 1954.

Mowry, George E. (ed.), *The Twenties: Fords, Flappers, and Fanatics.* Englewood Cliffs, N.J.: Prentice-Hall Press, 1963.

Perret, Geoffrey, *America in the Twenties.* New York: Simon and Schuster, 1982.

Sundborg, George, *Hail Columbia: The Thirty-Year Struggle for Grand Coulee Dam.* New York: Macmillan, 1954.

Woods, Rufus, *The Battle for the Grand Coulee Dam.* Wenatchee, Wa.: *Wenatchee Daily World,* 1944.

* * *

Special thanks to Doug Olson, Eastern Washington State Historical Society, Spokane, Washington, for his help.

Thanks also to the fine staff of the Cheney Cowles Museum.

PART SEVEN—TODAY

Daughtery, Richard D., op. cit.

Kirk, Ruth, and Richard D. Daughtery, op. cit.

* * *

Finally, of course, I would like to thank my family: my parents, who read each draft with careful, kind criticism, unearthing flaws with unerring but loving eyes; my sister and brother, Wendy and Rick, who make me feel that what I do matters; a whole host of friends and relatives who are supportive and who endure endless recounts of my ideas with patience and good humor. Thanks also to Roz Targ, the best of battling agents and a loyal friend, to Joyce Engelson, a valiant editor, who knew that "some things must be believed to be seen," and to Hope Dellon, who carried *Columbia* through to fruition.

And lastly, to the most valuable support of all, my heart to my husband, for simply everything.

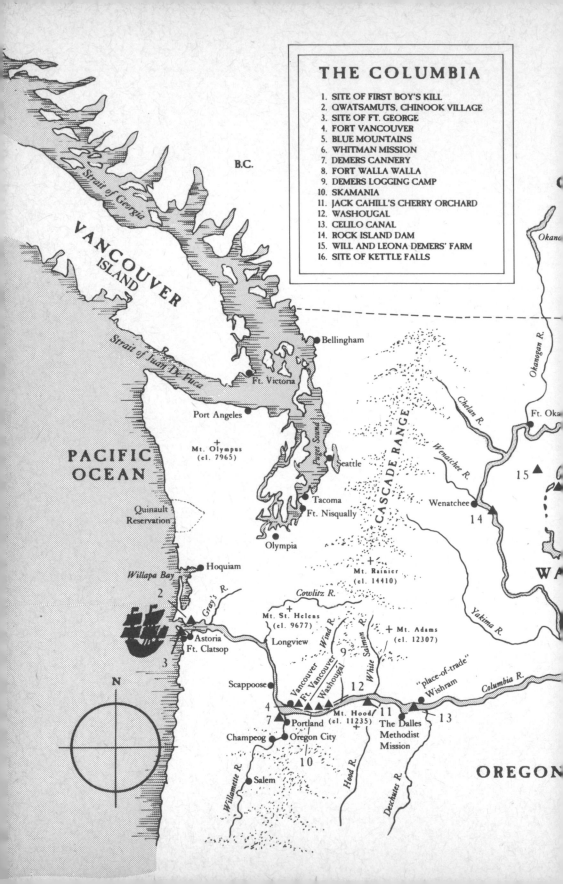

THE COLUMBIA

1. SITE OF FIRST BOY'S KILL
2. QWATSAMUTS, CHINOOK VILLAGE
3. SITE OF FT. GEORGE
4. FORT VANCOUVER
5. BLUE MOUNTAINS
6. WHITMAN MISSION
7. DEMERS CANNERY
8. FORT WALLA WALLA
9. DEMERS LOGGING CAMP
10. SKAMANIA
11. JACK CAHILL'S CHERRY ORCHARD
12. WASHOUGAL
13. CELILO CANAL
14. ROCK ISLAND DAM
15. WILL AND LEONA DEMERS' FARM
16. SITE OF KETTLE FALLS

B.C.

VANCOUVER ISLAND

Strait of Georgia

Strait of Juan De Fuca

PACIFIC OCEAN

Bellingham

Ft. Victoria

Port Angeles

Mt. Olympus
(el. 7965)

Quinault
Reservation

Seattle

Puget Sound

Tacoma
Ft. Nisqually

Olympia

CASCADE RANGE

Chelan R.

Wenatchee R.

Wenatchee

Okanogan R.

Ft. Oka

15

14

WA

Hoquiam

Willapa Bay

Grey's R.

Cowlitz R.

Mt. Rainier
(el. 14410)

Mt. St. Helens
(el. 9677)

Mt. Adams
(el. 12307)

Yakima R.

2

Astoria
Ft. Clatsop

3

Longview

Wind R.

White Salmon R.

9

"place-of-trade"
Wishram

Columbia R.

N

Scappoose

Vancouver
Ft. Vancouver
Washougal

12

Mt. Hood
(el. 11235)

11

13

4

7

Portland

The Dalles
Methodist
Mission

Champeog

Oregon City

10

Hood R.

Deschutes R.

OREGON

Salem

Willamette R.